MW00917751

Rapid Transit:
A Novel of Teleportation and Entrepreneurship

James Rolph Edwards

© Copyright 2009, James Rolph Edwards

All Rights Reserved.

No part of this book may be reproduced, stored in a
retrieval system, or transmitted by any means,
electronic, mechanical, photocopying, recording,
or otherwise, without written permission
from the author.

ISBN: 978-1-4452-7618-2

Cast of Characters in *Rapid Transit*

Thomas Alvin Wright (scientist, inventor, entrepreneur)
  Maria Santos (Tom's executive secretary at UTT)

Derek Martin (brilliant engineering graduate student)

Gina Barlow (Economics and Political Science graduate student)
  Adam (Gina's father, head of California branch of AAPS)
  Rachael (Gina's mother)
  Heather (Gina's teenage younger sister)
  Cindy Markham (Gina's roommate at the Edison Institute)

Edison Institute Professors
Mike Zidelski (Engineering)
Irwin Westholm (Chair, Department. of Physics)
Jacob Hansen (Chair, Department of Mathematics, UTT Board of Directors)
Lew Edleston (Economics, UTT Board of Directors)
Ludwig Rothman (Business, UTT Board of Directors)

The Skeleton Crew
Thad "Beowulf" Thorsen (engineer, 2nd year PhD program)
Hulio Sanchez (engineer, Thad's class, dropped out)
Billi Jo Jensen (engineer, Thad's class)

Dave Barret (physics, last year of classes)
Lynn Yip Ki (physics, finished PhD last year)
Parker Freeman (physics, long finished with PhD)
Phillip Adobo (math, last year of PhD program)
Angel BlackSnake (math, finished PhD)
Sean Nezbit (computers, finished)

California Senate ALP members
Bill Braxon (St. Senator, Minority Leader)
    Barbara (Bill's wife)
    Amanda (Bill and Barbara's teenage daughter)
    Ly Cam Hoang (Bill's secretary)
    Dexter Gibbs (Bill's Chief of Staff)
    Kyle "Spider" Webb (staff member)
Roger Galbraith (State Senator)
    Lillian (Roger's wife)
    Serena Michelo (Spider's girlfriend on Roger's staff)
Hally Arkwright (Senator, Minority Whip)

California Senate RepubliCrats
Samuel Hamilton Clanton (Senator, Majority Leader)
    Martha (Sam's wife - separated)
    Charise Meardon (personal assistant/call girl)
    Mark Mason (staff)
Gerald "Jerry" Foxly (Majority Whip)
Jake Gramm (Senate President)
Melvin Slanghorn (Governor of California)
Maynard Clairborne Hoffer (Director, Department of Transportation)
Eugene Neely (Democratic-Republican Party Chairman)

Investment Bankers
Marlon Gates (senior partner in Gates, Feldman, Vanderhoff, and Shapiro)
    Jenny (Marlon's wife)
Joseph P. Feldman (senior partner)
Remington S. Vanderhoff (partner)
Eli Shapiro (partner)

Lawyers for UR&F and UTT
Buzz "The Buzzard" Byrd (senior partner in Byrd, Rand, Epstein, and Ely)
    Ron Beck (young attorney)

3-V Network News Personel
CBC
    Chet Barker (New York)
    Wesley Frickman (San Francisco)
    Donald Burgley (Menlo Park)

NBS
    Rexford Grumman (New York)
    Bob Van Neff (Tokyo)
    Karl Rasmussen (economics consultant)
    Sloan Brinkerhoff (legal consultant)

Nucleonic Orbital
Dan Hargrove (CEO)
    June (Dan's wife)
    Mike (Dan and June's son, 20)
    Kira (Dan and June's daughter, 18)
Kumar Banerjee (young physicist and mathematician)

Japanese
Koichi Ono (Head of Sony Electrodynamics)
Yukio Hasimata (Head of Research, Section 5, Sony Electrodynamics)
Kiyoshi Tomiki (Lab assistant, Sony Electrodynamics, spy for a rival firm)
Ishi Harada (Aikido Sensei, Oakland Club and Pinkerton Agency)

Pinkerton Men
Harry Pinkerton
    Al Frandsen
    Dalton Pinkerton (Harry's nephew)
    Sergeant Slaughter
    Joe Bender
    Juaqine "Jack" Menendez
    Rod
    Pete

Menlo Park Police Department
Detective Burt Devlin

Officers, Universal Teleportation Transport
Thomas A. Wright (CEO)
Derek Martin (initial VP of Operations)
Richard Mathews (VP of Operations after Derek)
Lee Bricker (CFO)
    Managing Directors
    Hulio Sanchez (Freight operations)
    Lynn Yip Ki (Satellite operations)
    Parker Freeman (Passenger operations)

Sean Nezbit (Human Resources)
Angel BlackSnake (R & D)

Chapter contents: *Rapid Transit*

Anyone who wants to know how the author pictures Gina Barlow can imagine a combination of Robin Mead and Catherine Zeta-Jones, without Robin's irritating laugh, or Catherine's accent. Or maybe, as Pete thought, she looks a lot like Yasmin Bleeth. Of course Gina is far more athletic than any of those beauties.

- James Rolph Edwards

Chapter 1: The Puzzle and the Prize Appear

The utter darkness of deep sleep resisted the invasion of light and images that began to be thrown up randomly, and perhaps not so randomly, from the subconscious, and to take on the fluid associations and relationships of the dream state. As is often the case with young men, having the natural libidinal charge and yearnings of their gender, there came a woman into the dream. He could not see her face with any clarity, but he knew she was beautiful; tall, blond, lithe, incredibly sexy, and somehow, incredibly attracted to him. He strained, but could not get closer to her, though she yearned to also, and she began to fade.

Then there was a man, a young adult like the dreamer himself, who seemed to have no direct connection to the woman, but who seemed to have a terrible, and wonderful, driven, *purpose.* The dreamer could not clearly see or recognize the man either, and he felt a sense of loss at that, as though he might once have had a chance to meet him and had missed it. However, another opportunity might await. He felt a kinship of the soul, and that the man was aware of, and interested in *him.* The odd impression came to the dreamer that if he could somehow meet the man, and fall in with his purpose, it would be a route to the woman, who would complete him in other ways. He struggled to focus and understand, but that effort accelerated the trend toward consciousness, and the dream began to dissolve, perhaps having served its purpose after leaving one last impression: something was about to happen.

Derek awoke, grasping at the tendrils of the dream dissipating like smoke into the dim early morning light of the corner dorm room. Even the memory of the dream disappeared as he peered around and began to think of his agenda for the day. Rolling out of bed, the tall, lanky, young man shed his pajamas and fumbled in the closet for his running clothes, trying to be quiet. Sitting on the edge of the bed, he pulled the right leg of his sweat suit up as far as it would go, slipped his left leg into the suit and pulled it up likewise, then stood and pulled up the pants the rest of the way. Picking up the top of the sweat suit off the bed, he shrugged into it. His dorm-mate Rufus Mankew, a pre-law student, was snoring peacefully in his own bed and could barely be seen in the early morning light.

Pulling his running shoes on and tying them up, Derek stopped to get his NanoPod out of his jeans pocket, strapped it to his wrist, and headed out the front door into the hall. Almost no one was up this early, which was fine with him. He did pass one guy he knew just as he reached the bottom of the stairs on the first floor. The man appeared to a bit tipsy and was probably just getting in from some all night party. Surprisingly, given his condition, the guy recognized him. "Hey, Derek. You're goin' the wrong way," he said in a somewhat slurred voice, as he stopped and leaned back against the wall to watch Derek pass.

Derek nodded and waved, recognizing the guy as an English major he knew, but kept on going. "Yeh, right." he called back as he went on by and headed for the front door. "But it all depends on where I'm trying to go, doesn't it?"

Derek sometimes played cards with the guy and some of his friends, but to be frank, they were all, well, losers, both figuratively and literally. Sometimes Derek almost felt bad about taking their money, despite how easy it was. But he didn't feel *too* bad. Dustin and his friends, children of privilege with well-to-do parents, seemed to have a lot of money to lose, and didn't much mind. In fact, it was odd that they kept inviting him to play and to hang around with them. Derek was an electrical and computer- engineering graduate student who was almost feverishly focused on his subjects and kept his political views private. Dustin Malik and his friends, despite the upper class backgrounds of their parents, all seemed to be from the mushy-minded left radical mindset. They were always talking about social injustice and capitalist conspiracies to exploit the little guy, among whom they, oddly, seemed to consider themselves. Maybe they thought they could convert him. At any rate, they were useful to him. His scholarships and teaching assistant stipend paid tuition, housing, and even food, but not much else. What he got from the Dustin Maliks and their like on campus kept him in running shoes, nachos, and movies.

Outside the dorm, the early October morning central California air was just a little cool for comfort, but Derek knew that would pass as he began seriously burning off calories. So he started on his standard Monday, Wednesday and Friday jog route: down the grassy hill, past the Administration building, across the quadrangle, between the SUB and the business and economics complex, down Reagan Avenue, through the municipal park, and around the circumference of the campus until he passed the stadium and came back to the student housing. Derek had run track in high school. At six foot three, his long legs had been an advantage. Though he didn't have the time or inclination for competitive running now, he did like to stay in condition, and a two mile run every other morning helped.

The campus of the Edison Institute of Economics and Technology was relatively new. It had been endowed after most California University campuses had gone up in flames, along with many inner cities around the country, when the Social Security, Medicare, and Medicaid systems had collapsed and federal taxes had been raised to punitive levels in a failed attempt to salvage the systems. Stanford University, just a few miles away, had also been destroyed, which partly accounted for the building of a new university in Menlo Park. Stanford had housed the Hoover Institution on War, Peace, and Revolution, which many of its enemies had credited with a key role behind the scenes in the emergence of the American Liberty Party. Most of the money for the Edison

Institute had come from the Gates and Edison Foundations. That had occurred not long after the American Liberty Party had deregulated the economy and drastically reduced federal spending and taxation, ending the Second Great Depression.

This morning Derek did not get far on his run. As he jogged across the quad, past the big bulletin board that was covered with notices of upcoming political protests, campus activities, and other trivia, some intuition or impulse from his subconscious made him scan the board. Something distinctly un-trivial caught his eye. It was a simple one-page notice that began, in very large type, **$10,000 Neodollar cash prize, if you can make this work!** What followed was a page of extraordinary variable definitions and mathematical equations. There was just enough light from the approaching dawn to read. As the dollar sign in the notice caught his eye, something he intuited in the equations made Derek stop almost as if he had hit a wall. He looked closely at the odd posting and was drawn almost instantly into the logic of the math, oblivious to everything surrounding him. About half way down the page his eyes widened and his breath caught. "No. That can't be right," he said, though nobody was there to hear him. "It couldn't do that!" But the epiphany was too powerful. He was caught in the realization that he just might be able to do what this person wanted and couldn't breathe for several moments. Finally he did.

At the bottom of the notice was an offer of joint patent rights and an instruction that anyone successful at engineering a solution was to put an ad, including a name and address, in the classifieds of the *New Californian* (the student newspaper) so he could be contacted. Reaching for the paper, to tear it down and take with him, Derek stopped. Sliding his left sleeve up his arm with his right hand, he used his NanoPod to photograph the notice several times from different angles, to be sure he missed nothing. Then he turned around and headed back to the dorm, running on automatic pilot, still oblivious of his surroundings as he focused inwardly on the implications of what he had been forced to see.

Derek arrived at the door of his room without being aware of having traveled the distance. He tried to open it without unlocking, put his eye in front of the retinal reader for a moment, and jerked open the door. Oddly, Rufus, who seldom got up before Ten-thirty a.m., was awake and sitting on his bed.

"Dude," Rufus said when Derek stormed in, "there was a guy just here looking for you."

Derek stopped. He sensed another odd event, perhaps connected to what he had just experienced. "Who was it?"

"I dunno," Rufus responded defensively, "a guy. Maybe six-foot, sandy hair, about your age. Never seen him before. I thought he was a friend of yours, another science geek or something, only he looked a little too, well, athletic. He left a book. Said to give it to you." He pointed to Derek's bed and a soft covered volume on the edge.

Derek quickly went over and picked up the book. It was a new biography of Nichola Tesla, the 19th century Serbian electrical genius who invented alternating current and the Tesla Coil, still used in gasoline automobile engines. Tesla, who had migrated to America, worked for Edison for several years. Edison, having invented the light bulb, had established Edison Electric and begun wiring the East Coast cities using direct current. Tesla tried to get Edison to switch to AC, but Edison refused because of his heavy investment in DC equipment, so Tesla quit and went to General Electric. The outcome of the resulting titanic struggle between the two giant firms was, of course, the adoption of alternating current.

Derek had read a little about Tesla before. He was widely believed to have been a couple of hundred years ahead of his time in his understanding of electricity, and to have done some amazing things that had never yet been duplicated. The problem was, Tesla, fearing copycats and thefts of his ideas (as did nearly all inventors) left few records. However, some had recently been found. Several passages in the book were marked. The small hairs on the back of Derek's neck stood up.

*　　　　*　　　　*

An hour later Derek regained enough presence of mind to pull himself away from the Tesla biography and the math, which he had replicated on a notepad from the telephone pictures downloaded on his computer. A glimmer of a plan, or at least an initial course of action, had begun to form in his mind. He had things to do though, that would have to be worked around his existing schedule. So he took a shower and put on his regular clothes. Then he made himself a quick breakfast of eggs, toast, and orange juice, put the plates and silverware in the sonic cleaner, slung his book bag over his shoulder, and headed out the door. None of this even woke Rufus, who had gone back to bed.

Derek had an eight a.m. advanced electrical engineering stat class that he couldn't miss. As an advanced PhD level course, it only had eight students, and Professor Zidelski would notice, and not appreciate, his absence. Zidelski, who Derek was working for as a teaching assistant this semester, was almost certainly going to head Derek's dissertation committee and Derek did not want to irritate him. Derek would be through with all his PhD course work soon and was under pressure to get something decided quickly about the form of his PhD project. In fact, Professor Zidelski was just the guy Derek wanted to see right now anyway, and he had an hour between the stat class and his next class to do it in. So he hot-footed it over to the engineering school, arriving only a few seconds late for class.

Derek had a struggle keeping his focus on the statistical material, even though it was interesting, in terms of its engineering applications and also to a guy who liked to gamble, and Professor Zidelski's presentation was typically both lucid and animated.

When the end of the hour rolled around and everyone began filing out the door, Derek walked down the stairs one floor to the department office complex and was waiting outside when Professor Zidelski walked up.

"Doctor Zidelski, can I see you for a few minutes?"

The Professor looked up. "Oh, Derek. Have you got those test questions for CE 638?"

"No. But I'm almost done. I'll have them emailed to you in plenty of time for you to finish making up the test before three o'clock. It's about something else."

"Sure. Come on in."

Derek followed Professor Zidelski past the Department secretary's desk and into his office. It was large and spacious, with windows on the east side letting in the morning sun. Dr. Zidelski was a full professor with tenure and had one of the nicest offices in the building, which had been well designed from the first. It was rumored that several senior faculty members, including Zidelski, had worked closely with the architect on the design. Two walls of Zidelski's office had shelves of books, journals, awards, and certification plaques. A large desk, kept fairly orderly (unlike those of many professors) faced the windows. Along the south wall were a computer desk and a couch for visitors. Dr. Zidelski put his class materials down on his main desk, spun his chair around, and sat down, leaning back with his hands behind his head.

"Have a seat, Derek. What can I do for you? And what do I have to do after three years to get you to stop calling me 'Doctor'? Despite your predilection for gambling and a few other character oddities, you're one of the best students I have, and as I've told you several times, you can call me by my first name."

"Sorry, Mike." Derek sat on the close edge of the couch and handed Zidelski the notepad on which he had transcribed the math from the posting on the quad.

"What's this?" Mike asked, taking his glasses off to look closely.

"I'm not really sure," Derek responded, "though I have suspicions. Follow the logic and see what you think."

"It's physics isn't it?" Mike asked after he closely scanned the page, sub-vocalizing almost audibly as he read down. He reached behind him, got a note pad and pencil, and began copying the math and taking notes.

"I'm not sure I see. . . Wow." His eyes opened, and then narrowed again. "Did you do this Derek? Along with being my best engineering student, I knew you were good at math and physics, but some of this I can only partly follow, and I didn't think you were quite this good."

"No. It's not my work." Derek told him about finding the posting on the quad, though, oddly, not knowing whether it was a good decision or not, said nothing about the Tesla biography delivered to his dorm room. Too much about Tesla was essentially mythological. A hardheaded, common sense guy like Mike Zidelski might not relate.

"This is part of a much larger argument, isn't it?" Mike asked when Derek finished.

"Yes. I think so."

Mike leaned back in his chair. "So where do you think it all goes?"

Derek thought for a moment. This was another thing that Mike could not relate to, being an enormously competent electrical and computer engineer, but not really being into deeper physics. He decided to plunge ahead however. "I think, if we saw the rest, we'd see it's an enormously sophisticated extension of Einstein-Podolsky and Rosen entanglement, in ways that John Bell, Carver Mead, and Gregor Cherenkov only dreamed they could get to. Even what's here casts severe doubt on Bohr and Heisenberg. It's making me think of giving up gambling."

Mike would have laughed, but the thought of overthrowing Bohr and Heisenberg was no laughing matter. He considered Derek carefully while leaning back in his chair. "It's fairly clear and specific what this guy wants isn't it?"

"I think so. He wants a hardware solution to the modulation and regulation of this field, whatever it is."

"Can you do it?"

"I think so. I see a way. It came to me as I was reading it, down in the quad this morning. Design won't be the problem. I could basically knock that out on my ELECTROCAD program at home in a few days. Getting the materials and making some of the components will be time consuming and expensive. Testing the thing will also be tricky, since it is intended to be part of a much larger system we can only intuit, but its main function is pretty clear and actually has several applications that I can think of."

Derek took out his pencil and pad and started drawing diagrams and component relationships outlining his basic engineering solution, explaining things as he went.

"Right," Mike said, after a few minutes. "That's brilliant. That might surprise even the guy who wrote this theory. Hell, you could probably patent that with what you've got on that pad right now. So what do you want from me?"

Derek took a breath. Push had come to shove. "I want to make it my PhD project. That way I can use the equipment in the engineering lab and justify purchase of some of the materials."

Mike nodded, chuckling softly. "I thought that's what you were about. Well, I can't say this was anything I had expected. It's certainly not a direction I would have sent you in, but now I'm as curious as you are. I only see a couple of snags. Some of the exotic materials you need are gonna be expensive, as are some of the existing components you'll use, like that room-temperature super-conducting ring. This thing is going to use a lot of electrical energy in testing, too. We can cover it all through the department budget, but I think the University will need a piece of the patent to justify it. And I think that whoever wrote the theory is probably gonna want another piece."

"Right. He said so, but I can live with all that," Derek responded enthusiastically.

12

"It's settled then. If, as I assume, you want me to head the committee, we'll need at least two others. I suggest Mackelheney, but who else do you want?

Derek thought for a moment. "How about Helen Friedman? She's awfully good on the laser optics engineering and has a lot of friends in the Physics Department. The energy this thing is going to release, even on the scale we'll be using, is going to have to go somewhere and we might as well pipe it through the big laser over in the physics lab."

"Right. Okay. I'll talk to Ed and Helen, but you probably ought to go ask them personally. And you'll need to write up a formal proposal and justification of the project, of course. Take as much time as you need on that, though it would be nice if you finished it before the end of the semester, and make it good. When you get it done, if Ed and Helen agree, we'll think about scheduling a proposal defense for the faculty."

With that, Mike Zidelski stood up. "And, don't forget, I still need those CE 638 test questions fairly quickly."

"No problem, sir." Derek stood, shook Mike's hand, thanked him for everything, and headed out of his office door and past the secretary toward the hall. Things were coming together.

Chapter 2: The Mystery of Tom Wright

When Derek was gone, Mike shut the door behind him, went back to his desk, sat down, and punched in a code on his office videophone. It buzzed twice and was picked up by Professor Irwin Westholm, the chair of the Institute Physics Department. Westholm, whose picture appeared on the screen of the videophone, was tall, fifty-eight years old, with a prominent Adam's apple and thinning hair.

"Dr. Westholm, this is Mike Zidelski over in engineering."

"Right," the rather high-pitched male voice on the other end of the line responded. "What can I do for you, Mike?"

"Well. . . ," Mike hesitated, "something a little odd has happened over here. One of my grad students, Derek Martin, came to me with a PhD project proposal. As an engineering proposal, it's highly original, but it was based on some math he found posted on the bulletin board on the quad, of all places, just this morning. Apparently, someone posted it with an offer of a cash award for an engineering solution to a physics problem. Derek thought he would kill two birds with one stone."

"Hmm," Westholm muttered. "That is odd. One would think someone making an offer like that would post it in your building where the faculty and students would all see it, and not on the quad. But why does it concern me?"

"Well, the math is clearly an argument in abstract physics. Derek thinks it might be an extension of Einstine-Podolsky and Rosen entanglement in some esoteric way, which is much more up your alley than mine, to say the least. I thought you might have an idea who was responsible."

In his spacious, though cluttered, air-conditioned office on the top floor of the campus physics building, Westholm felt a chill on his forehead as sweat appeared. "Can you at least describe the argument?" he asked.

"I can do better than that. I copied most of it. The resolution on this phone might not be very good. Hold on. I'll scan it in and send it over to your computer." Zidelski held the paper in front of the phone scanner and punched in the computer system scanning command on his videophone.

In a moment the notes appeared on Westholm's computer screen, and through his optic nerves and logical faculties, impressed themselves on his brain. The sweat on his forehead got worse.

"Humph," Westholm squeaked in a voice somewhat higher and squeakier than normal even for him. He swallowed to clear his throat. "I've never seen this before, but it has a smell about it, a sort of . . . analytic style. Yes, I think I know who's probably responsible. He was a grad student of mine. Name was Thomas Wright. A troublemaker. I didn't know he was still around."

Mike sensed some of Westholm's stress. "I seem to remember hearing about him. Isn't that the student that you guys kicked out of the physics PhD program a couple of years back?"

"Yes. That's him." Westholm didn't bother to add that five other PhD candidates in Wright's class had also left the program in protest. From a class of only eighteen to begin with, that had hurt and the university administration had been quite upset. Only the return and reinstatement of two of the five had kept Irwin from losing his job, but some matters of principle had to be defended and he had, by damn, defended them.

"I never understood that," Zidelski pressed. "I heard Wright was a genuinely perfect student, brilliant, with a 4.0 GPA, who maxed everything and impressed everybody; maybe even a genius. I never got a straight story as to why he was expelled from the program."

Westholm gritted his teeth. "You wouldn't understand unless you knew and had to deal with him. You know how some pseudo-scientists are smart enough to make their nonsense seem logical? That was Wright. He wasn't as brilliant as everyone thought; just smart enough to make the crazy seem sensible to those of mediocre mentality. He was upsetting everybody, both faculty and students. He had to go. But obviously he hasn't entirely gone. My suggestion is that you put a stop to this nonsense. Don't let it proceed any further. After all, look at that energy field assumption here. Why it's like. . . phlogiston!!"

Mike was taken aback by the vehemence of Westholm's response. Westholm's reputation was one of a once top-flight physicist who had passed his prime and become somewhat set in his thinking. Some even said he hadn't had an original thought in over a decade. But he was still enormously competent, even influential in national and international physics circles, and his opinions were not easily dismissed. Still, Mike did not feel like being rousted.

"Well, as a purely engineering project, Derek's proposal seems feasible, even if there is something wrong with the cosmology behind the math that motivated it. I can't just revoke his authorization to pursue that without. . ."

"If you don't, there will be trouble," Westholm interrupted. "You'll see."

Mike decided it was time to end the conversation until he knew more. There were undercurrents here that he didn't grasp and Westholm wasn't going to enlighten him much. "Well, thanks for the advice, Irwin. I'll think it over and let you know what happens." He hung up and his view of a very distressed and somewhat irate Professor Irwin Westholm, PhD, disappeared as his videophone screen went blank.

Mike thought for a minute, then, rolling his chair over to his computer desk, he called up the DINOSAUR program that contained all campus records, entered the required codes and passwords, and shuffled files until he had the academic record and profile of one Thomas A. Wright on screen. Wright had been raised in Boise, Idaho. He was home schooled through high school, scoring perfectly on his GED. He had obtained his BS in physics at Oregon State University, graduating two years early. After a short stint in the army, where he had earned rank rapidly, and been awarded several impressive combat medals during the Disorders, he had applied and been admitted to the Edison Institute. As Mike had heard around campus, Wright's academic record here had been perfect clear through his PhD coursework. Amazingly, it turned out he had actually been pursuing *two* PhD's *simultaneously,* one in physics and one in math, and attained perfect grades in both fields. Disturbingly, nothing in the record explained his dismissal from the physics PhD program. Apparently, several members of the Physics faculty had threatened to quit *en masse* if the administration didn't uphold their dismissal of Wright. He *had* finished the math PhD program, however.

Surprisingly, Wright had not left the institution, as Mike had thought he had. Instead, Mike noticed that Wright had begun taking business and economics courses the very next semester under the name T. Alvin Wright, though he was taking many of them either online or through independent study. More oddly, he was only maintaining a 3.6 GPA. Mike felt a niggling suspicion that the guy was deliberately maintaining a low profile. His listed address was somewhere over in the industrial district on the other side of town.

Mike logged out of DINOSAUR and went back to his vid phone, punching in another number. The phone buzzed a few times in his ear before a sexy female voice answered and a young blond secretary's face appeared on screen. "Mathematics department. Doctor Hansen is out right now, may I help you?"

"This is Mike Zidelski over in engineering. Is Jake going to be back anytime soon?"

"Yes, I think so, Dr. Zidelski. He's teaching now, but his class is just letting out. He has a committee meeting at eleven, but I'm sure he's coming back to his office until then. In fact, here he is now. Hang on until he picks up."

It was only a few moments before her face was replaced on screen by that of the cheery, fifty-year-old, white-haired Math Department Chair. "Mike. What's the occasion? Haven't heard from you in a while. Almost never see you at the faculty meetings. What are you up to these days?"

Mike genuinely liked Jacob Hansen. The two had been friends for years, often taking their families on fishing trips together in the summer. But the frequency of those trips had diminished as they had both aged. "I'm fine Jake. Been busy as usual. And you know how I feel about most faculty meetings. But I got a question for you. You remember that dust up over in Physics a couple of years back, when that kid, Tom Wright, was kicked out of the PhD program? Back then I didn't know that he was in your program at the same time. What was that whole thing about?"

A little of the cheer seemed to go out of Jake Hansen's face. "Well now, that's a strange story, Mike. We never saw a natural mathematician like that kid.

Before he was even finished with the course work in the program, he was teaching *us* math."

Mike was surprised, despite all that he had heard about Wright on the physical sciences and engineering grapevine at the time. "You're kidding? You have three of the world's top mathematicians over there, including yourself, and a lot of other guys that are not far from top rank!"

"No, I'm not kidding. Wright's dissertation actually seems to have developed a couple whole new classes of mathematics, including some dynamic resonant field equations. It was so esoteric, that, truth be told, there was about a third of it that none of us could follow. There was actually some sentiment here similar to that felt by Westholm's crew over in physics. We wondered, for a while, if we were being scammed. Plus, there was the fact that here, as in Irwin's department, there were a lot of the better graduate students who got to be thick as thieves with Wright. They seemed to understand him. He had a sort of mesmerizing effect. Since we weren't sure ourselves quite what he was talking about a lot of the time, it was a little disturbing to have him influencing so many of the other students. But every time we figured out a piece of what he was saying, it turned out to be immensely insightful and to work. He solved problems that we couldn't handle and made it look easy. We had no choice but to give him his PhD. In fact, and I hope you'll keep this just between you and me, we're still mining that kid's dissertation like crazy. Several of us have already published peripheral applications; giving appropriate credit, of course. That kid will be famous in a few years whether he likes it or not."

"Do you know what Wright has been up to since then?" Mike asked. Not sure why, he decided not to tell Jake Hansen just yet that Wright was still on campus, apparently getting training aimed at some sort of career change.

"That's another disturbing part of the story, Mike. I don't know, and I don't know anybody else here who does. You can't have a student like that come along and people not find out about it. I know for a fact that about a dozen universities, research institutes, and large corporations were trying to hire him. Of course, that all ended when he was kicked out of the physics program. Then he just dropped out of sight, right off our radar screens. Never told any of us where he was going or where he went. Some of us who stood by him are a little miffed about it."

Jake rubbed his ear thoughtfully before continuing. "Just about as disturbing, we've lost several of those students that were thick with him. They dropped out of the program and out of sight over the last year or two, just like Wright."

"Do you think there's a connection?"

"It's possible. I heard a rumor - nothing more - that Wright might have gone into business for himself and started hiring talent for some big research project, maybe with business applications. I'll admit we haven't made much effort to find him or any of the others. Frankly, we've been a little relieved to get some normalcy back here. By the way, Mike, what got you interested in all this now?"

Mike thought again for a moment about telling Jake that Wright was still on campus, but decided again to keep that to himself for now. "Well, I don't quite know. This Wright kid might or might not be connected with an interesting doctoral project proposal a student of mine came up with this morning. I'm just a little curious. I talked with Irwin Westholm a few minutes ago and he was the one who suggested the connection."

On the vid screen, Jake Hansen turned and looked to one side. "Well, I'd like to hear more about all that, but I better ring off, Mike. Looks like some students are here to see me. Let me know if anything interesting turns up."

After he hung up, Mike thought for a few minutes. Despite the nagging questions, was there any point in pursuing this anymore? He didn't even really know if this Wright guy was behind the posting on the quad that had so animated Derek Martin. It might have been left by some corporate recruiter from the technology sector looking for talent on campus. And it might not matter anyway. Sighing, he rounded up the materials he needed and headed out to his meeting with the Chancellor.

*   *   *

After Mike Zidelski had hung up, Irwin Westholm sat nearly frozen in a cold, clammy chill, staring at the equations on his computer screen as his mind tried to come to grips with the ominous pieces of the puzzle just presented to him and to fit them together with the pieces of the past. Gradually a little of the paralysis wore off. Reaching into his pocket, he pulled out his NanoPod and checked his blood pressure, body temperature, and respiration. What he saw was not good and he forced himself to breathe, slowly and deeply. Gradually his shock began to be replaced by a burning anger and determination to somehow strike back at the madness that seemed to be surrounding and engulfing him again after he thought he had banished it once and for all. *If I can't stop it,* he thought, *maybe I can damage the one most responsible and profit in the process.* Picking up his phone, he rang up the department secretary in the anteroom of the office complex, disconnecting the video feed first. It wouldn't do to have her see him in the state he was in.

"Marge, I need to see several of the teaching and research fellows. Schedule them to see me separately, this afternoon and tomorrow morning. I'll only need about five minutes each with them." He then read her a list of ten of his most reliable graduate students, all of whom had office cubicles down in the sub basement.

"Then cancel my classes for the rest of the week. I'll probably be going out of town until at least next Monday. Then contact the corporate headquarters of Sony Electrodynamics in Tokyo and get Yukio Hasimata, the head of their Physical Research

Department, on the phone for me. If he's not available, ask to have him call me back. Tell them it's urgent."

Putting the phone down, he got up and began scanning a row of journals along one wall, looking for the latest issue of *Metaphysical Research Letters.* Pulling it out, he flipped through pages until he came to Hasimata's article, which Irwin had only scanned and scoffingly dismissed the first time he saw it, intuiting that it seemed similar in too many respects to Wright's madness. Now he began reading it carefully, marking the major passages and equations.

After a while, he turned back to his computer, opened a file he had not looked at in over a year and began scanning through Tom Wright's dissertation proposal for certain passages, which he soon found. At that point the phone rang. It was Marge. Feeling better now, he reconnected the video feed.

"Sir, I have Dr. Hasimata on the line. I'll connect you."

"Thanks, Marge." After a pause, "Ah, Dr. Hasimata. This is Irwin Westholm, from the physics department at the Edison Institute in Menlo Park, California. Yes, *that* Irwin Westholm. I read your article in *Metaphysical Research Letters* last month. Very impressive, Hasimata-San. It occurred to me that some recent breakthroughs made by a student of mine under my tutelage might provide a solution to your field modulation problem. I'd like to fly over there and discuss it with you, if you don't mind. I have a hunch it could be mutually profitable."

Chapter 3: Economics and Attraction

Thomas Alvin Wright arrived early for the ECON 588 midterm and took his usual inconspicuous seat, about half way back and a little toward the right side of the room, not far from the door. The room was already filling up with anxious students, many of which were talking nervously in low tones to one another. Some others were shuffling through either electronic or paper notes in the usual last minute effort to cram a little more information into their heads, and a few almost seemed to be praying. Tom took a stylus out of his pocket, and then he turned his desk computer on and initialized the stylus.

Economics had been a surprise for Tom. Entering the business program in the fall semester last year, because he realized that that particular expertise was going to be necessary for the project he had undertaken, he had signed up for microeconomic principles simply because it was one of three economics courses the business program required. He was quickly impressed with the insight and analytic power of economics. What astonished him most, initially, was how *economical* basic economic theory was; how much it was able to derive from a few sparse postulates about human nature and the physical universe.

From the social studies mush he and everyone else his age had been forced to suffer in the K-12 system, before his parents had taken him out and begun home-schooling him, it had never occurred to him that there was or could be a science of human action and interaction with the systematic rigor and explanatory insight economics had. It was embarrassing to him now to realize that all he had previously known about economics had the character of hearsay gathered from biased discussions by teachers in the 5-12 system who had all been unionized government employees and from ignorant 3-V network news analysts. It bothered him that this hearsay had turned out to be so misleading. His prior fixation on the physical sciences and math had also left him unprepared for the discovery that there was a nearly equally rigorous social science capable of providing immense insight on how the social and productive universe works. Now, whenever he could tear some free time away from the project, and wasn't plowing through math and physics journals, or completely relaxing with a novel, he read economics.

Tom also greatly enjoyed his business courses and unlike many business students, who resented having to take economics, he found the two subjects highly complementary. Economists did not say enough about management and marketing, but economics provided a crucial view of the larger social processes lying behind, and partly resulting from, the marketing, management, and other decisions made by persons narrowly focused on operating their business firms effectively and profitably. Tom had quickly decided to take courses in both subjects. In only a year he had completed a double major and was now working on a master's program in economics.

The Economics and Business faculty on campus, reputed to be among the best in the nation, seemed to be excellent teachers for a research institution, though Tom thought he was losing some of the benefit of this because he took most of his business and economics courses either on line or by independent study. That allowed him to work around his other activities, which took most of his time. Besides that, he seldom had to be on campus and run the risk of meeting somebody he didn't want to, who knew him in his prior student life as the famous, or infamous, physics and mathematics student. But some courses, including this one, were not offered on line or as independent studies, so he had to show up. That was okay. Occasionally he needed to be on campus for one reason or another anyway, as was the case today.

More students filed into the room, including the guy who had sat in the seat to Tom's right all semester. Rick French was a better than mediocre student who struggled with the math at times, though he also seemed to like economics and intuitively grasp most of its major insights.

"Hey, Alvin," Rick said, as he took his stylus out of his book bag and stowed the bag under the desk. "You ready for this?"

"Oh, you know me, Rick. I'll muddle through."

"Man, I've studied and studied and I still don't think I can replicate that matrix algebra proof of the short-run profit maximization formula. If he asks that I'm dead."

Tom shrugged. "Don't worry about it. You know Edleston's views are New Chicago and Proto-Austrian. He's probably going to focus a lot more on market processes and the entrepreneurial nature of resource use adjustments than on the maximization proofs. It'll be duck soup."

Rick muttered something in response, but Tom didn't hear it. A young women he had never seen before entered the classroom. Something a little less than an electric shock and more than a tingle went through Tom the moment he saw her and he lost all focus on anything else. She walked to the desk, moved the chair out of her way, and began scanning the students, some of whom were still finding their seats. She was a bit taller than most women, perhaps five-seven or eight, with medium length brown hair that seemed naturally arranged to accentuate a face Tom thought most angels would probably kill for (or would have thought had he been able to do anything more than gape at the moment). She also had generous curves packed into a modest but stylish dress. Her demeanor radiated a number of disparate elements: intelligence yet sensitivity, gentleness yet resolve, seriousness yet humor, restraint yet openness. All this combined and somehow *balanced* in a way that the most complex mathematical equation Tom could imagine (and he could imagine very, *very* complex equations) could never have described.

Tom had experienced all the same things going through puberty as every other male of the species, developing all the same urges and attractions. Nor was he a social eunuch. Perhaps it had been somewhat easier for him than for most guys because the almost obsessive love of physical sciences and math he quickly acquired had tended to dominate his attention, and because he had made a habit of burning off much of his sexual energy through rigorous and regular exercise. He had dated some, but never seriously, all through high school and college. Never, ever, however, had he felt an instant and powerful attraction like this one.

It was disturbing on several levels. In physics, Tom dealt with the most powerful and subtle forces of the physical universe. Yet, here was a powerful force he was experiencing right *now* that he could not even imagine how to describe in any such terms and all the talk in the world about "chemistry" could not explain why *this one,* and no other woman he had ever seen, did this to him. Nor were matters helped when, as the students settled down, she finally spoke in what seemed to Tom the most melodious and naturally sensual feminine voice he had ever heard.

"Good morning. My name is Gina Barlow. Professor Edleston is unavailable today and asked me to proctor the test. You have the usual fifty minutes. My advice is to take your time. If you finish early, however, feel free to leave. Be sure to enter the TEST COMPLETED command on your desk module before doing so, however. Good luck. And no cheating!" With that she inserted the test chip into the receptacle on her desk so that the test appeared on the desk-top units of the student's chairs, and they began.

With an act of will Tom had never previously have thought necessary, he tore his attention away from Gina Barlow and began working on the test. He flipped past the first several pages of multiple- choice, preferring to do the application problems first. They required the most concentration and hence helped him focus. Rick, as it turned out, was going to be disappointed. There was somewhat less of the market dynamics material and more of the mathematical maximization proofs on the test than Tom had anticipated. He wrote out those proofs quickly with his stylus in the appropriate answer blanks shown on the desktop screen. Their solutions were obvious, if you understood the economics as he did, and the math required was, to him, like first grade addition and subtraction would be to the normal college student. Next he turned to the graphic problem, drew that out with his stylus and filled in the question blanks.

Lastly, Tom went back to the multiple choice, true-false, and short- answer questions. Even the most difficult of these were so easy that, in fact, he had to make himself focus to be sure he *missed* the correct answers to a few questions. As near as he knew, none of the faculty or students in the business or economics departments had connected him with the Tom Wright who had so shaken up the physics and math departments two years back and more, and he would just as soon keep it that way. Anyway, it was information and understanding he wanted these days more than grades.

As he worked his way through the questions, Tom found himself losing concentration and stealing glances at Gina Barlow. Once or twice, he caught himself staring intently at her with his mind only half focused on the answer to a particular economics question. Dragging his attention back to the test, he finished up and glanced at the time readout on his computer. *Darn,* he thought. The whole thing had only taken ten minutes, and he couldn't log out and leave yet. The computer would record the log out time and taking something like the normal amount of time students take was another part of his cover desirable to deflect undue attention and questions. The problem now was, it left him with nothing but time for some undue attention of his own on the disturbingly attractive Ms. Barlow, who rendered the same intense tingle in him every time he looked at her; a fact he found strangely embarrassing.

Now that he thought about it, it occurred to him that he had heard of her somewhere once or twice. It was probably in some partly overheard fragments of conversations between other students in the business or economics programs. He seemed to remember something about her being a graduate student doing simultaneous doctoral degrees in political science and economics. That should have caught his attention from the first, and he wondered why it hadn't. He must have been distracted at the time. Yes, Lew Edleston had even mentioned her once when Tom was in his office to get help seeing some scale implications of Variable Elasticity of Substitution production functions.

She was tutoring for undergraduate economics that semester. Edleston, who was too busy to talk much at the time, had actually suggested that Tom look up Ms. Barlow, who had a cubicle down on the first floor with the other grad students, and who, he had said, was very sharp on isoquant analysis. Tom, who had been short on time himself (as usual), had not done so, which now, to say the least, he deeply regretted. *On the other hand,* he thought, *the last thing I need right now is this kind of distraction.*

Up front, Gina Barlow watched the class. She seldom sat in the seat behind the class command desk whether she was teaching a class for one of the professors or proctoring a test as now. And she never used a podium, though she had done so that one time when she had given her paper on the theory of optimal democratic electoral turnout to the Northwestern Political Economy Association last year. With her nervous energy, she felt more comfortable standing and moving in front of a class even when she was using LecturePoint 2025 on the front screen. Besides, it was necessary now to keep an eye on the students to minimize misbehavior and too little could be seen from behind a desk. So she wandered back and forth and looked up and down the columns and rows of seats.

Very quickly, Gina became aware of a prickly sensation that *she* was being watched, and rather intently. Of course, students often glanced up at her at random intervals, then back down at their work, and at age twenty-four she had long since become used to erotic male attention and scrutiny, but that was normally muted during class periods. This was different; a scrutiny that was only partly erotic, involving in addition an appraisal and appreciation of her character, personality, emotion, and intellect that felt almost psychic. She began looking back and forth among the students to see if she could see who it was, but could not find him, and it was definitely a him.

Suddenly questioning that intuition, in an effort to regain an objective mindset, it occurred to her that it just might be that the class monitoring system was on. All classrooms had visual and audio monitoring units connected to the school computer system, and classes were, by contract, randomly recorded and the information stored. Faculty tenure and promotion committees had access, and used the recorded information to aid in making their decisions. Faculty offices, in contrast, were private and by contract the university could not watch or record what went on in them, though, of course, it was often rumored that they did so. What happened in the classroom, however, was open season. But why would the Institute monitor a simple graduate student giving a test? She couldn't believe that was the source of her disturbing sense of being watched.

Ignoring the female students, Gina began systematically examining the men in turn and eliminating them as likely candidates one by one. Eventually her attention led toward the right side of the room, about halfway back, where a sandy-haired man, who looked to be in his mid twenties, just a little older than the average student, sat. She strongly sensed that he was the source of the attention, though he appeared to be focused on his test, not on her. She moved and looked away, then looked back several times, trying to catch him looking at her, but never did. Despite this, the feeling that this man was the source of the attention strengthened. It was odd. He was not quite, by objective standards, the *most* handsome man she had ever seen, though she felt an immediate, intense visceral attraction, and found herself admitting he was far, far from the least. It was hard to tell how tall he was, though she guessed he might be two or three inches over the average for men. From first appearances, he was in unusually good health and physical condition, not with the bulging and highly defined muscles of a weight lifter or football player, but with the smooth musculature of a swimmer, gymnast, or college wrestler. His whole bodily composure was one of restrained energy.

Going behind the command desk, she brought up the seating chart, and then touched the man's seat number to register his data. He had logged in as Alvin Wright and she could see that his test was already completed, making him probably the first student to finish. In and of itself, that meant little. Many students quit early simply because they realized they knew almost nothing of the required material, though the tests of such students were rarely complete. Others who finished early did so because they knew everything cold and just slapped it down fast. Paging through his test, she noticed something odd. He had completed all the really difficult parts perfectly. His mathematical proofs of the required economic theorems were impeccable. His graphic problem was finished without the slightest mistake, with everything labeled perfectly and the function shifts illustrated clearly. *But he had missed several of the more difficult among the multiple choice and true-false questions.* Apparently he was mathematically talented but had a problem with verbal interpretation.

Gina looked up at the man again to find that, this time, he was looking directly at her. Her eyes caught his, and if a two thousand-pound bomb had hit the Demsetz building at that moment she would not have looked away. She felt her pulse quicken. His eyes radiated a piercing intelligence she had never sensed before in any man; an intelligence that seemed to be examining and appreciating her, in an almost *hungry* way, to the bottom of her soul. His facial expression showed strength, kindness, and intense interest, and it held a slight, almost humorous, smile. Then it broadened into a discernible grin as he did something astonishing. He broke the lock on their gaze, looked down, and began working once more on his already completed test.

Gina quickly looked down at the classroom command desk, still showing his test, to see what he was doing. One by one he went back through all the questions he had answered incorrectly and changed them immediately in turn to the correct answers. Then, one by one, he went back through them and changed them back again to the wrong answers. Then he pressed the TEST COMPLETED command and logged out. Standing up, he walked, with the natural and unconscious grace and economy of a trained athlete, down to the front of the room and out the door, without looking at her. A moment later Gina noticed she was sitting in the chair behind the command desk. All of her life, she had heard her girlfriends talk about going weak in the knees from meeting some particularly attractive guy. She had never experienced it before.

Chapter 4: The Skeleton Crew in the Closet

The middle of the hour was the natural low point in student foot traffic around the campus, both too early to rush to the next class and too early for most students to be out of the current one. So, only a few people were strolling or lounging around in the bright sun and cool air of the mid fall semester central California morning. By the time Tom left the Demsetz Economics Building and made it over to the fountain on the Quad, he had nearly managed to put Gina Barlow out of his thoughts.

Thad "Beowulf" Thorson, a six foot two Nordic blond grad student two years behind Derek Martin in the electronic engineering PhD program, was lounging on one of the concrete benches placed at intervals around the fountain, waiting for Tom. He turned sidewise and grinned as he saw Tom walk up.

"Hey, Tom!"

Tom nearly always found Beowulf's cheeriness to be infectious. "Beowulf! What's the good word?"

Beowulf had fallen in rather quickly with Tom's Skeleton Crew, as they called themselves, somehow figuring out for himself that there *was* a Skeleton Crew and at least part of what they were about. Unlike some of the others, he had accepted Tom's suggestion to stay in the engineering program, not just to finish his PhD, but to be one of Tom's sets of eyes and ears on campus. So Beowulf just worked part time evenings, some nights, and when he could find time and a ride down and back during the day, on the project at the Asylum. Nevertheless, he was already a skilled and invaluable member of the Skeleton Crew.

Tom stuck his right foot up on the ornamental concrete retaining wall surrounding the pool, propped his arm on his knee, and divided his attention between Beowulf Thorson and the sunlight refracting through and reflecting from the water in the fountain.

"Well, boss," Beowulf waved his hand in the direction of a pair of lightly clad coed Frisbee players on the lawn south of the fountain, "I'm scoping out the babes here. There are some fine ones, too, as you can see. But that's not what you want to hear. I've got good news and bad news."

"You know me, Beowulf. Give me the good news first." What formal organization Tom had thus far given to the business side of the project was in the nature of a partnership and it bothered Tom to be called 'boss.' But the members of the Skeleton Crew, who were all equal partners, often did so and there didn't seem to be anything he could do about it. Tom never ordered, he only led, and despite the fact that the members of the Skeleton Crew were all highly independent sorts by nature, they followed.

"The good news is, Derek cracked it. Heck, he had it within a week after he saw your flyer on the board. For the last month he's been assembling the parts, ordering or machining what he didn't have, and putting the thing together in the engineering lab. Check it out."

Reaching into his backpack on the bench beside him, he pulled out a sheet of engineering schematics and handed it to Tom.

Tom turned around, sat down on the concrete lip, spread the schematics out over his lap and scanned it intensely for several minutes. A look of wonder and amazement lit his face.

"Wow," he said, "this is amazing. You're right. This will work. It will not only work, it will be cost effective."

"I'm telling you, Tom," Beowulf nodded, "the guy is preternatural. When it comes to engineering, he's almost as good as you are in physics and math. You know how long I and the other engineers in the crew have been trying to crack this nut and he does it in a week? I'm really starting to think now; we just might make the whole thing work. We'll all be filthy rich."

"Aha. Only now are you beginning to believe, young Padawan?" Tom kidded him. "Tsk, Tsk, Tsk. By the way, how did you get this?" Tom indicated the schematics.

Beowulf flushed visibly. "Actually, it wasn't hard. I asked him to tutor me for my comps. He's a good guy and was happy to help. We've gotten pretty friendly and I wheedled him into letting me see his project. He was actually glad to have another pair of eyes look it over since his faculty defense is coming up in a couple of weeks. He went through the whole thing and showed me how it would work. I actually made a helpful suggestion or two. See that part right there, I helped with that. He thought that was cool, made the change and ran me a copy."

"Hmm," Tom said. "He has to know at least some of the potential of this. If he gave you this in private, you really shouldn't have shown it to me. Did he say anything about where he got the idea?"

Beowulf snorted and laughed. "Yeh, he told me the whole story. It was kind of funny, since I was the one you asked to post the notice where he would be likely to see it that morning on his run. He's mystified, of course, but it's surprising how much of the basic physics and cosmology behind the project he's been able to intuit on his own. And I can tell you he's highly intrigued."

"Why hasn't he run the notice and claimed the prize? Doesn't he need the money?"

"Yeh, he does. He lost several shekels last week on internet horse races. But he's just too smart. He wants to finish the thing and run tests, be sure it will do what he thinks, and see what else it can do. I think he suspects that it might be worth a lot more than ten thousand NDs. Besides, now that it's an official PhD project and the university is involved in financing the thing, it's more complicated than that."

Tom fingered the blueprints nervously. "Right. I was hoping he wouldn't do that. In this case, trying to keep things on the sly has backfired on us. I hoped that if he saw a solution he'd just draw it out, make contact and show us his design. I'd give him his prize money and we could work out a joint patent and an agreement for us to knock it together down at the Asylum. The university wouldn't be involved."

"We could try recruiting him," Beowulf suggested.

"I guess that's the thing to do now." Tom agreed. "Up the ante and see if we can bring him on board. There are risks there. He could hold us up for a lot of money we don't have for the right to use his hardware. But it's our last option and we better do it quick. Entropy happens. Information spreads and we're in a race. We need that field modulator soon. Without it, we can't make the particles sing. What's the bad news?"

"What?"

"You said you had good news and bad news."

"Oh, yeh. Talk about information spreading. Dave Barret tells me something has Westholm all worked up again. He was out of town for a few days. Somebody said he flew to Tokyo. Since he got back, he's been making a lot of noise about you around the physics department and asking questions. Somehow he must have found out something about the flyer, too, because he sent some grad students out to scour the campus bulletin boards. Didn't find anything, of course, since I took it down right after Derek saw it. Dave heard some of them laughing about it."

"Damn." Tom fumed. "Westholm and his string theory acolytes have too much information already. If I could do it all over, I would have quit the physics program when I realized what I had and what I could do with it and would never have even submitted that dissertation proposal. Much as it scared them and they hated it, I'm sure they still have a copy. Westholm may be a slave to Bohr and Heisenberg mentally, but he's not a total idiot. If he sees those resonant field equations, he just might put two and two together and come up with something besides randomness."

A bright blue and white Frisbee flew past Tom's shoulder and splashed into the fountain. Beowulf was off his bench like a shot and into the water up to his knees retrieving the plastic disk. With a couple of feint tosses he finally threw it on a long, high arc out over the grass. The girls screamed and giggled and chased it. Beowulf stomped out of the fountain and made a halfhearted effort at wiping some of the water off his pants. "Well, what do we do then?"

Tom stood, shook some errant drops of water off the schematic, folded it up, and handed it back to Beowulf. Just then his NanoPod went off and he answered. "Yes? Okay. I'm coming now." Hanging up, he turned back to Beowulf.

"About Westholm, there isn't anything we can do. About Mr. Martin, I think it's time he and I had a man-to-man chat. But right now I have to head back to the Asylum. The guys got the relay unit together and in about twenty minutes they're going to try to power it up and calibrate it. If it works, we're one step closer with not many more to go."

"Rats!" Beowulf said. "I didn't think they'd have it done before five or six. I wanna be there for that. I've got an afternoon lab, but I think I can skip it. Can I ride over with you?"

"Sure, I was really hoping you would. Dave, Hulio, and Lynn are already down there; and we need you if you don't mind missing your lab. Dave said he'd give you a ride back later."

"That'll work. Let's go." Beowulf gave one last longing look and a wave at the Frisbee bunnies as the two men headed for the lot behind the Hayek Social Science Complex where Tom had parked his car.

"Say, Beowulf," Tom had to ask, "I know you've never spent much time on that side of the campus, but did you ever hear of a political science and economics grad student named Gina Barlow?"

Chapter 5: The Seduction
of Derek Martin

"Run another twenty-thousand amps into the induction field, Thad," Derek called as he eyed the power readouts and made an adjustment to his completed field modulator.

Beowulf Thorsen, working on the other side of the engineering lab, adjusted the generator as requested. "Okay, but I'm givin 'er all she's got, Captain," he called back in a mock Scottish voice. Then he rushed over to look at Derek's readouts as Derek made notes on his NanoPod.

In the field chamber above them, a purple nimbus sharpened into a nearly perfect and clearly defined sphere. As it did, a sound emerged from the inaudible range into the audible and crystallized into a pure note then faded back into inaudibility. Several other students working in the lab looked around in surprise.

"What was that?" Thad asked.

"About what I expected." Derek made another adjustment. "It's clear we're not going to need the laser. We're getting practically perfect energy conversion and the field is getting just tighter, more stable, more focused and more *harmonic.* I'm sure we aren't using the type of field this thing was intended for, but I just keep seeing more and more applications. You know one thing I could do? I could use this to make a whole new type of musical synthesizer better and cheaper than anything they have now. Bands would kill to have one. Look."

He turned to a computer on the table to his left, opened the ELECTROCAD design program and began drawing circuitry and peripherals. In a few minutes Beowulf was open-mouthed. He pointed to a part of the design and suggested several alterations. "Oh, that's good. How did you see that?" Derek asked. The two men worked happily for several minutes.

"You're right," Beowulf said. "This is cool. I played a synthesizer in high school, and there's nothing like this. A few refinements and you could make some money off this!"

"*We* could make money. I wish I knew a good patent attorney."

Beowulf looked thoughtful. "I think I know a guy. But we couldn't do anything without getting the rights to the field modulator settled first."

Derek left the computer and went back to his modulator readings. Jotting a few last readings and comments into his NanoPod, he said, "Okay, Thad, power down and we can disconnect."

Beowulf went back to the generator and cut the power. The purple sphere in the field chamber faded back into a haze and disappeared. The same pure note, in appearing and disappearing in reverse, hung in the air again before fading. Beowulf returned and began helping Derek disconnect the field modulator. "Wow," he commented, "all that energy going nowhere and the thing isn't even warm."

"We know a lot of the energy is going into field resonance," Derek responded. "We just don't quite know how. That bothers me. I've got to go back over those equations, maybe even see if I can work out a little more of the background theory and implications. I'm missing something."

Beowulf helped Derek carry the three main components of the modulator over and put them in a storage locker.

"You know, Derek, you could just ask the guy who developed the whole concept in the first place. Might be a bit easier. You're gonna have to look him up sooner or later. However, you figure it, this thing's as much his as yours. Besides, didn't you say you were short on cash? Somebody offered me ten thousand NDs for a piece of hardware I came up with that fast I'd think seriously about taking it. And he might even let us use it to build our synthesizer."

Derek locked the door on the storage unit, setting the palm print and retinal locks, and the two of them headed out of the lab, past a few errant students still working on their own projects or standing around watching him and Beowulf.

"Well, you're right, Thad. But I'm a little leery of meeting the guy just yet. It's like poker. I don't know what or how to bet until I know what my hand is and have some idea what the other players are holding. Speaking of which, I'm not going to be that short on cash much longer. I've got some sheep set up to be sheared down at the SUB tonight."

"You mind if I come and play?" Beowulf asked.

Derek was surprised. Thad and he had been palling around a lot lately, Derek tutoring Thad for his upcoming comprehensive exams and Thad helping Derek with the field modulator. The kid, called 'Beowulf' by most of his other friends, apparently because of his Nordic physique and parentage, was a talented engineer, soaking up everything his professors and Derek taught him at an amazing rate. And, of course, he was only a couple of years younger than Derek; not really much more of a kid than Derek himself. But Derek had never pegged Beowulf for a gambler.

"Sure, come along. The game usually starts about seven. But prepare to get shorn along with the other sheep. With me, poker is a blood sport."

Beowulf laughed. "I just play for fun. If I end up being one of the sheep, I'll quit early."

*   *   *

Since he planned on being up fairly late, Derek went back to his dorm room and took a nap. He woke up when Rufus came in and started cooking something at about four p.m. Then he spent an hour studying his advanced engineering statistics and was just about to start throwing a sandwich and some coffee together when the doorbell rang. It turned out to be Beowulf.

"Hey, Derek. I thought I'd drop by and we could go down to the SUB together. I'll spring for some burgers and fries at the cafeteria, then we can start playing."

Actually, Thad did a little better than burgers and fries. The cafeteria had some nice pork chops with brown gravy, potatoes, mixed vegetables, and a chef's salad. Derek topped his off with a piece of banana cream pie and Thad added a hot fudge sundae. Thad paid the cashier, they carried their trays to one of the four-place tables, and were just getting a good start when Beowulf looked up and waved at somebody over in the cafeteria line.

"Tom!" he called, and Derek looked over to see who Thad was talking to.

"Hey, Beowulf," the man waved back and started carrying his tray in their direction. He had sandy hair, an athletic build, looked to be about twenty-six or so, and walked much like some boxers and martial arts guys Derek had seen - carefully, with a controlled energy. Something about the guy pricked Derek's interest. Perhaps it was the intelligence in his eyes, or the look of discerning humor and good will on his face, or something else in his demeanor. But it occurred to Derek that this could turn out to be a man of surprising and unknown depths.

"Tom, do you know Derek Martin?"

"No," the man said, looking Derek in the eyes and shaking his hand in a firm and friendly grip that Derek felt could, if the man wanted, crush rocks. "I'm Tom. Are you one of Beowulf's engineering friends?"

Before Derek could answer, Beowulf jumped in. "That's an understatement. Derek's the best engineer on campus, maybe excepting a couple of the Profs. But he's more than that. He's an inventor. Tom here

48

is into economics. Set your tray down and join us, will you, Tom?"

"You mind?" The man asked Derek.

"No. Have a seat," Derek responded. "Nice to meet you, Tom. Economics, huh? Now that's an interesting subject. I took a few courses as an undergrad. Heard about supply and demand all my life, but the first time I really saw it explained, it was a revelation to me. Actually thought of going into the field, but finally decided on engineering instead."

"Say," Tom sat down, arranged the food and utensils on the plate to his satisfaction as he spoke, and started eating along with the others, "did you know that some of the very best French economists of the mid 19th century started out as civil engineers? They got to thinking about it because they had to deal with the cost side of their projects and not just the engineering aspects. They did a lot of marginal analysis very early."

"Right." Derek pointed over at Tom with his fork, before using it to spear another piece of pork chop. *I could get to like this guy,* he thought. "Jules Dupuit and, uh, what's-his-name . . . Cournot."

"Oh, I heard about them," Beowulf put in. "Doctor Salinger actually covers them in his Engineering History course. I had it last semester."

"Right." Derek agreed, chewing on his pork chop. "But Dupuit and Cournot gave the profession Oligopoly Theory, which I always thought was a mess."

"Oh," Tom chuckled, "that's one thing we definitely agree on. But the important thing was the techniques of analysis and the practical mind set they brought to the economics profession. Say, did you ever notice how inventing, engineering, and economics *always* go together? Think of the great inventors of the eighteenth and nineteenth centuries; particularly the early guys."

Beowulf hurried to swallow a mouthful of carrots, peas, and corn. "I know what you mean. Watt, John Fitch, Fulton, Oliver Evens, Shreve, Whitney, Colt, the whole Connecticut River Valley complex thing. They all not only had to come up with the ideas and solve the engineering and production problems, but do it in a *cost effective way.* And they had to find financing and develop the markets. Miss any of those things and you just wasted time and lost money, which a lot of them did."

"True," Derek agreed, "but thankfully some of them didn't. And if they did, the really good ones learned from their mistakes and kept trying 'til they got it right. But I see your point, Tom. Invention of something potentially useful isn't enough. It takes innovation, too, the practical engineering, manufacturing, and marketing. If invention is all you have, you end up like a Leonardo da Vinci, with drawings of machines that never get built, manufactured and sold until four or five hundred years later, and that entire time people just go on living in poverty."

"Whoa, Kimo Sabe," Beowulf objected. "I'm not sure I'd go that far. You can't blame poor Leo if the engineering technology of the sixteenth century didn't allow the production of the helicopter."

Tom put his fork down and chewed slowly as he thought. "You both have good points. Watt, Fitch, Evans, Colt, and the rest all made their efforts at a time when other people were working on similar problems and they could draw from each other on what worked and didn't work. But doesn't using Leonardo as an extreme case obscure the more fundamental question of why so *few* minds were focused on solving such problems in Leonardo's time and place, and why did so comparatively *many* minds start to be focused that way in Britain and the U.S. during the eighteenth and nineteenth centuries? It took the Watts and Whitneys and Colts decades to develop and refine their machining technologies, to the point they could go from unique craftsmanship to interchangeable parts and so on. But they just kept trying, over and over."

"True," Beowulf added. "Even though they lost money most of the time. But when they did get something right, it could pay off big. Did you know, by the way, that the ancient Greeks had the steam engine? An actual working model and didn't do a darned thing with it? Why is that?"

"Well, it seems to me that that's the second level at which invention, engineering and economics all go together," Tom responded. "Not many minds, from a given population, become focused on solving such problems *unless the economic incentives for people to do so, embodied in the law, are right.* Private ownership, so that if you make something people like you can gain personally. Low taxes. The rule of law, with governments limited mostly to preventing crime, providing defense, and enforcing private contracts. Seems to me those legal and institutional inventions and innovations were the most fundamental ones of all."

Now I know I like this guy, Derek thought. "Right on." He raised his glass. "Let's hear it for the boys at Philadelphia." Another thought struck him. "By the way, speaking of inventors and entrepreneurs, did you ever notice how *young* most of those guys were when they made their marks?"

"Oh, right." Beowulf caught his thought. "You gotta start early. Oliver Evans. Only seventeen when he invents a machine to make the wire teeth they used to remove cotton snags in textile mills. It knocked them out about a thousand times faster than they could by hand. Then before he's thirty-six he has the world's first automated assembly line in those flour mills up in Pennsylvania, making better quality flour at a fraction of the previous cost. That's about *seventeen-ninety,* if you can believe it, more than a hundred years before Ford!"

Derek was perplexed. "I thought Evans invented the high-pressure steam engine."

"He did," Beowulf laughed. "That came next. They say he got that idea when he was just a kid, though, from the son of a rifle maker who had fun putting water down a new rifle barrel, stuffing wadding in as hard as he could, then holding the end of the barrel in a fire until it blew the wadding out. Evens kept inventing things all his life and he was one who actually made money at it."

"Guess there's still hope, then, for any of us who might be thinking about revolutionizing the world." Derek noticed that Thad's friend was watching him rather intently as he said this.

A few minutes later the conversation wound down as they began to run out of food. Beowulf pushed his plate away, leaned back and stretched. "Say, Tom. Derek and I are meeting a few guys for a little poker in a few minutes. Wanna come?"

Tom seemed to think it over. "Well, I really have a lot of other things I should go do, but it is Friday night. I guess I can cut loose a little."

The three of them drifted down to the small casino the university maintained in the Student Union Building. Derek led them over to the table in a corner he usually used. A dealer came over, started arranging things, and they bought their chips. They were still getting comfortable when Dustin Malik came in with two of his friends from the English program. Derek waved them over and made introductions. They were apparently feeling flush, because they each bought over a hundred NDs worth of chips. Once they were settled play began. *Let the shearing begin,* Derek thought.

For a while it went that way. It wasn't correct to say that Derek was addicted to gambling, but it was his favorite spare time sport. He had practiced it into an art form and Poker was his specialty. Few people had good enough memories or were good enough at math to be able to count cards, but Derek was a far better than average card counter. He played a lot on the internet, but there was something a bit different, and more fun, about sitting around a table and looking into the eyes of the people you were playing, interpreting human cues as well as calculating the odds. It was especially fun taking money from Dustin Malik and his friends, since they thought they were good poker players and weren't. Like many mediocre players, they thought their repeated losses to a better player were just a run of bad luck and kept coming back for more.

True to his word, Beowulf Thorsen, down twenty NDs, had cashed out at about ten o'clock and was simply watching the others play. By then Dustin and his friends, Terry O'herlihy and a French-Canadian student named Reynaud 'Ray' Gosselin, had nearly lost the shirts off their backs and seemed determined to reverse things by betting more heavily on each hand. This was somewhat earlier than they usually tapped out, because Derek was not the only big winner so far. Beowulf's friend Tom was up even more than Derek was.

"Raise fifty and call," Ray said.

"That's it for me," Dustin muttered, and threw in his hand. "I think you guys are in it together." He nodded at Derek and Tom.

"Hey, I barely met this guy," Derek protested.

"I'm out, too," Terry said, throwing in his cards.

Derek thought Ray was bluffing again. "I'll take that bet." He tossed in a fifty ND chip.

Tom also slid his chip into the pot. "I'm in, too."

Ray had placed his cards face down on the table. He turned them over, revealing three tens.

Derek put his hand down, showing three queens, an eight and a jack, and thought he had won until Tom put down a full house, Aces and eights, the famous 'dead man's hand'.

"Well, I guess if Dustin and Terry are going, I am, too," Ray said. He cashed in his few remaining chips.

"We'll see you around the dorm, Derek," Dustin said as the three men picked up the beers they had been nursing and headed for the door.

Derek looked over at Tom. "You play much? You're awfully good."

Tom's smile was a bit enigmatic. "Oh, I often take gambles, but I seldom play cards. You can chalk this up to beginner's luck."

Derek's eyebrows raised a little, and then lowered. "Chilly day in purgatory before I believe that. Well, it's still early, and I'm still ahead. Let's see how this plays out." He nodded to the dealer. "Play on, Macduff."

By midnight it was clear it was not playing out well for Derek. Using every trick he knew, counting every card he could, and computing the odds from every angle, he had won only four of the last ten hands. Tom was relentless. Derek could not read him, could not bluff him, and he seemed to anticipate all of Derek's moves. Finally, chance favored Derek with a strong hand and he decided to bet heavily and see if he could make up lost ground. He pushed everything he had left into the pot. "Call."

Beowulf Thorsen had been leaning back in his chair with his feet propped up on another. He pulled his feet down and leaned forward over the table, watching his two friends closely. Tom put his cards face down, leaned his right elbow on the table and pinched his chin with his thumb and forefinger as he considered Derek. "Are you sure you want to do that?"

Derek swallowed, but kept his poker face on. "I'm sure."

Tom stared Derek in the eye for a few more moments before speaking. "I'll tell you what, Mr. Martin. I'll make you a different kind of bet I think you'll find to be a win-win offer. I'll put up everything I have here against what you've bet and if you win this hand, you take it all. If I win, you keep your money, but you borrow that field modulator you designed from the Engineering lab just for a little while Monday morning and you let Beowulf here take you across town to where I can show you what it's really for."

Derek sat back in his seat, stunned, unable to speak for a moment. Then: "You're the guy who wrote the math."

"That's right."

"You said you were an economics student."

"I am, right now, among other things. But my primary expertise is math and physics."

Derek nodded knowingly, squinted his eyes, and pursed his lips as some of what was going on began to become clearer to him. "The Tesla biography was a nice touch. It gave me some clues."

"That was the point."

Derek looked over at Beowulf. "You knew all along. You set this whole thing up." It was not a question.

Beowulf shrugged and nodded. "Take him up on it, Derek. There's more at stake than you think. The payoff for all of us is huge."

Derek looked back at Tom. The guy was right. It was a win-win set of options, even if Beowulf was wrong. He laid down his cards. Ten high straight flush, diamonds.

Tom turned his hand over. Ace high straight flush, spades.

Derek thought intently for a moment, straining to remember something that he had heard of a couple of years back; someone he had thought at the time that he would like to meet, but never quite had. He could feel the memory trying to coalesce out of his subconscious. Then it came to him. "You know," he said, "I didn't think to ask before. Is your last name Wright?"

Chapter 6: Wonder in the Asylum

It had clouded up and rained over the weekend, but the clouds had burned off late Sunday afternoon. Monday morning dawned clear and bright. Derek walked over to the engineering building early. It was usually open by about six, two hours before any classes started, and he wanted to get the modulator out before Mike Zidelski or any of the other professors were around to ask questions. They might have some objections to him and Beowulf borrowing, however temporarily, a potentially valuable piece of what was, at least in part, institute property. Zidelski certainly could be reasoned with and would probably be almost as curious as Derek to find out what was going on and just what central use the field modulator had, but a lot of people were clearly doing a lot of things they didn't intend other people to know about just yet. Derek felt it might be best to find out for himself what was going on and fill Mike in later, if at all. He couldn't see much risk in borrowing the field modulator unless it was somehow damaged or destroyed in whatever test or operation the mysterious Tom Wright was going to subject it to, and Derek would be there to see that no such thing happened, if he could. Nor could he see Thad allowing anything bad to happen to it and thereby jeopardize his standing in the PhD program.

Very few cars were in the lot in front of the building this early, but as Derek arrived an old green Chevy

Carnivore pulled up and two men got out. One was Thad, who had agreed to meet Derek there. The driver was Dave Barret, one of the better students in the physics PhD program. Derek had met him a few times and they knew each other by name. Oddly, neither Dave nor Thad looked like they had slept for some time, though they both appeared cheerful, with a sort of nervous energy.

"Dave," Derek nodded. "Don't tell me you're part of this whole conspiracy too? This just gets curiouser and curiouser."

Dave looked at Thad. The two men shrugged, and then headed up the steps with Derek. "Well, I wouldn't exactly call us a conspiracy, Derek; just a sort of covert project. Right, Beowulf?"

"Yeh. Just trying to manage informational entropy. You know how it spreads, Derek. Sometimes, to take advantage of something you know, you not only have to know it first, but limit that flow."

"And just what is the project, anyway?" Derek asked.

Again, Dave and Thad glanced at each other and something unspoken passed between them before Thad answered. "You'll see."

"Maybe we'll all see," Dave added.

"You ever know anything Tom said would work not to?" Thad asked Dave.

Dave became defensive. "Well, there *was* that time. . ."

"But that wasn't his fault," Thad shot back. "You got the circuits reversed on the discriminator. It's no wonder it blew up!"

"I designed 'em right! It was Lynn that snapped those circuits in."

"That's not what she says!"

The three men took the stairs up to the lab on the third floor. Derek opened the security locker and Thad helped him take the modulation unit out. They disassembled it into its three main components and put them each into a padded packing crate. Each carrying one, they took the elevator back to the first floor. In a few minutes they had them stowed in the trunk of Dave's car. Derek climbed in the back seat, the other two got in the front, and they headed out of the lot and off campus.

"Where we going, exactly?" Derek asked as they wound down Reagan Avenue and through town.

Dave, driving, glanced back over his right shoulder. "To the Asylum."

"The what?"

"The Asylum. Our lab. Our research and fabrication business." He looked pleadingly over at Beowulf. "What is it called? I forget."

"Universal Research and Fabrication is the official name," Thad explained to Derek. "Only we never call it that."

"Why do you call it the Asylum?"

Dave and Thad both laughed and high-fived. Thad answered as Dave kept one eye on the road and his left hand on the wheel. "Because so many insane things get thunk up there and so many even crazier ones get done. It's out past the warehouse district on the edge of town. We'll be there in another ten minutes or so. You'll get to meet the rest of the Skeleton Crew."

Derek shut his eyes and shook his head. "I don't even want to ask."

*   *   *

Dave turned off the state road onto what appeared to Derek to be a private airfield, only no planes were in evidence. The access road led down along the main runway toward a huge hanger off to one side at the end of the runway. On the other side there was a smaller hanger and some other buildings and sheds. There was also a small control tower. Seven or eight cars were parked at the close end of the main hanger. Dave pulled up and parked next to them.

The three men got out of the car and Dave walked back to open the trunk.

"Why an old abandoned airfield?" Derek asked Thad.

"Well, it was cheap for one. Plus, the hanger was big enough for our lab. And as for the runway," he grinned, "we figured that if everything goes right, we'll need the parking space."

Each man picked up one of the packing crates. Derek followed the other two through the door at the end of the building. Once inside Derek stopped and gaped as he tried to assimilate the scene inside the hanger. The other two men also stopped, waiting for him.

The place was huge and much of the first half seemed to be filled with physics and engineering lab equipment. Most of it Derek recognized. Some of the equipment appeared not to be new, but it was all well maintained and serviceable. Some of it, on the other hand, was strange and exotic and Derek suspected those items might be beyond the state of the art as he knew it. All of the computer equipment seemed up to date. Near the center of the building was what appeared to be some kind of large mainframe supercomputer, where several people were inputting data and monitoring processes. Derek was familiar with supercomputers of the Rubidium atom quantum memory chip design pioneered by Lafyatis and Christandl before The Disorders, but only perfected a decade or so back when the Second Great Depression finally ended. This one had one of the brand new holographic displays, but with a resolution and size he had never heard of. The spherical hologram had a circumference that easily spanned twenty feet in the air above the mainframe At the moment it seemed to be displaying complex circuitry in the walls of some cubic construction.

"Impressive, isn't she?" Thad nodded at the display. "Dave and some other members of the Crew helped Tom develop a new form of nano cubit memory chip for her CPU. We call her Zelda. She's at least a generation ahead of anything commercially available right now."

"Wait 'til you talk to her," Dave added. "You'll think she's human."

"You mean you've got true interactive verbal input and output?" Derek was amazed. "You're that close to true AI?"

"I think Dave's in love with her," Thad laughed. "Come on. Tom's waiting. We're almost ready."

"Ready for what?"

"Ready for you. Ready for us. Ready for this." Beowulf hefted his crate, stuck his tongue out, panted as if it was heavy, and began leading the way down the long axis of the building.

As he followed, off to his right, Derek saw something seemingly incongruous. The front right corner of the building was set aside as an open gymnasium, with rings, bars and a horse for gymnastics, weights and other exercise equipment. There was also a large exercise mat that was not of the rubber wrestling kind, but which seemed to consist of plastic covered rectangular sections, fitted together.

Just past the now unoccupied open gym was what might be a large shower and dressing room complex, followed by a set of offices that extended most of the way down the right side of the onetime airplane hangar. Actually, the whole front part of the building was currently unoccupied, except for Derek, Thad, and Dave, but as the three men walked down, Derek could see that there was frenetic activity at the other end of the building. As they passed the mainframe Derek was surprised to notice that he knew a couple of the computer programmers and technicians from classes in computer programming he had taken at the Institute. Apparently Mr. Wright had been poaching talent from more than the physics, engineering, and math departments.

Now Derek could see that the construction represented in schematic in the holographic display was actually in the final stages of assembly and testing at the approaching end of the building. It was a huge cube about two-thirds the width of the building and as much long, with the same height, ceramic walls, and the front open. The design appeared to Derek to be modular, for easy replication, he guessed. Both inside and outside of the cube there were panels off the walls and the ceiling in places, where work was being done, apparently on circuitry and components inside. Scaffolds had been set up where the circuits being worked on were too high to reach otherwise. Three people working up in the ceiling through an open panel stopped and looked back at the mainframe holodisplay, and Derek looked back also. A major circuit shown in red in the display changed to yellow and flashed several times, apparently indicating active status. The three men cheered and began fitting the panel up into place.

About a dozen people were working in teams of three or four, either on the cube or on a complex piece of electronic equipment and control panels outside the left front of the cube, which had a large power lead in and several other power leads out to the cube. Derek was even more surprised this time to realize that he knew many of the workers, the "Skeleton Crew" as

Dave and Thad had called them. Hulio Sanchez, who had dropped out of Derek's class in the Engineering doctoral program without explanation six months back, was working inside an open panel on the left wall of the cube. Among the three who had been working inside the ceiling panel and were now scrambling down the scaffold, he saw Lynn Yip Ki, a small third generation Taiwanese-American gal who had finished her physics PhD class work last year. She and Derek had been good friends, but he hadn't seen Lynn around campus in months. And there was Philip Adobo, the Nigerian Math student, Billi Jo Jensen, a very bright and attractive gal with coal black hair from Thad's class in the engineering program, and several others he knew. It struck him with some force that he not only knew these people, but that they were all highly skilled people he liked, trusted, and had been friends with. *All this going on,* he thought, *and why am I the last to know?*

Lynn Yip Ki, reaching the floor of the cube, turned around and saw Derek. A big smile lit her face, she squealed, and began jumping up and down in a most un-Chinese fashion, as she waved at him. Several of the others, hearing Lynn, waved and called out greetings to Derek. It was almost embarrassing.

"You're already popular here," Thad commented. "Hey, Tom, we made it."

Tom Wright, in conference with two members of the Crew working on what was apparently the control station next to the strange device at the left side of the cube, heard the hubbub and turned toward the approaching men. "Well. I'm glad to see you guys. I was beginning to wonder. We're almost ready. Just a couple more circuits to connect up and check. Here; set those down here."

The three men set the packing crates down and Dave and Thad began taking the modulator components out as Tom shook Derek's hand. "I'm glad you decided to come. Is this going to cause any problem with the Institute? Because we can stop right here if it is."

"I don't see a problem," Derek responded, "as long as we get it back and in good shape, before anyone up there asks questions. I don't see any harm done as long as it isn't physically degraded. In fact, I suspect that what I find out here might even enhance its value to the University."

Tom seemed a bit relieved. "Good, because we've been working in shifts all weekend to get ready for this and I'd hate to have to stop now. I really appreciate your willingness to let us try this."

Thad and Dave had the components out of the boxes and it only took a minute to connect up the completed unit. Tom looked it over admiringly. "Now that's an elegant piece of work. You don't know how hard we tried to solve that ourselves. Once we actually had something that we thought might have . . ."

A female member of the Skeleton Crew that Derek didn't know came up to Tom, put a hand on his shoulder, and spoke something to him quietly enough that Derek couldn't hear.

"Dave," Tom looked up. "They're still having trouble with the discriminator circuits on the number fifty-three West side module. Can you go help them? We get that fixed and get this connected I think we're finally ready."

Dave and the woman hurried off toward the west inside wall of the cube where a couple of other people were still working on the one remaining open panel. Other members of the Skeleton Crew were taking down scaffolding and removing tools as they cleared the area.

"You want to help me with this, Beowulf?" Tom asked. He and Thad picked the assembled field modulator up and carried it over to the large device next to the control station and began fitting it up to that device which Derek guessed was the central field generator, or at least the core unit that would generate the field within the cube. Derek followed along.

"If you could run those power leads through there and plug them in, Derek, we can connect this sleeve." It took the three men about fifteen minutes to mate the modulator to the field generator, then Derek watched as Tom, Beowulf, and another man Derek didn't know sat at the control stations and carefully tested all the circuits, connections, and functions to see that the completed unit was working harmoniously. By that time the last members of the Crew had cleared the cube with the last of the tools and equipment. Several, including Dave and Lynn Yip Ki, came over to watch what was going on at the control station, while others stood a ways back in front of the cube and looked in as if in anticipation. Lynn came over, stood on her tip toes, and gave Derek a big hug and greeting which he reciprocated. It always surprised Derek how demonstrative Lynn was. Derek still didn't know what kind of field was going to be generated in that cube, but from watching the dials, power flow units, and screens on the control panels, he was getting increasing suspicions. Looking back down the hanger at the holo display above the main computer, he could see that all the circuit segments shown there were now in the yellow.

Tom touched the throat mike he had slipped on, and his voice was projected all over the building. "Well, everybody, this is what we've been working towards for two years now. First time through we're going to take it slow and by the numbers. If this doesn't work, and you know I expect it to, but if it doesn't, I want you to know, a man never had better friends than you and it's all been worth it."

Alarmed, Derek turned to Dave. "What's he talking about?"

"Well," Dave looked a bit sheepish, "depending on how you read the equations, one of two things is going to happen. Either we are about to do something amazing and live to be amazed by it, or we and this facility and half of Menlo Park are going to be instantly transformed into heat and light. But cheer up. That second one has a lower order of probability."

"How low?"

"Oh, definitely less than fifty percent. We'll be able to calculate it better after a few trials. If we get through three or four, it becomes a vanishing order of probability."

Derek swallowed hard as Tom's voice boomed out.

"Okay, let's make the initial placement."

Two small wheeled robots Derek had not noticed previously moved into the cube, carrying in their pincers what appeared to be small ceramic posts, about three feet high. They wheeled the posts to opposite sides of the cube and set them carefully down. A third robot carrying something that appeared to be a small drinking cup then entered the cube, headed for the left side post, and carefully lifted the cup up and placed it on top, before following the other robots out of the cube.

"Run the dust screen sweep," Tom called out.

A light purple screen or field appeared at the back of the cube, from one side to the other and moved forward. Derek could see its edges as it crossed the pillars. At the front, open side of the cube it stopped.

"Modulating to zero-zero."

The screen either dissipated or shifted into the invisible part of the spectrum. Derek suspected the latter. Dave leaned over toward him and spoke softly. "We're just eliminating dust and all other contaminants from the space. Reducing computation, memory, and translation requirements. It's a pristine environment in there now. We debated getting rid of the air, too, at least for the first test, but decided we could handle it. It would have cost us too much field power maintaining a vacuum anyway."

"Powering up the D-R field."

"Check," Beowulf responded from the second station at the control desk. The device hummed and the inside walls of the cube glowed softly as a field began to coalesce.

"D-R field?" Derek quietly asked.

"Dematerialization-Rematerialization field, dummy," Lynn poked him gently with her elbow. "You mean you haven't figured it out yet?"

"Discrimination and resolution?" Tom called.

"Atomic and declining," the man in the third control station responded. "Zelda says subatomic imminent. Check."

There was a tension in the air that was something more than just the anticipation by Derek, Tom, and the members of the Skeleton Crew. It was something palpable, happening in the material universe around them.

"Field Harmonics now," Tom directed, adjusting the control.

Somehow it felt as if a pressure emerged from the cubic chamber, though it seemed more mental than physical as it swept through Derek and the members of the Skeleton Crew, and it had a profoundly resonant and *musical* character, of a tone, pitch, and harmony no one had ever heard before.

"Watch that feedback, Beowulf," Tom said.

"Got it," Beowulf responded. "Phase-canceling now."

The harmonic mental pressure wave diminished and disappeared, the absence somehow haunting and disturbing as the memory of an unearthly, *heavenly* tune almost grasped faded.

"What was that?" Derek looked around. "What's happening?"

There was a sense of wonder on Lynn's face as she looked up at him. "The particles are singing."

"Okay, folks," There was a touch of nervousness in Tom's voice, "Displacement in ten, nine, eight. . ."

"Should we be wearing dark glasses or something?" Derek whispered.

Lynn elbowed him again and Dave whispered nervously, "Shhh!"

"Four, three, two, one, displacement."

Maybe they should have been wearing dark glasses. There was a brief flash of light from the top of the pillar holding the coffee cup and an audible popping sound as the cup disappeared from the top of the left post, and *reappeared at the same instant on the top of the right side post.* Derek's eyes went wide and his mouth dropped open. Pandemonium broke out as every member of the Skeleton Crew began whooping, cheering, jumping up and down, dancing around, and slapping one another on the back. Tom jumped up from his station, rushed up to the edge of the chamber for a closer look at the cup, and then went back to his station.

"Scanning?" His voice boomed out.

"Zelda says the pattern's the same, boss," the man at the third station responded excitedly, "Right down to the last neutron and proton. The photonic emission seems to have just bled off from a few of the air molecules around the cup."

"Power down."

"Powering down."

Tom got up and rushed forward again, this time going into the chamber. Derek followed, along with the other members of the Skeleton Crew. Everyone wanted to see and they crowded around, but gave Tom a little room as he approached the right side post, slowly picked up the cup, examined its contents, then lifted it to his mouth and emptied it. An intensely pained look came on his face, and he said, "Coffee! All right, who's the Joker? You know I wanted hot chocolate!"

Tom waited a few moments for the laughter to die down, but now he was more serious. "Well, guys, we've just made the greatest scientific and technological breakthrough in more than a century. Whatever else happens, this moment is going to live in history forever. As soon as we can make a permanent arrangement to use Mr. Martin's field modulator, *if* we can, we'll start running more transmissions, scaling up size and mass. Assuming no glitches at that point, we'll start running live animal transmissions. Even if all that goes as we hope, remember, all we've done is beat the technical problems. We still have the crucial business and financial ones to go. As I keep telling you, making teleportation work and making it work *economically* are different things. But I think we can do it. For now, you're as tired as I am, so I suggest we wrap things up and take the rest of the day off."

It wasn't quite that simple, though. Everyone wanted to shake Tom's hand, slap his back, and congratulate him as well as each other. Most of the members of the Skeleton Crew also shook Derek's hand and thanked him, apparently convinced that his field modulator was crucial to the success of the experiment, which Derek suspected to be true. Finally the Crew began to disperse, and Tom pulled Derek aside.

"I'll get Dave and Beowulf to pack up your modulator. While they're doing that, have you got a few minutes to talk?"

*   *   *

Tom led Derek back down the hanger into the complex where the members of the Crew apparently had personal offices. The ceilings in the complex were hung about ten foot high and well lit.

"This is mine down here," Tom pointed. The office they entered was modest, though reasonably large and spacious. It held a couch and several chairs in front of a large desk with a comfortable looking office chair behind it. A computer desk off to the side of the main work desk held a state of the art Macintosh and a printer. Behind the office chair there was a floor to ceiling bookshelf, with very little remaining space on it, covering that wall. Between the computer desk and the couch was a second door which Derek surmised led to another office.

Tom waved a hand in the direction of the couch. "Have a seat. Be back in a minute." Then he went back out the hall door, returning shortly with another man, slim, average height, with a neatly trimmed beard and mustache, who, at somewhere between fifty and sixty, was the oldest man Derek had seen since he entered the Asylum.

"Derek, meet Buzz Byrd. His firm handles our legal work. You can speak freely. Buzz knows everything. He's an old family friend and, in fact, has been rather heavily invested in our project here from the first."

"Nice to meet you." Derek stood and shook the man's hand. He seemed to be a pleasant, though businesslike sort.

"You can call me The Buzzard. Everyone else on the Crew does."

"They all mean that affectionately, though," Tom said. "Buzz's firm does all our patenting work, too. That's one of our two main sources of income nowadays, so the guys all love him."

Tom took one of the comfortable chairs opposite the couch; and as the others made themselves comfortable, he leaned back, stretched, and closed his eyes for a moment before focusing again on Derek.

"You'll have to excuse me if I'm not my normal self. We've been at it all weekend and if I don't get some sleep soon I'm going to keel over. I'd go to bed now if we didn't have some important things to settle."

Derek's ears pricked up. "You live here?"

"Oh, yes. My quarters are through there." Tom indicated the door next to the couch. "I'm the only one actually living on site though some members of the Crew, like Dave and Lynn, are out here so much you'd think they lived here."

"So the gym is for you."

"Well, I had it installed, yes. On a normal day, I work out for at least a couple of hours in the evening. I think a lot like the old Greeks. A healthy mind and body go together. But a little of it must be rubbing off, because I usually have several other people working out with me. And some of the Crew members use it at different times."

Derek wanted to ask what the mat was used for, but decided to cut to the chase instead. "If I heard you right out there, you're out for a lot more than just technically demonstrating teleportation."

"Right. You remember our little discussion at the SUB. I love science and math as much as anyone who ever lived, the wonder of the universe, the joy of discovery, but I've never wanted just to be an ivory-tower scientist. From the moment the practical possibility of macrostate matter transmission hit me, everything I've done has aimed at not just inventing teleportation, but *innovating* it. This project and everyone I've managed to involve in it has that intent. If we accomplish what we expect, we're going into the transportation business. We intend to drastically reduce transport costs across the economy, increase world production and trade, significantly raise the living standards of ordinary persons, benefit mankind in general, and get filthy, stinking, and unapologetically rich in the process."

There was a quaver in Derek's voice. "Can I get in on it?"

Tom snorted, and looked at Buzz, who was chuckling himself, before looking back at Derek. "You're making this too easy, Derek. I thought I was going to have to twist your arm."

Derek's voice still quavered. "I saw what you guys did out there. I know what it means. If I can get in, I want in."

Tom grinned. "You're in then, Derek. In fact, I really couldn't keep you out since our success is vitally dependent on your component. But you ought to know, there are a lot of hurdles ahead. Some technical. We don't know for sure yet that we can transmit life. If that doesn't work, we'll be restricted to freight and won't be able to do passenger transport. But there are also other hurdles. For one, we're likely to face competition, and not just with existing transportation industries. Entropy happens. New information spreads no matter how hard you try to stop it. There are other smart people besides us out there and some of them are working in the same direction. There is a guy at Sony Electrodynamics, named Hasimata, who seems to have a lot of it figured out. There's also a German firm working very secretly in what we think is the same direction. Maybe even a couple of American firms.

"But the biggest thing is that we're going to make enemies. You can't shake up the world and change everything the way we're going to shake up and change things without making enemies. You sure you're up for all this?"

It was Derek's turn to grin. "Sounds like the biggest gamble of all to me, Tom. And you know about me and gambling."

Tom nodded. "In that case, it's just a matter of dotting the i's and crossing the t's. Buzz?"

The Buzzard opened his briefcase and handed Derek a sheaf of papers. "The first one here is a draft Tom and ah worked out of a patent application for your field modulation unit, in the names of you, Tom, and the Institute. We used schematics you gave to Beowulf. We hope you'll forgive us for that."

Derek thought a moment, and then nodded. "Even an hour ago that might have bothered me. Not now."

"Good. Take that up to the University, Show your Dr. Zidelski, and have him kick it around with 'The Powers That Be' up there. It'll raise some red flags when they see Tom's name on it, but that can't be helped at this point. The second document is a provisional contract over royalty shares, forty-five percent to you, same to Tom, and ten percent to the University. It also specifies a royalty payment from us, Universal Research and Fabrication, for rights to use your modulation unit. Run that past the University, too. If they want to dicker, have them get in contact with me downtown at Byrd, Rand, Epstein, and Ely. Here's mah card."

Derek put Buzz's card in his wallet. "What's this third document?"

"That one makes you a member of the Skeleton Crew," Tom answered. "It's our standard partnership agreement. We make a lot of our money these days from patent royalties, but we avoid patenting anything in the name of the firm in an effort to keep others from connecting the different threads of research and seeing what we're up to. You come up with something original while working on the project, with the firm's equipment, even if it's something peripheral - say like that musical synthesizer Beowulf tells me you and him designed - you patent it in your name or names, with whatever royalty shares you agree on. But your agreement as a partner is that ten percent off the top goes into a common pool to the firm, Universal Research and Fabrication. We manage to cover most of our research costs, even labor like our maintenance employees, from profits on our equipment fabrication business run out of the other building. So what is paid into the common pool from patent royalties is mostly paid out under the firm's part of the contract as salary on a pro-rata share to all the partners. That's salary and medical insurance benefits you'll start collecting as soon as you sign. Your synthesizer won't count, of course, since you weren't a partner when you did that. That's all yours and Thad's"

"What about time commitment?" Derek asked. I'm close to finishing my PhD, and I'd like to wrap that up."

"The time you commit to the business is up to you," Tom said. "You're a partner, not an employee. There is a clause allowing collective agreement to remove a partner if he or she proves unproductive, but it has never been invoked. We hope this will all change soon anyway. Assuming we really are able to teleport passengers and/or freight at competitive rates, it's going to take big bucks to even get a start setting up the transport network we'll need. Dematerialization and Rematerialization cubes like our prototype out there don't come cheap and there's a lot of other expensive physical capital we're going to have to have in place. That means incorporating and selling enough stock shares at a high enough price each to raise a really huge amount of money. At that point, all the members of the Skeleton Crew will be issued enough shares to be major stockholders."

"We're still tinkerin' with the details," Buzz added, "but it's lookin' like one percent of the IPO shares for each member of the crew and four for Tom, who will also become CEO. Right now, though, we're still a partnership. You still want in?"

Somebody knocked on the office door and Tom answered. It was Beowulf and Dave Barret. "We're heading back up to the Institute," Beowulf said to Tom. "I've got an afternoon class and Dave has to see his dissertation committee. Is Derek coming with us?"

Tom opened the door wider and Derek leaned forward so they could see each other. "Just a second, guys. I've got to sign some things."

Chapter 7: Ships Passing

"I'm telling you, Gina," the gray-eyed blond girl said as she slung her book bag over her shoulder and they filed out of the classroom with the other students, "you're *sooo* lucky to be done with everything this semester."

Gina smiled as she hefted her own bag and they headed out the door and down the fourth floor hall of the Demsetz building. "Just the class work, Cindy. I've still got the dissertation to do. Some people take years on those things. I'd be in real trouble if I hadn't talked both the poly sci and econ people into letting me do essentially the same project for both degrees. That's the advantage of specializing in public choice!"

Cindy gave Gina a look of mock suspicion. "I still don't see how you talked those old guys into that."

Gina made moon eyes and gave her chest and hips a little extra jiggle. "I have my ways," she said. Then she laughed. "No, really, it wasn't hard. Most of them liked the idea, particularly Edleston. Besides, Marilyn Hauser, who's PhD specialty was in public choice, is officially a member of both departments, you know. I just talked her into being on the committee, and she convinced the rest."

"Where are you going now?" Cindy asked.

"Professor Edleston asked me to see him about something or other. I don't know what. Probably something about the dissertation project. You?"

"I'm going over to the library. You know that Jimmy Heartman, the soccer player from our world politics class? He wanted me to help him study for the midterm. He's *sooo* cute."

Gina looked at her askance. "Cindy, you ought to look for a guy with some brains. Those muscle men are always breaking your heart."

"*Ohh,* brainy men are *sooo* boring," Cindy responded. "Besides, I'm not like you, always getting hit on by the law and medical students. I have to take my opportunities when they come."

At that, the thought of the mysterious Alvin Wright crossed Gina's mind, not for the first time in the last several weeks. "Oh, I don't think brainy men are boring at all," she mused, not realizing that she was biting her inside lip. "I even know of some who have muscles, too."

Cindy giggled. "Well, hook me up with one of those." As they passed the economics department office complex, she raised her right hand a little, wiggled her fingers, said "Tah tah," and headed on down the hall toward the stairway.

"See you back at the dorm, Cindy," Gina waved, and then went through the office door, past the department secretary, and back to Edleston's office, where she knocked.

"Come in," Professor Lewis Edleston called, then, when she did, "Oh, Gina. Glad to see you. Have a seat while I finish up here."

Professor Edleston was a middle-aged man, a little short and a bit rotund, with a full head of graying hair.

He taught most of the industrial organization and some of the monetary theory courses in the graduate programs, but also had a toehold in public choice. Gina had met his wife, who was a very nice lady, and knew that they had several children, including one who was now an undergraduate biology student.

Edleston's desk faced the window, and Gina could see his computer screen. Apparently he was running some kind of statistical analysis. It looked like a multiple regression of some kind. He exited that program, however, and swiveled his chair around to face her.

"I've been thinking a lot about your project. It's a great Idea, measuring rent-seeking and rent-extraction costs in the California legislature, and your attack on Tulloch's underpayment problem is brilliant. You're certainly right that the problem with attempts to measure rent seeking costs has always been researchers being restricted to the use of publicly available data sources. Too many of those payments are hidden and hard to measure, and your empirical methods are an advance.

"It occurred to me, though, that it might help if you could get an inside view of things. I've got a friend in the legislature, Senator Braxon. Bill Braxon. He's the minority leader for the American Liberty Party there. I actually did some work for him on his last campaign; issue papers and the like. I've talked to him. He's looking for somebody like you so I put in a good word. If you want, you can do an internship with him over the next legislative session. You'd be like a member of his staff, helping him out with things while working on your project. You could make a lot of contacts, get inside information and such. It would be very good, both for your project and, maybe, for your future career. If he likes you, and I know he will, I'm sure he'll offer to take you on as a full-time staff member at the end of the internship. What do you think?"

Gina's head swirled for a moment. Opportunities like this did *not* come along out of the blue very often. "I. . . I'd love to! My folks live in Sacramento. I wouldn't even have to rent an apartment, unless I wanted to. Yes. Yes. This is perfect!"

Professor Edleston grinned. "It's settled then. I'll get back to Bill and give him your answer. I'm sure he'll even kick in a little money for moving expenses if you want. He's been anxious to find the right person for the job. And I'll let the other members of your Graduate Dissertation Committee know what we're doing. There are only a few weeks left in the semester, you know, and then you can head out."

Gina shook her head. "I won't need moving money. All I've got is my books, my computer, a small 3-V, and a little personal stuff."

"Well, let me know if I can help with anything, Gina." Edleston stood, apparently indicating that he had other things to do now, so Gina, anxious to get back to her dorm apartment and start planning, stood also, shouldering her bag.

"How can I ever thank you, Professor Edleston?"

"Don't worry about that, Gina. Twenty-five years in this business and I can tell you, a student like you doesn't come along very often. I'm glad to help." Then Edleston had another thought. "Oh, by the way, Gina, do you know a guy named Alvin Wright?"

Gina's eyes widened. She hadn't seen this coming either. "N-n-n- no," she stammered, "should I?"

Lew looked a bit puzzled. "Well, I thought you might. He's been in the economics master's program, but he dropped out a couple of weeks back, no explanation. He's a fair student, no rocket scientist. Seems to have a good grasp of economics and math, but only runs a 'B' average. I just wondered what happened and thought you might know. Besides, didn't I send him down to see you in your cubicle once for mentoring on some technical issue in production theory a couple of semesters back?"

"If you did, he didn't come. I'm sure I'd know if he had," Gina said. Then she had a thought. "Do you want me to ask around?"

Lew apparently wanted to get back to his work. He sat down and started to turn his chair back around. "No. Not important I guess. Students come and students go. Just another minor mystery. I hate to lose even a mediocre grad student. See you tomorrow in I.O. Gina."

To say the least, Gina's feelings were mixed as she left Professor Edleston's office and started walking back to the dorms.

*   *   *

Early Wednesday morning, the second day following the amazing event at the Asylum, Derek was surprised to find Tom waiting for him in a sweat suit just in front of the dorm when Derek went out for his morning run. "Tom! Up for a little exercise, are you?"

"Morning, Derek. Can I tag along? I usually run up and down the runway outside the Asylum a few times when I want to jog, but I thought that if you didn't mind some company we could talk."

"Okay, but you'll have to keep up," Derek grinned and started trotting down the hill toward the quad at his normal mile-eating pace that usually left most joggers behind in short order. Tom started after him. And he did keep up, rather easily, to Derek's mild irritation. *Shees! Isn't there anything this guy isn't good at?*

This late in the Fall semester in central California the days were growing short, and it was somewhat darker and cooler at this time of the morning than it had been earlier in the semester. The morning sun, just reaching the horizon, was bleeding up into the intermittent clouds, casting a reddish light across the campus and the sky surrounding the clouds was already making the transition from black to blue. Few other human souls seemed to be up and awake this early, though lights were showing in a few of the buildings. Some squirrels, out scrounging an early morning meal, had to scamper out of their way as the two men jogged down the hill and onto the quad.

"How did it go yesterday with Zidelsky?" Tom asked.

Derek looked at him askance. "So that's what you're out here for. Answer me a question first. Who

85

put your flyer up on the board for me that morning?" Derek nodded at the bulletin board as they went past.

"Oh, Beowulf did that. He used to jog around campus in the mornings, too, before you and he really got acquainted. He saw you out here several times. I hope you aren't irritated about all that. He was convinced you were the one guy on campus who could solve that problem for us, but sometimes we've had to be a little careful about who we let in on things."

Passing the fountain, Derek could just begin to feel his muscles loosening up. They crossed the grass past the Business and Economics complex to Reagan Avenue and headed west. The Avenue had no traffic this early and their feet thumped rhythmically and solidly on the asphalt. Lights could be seen in some of the houses down in the valley, starkly yellow against the bluish-black haze of the horizon.

"No, I'm not miffed at all, over that. If I'm miffed at anything, it's just being about the last one to be let in on everything. On the other hand, I'm astonished and gratified that I *have* been let in on it at all. I never imagined in my life being part of anything as big as what you guys are up to. So, no, I'm not miffed."

"How *did* it go with Professor Zidelski?" Tom also seemed to have hit his stride, breathing comfortably and easily as they jogged down the Avenue.

"Actually, very well. I hope you don't mind, but I took Thad with me to talk to him. The only touchy part was, Mike wanted to know just what use Universal Research and Fabrication was going to put the field modulator to, but he was okay with it when we explained that that was sensitive business information at this stage and would become public knowledge soon anyway. I suspect he figured out quite a bit from that and from seeing your name on things. I think he knows now what happened to some of his lost grad students. But when he saw the royalty offer to the Institute on the contract, and we explained that they would also get a piece of what me and Thad get from our synthesizer, he came on board."

"What happens next?" Tom asked. "You know we're kind of stymied, right at a critical stage, until some of this gets settled. We want to continue our tests so bad our teeth ache, but we can't."

The sky was brightening rapidly now, becoming discernibly bluer. They began to pass other early morning joggers and walkers at random intervals, some of whom nodded or waved in greeting and some of whom didn't. Soon the two men reached the municipal park and followed the jogging trail along the creek and through the trees.

"I know. Seeing what I saw Monday, I'm as anxious as you. But you know bureaucracy, Tom, and University bureaucracy is as bad as any other. I'm sure that's one reason you wanted to go private sector so bad. Mike has to take it to the engineering faculty. He called a department meeting for Thursday afternoon. With their recommendation, it'll go to the Chancellor. Then the Institute's lawyers will hassle it over."

"So how long are we talking?" Tom asked.

"Possibly weeks. Maybe even next semester, if Christmas vacation distracts everybody. But why do we need to wait? If it's as critical as you keep saying, then *let's get going.* The modulator belongs to you and me. They might try to hold us up for a larger share, but they can't deny us majority rights. There's too much at stake to wait."

Tom seemed to want to think this over, so the two men jogged on through the park in silence and up toward the stadium. A few solitary cars carrying overachievers to work early or underachievers home from bars late drove past them on the road. Occasionally, a slight tang of carbon monoxide infiltrated the pristine purity of the early morning air, and then dissipated on the breeze.

Tom seemed to reach a decision. "Okay. Since you're all right with it, I'll tell the guys at the Asylum to start fabricating another field modulator as soon as I get back. But that'll take a couple of days anyway. Let's figure on Monday to start the next series of teleportation tests. It might actually be good to take a little time for other things anyway. We've been pushing so hard on the project lately that we have a backlog of equipment fabrication orders. I'll get some more members of the Crew working on filling those. We badly need the money. Then we'll get everybody together for a partner's meeting Thursday afternoon, at say one o'clock. See if you can make it. We need to do some thinking about the tests and what comes next."

Heading back up hill, the last half mile past the stadium and back to the student housing was the hardest part of the jog and both men were sweating and breathing harder when they reached the dorm, though neither was seriously winded. They stopped running and walked the last twenty yards, breathing deeply and allowing their heart rates to slow.

"That was fun," Tom said. "Why don't you come out to the Asylum one of these evenings and work out with me and the guys? I'll show you what the mat's for."

Derek wondered if he was being set up for something else. Tom sometimes seemed a little mischievous, and even devious. "Can't say I'm not intrigued, but that's gonna have to wait. Its twenty minutes out to the Asylum from here and twenty back and I have an early morning class tomorrow. But I'm all finished with class work in three weeks, and then I'll rent some digs closer to the Asylum. As for Thursday, I'll try to make it. In fact, I'll try to come out this afternoon and help start fabrication of the field modulator if I can find a ride."

"Good." Tom started down the hill again. "That'll make it go faster. See you soon then, Derek."

*   *   *

On Friday at noon, as he was going through the cafeteria line at the SUB for some lunch, Derek spotted Thad Thorsen and Phillip Adobo conversing somewhat animatedly as they chowed down at one of the tables. Paying for his sandwich, potato salad, and drink, he threaded his way through the noisy throng in their direction. Phil saw him coming first, grinned, and waved his hand at one of the empty chairs.

"Hey, hey, Derek," Phil said in his heavy west African accent, "put 'er there-a Yogi Berra!"

"Howdy, Derek," Thad added when he saw who Phil was talking to.

Derek set his tray down in the indicated spot and pulled the chair back far enough that he could get his long legs under the table.

"Beowulf," he deliberately used Thad's Skeleton Crew moniker for probably the first time, "you may have the physique of a John Wayne, but you're just two darned intellectual to be a cowboy! And as for you, Phil, you haven't been in this country long enough to know who *either* Yogi Bear *or* Yogi Berra were."

"Not so," Phil objected. "I love Saturday morning cartoon reruns, though I'll admit the old ones don't translate well into 3-V. And I've been here long enough that I'm going to be a rich American capitalist soon!"

"I'll drink to that," Beowulf agreed, and the three men clanked their plastic cafeteria juice glasses together.

"Say, Thad," Derek said, "I was out at the Asylum all yesterday afternoon. Have you heard how things went at the department meeting?"

Beowulf swallowed the last of the sandwich he had been munching and washed it down with the last of his juice. "Fine. They voted overwhelmingly to send the patent application and contract to the Chancellor as

90

written. Looks like you and me are in the chips on that synthesizer. We should knock off a prototype soon. But things aren't going quite that smoothly over in Math and Physics. That's what brought Phil up here."

"Yeh, that's right," Phil agreed. "Jake Hansen and some of the other Math profs were a bit upset when they heard, so Beowulf and me and a few of the math guys on the Crew went up and talked to some of them this morning. We think we got Jake and most of the rest turned around. In fact, it didn't really take much of an adjustment in Jake's attitude anyhow for him to start seeing Tom as their 'golden boy' again. Jake always liked Tom anyway."

"The big news, though, Derek," Beowulf interjected, "is that when Irwin Westholm heard, he went ape. Him and his henchmen over there - "Phil gave him a scowl at that, but he was unapologetic, "- well, *that's what they are* - have already started raising Cain with the Chancellor's office, lobbying for them to turn down the whole deal. They're even threatening to sue, Tom, UR&F, the University, everyone they can if the University goes through with it!"

"Can they really do anything?" Derek asked.

Beowulf and Phil glanced at each other, and then both shook their heads. "Nah, not really. Westholm lost a lot of credibility with the Administration clear back when they cashiered Tom without cause. I think that's why they're being so nasty. Tom being behind something big like this makes them look bad now for what they did then."

"Well, for them, worse to come," Derek said, and once again the three young men clanked their plastic glasses together.

*   *   *

Gina Barlow had begun training in gymnastics very young, and one of the great disappointments in her life was that she had grown up too tall, and at a hundred and twenty pounds, rather too heavy to ever become a first class Olympic gymnast. The very best were slips of girls who never got over about ninety-five pounds. Even at twenty-four, long ago having given up that particular ambition, she loved to burn off her built-up tensions and frustrations from life on the uneven bar, horse, and mat exercises. The gymnastics room was usually free and she took advantage of it whenever she could tear time away from studies. On this occasion, as often happened, Cindy came along and watched from the sidelines while Gina exercised. Gina had often tried to get Cindy to learn the basic exercises to no avail. Cindy was a dance major with a fast metabolism that also kept her slim, but she had no desire to learn gymnastics.

Usually, as today, several other people, mostly men, also watched, and not just because Gina was an excellent gymnast. She was used to that, too.

"You make me hurt just watching you, Gina," Cindy complained after Gina finished a set with a double back flip off the uneven bars.

"Well, sometimes it makes me hurt, too, Cindy," Gina said as she walked over and sat down by her room-mate, breathing heavily. "But it actually feels good. Besides, you know, I have to fight to keep from weighing a ton. And I have fun exercising anyway."

While Gina had been exercising, a black-haired girl about the same age as and just a little shorter than Gina had come out of the women's locker room and begun doing stretches while watching Gina. Now she began doing some floor exercises. She was actually pretty talented, though clearly a relative novice.

"Do you really have to go, Gina? To Sacramento?" Cindy half whimpered. "I can't afford all the rent, and I'll have to let Misty Parker move in. She wants to room with me in the *worst* way. But it won't be the same. If you think I'm messy, you ought to see her! Two of us just can't be that way in one dorm apartment. And how will I get any studying done without you there to nag me?"

Gina laughed. "You're the one that needs to move back with your parents, Cindy."

"Ohh!" Cindy was horrified at the thought. "What would that do to my love life?"

Just then the black-haired girl missed a back flip, rather badly. Picking herself up off the mat with a disgusted expression, she walked over toward the two girls.

"Hi," she said to Gina. "I'm Billy Jo Jensen. I was watching you. You're good. Could you show me what I'm doing wrong on my back flip?

"Sure. I'm Gina." It always delighted Gina when people sought her help and advice, which for reasons she did not entirely understand, happened frequently. One summer between high school and college, she had taught a children's gymnastics class at the Sacramento YMCA, and had a ball doing so. So she went out on the mat and helped Billi Jo with her exercises, showing her several tricks of the trade. Finally Billi Jo was as tired as Gina and the two sat down on the mat.

"Where did you learn so much?" Billi Jo asked.

"Oh, I trained a lot in middle school and at the high school in Sacramento after it went private. They had a good program. And my parents paid for some extra training at a gym downtown. I competed in the nationals and for a while I wanted to be an Olympic gymnast, but as you can see, I grew up too big. How 'bout you? You're not bad, though I get the impression you're pretty new to it."

Billy Jo smiled shyly. "No, little more than a year, a couple nights a week. This guy I work with, Tom, has been showing me. He runs classes in gymnastics and martial arts in his gym."

Gina was intrigued. "What gym? I thought I knew all the gyms and gymnastics coaches in town."

"Oh, it's actually at the place where we work; way over on the other side of town.

Gina was impressed. "Wow. A gym at work. Talk about enlightened employment policy. You must like working there."

"Oh, I love it. But I'm not really an employee, sort of a partner. You know, you ought to come down with me some evening and meet Tom. You'd like him. He's almost as good as you are."

Gina thought about it for a moment. "Well, that sounds like fun, but I think I'll pass. I'm moving to Sacramento as soon as finals are over anyhow."

Gina stood and started toward the women's locker, and Billi Jo followed. "Are you sure, Gina? Tom's an unusual guy. He almost redefines the word 'hunk'. And there are a lot of other nice single guys out there; including one big lug I've got my eye on."

Gina thought about Alvin Wright, reflected on the tragedy of missed opportunities, and how certain experiences changed one's standards, like the first time she had seen 3-V and had decided immediately that she never wanted to watch TV again. "No thanks," she said. I'm just not up for it."

Chapter 8: Beam Me Over Mr. Wright

It was a full court press at the Asylum Monday morning. Two carloads of Crew members drove down from the Institute. Derek, Dave, and Beowulf went in Dave's car. Other members of the Crew who lived closer were already there when the University component arrived. By eight a.m. the circuits on the D-R chamber had already been checked. Several members of the Crew responsible for monitoring Zelda's functions watched from her holographic display, which now simply showed the inside of the D-R cube. Most members of the Skeleton Crew, not directly involved in control functions, crowded in front of the chamber as before to watch directly. This time they *did* have dark glasses ready.

Most were nervous as well as excited. The successful test a week back could conceivably have been a fluke that could not be repeated. The second test was almost as important as the first. Everyone knew that replication of results was one of the hallmarks of science. The only thing different this time was that the first object they hoped to teleport was a container of pressurized Argon gas. One of the things worked out at the meeting on Thursday was the sequence of teleportation experiments to be run. It was necessary to test the process on different substances, masses, and sizes of objects. It was no accident that the cup of coffee was the first test subject, because it demonstrated simultaneously that both liquids and solids could be teleported.

Tom went through the firing sequence and countdown as before. The light violet dust screen swept through the chamber and disappeared when it reached the front.

"D-R field?" Tom's voice boomed out over the sound system.

"Five by five, boss," Beowulf responded from the second station.

"Discrimination and resolution?"

The man at the third station had anticipated him. "Subatomic attained."

Derek nudged Hulio Sanchez who was standing next to him. "Who is that guy, Hulio? I don't know him."

Hulio glanced that way for just a moment. "His name is Parker Freeman. Tom recruited him from a big corporate research lab a few months back. He was one of their top physicists."

"Field harmonics," Tom's voice boomed.

Again the same apparently psychic harmonic pressure wave seemed to sweep out of the chamber, though muted somewhat, and fading more rapidly than before, but leaving the same hollow feeling of lost beauty and harmony.

"Humph," Hulio muttered to Derek. "I wonder how far out that effect went. Remind me to ask the guys monitoring Zelda whether they felt it."

Lynn Yip Ki, on his other side, must have heard him. "What are you, worried about, Hulio? The neighbors complaining?"

"Displacement in ten, nine, eight . . ."

Everyone put their dark glasses on.

". . Four, three, two, one, displacement!"

It was a good thing, because the flash, though not blinding, was bigger and brighter this time, and the popping sound from displaced air at one location and vacuum filled at another was larger, as the Argon gas container disappeared on one side of the chamber and reappeared simultaneously on the other. The whoop that went up from the assembled members of the Skeleton Crew was nearly as large as the first time, as was the pandemonium of released tension and expressed excitement.

"Hold it down everybody," Tom's voice boomed out. "Beowulf, can't we dampen that flash any more?"

"Not with our current discrimination. Emission's as low as we can get without a vacuum."

Tom was apparently satisfied, at least for now. "Scanning?"

"Pattern at one-hundred percent, Tom," Parker Freeman responded from the third console station.

"How's the Argon tank containment pressure?"

"Identical to initial."

"Power down then."

"Powering down."

Two members of the Crew, apparently pre assigned, went into the chamber and started wheeling the Argon gas tank out. Several others started wheeling in and stacking hand-truck loads of old lead batteries until they had a pile nearly six feet high on the left side of the chamber. Then they started the whole sequence again and attained the same result as before. In all, they ran five tests before noon, in each case simply teleporting the test object or objects from one side of the chamber to the other. On the last of those they opened a back door behind the chamber that Derek had not been able to see, drove a car in and up into the chamber over a ramp. It was a three-year-old Makerov Spitfire, apparently belonging to some brave member of the Crew.

The driver, a gal Derek did not recognize, who appeared to have Native American heritage, got out of the car, cleared the chamber, and walked over to Tom sitting at the console.

"Tom. There's a fly in the car. I tried to shoo him out, but he wouldn't go. Should I try again?"

Tom thought about it, and shook his head. "No. That certainly wasn't my first choice for a live test subject, but leave him in there." Then he initiated his throat mike. "All right people, placement is ready for run number five. Run the dust screen sweep."

Derek found himself standing next to Billi Jo Jensen as the initiation sequence began.

"Why do we just keep beaming things across the chamber?" he asked. "Why don't we teleport it out onto the runway or something?"

Billi Jo laughed. "I keep forgetting, Derek, that you're behind on all this. You're going to have to spend some time with Tom going through all the theory

99

and engineering of the system. The thing just can't work like the old Star Trek shows. The pattern can't be reestablished anywhere but in and by a D-R chamber. When we get the second one finished, we'll teleport things from one chamber to the other. That's how it's designed to work in the first place. We're really straining both the resolution software and the hardware of the system to do it the way we are now."

"How far along is the other chamber?"

"Oh, we've got about eighty percent of the modules fabricated. The second field generator is the big holdup, but we'll have it finished fairly soon, too. Any luck, one of these days we'll have some manufacturing subcontractor turning them out like hot cakes."

"Field harmonics," Tom's voice boomed out, snapping Derek and Billi Jo's attention back out to the chamber along with everyone else. This time Derek was ready for the psychic harmonic pressure wave and he strained to *hear* the music he *felt* in every atom of his being. But it didn't work and the wave faded leaving only a lingering memory.

"Glasses on." Tom decided nothing would be sacrificed in shortening the countdown. "Displacement in five, four, three, two, one, displacement!"

Flash! Bam! The car caused the biggest flash and the loudest air displacement yet, as it was dematerialized and rematerialized simultaneously at the other side of the chamber. Quite aside from the noise and light, the air movement was noticeable, particularly to those standing closest.

"Maybe the neighbors *will* complain!" Lynn Yip Ki mumbled.

"Scanning?"

"One hundred percent, boss. Perfect. At this range we're not getting anything else. No sense worrying 'til we can try long distance."

Tom did not respond, but sat thinking for several moments.

"Should we power down, boss?" Parker Freeman asked.

"Not yet." Pulling his throat mike down, Tom turned to the gal who had driven the car into the chamber. "Angel, you willing to go in there with the power still up?"

"Sure, Tom. No guts, no glory. You guys shouldn't have all the fun."

"Good. Grab a volunteer and the two of you go find that fly."

"Who is that gal?" Derek asked Billi Jo as Angel walked back into the chamber taking Phillip Adobo with her.

Billi Jo was surprised. "The native gal? Angel BlackSnake. One of the math people. I thought you knew 'em all."

Phil and Angel approached the car rather slowly. Angel went around to the other side and they opened the doors, got in quickly, and shut them again. Tom and the Skeleton Crew watched as the two moved around inside the car, apparently looking everywhere for the fly. Finally Phil opened the driver side door.

"Can't find him, boss," he called over to Tom. "Either he flew out when Angel left the car or when we got in just now, or he wasn't transmitted."

Nobody liked the sound of the third alternative. It was not entirely impossible that somehow, life *force* would interfere with the D-R field. The notion of life being a form of energy, in some senses distinct from though integrated with the physical materials and energy composing the living entity was not uncongenial to Tom's metaphysic, however, and indeed this seemed to be *required* by many of his equations. Tom apparently mulled this over for several moments. Then he put his throat mike back up. "Lynn, bring Schrodinger up, will you?"

Lynn was apparently waiting for this. She picked up a cat carrier that held a very scrawny old cat and walked out into the cube toward the car.

"Who does he belong to?" Derek asked Billi Jo.

"Oh, he just lives around the air field off mice and birds. Took us a couple of days to catch him. We left some food out and he finally got greedy."

"And you named him Schrodinger?"

Billi Jo's response seemed just a bit defensive. "Well, it seemed appropriate. It's not exactly Shrodinger's thought-experiment we're running here, but he is a cat, and we don't know whether the poor thing will live or die."

Lynn put the cat carrier in the back seat of the car. Apparently at Tom's instruction, she powered the windows down, closed the door, and rapidly exited the cube. The cube had remained powered up, but the unfocused D-R field apparently had no effect on her or the cat at all, as Tom had apparently anticipated.

"All Right," Tom's voice reverberated through the hanger. "Retarget for reverse displacement."

"Already done, boss," Beowulf responded.

"Parker. Have we got enough resolution and discrimination to do without the dust screen?"

Parker consulted his console indicators and listened through his ear connector for a moment. "Zelda says she can handle it."

"All right. Focus the field."

"Quantum level achieved."

"Field harmonics," Tom called as he adjusted the control.

As the psychic harmonic pressure wave swept out, the cat yowled. Everyone froze and for a moment Tom thought of aborting the sequence, but the cat was indisputably still alive since he could be heard growling. Tom decided to continue.

"Displacement in five, four, three . . ."

When Tom reached zero and the car teleported back to its initial position with a flash and whump, there was dead silence.

"Scanning?" Tom called.

"We're at a hundred percent, boss," Parker responded, "but Zelda says Schrodinger isn't moving."

"Power down, then and someone go look."

The field glow faded from the inside of the cube. Lynn hurried forward, opened the back seat of the car, and lifted the cat carrier out. Schrodinger didn't move. Lynn later claimed that his legs were locked, his eyes were glazed, and he didn't even blink. Worried sick, she set the carrier down, opened its door, and reached in for the cat. With a sudden shriek and a yowl Schrodinger sprang from the carrier, clawed his way past Lynn's arms yowling all the way, and scrambled out of the cube past at least six members of the Skeleton Crew trying to grab him, to disappear into the back of the hanger behind the cube.

Most of the Crew rushed out to Lynn, and Tom was far from the last one there. Phil Adobo had the presence of mind to bring a first-aid kit, but it turned out that, save for a few scratches, only one of which was deep, Lynn was more rattled than hurt.

"Someone find that cat," Tom said as the tension began to dissipate and people started milling around. "Unless he's dead now, we can count this as a huge success. Everybody decide what you want for lunch. Let's order in and meet down in the conference room in a half-hour."

*   *   *

Some members of the Skeleton Crew began to gather in the office complex conference room about fifteen minutes later to engage in animated and excited discussion of the morning's events. The others drifted in over the next few minutes, mostly in small knots of two or three as food began to arrive. Derek sat down next to Beowulf and Dave and snagged a piece of pizza and some Chinese food being passed around. Tom was one of the last to arrive and the mutter of various group conversations muted somewhat when he did. He waited a while for everyone to find their favorite cuisine, but it was still only five minutes later when he called the meeting to order.

"Uh, 'scuse me, Tom," Phillip Adobo interjected. "Before we go on, I'm wondering, what we've done here already is pretty earth shaking and don't you think we ought to start putting together some kind of historical narrative of all this?"

"Yes, we should!" Billi Jo Jensen assented as did several other Crew members nearly simultaneously.

"Right," Tom agreed. "I was going to suggest that. It's a good idea. History needs to be kept straight right from the first or somebody will screw it up later. A lot of the raw data is time coded in Zelda and won't be hard to get. But somebody needs to do a narrative, from the personal views of as many of the people involved as feasible. You want the job, Phil?"

Phil felt a lot less enthusiastic about *being* the company historian than he did about *somebody* being the company historian, but he reluctantly assented. "Well, now I wish I'd kept my mouth shut. I'm a math man and what I don't know about writing histories fills volumes. Tell you what; I'll do it for now, 'til we find or hire somebody better suited, if Billi Jo and Parker will help. That'll spread the strain a little among the physics, math, and engineering groups and might give us a little more balanced view anyway. Okay?"

The others agreed and Tom proceeded with business. "All right. First off, how's Schrodinger, Lynn?"

Lynn choked down a bite of taco quickly. "The poor little guy's fine, Tom. As good as he was before, anyway. He's an old cat, you know, hardly in perfect health. But we got Zelda to isolate his part of the post translation pattern and compared it with the original. It's like she said at the time. No difference. Whatever happened to him wasn't any kind of physical degradation."

"What, then?" Tom asked. "Why did he freeze up like that, and then go ballistic when you opened the cage door?"

Several people started to respond almost at once, but Hulio Sanchez won out and the others quieted. "Well, he's a half-wild cat in the first place, Tom. Not exactly a willing test subject. But my guess is that he was simply startled by the whole displacement experience. That weird harmonics we're all feeling from *outside* the cube has to be intensified in the test subject. I don't think we have any way of knowing what the experience feels like until somebody goes through it who can tell us."

Most of the others apparently agreed with Hulio. Tom allowed the meeting to break down for a couple of minutes into free conversation on the subjective harmonic effect they were all experiencing. Then he brought it back to order.

"Suppose we find that the subjective experience is intensely disturbing to people in some way," he asked. "What do we do then? Any ideas?"

The relative silence around the table, as most members of the Crew even stopped eating for a few moments, indicated that few of them had considered the possibility or its implications.

"Well," Parker Freeman ventured, "that would knock a big hole in any passenger business."

"That's the point," Tom responded. "Is there a way we can deal with that? Passenger business is something we don't want to lose right off the bat, if possible. Sure as we write it off, someone else will figure out how to do it."

Everyone looked at each other and finally Dave Barret spoke. "Maybe we can't. You know very well, Tom, 'cause you're the one who showed us, that the field harmonics are the essence of the matter. That's what allows us to release the tension, the strong force, so we can temporarily break down the pattern and transmit it over the carrier wave. If that's innately subjectively disturbing to a person being teleported, well . . ."

Lynn, sitting on Dave's other side from Derek, nudged Dave and the two started talking animatedly in low tones for a few moments. Everyone else watched in anticipation. Finally, the two seemed to reach some consensus and Dave continued on a more optimistic note.

"Now that we think about it, there might be a way, without too great a modification of our field generator and a little software reprogramming, that we could introduce a sort of temporary unconsciousness, just for a few seconds spanning displacement. A sort of electronic anesthesia or amnesia. That might do the trick."

Tom thought about the math and physics of teleportation for a few seconds and caught Dave and Lynn's vision. "You know, I think I see what you're saying. We just modulate their alpha waves into the sleep mode for a few seconds. That'll work."

"Wouldn't people have to be warned?" Beowulf asked, "Maybe told to strap down to keep from falling over or spilling something?"

Dave nodded in agreement. "But all of this is jumping the gun, Tom. Until one of us goes through it, we just don't know."

Tom rubbed his chin as he thought this over. "Well, maybe, but we can make an educated guess, Dave. Theoretically, the best assumption for people might be a *variety* of subjective reactions. Essentially a normal frequency distribution, possibly with a neutral mean. People, say, outside the standard deviation in the left tail might find the experience unpleasant enough to need some relief. So could we do it selectively?"

Dave and Lynn looked at each other for a moment and nodded. "Yeh, that would take more sophisticated programming and they'd have to request it in advance, but I think we could work it out."

"Tom, pardon me," Derek decided to interject; "I don't know what's going on the way the rest of you do, but it seems to me we still might be jumping the gun. I've talked to Lynn, Billi Jo, Phil, and several of the others and we *all* found the harmonics of the pressure wave *pleasant*. So maybe the whole issue won't come up and we just need to send someone through to see."

"I felt the same way," Tom responded, "but we all felt it from the outside. Schrodinger's the only one who's actually experienced teleportation first hand. And there's enough human variation that even if the vast majority find it pleasant, there will almost certainly be some who won't. It's true; we'll know more once we send someone through. But in any case, Dave, and Lynn, work your idea up. And Derek, if you're willing, help them with any engineering aspects. You run the team, Dave, and if possible, have at least a preliminary feasibility report for us at the next partner's meeting.

"Let's move on and talk money. Based on our experiments so far, preliminary numbers for the energy use, compensation of *necessary* personnel, even amortized capital use cost, it looks like in total it cost us about twenty-three thousand NDs to teleport that cup of coffee sixty feet across the chamber."

"Yes, but how much is it if we fill the cube with coffee cups and send them, say, a thousand miles? Angel BlackSnake asked.

Trust Angel to see the upside, Tom thought. "That's the good news. As you know, it takes a certain minimum power use to generate the field and the carrier wave and then it doesn't matter how much is in the cube. It's still about twenty-three thousand total since our cube here is still using power for Rematerialization that the other chamber would be using instead in a long distance transmission. Labor and equipment costs at that end run it up; but still, with the cube full, the cost of transmission falls to a fraction of a cent apiece. So, volume is going to be the key to keeping costs down, just like any other form of transportation business."

Something struck Derek as wrong, or missing, from that argument. "Wait a minute, Tom. What about the cost of stacking and unstacking those cups?"

The entire Skeleton Crew, other than Derek, immediately broke out in raucous laughter and Derek found himself embarrassed, without knowing why, and hence irritated. "Hey, I'm serious. Somebody has to stack and unstack those cups. And they aren't gonna do it for free!"

Even Tom had laughed, a little, but he forced the grin off his face. "Yes, somebody has to load and unload, but it usually won't have to be us. Passengers mostly load and unload themselves, and as for freight, which is what you're asking about, the last thing we want is to hire a lot of laborers, put up with unions, and the like. Besides, it's inefficient and unnecessary. We can avoid it by systematically containerizing this business right from the first. We've had this discussion before and, as the new guy, you missed it. Sorry for laughing."

"But the question I want to ask now is," Tom continued, "can any of you see any modification of our equipment or procedures that would help us get that basic cost down in the first place?"

Hulio was quick to respond. "Boss, Phil and I noticed that just automating our control procedures more will help a lot. It doesn't just cost us to generate the field, but also to maintain it, so we need to streamline the sequence of operations to minimize that. We can design a simple feedback mechanism, adjusting the resolution by the difference between ideal and existing resolution that will kick in the field harmonics and displacement automatically. I'm surprised now that we didn't do that in the first place. Should reduce field duration significantly and save us some power use and money."

"What about problems occurring during the firing sequence?"

Hulio shook his head. "Shouldn't be hard programming Zelda to abort under all sorts of preconceived problems. Besides, we're not talking about automating completely and there can be a manual override in case something happens we didn't program Zelda to watch for.

"Okay." Tom responded. "Work it up. Anything else?"

Parker Freeman raised his hand. "We're going to run into computation and memory problems with Zelda down the road when we start packing the cubes full the way you want and transmitting multiple loads over different routes simultaneously. I think we need to anticipate that and start now looking for a way to expand her function by at least an order of magnitude."

"All right, Parker. I know you're busy on several other projects already, so I'll help you with this one. I've got some ideas, and I think Beowulf might be willing to help us, right?"

Darn, Beowulf thought. *When are me and Derek gonna get time to work on our synthesizer? Oh well, maybe over the holiday break. First things first!* He nodded assent quickly.

Tom thumbed through his agenda and notes for a moment. "Now, as you all know, assuming things go as anticipated on our last test run today, we're going to face some heavy outlays in the next few weeks, finishing fabricating the second D-R chamber, arranging a platform for the relay, getting set up in Seattle, and so on. Buzz is willing to invest another couple of hundred thousand, but that's still going to leave us way short. Any ideas?"

Somewhat confused, Derek leaned over and whispered to Beowulf. "What platform is he talking about, and what's this about Seattle?"

"The carrier wave is line of sight," Beowulf whispered back, "so it'll have to be relayed from an elevation for us to teleport long distance." Then he grinned. "And Seattle is one place where we're going to raise a heck of a lot of money for startup capital."

Billi Jo Jensen raised her hand and Tom nodded. "Well, if Buzz can do it, so can I, right? My Dad just inherited my grandpa's hardware business and he's selling it off. I think I could get him to let me invest it with us, no sweat."

A murmur of assent went around the room as several other Crew members indicated a similar willingness to put additional personal assets into the business.

"Good." Tom said. "Any of you who want to bring money to the table, see me later about specifics. Of course, all we can do is work out a deal for extra shares of the IPO, based on how much you put in, same as with Buzz, so you're taking a risk. The other thing I think we can do, since the fabrication shop has been running well into the black, is borrow against it. I don't like the idea of issuing debt at this point, but that would get us most of what we need. The only alternative is to sell it off completely and I don't think we want to do that just yet. Any objections? No? Okay. Anything else from anyone before we go make our last test run today?"

The room went silent and Tom sensed from nervous looks several members of the Skeleton Crew gave each other that it was not for lack of anyone wanting to speak, but precisely that many members of the Crew wanted to say something he didn't want to hear. Finally Lynn Yip Ki broke the silence.

"Tom, we've been talking this over and most of us don't want you to do it. We know you want to be the first and we know you *deserve* to be the first. None of us could have conceived any of this on our own. You conceived it and showed us how to get where we are. But that's the point. You're the one indispensable person here and the risks are too great. Please, Tom, let someone else go first."

Tom's shoulders slumped and he looked down at the table and drummed his fingers on it as he thought. After a while he looked up. "If we held a vote, would it go against me?"

About three-quarters of the members of the Skeleton Crew nodded.

"Okay, Lynn," Tom reluctantly assented, "You be first."

*   *   *

So at two p.m. that day, one last teleportation test was held and the results duly recorded, both in Zelda's memory banks, through her visual receptors placed strategically around the cube, and by about a dozen of the personal NanoPods of Crew members. Lynn Yip Ki, who said she wanted to go in style, sat in the front seat of the Spitfire with the window down. The field was generated, focused, and harmonized. The particles sang, and with a flash and a whump, *moved.* As the sound of the air displacement and the mental harmonics felt by the other members of the Crew faded, Lynn could be seen sitting with her mouth and eyes wide open. After several seconds she slowly opened the door, stepped out and faced the Crew. Her mouth and eyes were still wide open, but she seemed to be looking inward, and not outward. Then she focused. "Wow," she said. "Now that was a rush!!"

Chapter 9: Christmas Calm
Before the Storm

It was more than three weeks later, in mid-December, before the next test run was made. For one thing, it took most of that time to finish fabricating the second D-R chamber and field generator, which the available members of the Crew assembled in one end of the fabrication shop. In addition, they had to install transmission/reception dishes on the tops of both buildings. Another reason for the slowing of work was that the end of semester final exams intervened and kept the University members of the Crew away from the Asylum most of the time that week. Work was also slowed by a constraint of funds, which could only be alleviated short-term by filling orders from the fabrication shop and much of the time of the Crew members was spent doing that. Buzz worked on solving funding problems on a little longer term basis by meeting in San Francisco with investment bankers concerning the bond issue. Since UR&F had built up an excellent reputation and done a profitable business of fabricating cutting-edge equipment for scientific laboratories - a business they had gotten into naturally as they had begun nearly two years back fabricating their own equipment - the bankers finally decided they were willing to purchase two million NDs worth of UR&F bonds for resale. That and the promised personal investments by The Buzzard and several

Crew members gave them at least minimally adequate funding for the next stage of the project.

When the second chamber was ready, Tom convinced the Crew that, to reduce expenses, they should only run one more test before moving on to the next stage, and that it made sense to load up the chamber. It wouldn't make a difference, after all, how many were in the chamber, except perhaps to Zelda, who had to tie up a larger amount of her quantum memory for a few nanoseconds. Of course, every member of the Skeleton Crew wanted to go, so they had to draw straws, since someone had to man the control stations, even with Hulio and Billi Jo's more automated redesign of the procedure. Lynn was excluded, since she had already secured her place in history as the first person to be teleported. Angel BlackSnake and Sean Nezbit, a computer programmer on the Crew, drew short straws and helped Lynn at the controls. Two others had to man stations in the other building. In all, ten Crew members, including Tom, went into the chamber in the lab that morning. Repeated conversations with Lynn about her experience had convinced them they ought to be seated when the time came. So they wheeled and/or carried office chairs from the conference room into the chamber and made themselves as comfortable as possible given their quite natural anxiety and anticipation as they waited through the powering and preparation procedures.

Lynn, at the first station, keyed the displacement sequence and announced the imminence of displacement in "five, four, three . . ." as she watched Dave and Angel's new automatic feedback mechanism adjust the field resolution. When the countdown reached zero, none of them saw the flash as they disappeared from the chamber and none of them really remembered hearing the *whump* of displaced air as they instantly reintegrated in the second chamber. However, they all knew afterwards exactly what Lynn had meant when she called it a 'rush'. They each felt an indescribable moment of instantaneous movement or displacement without inertia, a rearranging of location and context, and an intense sense of order and harmony, literally transcending *symphony,* vibrating in every fiber of their being; persisting and fading over several seconds during which no one had the slightest desire or will to move.

Phil Adobo was the first able to speak, and his spontaneously expressed sentiment prompted an outburst of essentially identical sentiment from the rest as people overcame their psychic paralysis. "Yeow! I wanna do that *again!*" The room broke up into a cacophony of excited discussion as everyone tried to compare and describe their experiences. Phil, Billi Jo, and Parker started recording all this in their NanoPods for posterity.

Tom stood up, hands to his head, and turned slowly to Dave Berret. "Dave, I hate to admit being wrong, but I think you and Lynn can stop worrying about coming up with that temporary field unconsciousness program. Anybody who doesn't like this can just take an airplane!"

*   *   *

A half-hour later, when excitement died down enough, Tom got the members of the Crew to wheel their chairs across the field, into the lab and back to the conference room.   At Tom's suggestion it was decided to suspend everything but minimal necessary fabrication shop operations for the next two weeks. It had been a long, hard haul to where they were and what came next would require intense effort, but they all needed a rest first and it was "that time of year." Many of the Crew members had long standing plans to visit family or friends over Christmas and New Years, and those who lived close were willing to handle necessary things in the shop.   Tom cautioned everyone to try to bridle their excitement. At this stage of things it was still necessary to keep what they were doing under wraps, an endeavor that was getting more and more difficult.

Beowulf and Phillip Adobo stayed in town. It was too expensive for Phil to fly back home, and Beowulf's family was visiting his grandparents in Norway over the holidays. Derek could have gone back to Ohio to see his family, but decided to stay so he and Beowulf could use some of the time to start fabricating a prototype of their synthesizer in the company shop. But first he had to move. He had already found an apartment in an older, but still respectable neighborhood, only a few miles from the Asylum.The next day, Beowulf, Phil, and Derek hauled his stuff from the dorm to the apartment. It took three trips in Phil's old green Chevy *Carnivore.* The apartment was fairly large and well kept, despite being older, with two bedrooms and another room Derek figured to set up as a computer room. In addition, there was a large living room and a spacious kitchen. It was a first floor apartment and its side windows were shaded by some large leafed trees. Right now the brightly colored leaves were mostly on the ground. Derek felt It was a definite step up from his dorm accommodations and he could afford it with his UR&F salary.

To Derek's surprise, as they were hauling the last of his stuff up the steps and through the door, Beowulf asked if he could move in with him and share rent. "I can just as well be here and commute to the school," he said in explanation, "as there and commute here, and these are much nicer digs."

"Well, sure," Derek agreed with relief, "that'll keep my expenses down. But if you're a loud snorer or a late partier, out you go!"

Beowulf grinned slyly, deciding to kid Derek. "Oh, I'll get us both girls. Maybe we can play a little 'strip' Poker so *you'll* find it interesting."

"I can find my own girls, thanks," Derek scowled in mock indignity, "and there are some things I don't like gambling on."

"Hey," Phil asked as he dropped a box of Derek's jeans and shoes on the floor, "how are you guys gonna commute anywhere when neither of you has a car? If you think I'm gonna come out here and run you around every day you're nuts."

"Way ahead of you, Phil," Beowulf drawled. "I saw a nice little roadster in that used car lot we passed on the old highway a few blocks up. I got enough for a down payment and I figure that might make a nice Christmas present for myself."

"I was thinking the same thing," Derek agreed. "I'll be *Doctor* Martin pretty soon and I've gone long enough without my own set of wheels. Besides, there's no reason not to spend just a little of my future fortune right now!"

"Amen, brother," Beowulf said as he and Derek high-fived.

*   *   *

After sleeping in and taking life easy unpacking, setting things up in the apartment, and stocking the fridge for a couple of days, Derek and Beowulf went out to the Asylum in Beowulf's sporty new (to him) El-Zorro *Blade* to do some preliminary work on their musical synthesizer. Tom gave them permission to use the company equipment and use available materials at cost. Only a few other members of the Crew were around. Apparently the fabrication business itself had slowed to a trickle over the holidays. Having gotten a good start and worked out several snags, they knocked off at five p.m., drove to a fast food joint for some burgers and fries, and back to the apartment to watch the six o'clock news on the 3-V. The news, as usual, was not particularly good. President Morgan had given another speech about loss of American jobs due to cheap imports from Mexico made by low wage labor, and had threatened to introduce a bill raising tariffs again. The thin RepubliCrat majorities in both houses of Congress strongly supported such a bill as, apparently, did the CBC news anchor giving the story, who had a hard time keeping the sneer out of his voice as he reported the opposition to such a bill by the minority American Liberty Party.

Beowulf, on the couch with his head back, while slowly feeding a long french fry down into his intermittently chomping teeth, stopped and stared at the 3-V. "What in the world is Morgan talking about? Didn't I hear just the other day that the national unemployment rate was only three percent? And would it even be that high if the RepubliCrats hadn't raised the minimum wage to four NDs an hour last year?"

Derek, similarly comfortable in his old easy chair, leaning back with one long leg lopped over the arm while he worked on his triple decker burger and malt, nearly lost a mouthful as he snorted. "Like other facts of reality, that doesn't matter. Even if Mexicans are taking all those NDs they get selling us their stuff and using them to buy stuff of ours or invest here, *as, of course, they are,* those network slugs won't have any trouble finding some poor American schmuck who just got his pink. . . Whoops! There they go!"

Sure enough, the 3-V scene switched away from the droning CBC anchor, Chet Barker, to another reporter, filled with righteous indignation, who was just sticking a mike in the face of an auto worker standing in front of a GM plant that had just announced coming layoffs due to increased Mexican automobile sales in the U.S.

"Damn you, Beowulf!" Derek nearly shouted. "Look what you did, buying that El-Zorro! You outta be ashamed!"

"Oh, I'm filled with remorse," Beowulf moaned in mock contrition. "I'll never live with myself. I'm gonna feel guilty every time I drive that powerful, finely-machined, sixty mile-per-gallon beauty anywhere. Might as well kill me now. Just be sure you bury me in that car."

When they finished snickering, Derek waved vaguely at the 3-V. "Really, I think the RepubliCrat leaders are just jealous 'cause the Mexican economy recovered first and grew even more rapidly than ours over the last decade. Last I read, the mean real wage down there was less than twenty percent below ours."

Beowulf finished off the last of his burgers and fries. "Don't ya think that's because when the Mexican LP gained power it went even further than the ALP did here freeing their economy? And they haven't lost majority control like the ALP has. Like you said, facts don't mean anything to the RepubliCrats. If they did, they'd notice all the Latinos going back to Mexico from here nowadays. Heck, even I'm old enough to remember hearing about Latinos flooding *into* the U.S by the thousands every day and how everyone was in a panic."

Derek sat up. "Well, you're right. And it isn't just Latino-Americans with family down there. Three guys in the graduate class ahead of me, none of them Latinos, took jobs with Mexican firms last year. You're forgetting a big part of the historical equation, though, Beowulf. If our ALP hadn't legalized all chemical euphorics and ended the U.S. war on drugs a lot of that reform wouldn't have happened. Legitimate businessmen took over and It took the money and power away from the Mexican drug cartels. That's why Colombia is prospering now, too."

"Beowulf nodded. "That's true. It's amazing what open markets will do. All in all, Mexico is an even freer country than the U.S. these days. Tom says that's one of the first places we'll go international once we get going. He wants to set up a San Francisco to San Diego run and then build a chamber in Mexico City. Speaking of Tom, once this food settles a bit, I'm going out to the Asylum for a workout. You want to come along?"

Derek thought it over as he scooped up the paper and plastic remnants of their meal and walked out to the kitchen to look for the garbage can, and then back to his chair. "Well, I would like to see what you guys do out there."

*   *   *

To Derek's surprise there were at least seven other cars parked at the end of the main building when they got out to the Asylum, including Phil's old green Chevy

Carnivore. One of them was a beat up Honda *Pilot* about five or six years old.

"Who does that belong to," Derek asked as Thad got his gym bag out of the back seat and they headed in.

"Oh, that's Tom's. He lives cheap and puts everything he's got into the project."

Inside it appeared that a workout was already in progress. Tom, dressed in gymnastic garb, was going through a series of exercises on the uneven bars with Billi Jo Jensen and a guy Derek didn't know, probably one of the programmers on the Crew. Derek pulled up one of several folding chairs that were around the periphery of the workout area and sat down to watch. Beowulf, carrying his gym bag, headed back into the dressing room.

Derek had never done anything more than elementary gymnastics, but he could still see that Tom was highly skilled. When Tom dismounted with a perfect front flip from the bars, Billi Jo and the other guy took turns trying the various exercises he had demonstrated. Tom watched and intermittently helped and critiqued. Looking over once to notice Derek sitting there, Tom waved then turned his attention back to the others.

In a few minutes the session ended, however, and all three headed back into the dressing room and shower areas. Over the next few minutes they all trickled back out, however, with Beowulf and Phil. This time they were all wearing the white uniforms traditional to Japanese and Korean versions of the

Oriental martial arts, tied in the front with soft white belts. These looked a little heavier than the uniforms Derek had seen in thousands of Karate movies, however. Six other people, who Derek had never seen before and who seemed somewhat younger than the Crew members, also came out. That included a young girl about sixteen who walked out from what was apparently the girl's side of the lockers with Billi Jo. Derek noted that Beowulf and Billi Jo's belts were brown; Phil and the others had white belts, while Tom's was black.

Each of them stopped and did a standing bow before stepping on the large plastic-mat-section away from the gymnastic bars and other exercise equipment. They lined up by rank facing Tom and at a soft command, apparently (since Derek could not really hear it clearly or understand what he did hear) delivered in Japanese, they knelt down, first on their left leg and then on their right, to sit between their heels in the Japanese fashion. Then Tom, looking over at Derek, stood up in the reverse fashion, and walked over to him while the others sat looking ahead with their hands relaxed on their knees and their backs straight.

"Derek," Tom asked when he reached the edge of the mat in front of him, "Do you want to try this? I guarantee it's a lot of fun. I'm sure I have an extra *Gi* and a clean jock back there that'll fit you and there are plenty of towels for a shower after."

Somewhat embarrassed, since the others were no doubt listening and he was no stranger to rigorous physical training, Derek demurred. "No thanks, Tom. This time, at least, I'm just gonna watch."

"Okay," Tom smiled and winked, "but you don't know what you're missing." Then he went back to his position in front of the students and knelt down as before. At another soft command that Derek could not really hear or interpret, the students and Tom all leaned forward, put their hands on the mat and bowed, then sat back up, then they all stood, and exercise began. Tom led them through about ten minutes of rigorous stretches, pushups, and oriental calisthenics. Then Tom lined them up in three lines and they each did some odd forward rolls of a type Derek had never seen before down the mat, stepping off on their right foot and rolling on their right arm and shoulder, slapping the mat with their left arms, and coming up in a natural position before stepping off for another roll. When they reached the far end of the mat and rolled up into a standing position, they walked back down to the end of the line. After a few minutes, Tom had them switch to stepping into the rolls with their *left* foot, going over on their *left* arm and shoulder, and slapping the mat with their *right* arms to absorb impact, in sequence down the matt. Then they took turns doing their rolls by taking several rapid steps and diving over a couple of their fellows who were down on the mat on their hands and knees next to each other, so that they had to stretch out into the roll.

After the rolls, technique practice began. Tom divided the students into pairs, one of which would perform a specified grabbing, holding, punching or kicking attack and the other of which would practice a specified defense. The pairs were shifted often. The techniques quickly struck Derek as having a different style and form than he had seen before though he had never been a great observer of, or a participant in, the Oriental martial arts. These techniques nearly all involved either a body turning or sliding *in* motion by the defender, designed to avoid the thrust or escape the grab, and put him or her in an advantageous position on the side of the attacker's body away from the hand still free to punch or otherwise attack. Many of the techniques also involved, along with the turning and sliding *in* motions of the defenders, some form of - at least potentially painful - arm or wrist twist which put the attacker in an unbalanced position and forced him or her to essentially *throw themselves,* or at least submit to being thrown, to avoid injury.

Other techniques involved the defender directing or deflecting the attacker's momentum into an odd, unbalancing circular motion until he or she was thrown. In all of these, of course, the attacker had to employ the rolling and arm slapping techniques practiced earlier to keep from being hurt when slamming into the mat. In many cases the defender's throw was combined with one or another odd form of pinning technique designed to immobilize the attacker, often face down on the mat, and sometimes with his arm twisted up behind him, while the defender remained in a standing or sometimes kneeling position on one knee ready to respond to possible additional attackers.

Some of the defensive techniques employed a counter punch, but here again the style was different than Derek had seen before. The defenders stood with hands open in front of them and delivered the punch *as their opponent attacked,* closing the hand into a fist only as the hand moved. Of course, for purposes of practice, the punches were all pulled short of actual contact. The point appeared to be mostly to stun the attacker an instant before applying the wrist or arm twist or body spinning technique. Derek decided this was definitely not any form of Karate, Kung Fu, or Judo. Though it seemed a closer cousin to Judo than to any other martial art he had seen. He had watched a few competition Judo matches at a local YMCA when he was younger. It must, he decided, be some form of Jujitsu and it definitely did look like fun, at least assuming one first learned the rolling and falling techniques to keep from being hurt.

Derek almost changed his mind about how fun it looked as the session neared its end. Tom had the students surround him in a circle. After saying something that sounded like *hajime,* they began rapidly attacking him with an attempted punch, kick or grab, sometimes in sequence as they saw an opportunity, and sometimes two or three together. With each attack, he spun around or slid between the attacker(s) and one or more of them flew out and/or flipped over to slam into the mat, jump up, and rejoin the circle to try again. For over three minutes Tom danced between the attackers, throwing them back and forth. When Tom finally called a halt, Derek could see he was drenched with sweat. After two shorter sessions involving the brown belts, Beowulf and Billi Jo as the defenders, in which the attackers were restricted to attempted grabs and slower punching or kicking attacks, Tom lined the students up. They did some deep breathing in unison to slow their heart beats and respiration, and then he had them kneel and go through the bowing ceremony as at the beginning. Finally, on command, they all stood and left the mat, each turning back and bowing before stepping off backwards and heading to the respective men's and women's locker and shower rooms.

In about fifteen minutes they began coming out, showered and dressed. The youngsters headed out the front door, a few nodding and speaking politely to Derek as they passed. When Tom and Beowulf came out, they headed over to Derek, who was now standing.

"Hey," Tom said, "it's only nine and the Celtics are playing the Mavericks tonight. I think it's only about second quarter. You guys want to come down to my place and watch the rest of the game? I've got a couple of frozen pizzas we can heat up and I think there's even a can of soda or two Dave left in my fridge last week."

Beowulf and Derek exchanged glances before answering. "We already had supper, Tom," Beowulf said, "but watching the game sounds like fun." The three headed down the hanger toward the offices.

"I'd rather play basketball than watch it," Derek added, "but I do like the Mavericks this year. What do you call that stuff you were doing out there?" Derek nodded his head back toward the mat.

"Oh, it's a form of Aikido; one of the lesser-known Japanese martial arts, derived from some older forms of Jujitsu. It's a little harder to conceptually grasp than Karate, so it hasn't gained the same popularity. Plus, the people who invented and developed it were always somewhat secretive. I spent a couple of years in the army and actually had to use it a few times."

"Tom's parents started him out at an Aikido club in Boise when he was ten," Beowulf interjected. "They even sent him to Japan for several summers. Weird parents."

"In that and other ways," Tom agreed. "My dad is a former science teacher and amateur inventor-turned-rancher. My mother taught women's gymnastics and English at the same school. They knew what went on in the public high schools, so they took me out and home-schooled me."

Derek opened the door of the office complex, and they headed down the hall toward Tom's apartment. Tom's comments reminded him of his own early education. "When I was ten, the Ohio ALP won control of the legislature and instituted a universal voucher system. We were one of the earliest states to try it. Governor Stinson signed the bill. My folks took me out and put me in a private school. It was a pain then - all the discipline and everything, but I'm glad now. Did you guys know the teachers unions tried three times to assassinate Governor Stinson?"

Beowulf nodded. "Yeh, I heard about that. It was national news. That was one of the things that helped break their power nationwide. When Montana adopted vouchers, a lot of parents there took their kids out of the public schools. My folks just left me in. I don't think it made any difference. It was amazing how much those schools started improving when they had to compete for students and funding. They dropped all the multi-culturalism, sex mis-education, and political correctness junk, kept order for the first time, and actually started teaching us math, reading, and science. They didn't like it, but they had no choice."

The other two men snorted and nodded agreement.

Tom led them into his apartment and turned on the 72 inch 3-V on his living room wall and turned to ESPN. Derek and Beowulf settled onto a large couch. "Who were the kids that were practicing with you guys tonight?" Derek asked.

"Some of them are from the Baptist Church Billi Jo goes to," Tom answered. "She invited a few over with my permission, and then some other kids in the neighborhood heard about it. I thought it was a good idea to turn the whole thing into a local club. They're all good kids, and some of them have potential. It's more fun with more bodies anyway. By the way, Derek, you know we do have a backboard and hoop down by the other end of the building. Beowulf put it up and painted a half-court on the runway. Maybe tomorrow we can find enough of the Crew for at least a three-on-three."

Beowulf was enthusiastic. "I'm up!"

"Me, too," Derek agreed. "Say, Tom, I'm nearly twenty-six, but I'm still in pretty good shape. Do you think I'm too old for that - what is it - Aikido?"

*   *   *

They did manage to play their scratch-basketball game the next morning, and Derek found one more thing - besides engineering - at which he was at least slightly better at than Tom. In the afternoon, Tom caught a flight back to Boise to spend the holidays at the ranch with his family. Derek and Beowulf spent some time the next few days working on their synthesizer, but gradually lost interest as the Christmas spirit seeped in. They spent most of the time shopping, wrapping gifts, and mailing packages home to their families. A day or two before Christmas, Beowulf brought a small tree that the two men set up and decorated in a corner of the apartment living room.

Unusual as it was for central California, the weather turned cold enough to actually snow a few flakes on Christmas Eve and Derek and Beowulf spent much of Christmas day itself with Billi Jo, who lived just a few blocks from their apartment. Billi Jo's parents and family were nice. Her dad was a jolly old Baptist preacher, recently retired, who took an immediate liking to Beowulf and Derek. He spent an hour just showing them his gun collection. Billi Jo's mother cooked a huge turkey dinner with vegetables, scalloped potatoes, and apple pie, and stuffed them all until they could barely walk. Watching them, Derek began to get a suspicion that Beowulf was sweet on Billi Jo and that she was more than a little interested in him. He suspected maybe it was all that contact in the Aikido class.

Over the next few days, the two men spent some more time working on the synthesizer, but couldn't get far because some parts had to be ordered in to get them more cheaply than they could fabricate them in the shop. So they spent a morning downtown talking with The Buzzard to begin the patent-application process for the synthesizer and to see how negotiations were going with the University on the field modulator. The surprise was that leaks from the Institute had already resulted in Buzz hearing from two high-tech firms offering royalties for use of the modulator. Derek didn't know whether that was good news or bad news. On the one hand, it meant more money in his pocket before long, but on the other, it meant another piece of the teleportation puzzle was now out there for other people who might know what to look for to see.

Afterwards, Derek had Beowulf drive him around town to car lots until he found a fiery red, three-year-old Ford *Banshee* that made his own motor run. The *Banshee* would only get him about fifty miles to the gallon, but it was well engineered and would do a hundred and seventy in nothing flat, almost as fast as Beowulf's El Zorro *Blade*. With his lanky frame, he had always wanted a nice, roomy muscle car. Besides, with Canadian Tar Sands and U.S. Shale Oil in full production, along with the new Wyoming, Gulf Coast, and Asian fields, gasoline was relatively inexpensive these days. So Derek made a down payment on the *Banshee* and drove it off the lot.

As the year wound quickly down, the two men began to get antsy and anxious for the holidays to end and the next stage of the project to crank up. On New Year's Eve, however, sure enough, Beowulf took Billi Jo to the SUB for the dance and celebration. If Lynn Yip Ki had been in town, Derek thought he might have asked her out and gone with them. But she wasn't, and he didn't want to be set up for a blind date by Beowulf, so he had to fend for himself in the apartment. He thought of going out to a casino and doing a little gambling, but somehow the urge seemed to have left him. *Or maybe, he thought, it has just been redirected.* He wasn't kidding when he had told Tom that the idea of innovating a teleportation industry struck him as the biggest gamble of all. *Whatever happens,* he thought, *maybe it's good for me to have that urge focused in a constructive direction.* Finally he drove out to a mall and took in a movie - the newest Hanse Remke sci-fi flick - but was still home before ten. Hitting the sack with nothing else to do, he fell asleep at least an hour before the ball dropped.

Chapter 10: Trepidation and Determination

Derek was not the only member of the Skeleton Crew anxious to get going. Tom was due back on January third. Derek awoke early that morning and couldn't get back to sleep. It wouldn't take long to get breakfast and a shower, he thought, but that would leave him with nothing to do but waste time staring at the 3-V, which he didn't want to do, so he decided to go out for a run. Though it was still a bit on the cool side, the weather had warmed up some and the snow was long since gone. He had already scouted a two mile scenic route around the neighborhood and hoped to get back on his normal three-day-per-week jogging schedule. Before he finished getting his sweat suit and running shoes on, however, Beowulf knocked and stuck his head inside Derek's bedroom door.

"Morning. You going out for a run?"

"Yeh." Derek finished tying his left running shoe and felt around under the bed for the other. "Can't sleep."

Beowulf ran his hands through his unruly hair. "Me neither and I don't wanna sit around here. Mind if I go along?"

"No. I don't mind running alone, but frankly, I'd just as soon have some company. If you wanted, we could make a habit of it."

"Give me a minute. I haven't found where I put my running gear yet." Beowulf still had much of his stuff packed in boxes or piles stacked on top of one another around his bedroom. His head and upper body disappeared from Derek's door as he headed back in that direction.

Derek went out to the kitchen where he grabbed a glass from the cupboard, poured himself some orange juice from the fridge, and reluctantly turned on the 3-V to watch the news. He switched it right back off in only a couple of minutes, however, as Beowulf came out of his room dressed and ready to run. The two men went out the door and started jogging down the street.

"Thank heavens for California weather," Derek remarked. "If it was much colder, I wouldn't want to do this. Back in Dayton, I used to see people out jogging when it was twenty below zero."

They nodded as they passed another early morning jogger going the other direction.

"That's one of the reasons I let Tom talk me into doing Aikido, Derek," Beowulf observed. "Hot or cold, rain or shine, I still get lots of exercise."

Derek grinned. "And you get to hang around Billi Jo."

"Well, there's that, too." It was Beowulf's turn to grin before turning somber. "But I don't think any of us are going to get too much exercise the next week or ten days. A lot of things have to get done before the semester starts and some of us have to start dividing our time again."

"When's Tom getting in?" Derek asked.

"Came in last night near as I know. Should already be there. We're gonna meet at ten and line things out."

For a while they jogged only with the sounds of random early morning traffic and an occasional dog barking from behind a fence in defense of its territory as they went past.

"Have you thought about the enormity of all this?" Derek asked Beowulf as they rounded a corner and started the third leg of their neighborhood circumnavigation. "The world went through a wringer and has really only partly recovered over the last decade. Now we're going to shake it up and change things in ways I don't think even Tom can completely imagine."

Beowulf recognized the seriousness of Derek's thought and was sympathetic, but also leery of its pessimistic connotations. "What do you wanna do, *Kimo Sabe,* put the genie back in the bottle? I don't think she'll go. Yeh, we're gonna change everything and some people won't like it. There're always Luddites trying to stand in the way of progress. But that's what it'll be. We're gonna benefit a lot more people than we're gonna harm and the world will be a better place for it. The evidence for that will be precisely that they'll gladly pay us to do it! I don't frankly see much reason for agonizing over it."

Derek couldn't help being cheered as he considered that. "I guess you're right. In fact, the whole prospect is as exhilarating to me as it is to Tom, or you, or anybody. I can't wait to get out to the Asylum and get started. That's why I couldn't sleep this morning. It's just that, sometimes I find the thought of actually being one of the personal agents of this kind of shakeup a little intimidating."

"Well, onward and upward *Kimo Sabe.* If the Luddites win, the world stays poor. We might even stay poor *ourselves* and we don't want that!"

"*Kimo Sabe*? If it isn't John Wayne with you, Beowulf, it's the Lone Ranger. Didn't he end up shooting Tonto because he found out that *Kimo Sabe* meant *horse manure?*"

In another few minutes they were back at the apartment, their breathing slowing returning toward normal as they walked up the steps.

*   *   *

Even after showering and getting breakfast, Derek and Beowulf got out to the Asylum early in Derek's *Banshee.* Other members of the Crew were also arriving early, apparently also anxious. Inside, they met Lynn Yip Ki, who greeted them each with a hug and told them Tom was in his office. In the office complex, several members of the Crew seemed already to be working in their cubicles while others were talking in the hall. Waving greetings to those they could see, Derek and Beowulf poked their heads in Tom's office door, which was open. He was standing over his desk with Parker Freeman, going over some math and hand drawn line schematics. When he looked up and saw them, he waved them in.

"Derek, Beowulf! Happy New Year. You guys all rested up and ready to go?"

"Ready, willing and able, boss," Beowulf responded.

"Same here," Derek agreed. "Did you have a good time in Boise?"

"I did. And I think the rest did me good, because I had some inspiration on our upgrade of Zelda. Parker and I were just working on it. I think we found a way to pack a lot more information into Rubidium atom cubits and get it out faster."

For a few minutes, Tom and Parker explained their insights and ideas to Beowulf and Derek who were not as astute on the physics and math, but whose understanding of the more practical engineering requirements and methods were superior. Modifications were suggested and new observations incorporated. Tom wrote it all down when the other three talked, scratching some things out and rewriting others on his pad as problems were found and eliminated. Gradually, an understanding came, and Derek realized that, in those few minutes, the boundaries of possibility in computing technology just might have been shoved back materially.

"I think that'll work!" he said. "It's going to be very tricky fabricating that nanocubit logic matrix and mating it up to these broad spectrum sensory feeds on the AI processors. It'll be darned expensive until we've run the learning curve down a little, but we can do it!"

"How long, do you think, before we can incorporate this into Zelda?" Parker asked.

Beowulf and Derek looked at each other for a moment. "Oh, I don't think we're really talking upgrade," Beowulf said as Derek nodded. "This is a whole new system. It'll be easier to start from scratch then download Zelda's memory and reprogram her cognition files into the new system. I'd say we're talking a year or more to get this together."

"That's roughly what I thought, too," Tom observed, "and that's about the right time frame if everything else goes the way we hope. But for now, we better focus on those other things. You two guys want to work for a while this morning on some of the engineering details, line out the work, cost out some of the materials, plan out the project? We can think later about organizing a team. But don't anybody get so wrapped up in this you forget the meeting at ten. And Beowulf, I keep forgetting. Show Derek his office space."

Derek was startled. "I have office space?"

"You're a partner," Beowulf laughed as they headed out of the door. "Sure you have office space. Everyone else does. Come on, it's the last one down the hall to the right. I thought Tom had already shown you. I kept wondering why you never went down there."

"Hey," Derek asked as they walked down the hall. "How come there's no secretarial support around here. How does anything get done?"

"Ah, that's an easy one. We wrote a program. Zelda does most of that. Not quite as good as real secretaries, but it saves us money."

*   *   *

The conference room was packed and noisy, but quieted down fast when Tom called the meeting to order. Dave, who was responsible for scheduling Crew members to work in the fabrication shop, reported on work completed, orders filled, costs incurred and revenues generated there since the last meeting. Then Parker Freeman gave a brief report on the computer system breakthrough in the works and a few other reports on ongoing projects were given.

Checking on down his agenda, Tom came to the matter of the second D-R chamber.

"Dave, how are the second cube and field generator coming?"

Dave cleared his throat. "We got the cube almost all taken down and packed last week, Tom. I think we can finish that and get the generator packed and ready to go today or tomorrow morning at the latest. Just let me know when and where and we'll have it shipped out of here in nothing flat."

"Good." Tom breathed a short sigh of relief. "Zelda did a preliminary survey of feasible alternate sites currently available in Seattle over the break using the criteria we fed her, and I've got a flight out of here at two this afternoon. Derek, Beowulf, you want to go with me?"

Derek wasn't yet entirely sure what was in the works, but a flight to Seattle sounded like fun. He and Beowulf glanced at each other, and then nodded enthusiastically. "Sure. We'll need to drop back to our apartment to pack a few things, but that's no problem, Tom."

"Okay. Between this afternoon and tomorrow, we'll find the best site and make arrangements. I can't see us being longer than a couple of days doing that. Then I'll ring you up, Dave, and give you the details. You get the cube, the generator, and the assembly tools and equipment shipped out, and then get your team up there so we can start setting up. The three of us will stay up there for a day or two at least to help get you started."

Dave nodded and looked around the table at his team members. "We'll be there at warp speed, boss."

Tom snorted. "If you could already do that, Dave, there wouldn't be any point to this. Light speed is all I ask, and that only *after* we get set up in Seattle! Lynn, how are you coming on platforms for the relay units?"

Lynn squirmed, apparently a little nervous, before answering. "Well - uh - finding an air freight service with planes big enough to not only carry the relay units, but get them up as high as we need, hasn't been much of a problem. But they all want a lot of money for the modifications to mount them the way we need. It's a big expense for a one or two time thing. Are you sure we shouldn't contract for satellite delivery instead and just put one up in a geosynchronous orbit? We're going to have to have to do that anyway once we're in business."

Tom was a little exasperated. "You're right, Lynn. In the long run it would save us money to orbit the relays, and eventually we'll do that. But all we can do for now is what's possible now, and satellite delivery just isn't in the budget. And it won't be *until* we demonstrate the practical feasibility of teleportation to a lot of people, or at least to enough of the *right* people. That's the point of our whole effort now. So unless you want to call for a vote and overrule me, find your best contract offer, Lynn, get Buzz here to cross the I's and dot the T's, then take your team over to modify their birds and install the relay units as quick as you can."

"All right, Tom," Lynn assented. "You know us gals; we just like to spend money. But if I can't have a Chaniel Foran gown, I'll be happy with a FredMart dress."

When the laughter died down, Tom turned to The Buzzard. "Now that we're talking about money anyway, how's it coming with the financiers, Buzz?"

Buzz, who had been lounging back in his chair to this point, sat up straight as he gathered his thoughts. "As you know, Tom, we've been checkin' out all the investment bankin' firms. Ah think we ought to go with Gates, Feldman, Vanderhoff and Shapiro. They have offices in 'Frisco, Sacramento and Seattle, and excellent contacts with a lot of people and institutions that have very, very deep pockets. Ah'v done a lot of business with them and Ah think they're the only ones on the West Coast who can handle an IPO of the magnitude we're plannin'."

Tom eyed The Buzzard seriously. "You understand, I need as many of those people with deep pockets as possible to actually come either out here or to the

143

Seattle module at the appropriate time. There's a good chance we'll be in competition more quickly than we like with interests that already have deep pockets of their own. And *we* will have already established the reality of teleportation. They won't have that hurdle. We've got to come up with a lot of money in a hurry and we need to be able to convince people to give it to us."

Buzz nodded. "Ah know, Tom. You've told me often enough. And if anyone can do that, it's Gates, Feldman, Vanderhoff and Shapiro. But you may need to convince *them* first. Just tell 'em and they'll think you're crazy, or some kind of a scam artist, and they won't even accept a contract to market our IPO. Hell, if Ah was them, *Ah'd* think that even if it was *me* that told 'em. That may require a special run just for them."

"What do the rest of you think?" Tom asked. A murmur went around the room for several seconds as Crew members talked among themselves, before Phillip Adobo offered a comment to the group. "Seems like that might let the cat out of the bag a little early."

"I don't see that," Angel BlackSnake responded. "It has to come out sooner or later and that would sure motivate them to sell to the investors!"

Tom was not so sure. "I don't know, Angel. If the bankers are going to be as hard to convince as Buzz thinks even when he knows it works, why would investors be any easier for the bankers to convince even if they knew?"

"It means another run with the planes," Lynn put in, "and more expense there." The remainder of her thought, that they ought to reconsider orbiting the relay right off, did not require verbal statement.

"Yeh," Tom admitted, "but we have to incur the fixed cost anyway, and the marginal cost won't be that much. Buzz, can you get the bankers out here just on your reputation without telling them the specifics that would make them think you're crazy?"

Buzz thought it over and nodded assent. "Yeh. Those people know me. You probably ought to come with me to talk to 'em though."

"And can the bankers, once convinced, get the money men out to our chambers based just on *their* reputations?"

Again, The Buzzard nodded. "Ah think so."

It was Tom's turn to nod. "And then we'll convince them."

Chapter 11: Insights in the Air

By half-past noon Tom, Derek and Beowulf were out at San Francisco International checking their carryon bags through security. That didn't take long. Security procedures were significantly relaxed compared to what they had been before the Disorders and the accompanying Second Great Depression. The near total collapse in international trade that had been a part of those events had hurt third-world countries, including the Arab world, even worse than the developed nations. Islamic militancy around the world had been overwhelmed with more basic concerns of survival as real incomes collapsed worldwide and famines, plagues, and riots had reduced populations everywhere. Some said the old militancy was on the rise and terror networks were reforming as the Arab nations recovered, but little evidence of that existed thus far. In addition, reforms of the National Air Transport System under the ALP had included not only the privatization of both airports and the Air Traffic Control System, but the arming of all willing airline pilots, which also reduced the likelihood of hijackings and hence the stringency of pre-loading security procedures.

By one thirty-five they were on the plane stowing their gear in the overheads and settling into their seats. Derek had the window, with Tom on the outside and Beowulf in between. Their aisle was forward of the wing enough that Derek had a good view, but there was nothing to see at the moment other than maintenance and baggage personnel doing their thing, an uninspiring side-view of the terminal, and a few other passenger planes on the tarmac. Right on schedule, however, the plane started powering up, the chief stewardess went through her spiel about the use of oxygen during an emergency, location of exits, etc, the seat belt sign went on, and the plane began taxiing onto the runway. With a brief pause, the pilot apparently got the go-ahead and the big plane started down the runway, accelerating rapidly. Then, with a rush of power, they were airborne with the ground receding below them and the plane making a lazy turn to head north. The day was bright; the sky was blue, with only a few intermittent cumuli to break up the expanse. Before long, cars on the ground appeared smaller than ants and they were on their way.

"You know," Beowulf commented, "I'm actually gonna miss this. It sorta has its own rush."

Derek was watching the ground through his window, noting the patterns of habitation and land formation that only became observable from this kind of elevation with their unique symmetry and beauty which changed as it moved under them. "I know what you mean. There certainly isn't going to be this kind of view from the matter-energy stream inside a teleportation carrier wave."

"Nor *that* kind of scenery either," Beowulf noted, indicating a shapely stewardess working her way down the center aisle, who briefly reciprocated the attention of the three young men as she did.

"Oh, I don't know," Tom contributed, "I think we could hire a few of those to help get people seated in the transit cubes and help 'em get out at the other end. 'Customer relations' is always important," he winked. "On the other hand, nobody is gonna to miss airline food!"

On that they all agreed.

"You do have a point about the view from up here though, Derek, and some of the other pleasant aspects of flying. If enough people miss those things, and I think more than a few will, air passenger transport won't completely go away. But when we get going, as fast as we can expand, air freight between metropolitan centers is done. Of course, smaller communities that can't generate enough volume to make use of a D-R cube economically will probably still have some."

Derek thought about that and shuddered slightly. It had occurred to him before that the transportation revolution they were contemplating would have major displacement effects on existing transport industries. "Same goes for ocean transport, right?"

He was asking Tom, but Beowulf, having been involved in the project longer than Derek with more time to contemplate its consequences, responded. "Same thing, probably. Right, Tom? Everywhere we go international, coast-to-coast, about as soon as we go, ocean freight'll disappear. Won't be able to compete at all. On the other hand, with pleasure cruises, it's all about the travel. We won't affect that."

Tom was not so sure. "Well. . . maybe we will, Beowulf. We knock transport costs down as massively as we expect, *ceteris paribus,* people's real incomes rise. Wealthier people tend to take more pleasure cruises. Might even pay a guy to invest a little in some of those firms."

"What about trucking," Derek asked.

Tom shrugged. "I think the story will be a little more complex there. Between the population centers we serve, long-haul trucking and rail transport should diminish severely, but short-haul trucking at the termini won't. In fact, it'll increase as we knock costs down and shipping volumes rise. A lot of goods will have to be shipped short haul to the transit points and shipped out for distribution when they arrive. I can't see overall trucking employment changing much, at least not away from its current growth path. But Beowulf is right. There will be a lot of employment loss in ocean shipping, more than a little in air freight, and maybe for the railroads. We probably won't offset all that entirely as we expand, since our operation is going to be so comparatively capital intensive."

"But doesn't your point about the real income change operate there, too?" Beowulf asked. "When suppliers and shippers of all kinds find their transport costs reduced, making 'em more profitable, won't they expand and employ more people?"

"Right," Tom agreed. "I'm not saying we're gonna create unemployment on net. We won't. But a lot will

149

be shifted and you can't expect anyone knocked out of his job or losing his business to like it. We might have to do some thinking about how to minimize some of that displacement. I've got a few ideas."

He didn't get to explain himself any further on the matter, however, because the stewardess came around with a cart of peanuts and soft drinks and the conversation turned in other directions as the three men munched and sipped along with the other passengers. Not too long after that, they made a stop in Portland where they sat on the ground for thirty minutes while some passengers got off and others got on before the big plane accelerated down the runway, blasted back into the air, and headed for Seattle.

North of Portland they ran into cloudy weather and began traveling through gray haze and occasional rain. *Now this I won't miss,* Derek thought. The air was not turbulent, however. Tom read and Beowulf dozed off, but Derek was wide-awake, his mind churning as he stared out through the clouds. After a while a puzzle floated to the top of his contemplation.

"Say, Tom, remember a few weeks back when I was asking about loading and unloading freight from the cubes and you said we were going to containerize this business to save those costs? I didn't quite catch what you meant."

Tom moved the slip of paper he was using as a mark forward to where he had been reading and closed the book as he marshaled his thoughts. "Well, you know as well as I do, one of the stories of the astonishing economic growth of this country over the last two hundred plus years has been a series of technical revolutions and commercial innovations that drastically reduced transport costs. Think railroads, and so on. But the one that's relevant to your question started out with ocean shipping.

"The first real revolution there, as I understand it, was the Yankee Clipper ships. Steam power was invented early, but, odd as it seems, before the Civil War the cost-reducing effects of steamboats were almost entirely on *river* transport, not ocean transport. But ocean transport costs fell a lot anyway, because American ship builders found ways to design sailing ships that would cut *through* the water better so they spent less time traveling up and down over the waves and more time going forward. Then after the Civil War, steam engines finally got reliable and powerful enough to replace sails on ocean ships. After that, diesel replaced steam, and so on. And of course, that was the great period of free trade and extension of classical liberal thinking and institutions. Most of the world globalized and prospered rapidly until World War I reversed all that. But that's all another story.

"Anyway, well into the twentieth century ocean transportation of goods was still very expensive. One reason was all the handling involved at the docks. The trucks, or rail cars, or whatever that shipped the goods to the docks had to be unloaded by the longshoreman, hand-loaded onto pallets, then, as I understand it, winched onto a ship, unloaded by hand, then carried down and loaded into the cargo hold. The shipping company only made money while they were in transit.

At the other end, everything went in reverse. Very labor intensive process, very costly, even when the labor market was competitive, before the dockworkers unionized, which they eventually did, not only in the U.S., but also in a lot of other nations.

"And that's another reason ocean shipping was so costly. The Longshoremen's Unions in the U.S. became monopoly suppliers of labor on the docks. They were able to force the shippers to pay enormous wages and benefits that rose continuously in real terms without any increase in labor productivity. On the East coast it was the International Longshoremen's Union, or ILU, run by a guy named Teddy Gleason. Here on the West coast it was the International Longshoremen's and Warehousemen's Union, or ILWU, run by Harry Bridges, who was a Communist. The ILWU was actually kicked out of the CIO. Or was it the AF of L? I forget which. Anyway, both the ILU and the ILWU were extremely militant, violent, and essentially criminal organizations. Theft by the dockworkers was massive and that ran costs up even more.

"Maybe even worse was their bitter resistance to anything that would increase productivity and reduce costs. For example, when shippers contracted with some of the trucking firms to ship goods already put on pallets with their own labor, the Longshoremen's Unions on both coasts insisted on *unloading* and then *reloading* the pallets on the docks. Pure, wasteful featherbedding, negating any of the possible cost savings. That was the way they treated any labor saving idea."

"In the 1950s, though, along comes a guy named Malcolm McLean. He'd built a very successful trucking firm in the late nineteen forties, mostly hauling freight up and down the East coast. About nineteen fifty-three, he got the idea of building waterfront terminals so his trucks could drive over ramps onto ships, deposit their trailers, and he could just ship the trailers along the coast and avoid the traffic jams on the freeways. Note that that would eliminate *all* of the labor intensive loading and unloading. Of course, the Interstate Commerce Commission, which regulated rail, ocean and truck transport in the U.S. at that time and didn't want any one firm in more than one of those businesses, rejected his proposal. But McLean was so entranced with the idea of using containers to get ocean shipping costs down, that he essentially sold off his trucking firm and acquired an ocean freight firm through a leveraged buyout.

"A couple of years later he decided that instead of shipping whole truck trailers, which wasted valuable space under the beds, he would just ship the beds. But he needed beds that could be easily lifted off the trucks by a crane and deposited on a ship and vice versa, and nobody made such a thing. So he hired this genius of an engineer named Tantlinger to design such a bed, which he did. They could actually be shifted easily between ships, trains, or trucks; and he designed them to *stack*. Then they had to buy and Tantlinger had to modify a pair of huge revolving cranes with booms seventy feet high from a shipyard in Pennsylvania and move them to McLean's docks in Newark and Houston, so they could load and unload their containers to and from the ships. As I remember reading about it, Tantlinger even redesigned their ships for ease, efficiency and safety of moving and storing the containers. Eventually they were stacking them five to seven high. Now you know why I've recruited so many of you engineers for this project. Anyhow, their very first ship essentially reduced the loading cost of cargo from nearly sixteen *dollars* a ton - that's old dollars, of course, not NDs - to about sixteen *cents* a ton!

"The short version of this story is that despite a lot of obstacles and resistance those potential savings eventually caused other shippers to copy and even improve on McLean's methods and the pressures for containerization became strong enough to break the resistance of the Longshoremen's Unions and the government regulators. Plus, over the next decade or two, inland shipping, both truck and rail transport, also switched to containers for all the same reasons."

Derek was amazed. "Why don't they tell us this history in the schools? I never heard of any of this. I'll bet the dislocations were enormous."

Tom snorted. "You're not kidding. But most of those hurt by the whole thing were those unwilling to adjust. For example, the ILU in New York resisted container automation to the bitter end, but McLean got the Port of New York Authority to allow him to automate the New Jersey docks. The result was that by the mid sixties the New Jersey docks were prospering and *adding* employees while the New York dock economy, despite massive subsidies from the city government, collapsed.

"The story for the west coast has a twist. Surprisingly, Bridges turned out to be more reasonable in the face of shipping company pressures for container automation than Gleason was. In nineteen sixty, Bridges actually talked most of the ILWU membership into accepting an agreement with the shippers that bought off their resistance. If I remember right, the shippers agreed to pay part of their cost savings from automating into a fund that would provide a guaranteed annual income to current active dock workers. For their part, the Union accepted containerization of the ports, gave up costly work rules, and agreed not to require any unnecessary labor.

"Amazingly the income guarantees turned out to be unnecessary. The cost savings and competitive reductions in ocean freight rates were so large, and trade and shipping increased so much as a consequence, that employment of dockworkers at the LA docks and some others actually *increased* as a result of containerization. I used to think union leaders and organizers were just lying when they claimed to believe the number of jobs is fixed and resisted every proposed labor cost saving innovation, but apparently they really *don't* understand the demand law.

"And that's the bottom line of the whole story. Yes, there were a lot of dislocations generated by containerization. Whole communities where people earned their livings at ports unwilling to modernize ceased to exist. Factories located close to ports to keep shipping costs low often moved away as costs fell, hurting some communities and benefiting others. Some people say it even gave businesses the edge in labor negotiations by increasing international capital mobility. But far, far more people were benefited than hurt worldwide over the rest of the twentieth century and into the twenty first as transport costs fell, production increased, and trade expanded everywhere."

Apparently Beowulf woke enough to hear part of what Tom had been saying. He yawned hugely. "Yeh, but Tom, isn't that laying a little too much on this guy, uh . . . , McLean? I mean, you had all the post World War Two multilateral tariff reductions, GATT, NAFTA, di-dah, di-dah, going on, too."

Tom simply shrugged at the accusation of having oversimplified history. "Of course McLean shouldn't get all the credit. A lot of other things accelerated the trend, particularly in the eighties and nineties. Not just the tariff reductions, but the personal computer and the internet. So throw Bill Gates in there, too. Think seriously, though, about the fact that from the end of the war to the mid 'sixties, before containerization really took hold, the Longshoremen's unions were forcing labor costs up so much that U.S. international trade, as a fraction of GDP, was actually *declining*. McLean doesn't deserve all the credit, but he should get a lot!"

Again, Derek was impressed with the enormous implications of their teleportation project. "We're going to make all that happen again, aren't we?"

Tom nodded solemnly. "All that and more, Derek. All that and more."

*   *   *

King County International Airport was huge, of course, and it bustled with the activity typical of large city airports. Derek was always amazed by airports, just as he often was when he drove over interstate highway interchanges. It wasn't just the sophistication of the physical engineering displayed in airports and interstate highways that repeatedly astonished him, but what that said about the capacities of human beings who so oddly were also responsible for wars, crimes, political oppressions, and other brutalities. With airports, in particular, it was the immense complexities of the social, legal, and economic relationships and, even more, the harmony and *coordination* of interactions underlying all the apparent randomness and bustle of activity. All this impressed Derek again during the nearly fifteen minutes it took the three men to walk from their disembarkation gate to the baggage pickup. They actually spent more time than that on route because Tom wanted to spend a few minutes looking at some currently unused gates along the way. When Derek got curious enough to ask him what his interest was, Tom just winked and said, "The fact that we've invented one thing doesn't mean we have to reinvent everything."

At the baggage pickup they had to wait another twenty minutes before their suitcases came down the chute and around the carrousel. Beowulf, as usual, entertained himself by checking out some of the young adult females of the species in the area, more than a few of whom also checked out Beowulf, Derek, and Tom. Tom waited patiently apparently lost in his own thoughts, but Derek, as always, despite intermittent attention from passing females, found baggage waiting one of the less pleasant things about air travel.

"Maybe this is one of the things you ought to reinvent, Tom," he grumbled as their bags finally arrived and he grabbed his.

"Actually, I think I'll pass that one off to you and Beowulf here. So far I haven't been able to think of an improvement."

Beowulf grabbed his last bag off the carrousel. "How 'bout we just let everybody carry *all* their bags in and out of the chambers with 'em. That'll save us any baggage handling. 'Course we'll get fewer people in that way on each run, but the alternative is to have separate runs for the baggage. That'd not only cost more, but we'd probably have to pack the bags in at the sending end and unpack 'em at the receiving end. Even that wouldn't be economical because the handling would be ridiculously expensive."

Tom nodded as he started down the terminal. "I don't know, Beowulf. There must be a reason airlines separate most baggage and passengers and store them separately. It must actually be cheaper that way or they wouldn't have done it all these years. Keep thinking, though."

Suddenly it came to Derek. "Wait a minute! You guys aren't thinking about . . . ?"

Tom and Beowulf both stopped and looked at him in amazement. "Well of course we are," Tom said. "You don't really think we should invest millions and millions of NDs recreating facilities and systems like this when they *already exist* do you?"

"Where would we come up with that kind of money?" Beowulf asked Derek. "It's gonna take almost everything we can raise just to build and locate our chambers and put our relay satellites up."

By the time they got to the rental car desks, Derek almost had his head wrapped around the idea and, by the time Tom had rented a new Lexus from the MAVIS representative and they were stowing their bags in the car trunk, he was to the point of asking himself why it hadn't been obvious to him earlier.

Tom got in on the driver's side and Derek and Beowulf flipped a coin to see who would ride shotgun. Beowulf lost and slid in the back seat with a suitcase that wouldn't fit in the trunk with the rest. It was only a short run over to the airport Ramada Inn, but before they were there Derek's attention began to turn to food.

"It's too late to look at any of the sites today isn't it, Tom? I'm famished. Two bags of airline peanuts and a couple of sodas just doesn't get it. My big intestine is hungrily eyeing my little intestine. Is there a decent eatery in this Ramada?"

Tom's eyes twinkled. "Hate to tell you, Derek, but you might be on your own tonight unless you want to come with Beowulf and me and eat later. There's a good Aikido club here in Seattle. Several, actually, but one in particular. I know the Sensei. Beowulf and I both brought a *Gi* and, as soon as we get our stuff in our rooms, we're driving in for a workout. We'll start tomorrow checking out the site options around town."

Beowulf leaned forward and stuck his head between the front bucket seats. "They do have good food in this Ramada. Tom and I've stayed here a couple of times when we came up to talk to some firms we were doing fabrication work for. But you otta come along, Derek. The Aikido club here is cool. The Sensei is a Go-Dan. Even Tom's only a Yon-Dan."

Derek sighed. "I haven't even taken one lesson yet and I don't know what a Go-Dan or a Yon-Dan is, but I'm already beginning to feel left out. All right, I'll come along and watch, but you gotta stop somewhere and let me get a sandwich on the way."

Chapter 12: Excitement in Seattle

Even given the distances involved in checking out alternate locations in a large city it really didn't take long the next day for the three men to find a nearly ideal temporary location for the second cube. Actually, they found at least three that would work, but the best seemed to be an older, now empty, hotel down on Pike Place with a nice view of Elliott Bay. The hotel had ceased operation only a few months earlier and the building was still being maintained while the owners tried to sell. It was just a few miles from the Seattle Center, much of which was still in operation. Tom had made previous arrangements with the owners and they were met by a maintenance man who gave them access to the building. The hotel had a huge ballroom that immediately struck all three of the men as essentially perfect for installation of the teleportation chamber and it was only a short trip from the hotel to the Space Needle. Indeed, from the upper floors on the north and west sides of the building that landmark could be easily seen.

The electrical power to the hotel itself turned out to be adequate for powering the chamber and it would not be hard for the Crew to get sufficient power over to the ballroom. The freight elevators appeared capable of hauling the cube sections and equipment they would need up from the parking garage to the ballroom floor. Satisfied, Tom got on his NanoPod to the corporate headquarters of the Westmark Inns and started arrangements to rent the parts of the building they needed, to make the necessary modifications and to get the power and water turned on. Then he called Dave Berret at the Asylum to get the Crew in motion. Those things took a while, but when they were done the three men brought their bags and suitcases up from the parking garage and set themselves up in the Presidential Suite.

The suite was luxurious and easily big enough to accommodate them. After unpacking they wandered around the rest of the suite and eventually congregated in the huge main living area. Beowulf flopped back in a large, comfortable easy chair and stretched out. "Now, this is the lap of luxury. Did you see the size of that spa? The other guys'll be green with envy when they get here."

Tom opened the drapes along the huge windows looking out over the bay. "I rented them rooms just down the hall that're almost as good. I don't think they'll complain too much. The big thing is, we'll have to get a catering service in here. We three can easily go out, but the others will be here in two days. Then it's work, work, work, for like the next couple of weeks and we're gonna need food delivered. Remind me to take care of that before they get here."

Derek stretched out on a huge couch and looked around the suite. "You're right, Beowulf, this place is nice, but a little on the older side. I guess that's why Westmark is letting it go. If a guy could find a way to increase occupancy, though, it might pay to renovate the place."

Tom glanced over at Derek from the window. "What? Are you thinking about going into the Hotel business, Derek?"

"Well, maybe. I was thinking about what you two were insinuating yesterday afternoon about renting gates and ticket counters and setting up teleportation cubes at airports. I mean, I see the logic. There's no reason we should duplicate a lot of that system. Too costly for us and it would generate a lot of unnecessary displacement for other people. The airports already have systems for handling passenger auto traffic in and out, parking, ticketing, baggage-handling and we just as well make use of all that. By the way, I had some thoughts on the whole baggage-handling thing. If it really is best to separate the passengers and the baggage, we'll need a redesign of the D-R chambers into upper and lower decks to keep from wasting space. I did a little thinking last night on the engineering of that that I'll run by you later.

"What struck me as we've been looking this place over is that airports aren't the only places with similar systems already operating. Hotels are designed to accommodate a lot of people always coming and going. They have parking lots for their guests and ticketing systems, or at least registration desks that could easily have ticketing added. Plus, they have one thing on site that airports don't: rooms for rent. With an airport, people transit in and then have to *drive or be driven off* to find accommodations or to get into the city. So, I guess what I'm saying is, instead of just renting this place so we can set up our chamber, use it a couple of times, and take it back down, why not *buy* the hotel and make it permanent? Even make it a general strategy to locate teleport chambers at hotels?"

"Hey, that might be a good idea, boss," Beowulf jumped in. "If we owned the hotel, we'd not only generate revenue from 'porting people in and out, but from renting rooms, food sales, the whole works."

"Yeh, and even if we didn't own 'em," Derek added, "I'll bet the hotels would make us a deal on rent to install teleportation chambers because we'd be increasing their occupancy. We could get the travel agencies to give people package deals for the travel and the hotel rooms, too."

Tom looked surprised. "That *is* a good idea, and we could certainly try it. I'm surprised that it never occurred to me. You may have missed your calling, Derek. Good an engineer as you are, you might be a just as good a businessman. My suspicion is, though, that we *will* have to have gates at the airports, and they probably will do more passenger business. The airports have much more parking space. You're probably right, though, that a lot of people might like to 'port right to a hotel, saving taxi fare and time into the city, even if they were just passing through to go other places."

Tom checked the time on his NanoPod. "I'll tell you what, guys, if we're gonna be at loose ends for a couple of days here waiting for Dave and the Crew, we just as well put it to good use. I wanna go down and tour the docks. I think we've got time this afternoon if we head out now. We can talk about all this on the way."

Leaving the suite, they took the elevator down to the parking garage to Tom's rental car. It was only a few miles from there down highway 99 to Spokane, then west a short way to the docks on the inlet southeast of Duwamish Head. They parked and joined a tour group that was just starting out. Though Beowulf had been to Seattle several times with Tom and both Beowulf and Derek had seen San Francisco bay several times, neither of them had ever toured a modern container port and seen its operations up close. Tom had apparently seen and pondered it all before, but Beowulf and Derek found the scale of the equipment and operations astonishing. There were dozens of ship berths, each with a huge ship tied up that had large metal containers stacked six or seven high on the deck, with more, the guide told them, in the holds. Occasionally a ship with an outbound load would move out into the channel to be replaced by another.

The loading and unloading was done entirely by cranes on the wharf, enormous steel structures which the guide told them were two hundred feet high and weighed more than two *million* pounds each. The cranes moved on tracks next to the ships. Each crane had an operator who controlled a trolley from which hung a steel frame called a "spreader" which locked on to the corners of a container. The container, weighing up to forty thousand pounds, was lifted up and swung over to the dock, where it was placed on a wheeled vehicle, called a transporter, which moved the container to an adjacent storage yard. As the crane placed one container on a transporter, it picked up an outbound container from another transporter and placed it on the ship, so that the ship was being *simultaneously loaded and unloaded,* each cycle taking less than two minutes.

"How in the world does all this work, Tom?" Beowulf asked. "How do they know what order to offload the incoming containers and load the outbound ones?"

Tom just shook his head in wonder even though he had seen it all before. "Everything here is coordinated through an immensely sophisticated computer tracking system that controls the movement and placement of every container. I wouldn't say nothing ever gets lost or misplaced, but very little does."

"But we're going to put those ships out of business."

"We certainly are," Tom agreed. "They're dinosaurs."

"What about the rest of this?" Derek asked.

"Well, that's what I wanted you two to see. When we start shipping freight internationally, that's where we want to set up our first chambers." He pointed right down to the docks. "We'll build chambers as big as those ships and we'll put 'em right there. Of course, we'll have to start with some surplus docks down the way, but you get the idea."

Both Derek and Beowulf were astonished, and had to think for a few moments to allow the insight to gel. Derek recovered first.

"It's the same point as at the airport last night, isn't it?"

"Well, yes and no. There's no reason a teleport chamber couldn't ship freight in from Rangoon to the middle of Kansas and after a while it'll evolve that way in order to reduce truck shipping costs from suppliers to markets. After the coastal cities, we'll be building container *teleports* a lot like this in big cities all over the country. I suspect that's what we'll be using a lot of the airport runways for in a few years. We can't immediately and costlessly duplicate this system for loading and unloading, storage, and distribution, though, and we shouldn't. By far the best thing we can do is, at least, start out with ocean port cities, using the existing system and facilities. That'll ease the pain of displacement and disemployment anyway, which might be important for several reasons."

Beowulf looked sharply and pointed at the cranes unloading the ships. "How're our cubes gonna work with those cranes without major physical redesign?"

Tom nodded grimly. "They won't. That's the second reason I brought you two out here and why I specifically needed engineers with me on this trip. We had to make D-R prototypes based purely on scientific considerations to get teleportation to work. Now that we know we can do that, we have to design them for actual industrial use, in particular to work with that type of crane. The top section and probably the sides are going to have to retract or fold down out of the way, immediately after 'porting in a load of containers. Once an outbound load is stacked on the chamber floor, the chamber will have to fold up and reconnect so that it works. So I think you two shouldn't stay more than a few days after Dave and the Crew get here. As soon as you get back to the Asylum could you two start designing a class of chambers that'll work out here?"

"I gotta be back for the start of classes in another week or so anyway," Beowulf told him. "Next semester I think I'll start taking as many of my courses as I can on-line, the way you did your economics. That'll keep me closer to the Asylum and save me a lot of commuting."

."Good. But right now, would you help Derek on this as much as you can? We're gonna need this redesign pretty fast. I can give you guys all the information you need on standardized container dimensions, normal shiploads, and everything. In fact, Zelda has it all. Just ask her when you get back. Derek, I know you're still finishing up details on your PhD, but would you head the team? Besides Beowulf, you can recruit anyone else on the Crew you think'll be helpful that isn't already wrapped up to the gills in some other aspect of the project. Let me know who you get, but don't raid Lynn's team."

"Okay, Tom. I'll start thinking about it fast. Whoops, looks like we're losing the tour. They're way ahead. We better move along."

Tom agreed, and the three men followed the tour group out into the storage yards, where literally tens of thousands of containers were stored in orderly rows over a huge concrete landscape. As they caught up, they could see trucks loaded with containers, constantly coming through the gates. The guide was pointing out how the numbers on each container were scanned into the computer system and compared with the manifests of the ships contracted to deliver their goods up or down the coast or across the ocean before the trucks were told exactly where to unload so that those containers could go on those ships in exactly the right place and order. Moving on, they could see rail yards where trains were constantly being unloaded and loaded by huge cranes that literally straddled the trains with the same degree of order and systematic tracking of the containers. Long before the tour ended, Derek felt nearly overwhelmed by the immense scope, scale, and sophistication of the movement and tracking of goods involved. *Here,* he thought, *is another example of the amazing capacities of human beings at their best and of the spontaneous, orderly nature of the voluntary interactions of literally thousands and thousands of people which comes to be, despite the fact that not one of those people, and not even a subset of them, ever really plans the whole thing out. Hayek would be proud. Just stop crime, enforce contracts, and let 'em be free. That's all it takes.*

*　　　　*　　　　*

Dave really pushed it. When Tom phoned him at the Asylum to give him the site location in Seattle, the trucks carrying the second D-R cube sections and teleportation field generator had already been on the road for hours and were nearing the Oregon border. Dave simply rung up the trucking firm on his NanoPod to give them the Seattle location, which they relayed to their drivers. Dave, Hulio, Parker, and Phil caught a plane later that night and showed up at the hotel early the next morning, much to the surprise of Tom, Beowulf and Derek, who hadn't expected them yet. The trucks arrived before noon. Tom had time to call around to temporary help agencies to arrange for local labor so that the Skeleton Crew could mostly supervise the unloading of the trucks and the movement of the cube sections, field generator, tools, etc., up the freight elevators to the ballroom. Over the next two days, the main glitches involved in getting power to the cube were solved and the cube began to take shape. Tom arranged for dedicated connections with Zelda so she could control and coordinate the teleportation operation at both ends and got a start installing the carrier-wave reception dish on the hotel roof and routing the connections down to the ballroom. Getting the cube complete and all the circuits tested would take another week at least. Tom decided to stay for another few days before leaving the rest in the capable hands of Dave and the Crew, but Beowulf and Derek caught a flight back to San Francisco International.

Chapter 13: Gina Goes to Sacramento

Gina Barlow had a wonderful Christmas with her parents and family. Her father, Adam, a renowned surgeon who was only slightly disappointed that his precocious daughter had not followed him into the field, and her mother, Rachael, who had devoted her own life to homemaking and child rearing and had never had any other occupational aspirations, were both overjoyed to have Gina back. Gina's younger sister, Heather, just in her freshman year of high school, with whom Gina had always had a special relationship, was also overjoyed. Even Gina's younger brother, Johnny, just out of high school and leaving in a few days for a hitch in the army, seemed to be leaving his bratty-young-male stage behind and was glad to see her. The whole family helped her move in and virtually everything fit in her old room just as before. Then the spirit of the holiday season took over for a while, dominating her attention.

A few days after Christmas, though, Gina decided to go to the Capitol building and introduce herself to Senator Braxon. The session of the California legislature would begin on the first Monday in January, which was coming up very fast. Under the terms of her internship, she wasn't really required to be on the job at the Senator's office before then, but she had always thought that it was a good thing to be early and do more for employers and benefactors than they expected. Besides, she was already anxious to get a start on her dissertation project. That would initially require finding relevant public data sources and equipment to tabulate, store, and process the data as she acquired it. Any start she could get on any of that would put her just that much ahead. So, she borrowed her mother's car and drove from Rancho Cordova, the suburb of Sacramento where they lived, down Fair Oaks Boulevard, then south on Watt Avenue and caught the new Parkway into the city. Traffic was light and there turned out to be plenty of visitors parking at the Capitol parking terrace.

This was the new Capitol building, built after the old one was partly destroyed in the Disorders and the remainder torn down early in the Second Great Depression. She had heard that for a couple of years after the Disorders the legislature had actually met in a private convention hall. Security let her into the building and through the metal and explosives detectors with only a fingerprint and retinal scan, which reminded her how much times had changed since then, even though she was way too young to remember more than the general unpleasantness and tension of those days. They even had a staff pass waiting for her and gave her directions to the Senatorial Offices.

On her way up, Gina passed first the House floor and then the Senate chamber, where a few lonely souls seemed to be moving about for reasons she couldn't fathom. It had been several years now since she had been subject to such romantic illusions as that democratic process somehow distilled the 'will of the people' into legislation. She knew that the dominance of the special interests in affecting and effecting legislation is not just occasional. Her belief now, after years of study of public choice economics, was more like what Winston Churchill was reputed to have once said, to the effect that "Democracy was the worst form of government on earth - except for all the others." But still, like Capitol buildings almost everywhere, this one exuded an air of permanence, grandeur, and consecration to the attainment of eternal principles of law and public well- being transcending any narrow personal interests. *If only,* she thought, *that was so.*

When she entered Senator Braxon's office complex, there were at least a dozen members of his Senatorial staff already on the job, working at computers, talking to constituents on their videophones, and so on. One young lady, who looked to be about Heather's age, immediately spotted Gina, smiled, and asked if she could help her.

"Hi. I'm Gina Barlow. I'm here to see the Senator."

The girl's eyes widened. "Oh, you're Gina! Pop said you might be in soon! Hi. I'm Amanda."

"P-Pop?" Gina stammered.

"Oh yeh. Bill. My dad. Didn't you know Sacramento is actually in his district? Come on. He's in his office back there."

"You work here?" Gina asked in surprise as they walked back toward the Senator's office.

"Oh sure. But only on my days off. I'm just starting high school, you know. I don't get paid. Oh, he could

173

pay me, the old skin flint! But he says it'd be a conflict of interest. Not that a lot of the other Senators don't have relatives on the payroll, but he won't. So I do it for fun. He use'ta try to keep me out, but I keep coming in whenever school's out. I'm gonna be a Senator just like him someday, 'though he says I should get honest work instead! Here he is."

Amanda walked right past the secretary's desk, knocked twice on the partly opened door, pushed it open wider, and spoke to the man behind the desk. "Dad, Miss Barlow is here." Then she flashed Gina another smile and an admiring glance and headed back out.

Later in her life, Gina often reflected on the nature of first impressions. Sometimes they were nothing; sometimes they were everything. The man sitting behind the desk, who looked up at the sound of his daughter's voice, was obviously tall, in early middle age, in good shape, with a shock of unruly white hair. The air of masculinity around him was definite, but she also immediately sensed a kind, gentle disposition. The smile that lit his face and the interest in his eyes as he stood quickly and came around the desk to shake her hand was instantly charming and disarming.

"Hi, Miss Barlow! Come on in. I've been hoping you'd get here before the craziness starts on Monday. Have a seat and let's talk a minute."

There were two comfortable chairs in front of the Senator's desk. Gina sat in one and the Senator sat down in the other, leaned back and crossed his right leg over the left knee.

174

"It's nice to finally meet you, Senator. My Dad is an admirer of yours and Professor Edleston thinks very highly of you. I want you to know how much I appreciate the opportunity to do this internship. It means a lot to me." Gina was surprised at all this gushing out of her, something in excess of her normal reticent conversation with people she had just met.

"Well, I'm glad to have you here, Miss Barlow. You don't mind if I call you Gina, do you? We're pretty informal around here."

"That's fine, sir."

"Good. How is Lew Edleston these days? He sung your praises to me to the point that I figured I had to meet you just to believe him. I rather badly need a person around here who has some of the skills he says you have. A lot of economic research and statistical work goes into some of this legislation."

"Professor Edleston is fine," Gina answered. "He had a bout of appendicitis in the middle of last semester and had it taken out. He had me teach a few of his classes for him, proctor a few tests, things like that. Then, in a few days he was right back."

"Do you mind if I ask about your family background? I understand you live in my district."

"Yes, sir. My father is a surgeon. He and Mom - Rachael - have been married forever. We live out in Rancho Cordova. I have a younger sister and brother and we're all very close."

Senator Braxon's eyes narrowed as he looked at her closely. "Your dad wouldn't be *Adam* Barlow, would he? The President of the state branch of the Association of American Physicians and Surgeons?"

"Yes, sir." Gina was surprised. "I didn't know he had ever met you."

"Oh, we haven't. But he put some money into my campaign last time around, and I've heard a lot of good things about him. He got a lot of doctors around the state to help the ALP with that medical deregulation and liability reform legislation we pushed a few years back."

"Yes, sir. I remember that. It's too bad we lost."

Senator Braxon smiled knowingly. "Lew told me you came by pro- ALP sentiments naturally as well as by training. I think you'll be an asset around here."

The videophone buzzed and Senator Braxon stood quickly, reached over the desk, and picked it up. "Braxon," he answered. "Yes, I'm aware of that, Fred. I've got my ducks in a row already. Don't worry. Yes. See you there."

Putting the phone down, he turned back to Gina. "The madness is starting already so I better make this brief. I understand you're going to need time to work on your Doctoral Dissertation. Would part-time be okay with you? You do staff work for me in the mornings, take a lunch down in the cafeteria, or even go out to eat if you want, and then work on your project in the afternoons? The way Edleston described your dissertation I really think it'll all dovetail together anyway. Like I say, I'm *not* gonna have you answering phones, doing campaign work, or handling constituent problems anyway. You'll be working with me instead on the statistics and economics of legislative issues and helping me deal with some of the lobbyists."

Gina couldn't imagine a better arrangement. It was almost too good. She was going to have to remember to thank Professor Edleston again when she saw him. "That'll be fine, sir. I'm excited. It sounds perfect."

"Okay. I've got to run down to a meeting right now with some of the other ALP leaders and help them hash out some committee assignments for the session. But I'd like to talk with you some more. Could you possibly come out to my place tonight about six? I'm having a little get together with the staff and some political colleagues. My wife and a few of the other gals are fixing steak and potatoes and you'll get a chance to meet everybody."

"Oh, I'd love to!"

"Good. Dress is casual. Most of the guys will be wearing jeans. See Mandy and she'll give you directions. In fact, have her show you where your desk and computer equipment will be. Then tell her I said to give you the cook's tour of the building, show you the chambers, committee rooms, cafeteria, even the gym. I'm gonna be gone a while, but I'll see you tonight, if not before then."

*   *   *

Gina drove her mother, Rachael's, Hyundai out to the Braxon household early for the same reasons she had gone to the Senator's office before it was necessary. In only partial concession to Bill's admonition of casual dress, she wore a nice pantsuit. The house was a large ranch style in a good neighborhood not far from downtown. It was obviously built since the Second Depression. There were already several cars parked out front that didn't look like they could all belong to one household. Gina went up to the door and rang the bell. After a minute it was answered by a pleasant looking middle-aged lady in an apron who looked at Gina a bit oddly for a moment.

"Hi. I'm Gina Barlow," Gina said. "Senator Braxon invited me out to his staff party. Do I have the right place?"

Just then the Senator came up behind the woman, saw Gina, and opened the door further. "Gina. I didn't expect you yet. This is my wife Barbara. Barbara, this is Gina Barlow. She's the economics and political science grad student I was telling you about who is doing an internship with the office."

"Well, Bill, when you told me you're putting an economist on the staff, this isn't what I pictured!" Then Barbara stepped back to make room in the doorway. "Come on in, Miss Barlow. I'm Bill's wife. Nice to meet you. You'll have to pardon me. I know most of Bill's staff members and colleagues and their wives. I thought maybe you were a party crasher. We've gotten those once or twice in the past. Usually news reporters who want to get an inside scoop."

"Please call me Gina, Barbara. I'm sorry for coming early if it's a problem," Gina said as she entered. "The Senator gave me the impression quite a few people would be coming out and you'd be getting things ready beforehand. I thought maybe I could help."

Barbara's eyes lit up and she led Gina into a large living room where three young men were watching a football game on a huge screen 3-V and on toward the kitchen where a couple of other ladies were already engaged in food preparation on a rather impressive scale. All three of the guys lost interest in football for a time as Barbara led Gina through. One of them sat up so fast he spilled part of his drink and was embarrassed over it. Bill went over to help him wipe it up.

"Well," Barbara said, "the steaks are on and the pies are in the oven. Do you know how to make a salad?"

"Actually, that's one of the few things I'm good at," Gina answered modestly.

The kitchen was almost as large as the living room and clearly designed for mass production, or at least for a very large family. It had a huge food service island in the middle. On the walls, pots, pans, and utensils hung down from hooks on overhead cabinets. One of the ladies was carrying plates taken from a cabinet on one of the walls from the kitchen toward an adjacent dining room Gina could just see through the connecting door, but she stopped for a moment or two as Barbara introduced them.

"Gina, this is Senator Arkwright. Call her Hally. She's going to be the new minority Whip. Her district is around Big Sur. Hally, this is Gina Barlow, an economics student Bill put on the staff."

Hally's eyebrow twitched. "Economist, my eye. You better keep an eye on that old goat of yours, Barbara." Then to Gina, "Nice to meet you, Miss Barlow. I'd shake your hand, but I'd drop these plates."

"And this gal," Barbara indicated a lady in her mid-thirties who was stirring some sort of frothy Jell-O dish, "is Esther Lowe, the wife of that klutz in the living room who just spilled his drink. He's on the Senator's staff, too. Esther is an LPN, but I assure you, we don't let her make hospital food here."

"Ha, ha, poor joke," Esther said before waving a greeting at Gina.

Barbara opened a cabinet and took out huge salad bowls, which she handed to Gina. "I stocked up yesterday, so there should be lots of salad material in the 'fridge there, dear, and mixing forks up there. We'll need at least two large bowls. See what you can put together while I get the glasses on." Then she started taking crystal out of another cabinet.

Gina set the salad bowls on the food island and started looking through the refrigerator. She found several heads of Romaine, plenty of tomatoes, celery, radishes, and a little cabbage. She put it all on the island, found a knife and some mixing forks, washed her hands in the sink, and started mixing. Barbara, carrying a tray of crystal glasses to the dining room, smiled satisfaction at Gina as she went by.

Just then Amanda came out of the dining room, dodged around her mother, and spied Gina. "Gina! You made it! Hey. Come meet Spider and Dex!"

"Hi, Mandy," Gina said, without stopping. "Come help me make this salad first. Here. Wash your hands, then slice some of these radishes, this way, and put 'em in."

"Ugh. I hate radishes," Amanda said as she sliced them. "They're hot!"

"We'll add this celery I'm cutting up. Eat 'em together, you'll like 'em. They're what we economists call *complementary* goods. Do you think your mother would mind if I put some of her Cheddar in, too?"

The two girls yakked and sliced happily for a few minutes, piling everything into the first of two large bowls. Then, Gina had a sly thought. Looking out to the living room to see if anybody was watching, and then up to the ceiling to insure that it was high enough, she said, "Let me show you my secret way of mixing, Amanda. Only the best chefs use it!"

Stepping back from the food island and gauging the distance, she jumped up, bent forward, and pressed herself up into a handstand. Then she shifted her weight to her left arm, picked up a mixing fork with the right, and started mixing the salad upside down. Amanda's jaw dropped open and her eyes widened as she watched Gina in amazement. Hally Arkwright, coming back to the kitchen with some extra plates, stopped suddenly and nearly dropped them when she saw Gina. Seeing the look on Senator Arkwright's face, Gina dropped back down to the floor, and she and Amanda began giggling nearly uncontrollably. "I'm sorry," Gina said to Hally. "I was just showing Amanda how to. . ."

James Rolph Edwards

Barbara Braxon, coming into the kitchen behind Hally, stopped also and wondered what was going on, but didn't ask.

"That's fine, dear," Senator Arkwright said as she recovered her composure and went to the cabinet to put the plates back. "I'll bet that will be a wonderful salad." In a few moments she and Barbara, who was still puzzled at what had gone on, headed back to the dining room with handfuls of knives, forks and spoons.

"You'll have to show me how to do that, Gina," Amanda whispered. "That looks like fun. I've never seen Hally Arkwright at a loss for words before."

In a few minutes they carried the two bowls of salad into the dining room. Barbara, Esther, and Hally Arkwright were placing the silverware and glasses around the tables. Heading back to the kitchen for more glasses, Barbara winked at them as Gina and Amanda entered. "Wow, Gina. You really can make a salad! I hear you have unusual culinary techniques, but it does look scrumptious."

Gina smiled and reddened with embarrassment. "Mandy did most of the work. I just supervised."

Two long, beautiful oak tables had been put together in the dining room to accommodate all the guests, a few of whom were standing around and talking in small groups. Others were still out in the living room watching the game. Gina wanted to go back to the kitchen and help with the silverware, but Mandy insisted on taking her around and introducing her to other members of her Dad's staff whom Gina had not already met. "Dex" turned out to be Dexter

Gibbs, Bill's Chief of Staff, a single man in his early twenties who Mandy seemed to have a bit of a crush on, and "Spider" was a junior staff member whose real name was Kyle Webb. The three of them seemed to be thick as thieves. Though Gina was a little older, on Amanda's recommendation, Spider and Dex seemed more than willing to welcome Gina into their coterie.

The front doorbell rang yet again. Bill, who seemed to be the designated greeter, opened it and stood back as one of his closest friends and colleagues in the State Senate, Roger Galbraith, a big bear of a man in his forties from a district south of San Francisco, bustled in.

"Hey, Bill. The food ready?"

Bill grinned. "Trust you, Roger. I always know what the first thing on your mind is going to be. Where's Lillian? Isn't she coming?"

"She's in Rio Linda with the kids visiting her. . ." Roger suddenly stopped as if he had been shot and just felt the shock, and stared through the door to the dining room. "Holy Toledo. . . Bill, who in heaven's name is that brunette Venus back there talking to Spider and Dex?"

Bill glanced back where Roger was looking. "That's Gina Barlow, my new staff economist. If you'll reel that tongue back into your mouth, take a few deep breaths, and try to remember what a cold shower feels like, I might even introduce you."

"Wow," Roger mumbled. "I'd like to get her in a committee room full of the RepubliCrat crowd. We could walk off with all their wallets if we could stop drooling and staring for long enough ourselves! Heck, they'd think it was worth the money!"

Bill grimaced. "More likely they're gonna walk off with *our* wallets and everyone else's if we don't stop 'em from passing Governor Slanghorn's tax bill this session. Come on. Let's go watch a little of the game. Food'll be on soon and you can satisfy one of your hungers, anyway."

Sure enough, they only got to watch ten minutes of the game before Barbara came over and whispered in Bill's ear that it was time to herd everybody into the dining room. So he herded.

Gina found herself seated across from Bill and Barbara with another State Senator whom Bill introduced as Roger Galbraith on her right and Mandy on her left. Hally Arkwright was sitting across the table to Bill's right. Apparently, Bill's staff had been consigned to the second table. Before anyone got past the stage of passing salad, vegetables, and baked potatoes around the table, Barbara picked up her goblet and rang it with her fork to get everyone's attention.

That was apparently Bill's cue. He spoke up in a loud voice that could probably have been heard by a passing mailman. "Welcome, everybody. Except for Gina Barlow here, the new intern on my staff, you've all been here before and you know the S.O.P. So all you ALP atheists and agnostics put your fingers in your ears 'cause I'm gonna say grace." Then he folded his arms and bowed his head before speaking in the same voice. "Dear God. We thank thee for good friends and the bounties of the earth. Please bless this food so that it may nourish our bodies and consecrate it that the energy we derive from it may be used in serving thee and attaining thy purposes. In the name of thy Son, Jesus Christ, Amen."

A murmur of assent went around the table. Apparently, it seemed to Gina, any convinced atheists in this crowd were keeping their peace. Barbara, Hally, Esther, and Amanda slid their chairs back and stood. Barbara spoke to the crowd. "The steaks are at the rare stage. Any of you who like them that way, please raise your hands and let us know now. We'll leave the rest on the fire for a while." Then the four women went to the kitchen to bring in the rare steaks and steak knives. The rest resumed talking and passing food around. Gina wanted to get up to help serve, but Bill leaned forward and said, "You're a guest of honor here tonight, Gina. Stay put. Let Barbara and the other gals do it."

Senator Galbraith leaned over toward Gina just a little. "This salad is delicious. Say, Miss Barlow, Bill, Hally, and I are going to be fighting the governor's bill to reinstitute a progressive income tax. Got any ideas as to how we ought to go about that?"

Gina thought for a moment. "Well, sir, on a purely rational matter of economic logic, a flat-tax like we have now that will raise a given amount of money is better than a progressive income tax that will raise the same amount. The disincentive effects and deadweight losses to output and employment are smaller for the flat tax, other things equal, and, of course, the costs of taxpaying and tax preparation are much smaller. So the progressive tax makes us worse off, overall. I could write out the equations and show you the substitution and income effects on work, investment, and the capital stock very easily. But the problem is, that's abstract. A lot of voters will think about it more personally. That is, whether they're going to be a winner by being in a bracket where their tax rate will be reduced or a loser by being in an income bracket where the rate will rise. There are gonna be more voters in the former position than in the latter. That's where the RepubliCrats will make their appeal, of course, and that's the appeal you have to counter."

"Don't you think voters will I see through that, Gina?" Bill asked as he worked on removing the skin from his baked potato. "It's been more than eight years since California and most other states instituted universal vouchers for education. Over forty percent of K-12 students go to private schools now. Reading and math scores are way up nationally, particularly for minorities. I think a lot of those kids know we came out of the Second Depression precisely because the ALP got rid of progressive taxes, abolished the welfare state, and deregulated a good deal of the economy."

Hally Arkwright shook her head and growled. "You may be counting a little too much on the rising generation, though, Bill. They aren't that big a part of the franchised electorate yet. Most voters are still 'old farts' like you and me, who were mis-educated in the public indoctrination system. Only, unlike us, they never saw through it. They were willing to accept deregulation, expenditure reductions, and tax reform when things were desperate enough, but *they're not desperate any more.* Hell, Bill, why did we lose our legislative majority last year if not because we underestimated the appeal income-redistribution still has to most voters?"

"Well, all of us here managed to get reelected didn't we, Hally?" Roger put in. "Looks to me like a temporary setback. Us 'old farts' are dying off and those younger voters are getting to be a larger part of the voting demographic all the time. That means the future lies with the ALP, not the RepubliCrats."

It seemed to Gina they may have all missed a crucial point. "You know, when I said we need to counter the redistributive appeal to most voters of going from a flat rate tax to a progressive income tax, I didn't just mean the self-interest aspect. Yes, we need to get them to see that even those having their tax rates lowered will be losers from the contraction of output or lower growth trend resulting and remind them that most of *them* will be richer some day and pay those higher tax rates. But the moral argument may be even more important. After all, do the RepubliCrats openly say 'vote for us because we're going to give money to you by lowering your tax rates and pay for it by raising the rates on the rich' or do they really cover that appeal by saying 'the richer *should* pay more, being rich, and the poorer *should* pay less, being poorer, and you should vote for us to establish that just principle in the law'?

"But don't they have a point?" Hally asked. "I always have trouble dealing with that. I mean, even if it's mostly a rationalization for self- interest, isn't that pretty hard to deny?"

Gina shook her head. "Not if you get the issue straight. The principal at issue, known as Vertical Equity, simply says that those who earn more should pay more and those who earn less should pay less. What you have to see, Senator, is that the principle is satisfied *perfectly* by a single flat-rate income tax like we have now. X-percent of an income of one hundred thousand NDs is precisely, *proportionately* more than X-percent of a twenty thousand ND income. The rich *do* pay more and the poor *do* pay less. No *moral* or *ethical* principle *whatever* requires the rich to pay a higher *percentage* of their income."

"Well, I'll be darned," Hally Arkwright responded. "Once you think about it that way it's obvious, isn't it? And if we take the *moral* argument away from them, they're done. Their majority is thin anyway. I think we can split off two or three of those RepubliCrat Senators just elected in the northern districts. We have a lot of support up there and they won by the skin of their teeth."

"Yeh, she's right," Roger agreed. "The RepubliCrats are wrong on both the economics and the ethics, and we need to fight both those fronts. Maybe even more important, though, is that we have a positive agenda of our own, not just oppose everything. Which reminds me, how is your second draft of our automotive deregulation law coming, Bill?"

188

"Staff's working hard; 'bout got it Rog." Bill said around a mouthful of potatoes.

Gina was intrigued. "May I ask what that's about, Senator Braxon?"

"Drop that Senator stuff, Gina, and save it for the office, if you want. Anyplace else, I'm just Bill. We've been working on a proposal to abolish the Department of Motor Vehicles. A transportation economist named Semmons came up with a plan back some time before the Disorders, but it's never been tried before. The basic idea is to solve the problem of so many underinsured drivers on the roads by turning licensing and registration of drivers over to auto insurance companies while making those companies liable for damages caused by anyone they issue a license."

Gina pondered that for a moment. "Oh, I get it. The companies wouldn't license or register cars to drivers, based on their demographic characteristics, physical ability, knowledge of the rules, driving history or whatever, unless they bought adequate insurance. Neat idea."

Bill swallowed and waved his fork. "Right. That would make a lot of drivers that are prone to risky behavior and underinsuring their vehicles think twice about their driving. Probably reduce accidents quite a bit. Plus, it'd save the taxpayers the cost of financing the DMV. In fact, I'm thinking of adding that tax reduction right into the bill."

"We'll run into a lot of resistance from those bad drivers, Bill," Roger commented, "and maybe even from the insurance companies until they figure out they're gonna benefit financially in the long run. And the RepubliCrats will go ape."

"Well, you know, Rog, we're probably not gonna get it to pass in this session. But down the road. . ."

Amanda and Barbara came in and passed steaks around to those, including Gina, who wanted theirs well done, then took their seats. Amanda started spearing salad with her fork as she listened to the discussion and sensed the lull. "Why do you always call them 'RepubliCrats' Daddy? Aren't they the Democratic-Republican Party?"

"Well, yes, honey. That's their official name."

"Weren't they different parties at one time?" She persisted.

"Well, that's an interesting bit of history, Amanda. People used to think so, but for a long time they weren't. It wasn't just the collapse of social insurance and the welfare state that caused the Disorders, the Second Depression, and the political party realignment to what we have now. When that collapse occurred, somebody in the Council on Foreign Relations lost his statist religion and released files and documents over the internet showing that over the whole post World War II period a secret committee of the CFR had picked, at least two years before each election, the Presidential candidates of *both* parties. Later the actual documents were sent to the FBI and authenticated. The committee included key leaders of both parties, the presidents of the major TV networks, and the Federal Reserve Chairman, among others. Their only failures were Barry Goldwater in nineteen sixty-four and Ronald Reagan in nineteen eighty. Goldwater they managed to defeat and Reagan they tried to kill, but failed. When all that came out, the public was outraged. Both local and national Republican leaders with Libertarian leanings bolted and joined with the Libertarian and Constitutional parties to form the ALP. A lot of voters went with them. Meanwhile, the welfare state and warfare state Republicans joined the Democrats and reformulated that party. The RepubliCrats dominated for a few years and tried to salvage the welfare state through tax increases and inflation, but that made things worse. When the chaos and Depression got bad enough, the ALP swept the national elections, won power in most states, and here we are."

"Fighting to stop a counterrevolution," Hally Arkwright said, "and hanging on by our toenails."

"Well, yes," Bill agreed, "but the future is still with us."

Barbara had finally managed to sit and eat enough to feel ready to join the conversation. "I'd like to hear about this project of yours, Gina dear. Bill said it had something to do with, what did he call it. . . rent-seeking? What is that about, the apartment market?"

Gina couldn't help giggling, and some of the others had to suppress laughter. "Sorry, Barbara. No. I *am* thinking about getting an apartment, but in economics, a rent is any payment to the owner of a factor of production that's *above* the minimum necessary to motivate him or her to willingly supply that factor on the market. So, a worker supplying his or her skills, a businessman with invested capital selling a product, or a lender, anyone might earn an economic rent."

"Well, okay, I see the idea, but why use that term for it?" Barbara asked. "The word rent already has a common meaning, paying for the use of something over time without just buying it. Right?"

"You're right, Barbara. Our use of the term is confusing to non-economists. But it goes back to the late medieval times, when a lot of common people rented farmland from aristocratic landlords. Early economists thought that *all* of the landlord's earnings from rents were excess in the economic sense, since God created the land and it would still be there if the landlord didn't exist. It wasn't a very good argument, but that's the connection. Later on economists generalized the concept to think of excess factor payments of any kind as constituting rents."

"I remember hearing about economic rents in my college economics course," Roger put in, "but I've forgotten what rent-*seeking* is."

Gina wiped her lips with her napkin before answering. "That's simply using scarce resources in some kind of effort to *obtain* an economic rent. A lot of rent-seeking is beneficial. We call the beneficial kind *productive* rent-seeking. Somebody investing in research and development in hopes of inventing a product people will like and pay a lot for, or a more efficient tool or method of production or transportation would be one example. Or, someone investing in education to make themselves more productive and valuable on the market. Or, a businessman simply transporting or shifting goods or resources - at a cost - from one location or use where they're less valuable to another where they're more valuable to consumers. All those are beneficial and productive efforts to obtain economic rents."

"But, by implication," Bill grimaced, "there must be *unproductive* rent- seeking. I know where this argument is going and, as legislators, we deal with it every day."

"Yes, Senator - Bill," Gina agreed. "It's something legislators do deal with every day. Unproductive rent-seeking is when people use scarce resources in the form of lobbying expenditures, campaign contributions, wining and dining, bribery, or whatever, in an effort to influence people in government to grant them some sort of special legal privilege at the expense of others, say a monopoly franchise over some market, a targeted income transfer, or whatever. The social problem, of course, is that *resources used to influence political decisions for the benefit of special interests are diverted from productive uses* and the real output and income they *would have* generated in those other uses is lost."

"Well, you can't do anything about that can you?" Roger Galbraith asked. "Isn't that just inherent in democratic politics? Even we ALP types who want to limit government have to get elected. Whatever position we take on whatever issue comes up it seems like some people are hurt, others helped, and a lot of lobbyists come out of the woodwork."

Bill nodded agreement to at least part of what Roger was saying. Gina, too, seemed to agree, in part. "Well, yes and no," she said. "You could never get rid of all of it. Even for genuine public goods, like, say, military defense, that have to be provided collectively because they can't be provided privately in the market, decisions have to be made as to their form and magnitude and people like private contractors will lobby to influence those decisions; so, no, you can't entirely eliminate it. Public goods, though, like provision of military protection, contract enforcement, crime suppression, and so on, have actual productive effects on the economy, offsetting their costs. The far bigger problem is with the sort of income transfer programs and regulation that simply reallocate property and rewards arbitrarily and have no productive effects, or, worse, even harm the economy overall, while benefiting relatively few people. Private resources used to influence those political decisions are a pure economic loss."

"Oh, I think I see it now, dear." Barbara said. "I was young at the time, but I remember my dad talking about all the lobbying that went on to get part of the money from those huge federal bailout bills way back in 2008 and 2009. The money was supposed to go to financial firms that should have just been allowed to go bankrupt. That was bad enough, since it redistributed income upwards from ordinary taxpayers. But the lobbying frenzy from every industry in the slightest distress was enormous. Everyone with any influence over how the money was spent ended up rich. It was a scandal, and we still had the Second Great Depression not too much later."

"Yes, Barbara," Gina nodded, "that was an extreme case. The general problem, though, is the *power*, the *discretion,* to use the law that way, to benefit some at the expense of others rather than simply applying law and contract enforcement neutrally and impartially. Anytime that *discretion* exists, people will apply scarce resources - diverting them from productive uses - in an effort to influence its use in their favor. *But that discretion can be minimized constitutionally.* It's been done. That's what happened in Philadelphia in seventeen eighty-seven and that's what the ALP did in the Second Great Depression, with immense benefits to the country as more private resources were shifted *out* of unproductive rent-seeking and back into productive uses. Almost nobody even *tries* to bribe a legislator who has no power to use the law to benefit them at the expense of others."

Everyone murmured assent, but Barbara was still unsatisfied. "Well, dear, now I see what you're talking about, but I still don't quite see what your particular project is."

"Well, Barbara," Gina responded, "Science isn't just theory, it's prediction and measurement. We try to put numbers to things. I'm going to try to measure the actual amount of rent-seeking in the legislature here. The problem is, studies in the past have been restricted to publicly collected data, like the registered expenditures of lobbying groups, and *that has always measured out as being less than theoretically predicted* given the amount of income actually redistributed through public policies."

Everyone more or less waited while Gina took a small bite of steak, chewed, and swallowed before continuing. "I think that part of the problem is that so many of the actual payments used to influence public policies are in hidden forms not reported. Literal bribes are just one form. High paying jobs given to legislators after they leave office in payment for services rendered in office is another. Paying for legislator's travel; purchases of their property at above market prices. There are a thousand ways people are paid off that are designed *precisely to hide the fact that they're payoffs.* No one can possibly list them all so nobody can measure them all, but I've developed some theories on how to statistically estimate some of the larger categories."

Hally Arkwright blanched. "You're talking about measuring corruption!"

Gina nodded. "Partly, yes. Some of that is not illegal, though, just unethical, at least in my view. And I'm not going to be partisan."

"This could make you a lot of enemies, though," Roger commented. "You might even irritate some members of our own party. I know a few that have taken jobs with firms that benefited from legislation they helped write. And I even know some current ALP legislators that have taken some perks from special interests that I didn't think were exactly ethical."

"If any of our people are doing anything illegal, immoral, or even unethical, Roger, I wanna know about it," Bill responded somewhat gruffly. "If we keep our own hands clean, anything that comes out will hurt the RepubliCrats more than us. They're the ones that're into expanding political power and income redistribution, anyway. Starting right now, I suggest we make it a priority to clean up our own act."

"Not everybody's as puritanical as you, Bill," Hally Arkwright agreed, "but you're right. If Gina, here, is able to find and document what she's trying to find and document, we better be as small a part of it as possible. Not just on strategic grounds, either. We have to live with ourselves."

*   *   *

About two hours later, with dinner over, after dinner conversation winding down, and most guests already gone, Gina thanked her hosts, said goodbye to Amanda, and left.

"She's a lovely girl," Barbara said to Bill as they walked back toward the kitchen to start cleaning up. She circled her arm around his waist from the left side and he put his left arm over her shoulder as they walked through the living room. "I like her and Mandy likes her. She's smart and seems to enchant everyone. Even Hally likes her, and you know Hally. I wonder where she'll find a man good enough for her, though, when I've got the only one, and you're too old anyway."

Bill just grunted and raised one eyebrow. "Actually, I've kinda been wondering that myself."

Chapter 14: Convincing the Bankers

The morning after they got back from Seattle, Beowulf went up to the University to make some last minute arrangements on his class schedule and Derek jumped in his *Banshee* and went to the Asylum to his office. Lynn's team was off working on the relay unit end of the operation, so few people were around and most of those were working over in the fabrication shop. Opening his computer and connecting to Zelda, Derek found all the files Tom had said he would find on standardized shipping containers and container operations. He spent much of the morning learning everything he could from that material. Then he began going through the files Zelda had on present teleport chamber design, materials, and physical and electrical stress factors. In a few hours he at least had a good idea of the size of the chamber they should be thinking about.

About noon, Beowulf came in with some fast food he had picked up on the way down from the Institute and he and Derek shared a quick lunch before getting down to business: thinking about how to design a D-R chamber with wall and roof sections that would fold out of the way, then fold back together and make reliable electrical connections for container operations like they had seen at the Seattle docks. Hulio Sanchez came back temporarily from Seattle for some reason and poked his head into Derek's office, so they picked his brains on the problem for a while until he left again.

Around three o'clock they decided to take a break. Derek got a 'wild hair' and suggested they go up to San Francisco International and see if they could take a look at some air freight operations. Beowulf wanted to drive, so they took his *El-Zorro.* It was about forty miles to the airport, but with the hundred miles per hour suggested speed-maximum on the new toll way, it didn't take long to get there, particularly since Beowulf actually cruised at about a hundred and twenty.

"You know you're gonna pay extra for that when you get your bill from the toll way company don't you?" Derek asked.

Beowulf just laughed. "Sometimes a man's got to do what a man's got to do. Heck, my foot wasn't even on the peddle anyway. That was just cruising speed for this baby!"

Though the air freight companies did not conduct guided tours and were somewhat suspicious of their intent, they finally got permission for an off-duty guard to show them around the main terminal for American Parcel Service. APS, formed by merger of UPS and Fed Ex during the Disorders, had since operated the largest commercial aircraft fleet in the world. It didn't take Derek and Beowulf long to see most of what they wanted to. APS's version of containerization, at least between big cities, seemed to be to load all the packages going from city A to city B into one or more trucks, back the trucks into the holds of the big cargo planes, where the truck boxes were lifted off by a small internal crane that moved along a track at the top of the cargo hold, which then set them down where they were automatically locked in place. Each truck then moved and was replaced by another until the cargo hold was full. At the destination trucks would, in sequence, back up to the cargo hold and have a box lifted up and placed on the truck by the crane. The boxes were then driven off to the local APS building where they were, no doubt, unloaded and sorted for local delivery. Derek surmised given planes would probably have truck beds destined for more than one city, and would make a route being serviced at intervals. At each stop, after unloading, beds would be loaded for delivery at succeeding destinations along the route, with everything being tracked and coordinated by computer.

"You know," Beowulf commented, waving his hand in the direction of a large cargo plane that was being unloaded, "we could save these people a ton of money and make a profit doing it. We could not only save them delivery time, but eliminate their whole need to own, operate, and service a fleet of planes. On top of that, we could design or find a commercial model of a crane that would work with our cube and stack those truck boxes several high."

Derek nodded an affirmative. "Definitely. That'll work, particularly if competition forces some of the savings to be passed on to customers so that freight volume rises. My guess, though, is that Tom has already thought about all this. Let's head back."

Back on the toll way, Derek leaned back and relaxed while Beowulf drove. "You know, Beowulf, I've been thinking about what Tom said out at the Seattle-Tacoma Airport, that there must be a reason the airlines separate passengers and freight. It must have to do with the time of loading and unloading. It must actually be much more time consuming and costly if passengers carry all their own baggage on and off. You can see that if you think about the design of planes - narrow aisles, passengers loading and unloading through narrow doors in the plane, and the narrow gates - it would be a mess. But we can generate a D-R field with a cube with the front section open. It only takes five of the six sides. The D-R chamber could literally be a separate section of the waiting room at the gate. People could just walk over in a mob with all their baggage."

Beowulf glanced at Derek briefly, before focusing back on the toll way. "Maybe, but it'd still be a mess, Derek. More baggage on the deck, fewer passengers, and we'd be wasting overhead space. We can't stack passengers several high like you can stack shipping containers. Wouldn't it be better to have a two or three-level chamber, have baggage- handlers load and unload the baggage in one of the levels - maybe from the back out of sight - and deliver it to the terminal carrousel just like the airlines do?"

"But that doesn't follow, does it?" Derek objected. "If we have two or three levels, can't we just pack passengers and all their bags in all of the levels and get just as many passengers in?"

Beowulf snickered. "How do we get 'em up there, Kimo Sabe? Stairways? Escalators? We'd be right back to narrow access and it'd be a mess. Besides, we can't make the chamber just a separate section of the gate waiting room. The flash and noise will be disturbing. We'll *have* to have the chamber separate, with some kind of gate access, though it certainly could be wider gates and more of 'em than the airlines use."

"Oh, yeh." Derek responded. "I forgot about that. Anyhow, we've got another design problem on our hands. Either way we're going to have to have some kind of two or three level passenger and baggage construct to fit *inside* the cube. We'll have to run it past Tom when he gets back, to see what he thinks."

Beowulf sighed. "Seems like we just keep making work for ourselves, doesn't it? And I only have a week before classes start."

They got back to the apartment in time for a light supper before Beowulf drug Derek, with only minimal reluctance, over to the Asylum for his first Aikido class. Tom being in Seattle and Billi Jo being out of town with Lynn's team, Beowulf ran the class. Derek spent the whole time being tutored in basic falling and rolling techniques, bowing and other Japanese courtesy protocols, basic stances, and movements. Apparently, one almost had to learn a whole new way of walking. It might have been mortifying except the neighborhood kids in Tom's club came and one of them was also new to the art, so Derek had company in his corner of the mat where the more skilled white belts, at Beowulf's instruction, took turns showing them what to do. In the end, he realized that it *was* fun, even for a beginner.

The next couple of days went similarly. In the mornings after their jog, Beowulf went up to the school and Derek went out to the Asylum. About noon, Beowulf would come out to help work on the new teleport cube designs. One evening they spent working on their synthesizer in the fabrication shop, and the next they worked out at Aikido. The next morning, Friday, Tom came back and reported that Dave and the other members of the Seattle Crew contingent were going to work on through the weekend and expected to have almost everything finished and ready by Monday. Dave and Phil, both in the last year of their respective PhD course work, expected to be back just in time for the start of their last semester, leaving Hulio and Parker to keep an eye on things in Seattle until they were ready to put the cube into use.

Tom didn't stay long. He talked with Derek long enough to become satisfied with the progress Derek and Beowulf were making on the new cube models, adding a few suggestions of his own, then left to catch a flight out to deal with some glitch that had come up with the relay platform. Before he left, though, he gave Derek some other good news. Buzz had called him in Seattle and told him the University had approved the deal on Derek's field modulator. That left one less thing to worry about.

Not long after Tom left, Beowulf came down from the Institute and barged into Derek's office without knocking. Derek was just leaning back and wondering about lunch when Beowulf slung himself into one of Derek's office chairs.

"Hey, Derek, guess what?"

"Well, let's see, Beowulf.   There's corruption in politics, some crazy guys invented a teleportation machine, and the Institute approved the deal on the field modulator."

Beowulf was crestfallen. "How did you know? I just dropped in and saw Mike Zidelsky. He told me it only happened yesterday."

"The Buzzard told Tom and Tom told me. You just missed him. He flew in this morning and just flew back out to help Lynn on something. You bring anything to eat? I'm famished."

Beowulf pointed at him. "It's your turn to buy."

Derek sat up and lifted his lanky frame out of the chair. "Well, okay. Let's drive over to the apartment. I got plenty of sandwich material in the fridge and I think there're some chips left. We'll take my *Banshee*. This afternoon maybe we can rethink that connector design. We get that straight, I think we could run some simulations on Zelda and watch 'em on the big holodisplay."

"Did Tom have any other news?" Beowulf asked as Derek grabbed his jacket and they headed out into the hall.

"Yeh.   Everything's copacetic in Seattle and, as soon as they fix this last glitch on the relay unit mounting, it looks like we're almost ready for the demonstration run. He's thinking of maybe doing it on the twentieth."

Beowulf shook his head. "Well, Kimo Sabe, that's the day the cat will be out of the bag. And I don't just mean Schrodinger."

*   *   *

On Monday morning, Tom came back and, with him, most of Lynn's team. Dave and Phil also got back from Seattle before noon. Both of them had to go up to the University to deal with registration matters, buy texts, etc. Those members of the Skeleton Crew who did not have to spend time at the Institute went to work in the fabrication shop to deal with a backlog of orders that had built up while almost everyone had been out of town. With Tom's okay, Derek kept working on the new cube designs, with Beowulf's help when he could break loose from the Institute, and Derek helped out in the fabrication shop part of each morning.

Tom, himself, spent most of Monday in conference with Buzz. The investment bankers, Gates, Feldman, Vanderhoff, and Shapiro had been perfectly willing to market bonds against the fabrication shop and that had gone well. UR&F had more than enough money to pay its debts to the trucking company, to the air freight firm that was going to handle the relay, to Westmark Hotels, etc., and to pay for the things they still needed to do over the next few months. But, as Buzz had predicted, the bankers were reluctant to handle a large IPO just on Buzz's word that the proposed corporation had a revolutionary technology that could be immensely profitable.

There was no option but to let them in on the details. Tom had worked hard for several months putting together a business prospectus in his spare time. Buzz extracted a solemn promise from the bankers to keep what they learned secret until a deal was struck, then had his people deliver copies of the prospectus to the San Francisco offices of Gates, Feldman, Vanderhoff, and Shapiro. The senior partners then distributed copies to others they decided they wanted involved in their Seattle and Sacramento offices with similar promises of confidentiality. Before noon on Wednesday, they made a call to the offices of Byrd, Rand, Epstein, and Ely to talk to Buzz. They were incredulous at the whole idea of practical teleportation, and wanted a meeting, to find out if they were being scammed. So Tom and Buzz set one up for Friday at one p.m., at the San Francisco office.

Tom and Buzz arrived five minutes early at the fifteenth floor office in the Atlas Building, announced themselves to the secretary at the huge desk inside the glass doors marked Gates, Feldman, Vanderhoff, and Shapiro, Investment Bankers, and were immediately shown into a conference room. The room was impressive, well lit and had beautiful wood wall paneling. The senior partners, Marlon Gates, Joseph P. Feldman, Remington S. Vanderhoff, and Eli Shapiro were already waiting, with what appeared to be some nervous anticipation, along with four other important partners from the Seattle and Sacramento offices. When Tom and Buzz entered and walked to the large table, everyone stood and shook their hands. Tom's sense of nervous anticipation in the room was confirmed in their grips.

Everyone had a copy of the prospectus in front of them and the partners had apparently been perusing and talking about them before Tom and Buzz arrived. Marlon Gates, one of the senior partners, had been designated primary spokesman from the Banker's side, so he introduced everybody and started the meeting.

"Buzz, Mr. Wright, thank you for coming. As you might understand, we here at Gates, Feldman, Vanderhoff, and Shapiro are in a bit of a quandary regarding your proposal. On the one hand, we've had a long and highly satisfactory relationship with Mr. Byrd. In the majority of cases it has been highly profitable and in no instance have we ever found reason to doubt his word in the slightest. And you, Buzz, vouch for Mr. Wright. If it wasn't for that, we wouldn't be having this meeting despite the fact that your business plan, Mr. Wright, is, on its own internal merits, highly impressive. Your numbers add up, and your plan for initial operation and expansion, while extraordinarily daring, would seem to be justified given the claimed technology and the assumptions on cost and revenues on which it's based. We also think your proposal of a five-million share IPO would make sense based on those same assumptions."

He glanced at his partners, who nodded agreement, before he continued. "Our reluctance, of course, stems precisely from those assumptions. It's not that we don't have some impressive information on, and recent experience with, you and your firm, Mr. Wright, that lends some credibility to your claims. Your fabrication business has built an excellent reputation in the scientific equipment industry. You service some of the most cutting edge corporate, government, and university labs in the country. We had no problem marketing the recent bond issue which I understand is being used to complete preparations for the incorporation. On the other hand, we understand that you were,. . ah, . . let us say, ejected from the Physics program at the University, which doesn't exactly instill us with confidence, though Mr. Byrd has done everything he could to back you up on that matter. Still, everything depends on what you are claiming you can do and the costs at which you claim you can do it. So we just have to ask: are you serious? This is not a joke? You have practical, cost-efficient teleportation?"

Both Buzz and Tom nodded affirmatively, and Tom answered. "Yes, we do. We've already teleported both objects and people successfully, short distances and we're set up, or will be in a few days, for a long distance transmission. Of course, we have to be careful about letting details of the technology out, but I brought visual data chips in formats compatible with what Buzz tells me your firm's computers handle and you can watch our prior experiments at your leisure."

Gates looked pained. "No offense, Mr. Wright, but any kid with a computer knows that kind of thing can be faked. In fact, these days *any kid with a computer can fake them.*"

"True," Tom responded, "and even though there are computer programs for detecting such things, which

I'm sure you'll use on our audiovisual recordings, I don't expect you to believe any of that. The only way you're really going to be convinced is to come out to our facility and either watch it happen or try it yourselves."

The thought of actually being personally teleported apparently shook several of the partners, but it was also exciting to at least one or two, and the offer itself made them consider the possibility that they might just be right in front of an earth-shaking opportunity after all.

"You mean, actually be teleported ourselves?" one of the partners asked. The man had a slight Jewish accent. Tom thought he was Eli Shapiro. The thought crossed his mind that Jews might have some religious objection to teleportation, perhaps biblical, but he couldn't think what that could be.

"If you want. I'll be right up there with you. Nothing will happen to you that doesn't happen to me. We've done it enough already to know the technology is reliable."

"You've actually been. . . teleported yourself?" another of the partners, probably Feldman, asked in amazement.

"Yes, once."

"Was it. . . unpleasant?"

Tom grinned. "No, almost all of us have found it rather the opposite, but so far I haven't been able to get Buzz to try it."

Buzz gave Tom a mortified expression. "I saw it, that's enough. To tell the truth, I'm not sure I like the idea of my particles being rearranged. At my age, they're rearrangin' enough all by themselves."

"I'm not going if he doesn't," one of the other partners said and the rest laughed, except for Marlon Gates, who drummed his fingers on the table, either in nervous irritation or from a desire to regain control of the meeting.

Looking Tom squarely in the eyes, he said "Let's suppose you're telling the truth, young man. Let's suppose you can do everything you say you can do and right now I'm inclined to at least consider that as a remote possibility. That still leaves us with a problem. How in heaven's name are we going to sell five million shares of an IPO to people who regard the whole idea of teleportation as science fiction?"

"Well," Tom said, "you said it yourself. You wouldn't be meeting with Buzz and me if you didn't trust Buzz. Business is built on trust and you gentlemen have been in business a long time. If we convince you, then you have to do the same thing we're doing. You get investors who've learned to trust *you* out to our sites in Menlo Park and Seattle and we'll give them the same opportunity I just offered you."

All the partners sat silent for a minute as they considered Tom's proposal. Finally Gates spoke. "That'd be the damnedest thing that ever happened in the history of business finance. We're going to have to think about it. We'll get back to you."

The meeting was over.

*   *   *

The next day Marlon Gates called Buzz and said the partners had viewed Zelda's audiovisual recordings of the prior teleportation tests and had voted in favor of coming out to the Asylum and at least seeing tele- portation demonstrated in person. The vote had *not* been unanimous. One of the partners thought the whole thing was a fraud and a waste of time and another was highly skeptical, thinking that such a new and revolutionary technology would be highly risky and unlikely to be cost effective. As per prior instruction, Buzz set the visit of the partners up for the twentieth at ten a.m., which gave Tom and the Crew several days to make last minute preparations and equipment checks.

Chilly, rainy, and windy weather rolled in to central and southern California for several days and Tom thought briefly of trying to cancel and reschedule the demonstration. None of their prior tests had taken place in bad weather and it was possible that high electrical activity in the atmosphere could interfere with the carrier wave, with possible disastrous consequen- ces. Of course, the probability of the carrier wave passing through a lightning strike was small and every form of transport had its risks. He certainly did not want to scare the investors, though, so he decided to go ahead on schedule. It turned out he didn't have to worry. On the eighteenth, the weather cleared up for what the forecasters said was likely to be an extended period.

On the morning of the twentieth, every member of the Skeleton Crew except Angel BlackSnake, who was home in bed with the flu, Parker Freeman, Derek, and two of the computer geeks on the Crew who were running the equipment in Seattle, and Lynn who was up in one of the planes with a relay unit, was out at the Asylum. Spring Semester at the Institute had been going for over a week, but Beowulf, Dave, Billi Jo, and Phil all skipped classes to be there. When The Buzzard and the partners arrived in their limousines and business suits, Tom greeted them and led them into the Asylum and down through the lab to the teleportation chamber giving them a brief tour and explanation of the key equipment and facilities on the way, including an introduction to Zelda.

The day before, Tom had had the guys temporarily remove enough of the office and hallway wall paneling to get the table out of the Asylum conference room and set it up in the cube with all the most comfortable office chairs they had placed around it. The idea was to put the partners at ease and make them as comfortable as possible in a familiar environment. Tom led them right up into the chamber.

"Gentlemen," he indicated the seats, "if you'll make yourselves comfortable, please, I'll take a few minutes and explain the nature of the demonstration we're going to give you."

A couple of the partners milled around nervously for a few seconds as the others sat down, apparently sensing that the chamber was something other than a normal room, and wondering what was going to happen. Eventually they, too, sat down and turned their chairs to watch Tom.

"Thank you," Tom continued, and waved his hand at the walls of the cube surrounding them. "As you might suspect, the large cubic chamber we're in is a key part of the transportation technology we're going to demonstrate to you today. We've been calling it a D-R chamber, or Dematerialization and Rematerialization cube, though I think in the future they'll simply come to be called teleport chambers, or teleports. That equipment out there, controlled by our quantum mainframe, Zelda, causes the cube to generate a field in the chamber that maps the particles of the matter to be transmitted, storing the pattern momentarily in Zelda's memory without disturbing the pattern itself. Then when the field is properly focused and harmonically tuned, it releases the strong forces binding the particles and allows the strong force *itself* to transmit the particles along a carrier wave to the destination chamber where the energy and matter pattern is instantly restored. The process is completely painless and occurs at light speed. You will experience some unusual sensations in your mind, and you might hear some sound of air displacement as you arrive. There is no inertia. This is not an airline, so nobody needs a seat belt."

A titter of nervous laughter went around the table. One or two of the partners looked more than a little uncomfortable at being put in the center of an experiment without any more advance warning than they had been given at their earlier meeting and were considering getting up and leaving, but Tom went on before anyone did so.

"What we are going to do today is offer you a free and very, *very* quick trip to Seattle, Washington, where we have a second chamber set up with its support equipment and personnel. Those of you choosing to go will be gone at most two hours before we bring you back and nearly all of that time will be spent on a brief tour of the Seattle Center and a luncheon we've arranged at the recently restored Space Needle. From there you can look out over the whole city, so there won't be any doubt where you are."

"Excuse me," one of the partners, Remington Vanderhoff interjected.

"Yes, Mr. Vanderhoff?"

"Uh . . . it's at least a thousand miles from here to Seattle, isn't it? I mean, I don't see how you'll. . ."

Tom had hoped the question would not come up, but now it had. "You're right; we can't transmit your signal directly to Seattle for reasons explained in appendix three of the prospectus. The carrier wave will be relayed through units designed for that purpose that are now in airplanes flying at high altitudes between here and there. After the IPO is marketed, of course, one of the first priorities will be putting our relay units in orbit."

Vanderhoff was not entirely satisfied. "Well . . . what if you miss?"

Tom grinned. At least he had not asked if they had ever done this before. "We won't miss and, if somehow we did, nothing will happen. We have a

214

failsafe built in. The carrier wave is generated a second before dematerialization is to occur, and if a dedicated connection isn't established, Zelda aborts automatically. Any other questions?"

The partners looked at each other nervously, but there were none.

"All right, gentlemen," Tom continued, "it'll take just us a couple of minutes to power up the equipment. While we're doing that, there are two things I would like you to do. First: any of you who wish only to observe, and not make this trip, please get up now and exit the chamber. You'll notice we have several comfortable chairs set up over there for a front row seat. While you gentlemen are thinking about that, I'd like to invite any of my associates not immediately engaged in critical functions to go along on this trip with us."

Remington Vanderhoff looked very much like he wanted to leave and actually started to get up as did Eli Shapiro. They might have been followed by some of the other partners except that several members of the Skeleton Crew, including Derek and Dave, enthusiastically accepting Tom's unexpected invitation, scrambled quickly into the cube and took seats at the far end of the table, chattering happily. Seeing that, Vanderhoff and Shapiro sat back down, though they did not seem happy about it. Tom, himself, swallowed in relief. He had been more than a little worried about a mass exodus of the partners at that point. The inspiration to invite the loose members of the Crew to forestall that had been fortuitous.

Looking over to Beowulf and Billi Jo at the console, Tom gave them the 'high sign' to power the system up and they began doing so. Then he turned his attention back to the bankers. "The second thing I would like you gentlemen to do is, please take your NanoPods out and call your wives, or a close friend, and ask them what time it is."

The partners all looked puzzled. Marlon Gates beat the rest to the punch. "I don't get it. Any NanoPod tells the time, right on by the atomic clock! That's one of the simplest functions."

"Please indulge me," Tom asked politely. "It's a matter of having what *you* will regard as reliable witnesses."

Marlon slowly pulled his NanoPod out, switched on its cell phone function and called his wife, as the others did the same. Jenny answered on the second ring. "Hello, Marlon, what do you need, darling? You seldom call me this time of day."

"Can you tell me what time it is, Jenny?"

"Well, sure. It's ten twenty-one. But why do you need to know? Are your NanoPod and office clocks on the fritz?"

"No, honey. I just needed to hear it from you. See you at supper. 'Bye." Before clicking his NanoPod back together, he switched to its respiration and blood pressure functions and noted the readings, just to make sure he was all right. It occurred to him that he might be a little old for adventures that made him this nervous.

After a minute or two, everyone seemed to have completed their calls. Tom knew it was time to either fish or cut bait.

"All right, gentlemen, if you'll just relax now, we'll be on our way. Where are we, Beowulf?"

Beowulf's response boomed back over the microphone. "Subatomic discrimination attained and carrier wave connection is imminent. Displacement in five, four, three, two, one . . ."

Nobody in the chamber heard zero. Nobody heard the "whump" of air displacement either, though they might have had their entire attention not been focused on the sensation of instant locational transition; and the indescribably beautiful harmony being generated by every atom of their being, which faded slowly, leaving each with a simultaneous sense of marvel and loss.

"What in the world was that?" Joseph Feldman asked, as much to himself as to anyone else, as the partners looked at each other in shock and amazement. "Where did the music go?" Then they looked out the front of the cube, to see that they, the chairs they were sitting in, and the conference table, were unambiguously, indisputably, *not* in the same place as they had been before. This cube seemed to be located in some kind of hotel ballroom. And there were several men and women who were apparently employees or partners of Tom's, jumping up and down and whooping it up just in front of the chamber. The partners didn't understand, and would only much later find out, that those people were celebrating the first *really* long-distance teleportation.

Tom decided to speak while the partners were still speechless, first to the Seattle contingent of the Crew celebrating in front of the chamber, then to the bankers themselves. "Hold it down little, guys, hold it down. Gentlemen, welcome to Seattle. Before we leave on our tour, I would like to request that you use your Nanopods to call your wives, families, or significant others, and ask them again what time it is."

Marlon, shakily, took his NanoPod out of his pocket, opened it up, and called Jenny. He understood now the purpose of the whole thing. If he got the answer he expected, there could be no fraud. She answered, as before, on only the second ring.

"Marlon? Did you forget something, honey?"

Marlon had trouble talking. He was still trying to get himself together. "J . . . J . . . Jenny, can you tell me what time it is?"

"Marlon, what's wrong? Are you okay? It's only been about three minutes since you called me before. Are you at work?"

Marlon thought that over. "No, honey. I think I'm in Seattle." Without further comment he disconnected, folded up his NanoPod, and put it away.

"Now, if you'll come this way, gentlemen," Tom beckoned, "we have to go down several floors. Transportation is waiting out front."

The members of the Crew along for the ride had recovered much more rapidly than the bankers, having known what to expect, and immediately began following Tom out of the chamber toward the front doors of the ballroom, talking excitedly. The bankers, still in some shock, followed along behind. As they went down the hall toward the elevators, they passed a window, and Marlon looked out. In the distance he could clearly see the Space Needle. He stopped several of the partners and pointed. They gawked, and then hurried to catch up with the rest who had stopped to wait. Marlon walked up to Tom and leaned close.

"Mr. Wright," he said shakily, "we've been thinking over that five million share IPO. We think it's too small. Let's go for ten."

Chapter 15: The World Changes

Gates, Feldman, Vanderhoff, and Shapiro decided they needed two weeks to line up potential buyers of the IPO and convince them to come for a demonstration run. In fact, there had been a long history, going back to the beginnings of the industrial revolution, of inventors and innovators giving demonstrations of new technologies for potential investors in hopes of weaning money out of them, but it certainly wasn't a normal practice of modern business finance. It was not an easy thing to convince hard-nosed investors to actually travel to Menlo Park or Seattle to see or even participate in a demonstration of a revolutionary technology. In this case, however, Tom, Buzz, the other members of the Skeleton Crew, and the bankers themselves all thought it to be necessary. The bankers put on a full court press, suspending for the period all of their other projects, and involved every partner and employee in the firm in the effort. The enthusiasm of the partners, bordering on fervor and their personal testimonials of what they had been through, at least intrigued many wealthy potential investors enough to attend the demonstration, even if most were not initially made into complete believers. Few savvy investors could completely discount the reputation of Gates, Feldman, Vanderhoff, and Shapiro. Even if what they were saying sounded like pure science fiction, one had to wonder what would cause staid members of an established and conservative firm to make such astonishing claims.

Word began to spread, as potential investors being solicited by the bankers relayed those bankers' testimonials to their wives, husbands, families and friends. The claims of practical teleportation were heavily discounted outside the community of high flying investors, however, even more than inside and hence took on the status of rumor or urban legend that nobody in the news media thought worthy of reporting, except on the internet where all sorts of wild rumors were always circulating anyway. Nevertheless, in mid-February two large groups of potential investors, mostly drawn from the west coast, but including many from Texas, the Midwest, and even a few from the eastern states, arranged to show up at the appointed times and places, one at the Asylum and another at the old Westmark Inns Hotel in Seattle.

The results were just as they had been with the bankers themselves. The demonstration in Menlo Park occurred first so the financiers assembled in the Westmark Inns ballroom in Seattle were actually able to see them arrive and talk with them before being teleported down to Menlo Park themselves. After both groups had taken their tours, been treated to dinner, and given a presentation of the business plan of the proposed corporation to be named Universal Teleportation Transport, or UTT, they were 'ported back to their city of origin. All doubt, at least about the technical feasibility of teleportation, was removed from the mind of every one of those participating in both groups and the prospectus they were given convinced nearly all of them that it was not only economically viable, but likely to be highly profitable. Nobody found the teleportation experience itself other than amazing and exhilarating. One person did have a nervous stomach afterwards but that was understandable, and was discounted by the investor herself.

When the investors went home, the rumors took on a completely different status. Word spread like wildfire. Too many people had been involved for the whole thing not to be believed. The 3-V networks made the Seattle and Menlo Park teleportation demonstrations the lead story the morning after they occurred and they never stopped being the lead story for a week, pushing news of the guerrilla warfare resistance to the recent U.S. occupation of Rwanda, and the efforts of the Mexican president to reduce border tensions with the U.S. into the background. Bidding began immediately for shares of the IPO, even though - by design of Gates, Feldman, Vanderhoff, and Shapiro - shares were not formally to be offered for another five days. Long before the five days were up they had firm commitments for all ten million shares, at prices more than forty percent higher than they had anticipated.

"Damn," Marlon Gates muttered. "We should have gone for *fifteen* million shares!"

*   *   *

Mike Zidelski was just coming out of his ten a.m. class when he got the news. He knew something was up when he walked into the department offices. Several professors were standing in the anteroom talking excitedly and the department secretary, Fran, was not at her desk, but was talking just as excitedly with the secretary from the graphic design department down the hall. Wondering what was going on, Mike decided to stop and ask.

"Fran, what's the excitement?"

"Oh, didn't you hear, Dr. Zidelski? Somebody right here in Menlo Park invented a teleportation machine! You know, like they used to have on the old Star Trek series, only it really works! They teleported a bunch of people up to Seattle yesterday. It's all over the news!"

Mike was shocked. "Who? Where? Who did it? Was it the Physics department? How come I didn't hear of *that* project?"

"No, no," Fran shook her head. "It was some private lab, over on the other side of town. Universal . . . something-or-other. I never even heard of 'em."

Mike froze and stayed motionless for several seconds as various pieces of information he had garnered over the last few months began to crystallize into a coherent insight. "Wright! I knew he was up to something big! Fran. Get on Dinosaur and download Thad Thorsen's class schedule for me. And if we have a current videophone or NanoPod code for Derek Martin, I want it fast."

Rushing into his office, Mike tossed his class materials on his desk and began punching Jacob Hansen's number in on his videophone.

*   *   *

Irwin Westholm happened to be watching the 3-V in his office wall when the first report of the teleportations by Universal Research and Fabrications in Menlo Park was reported by CBC. Even though the report was fairly sketchy, consisting of barely coherent interviews with three of the investors who had participated, and Tom Wright's name had not been mentioned, Westholm knew exactly what had happened and exactly who was responsible. He had been preparing himself for something like this for months and was not shocked, though he had been hoping it would take more time. He was filled only with a cold hatred and determination.

Picking up his videophone, he keyed the department secretary out in the anteroom. In a moment, she picked up.

"Marge, get me Yukio Hasimata on the phone."

"Sir, I can't do that. You know what time it is over there now. He doesn't like to be disturbed at this time of day."

"Marge," Irwin repeated himself in a voice cold with menace, "get me Hasimata on the phone. I don't care if he's at home asleep, I don't care if he's in a meeting, or eating supper, or with his mistress. I don't care if he's *dead;* you get Hasimata on the phone!"

Marge did, though it took some time, over which Irwin Westholm waited in silent contemplation of the tortures he might inflict, were he not a civilized man, on Thomas Alvin Wright. Eventually the phone buzzed and he picked it up.

"Dr. Hasimata is on line two, Dr. Westholm," Marge spoke.

"Thank you, Marge," Irwin said coldly before punching up line two. The Japanese scientist, looking tired, haggard, and irritated, appeared on the screen. "Yukio? Have you heard the news? Yes, yes, I know what time it is. Turn on your 3-V and find out what's going on. We're on the Institute's dime, and I'll wait."

It didn't take more than five minutes for Hasimata to return to the phone. "It would appear, Westholm San, that they have beaten us to it," he said in broken English.

"How far away are we?"

Hasimata looked troubled. "Even with the schematics for Mr. Martin's field modulator, which you managed to get for us, we may need another several months. Our quantum computer and field generation system are still an order of magnitude away from sufficient resolution, and we have not found the proper field resonance for releasing and directing the strong force anyway. Unlike Mr. Wright, who was apparently able to derive it mathematically, we have to search for it and that may take some time. Is there any way you can help us further with that?"

Westholm grimaced with frustration. "No, Yukio. The math in his dissertation proposal relating to the strong force harmonics is maddeningly dense and appears incomplete. I think he deliberately withheld something at that point. You and your people will just have to keep searching. As for the computer problem, have you tried x-ray splicing of the cubit sections yet, as I suggested?"

Yukio Hasimata had to struggle to keep his disdain and irritation from showing. He had tied up many of the resources of his research team for over a month pursuing that blind alley at Westholm's insistence and had known beforehand that it wouldn't work. "Yes, Westholm San, we did. Thus far that has not generated a stable four dimensional information matrix."

"Well, keep me apprised. We both have a lot riding on all this."

*   *   *

Samuel Hamilton Clanton, the Majority Leader of the California Senate and perhaps the second most powerful person in the state after the governor, was on the couch in his office having sex with his public relations and research assistant while talking to his wife on the phone - with the video feed discretely disconnected, of course - when he first heard the news. The assistant was actually a very, very high priced call girl named Charise Meardon, whose sexual services to him were completely and secretly paid for, on a permanent basis, by the California Brotherhood of Teamsters, to whom he, Samuel H. Clanton, had provided very valuable legislative services in exchange. 'Tit for tat', as he liked to say; and it cheered him no end whenever he heard the ALP crowd nattering on about the wonders of free markets. Sam thought it was a nice touch on his part, however, to also put Charise on the public payroll. She was more than willing to kick back half of her state salary to him, in cash, for the hour or so a day she actually spent in the office, and she gave a whole new meaning to the phrase 'public relations.' The other staff members all knew what was really happening when Charise went into the inner office, of course, though nothing could be proved.

"No, Martha," puff, puff, "for the last time," puff, puff, "I will not sign the divorce papers." Puff, grunt. "You think it was an accident we repealed the no-fault divorce and community property laws last year?" Puff, puff.

It was another rather delicious irony to Sam that the ALP had been so split on that issue. Some Libertarians had rather strong conservative streaks and, like other conservatives, thought that those laws had caused some serious social decay over the last half of the 20th century. That had motivated a lot of them to vote with the Democratic Republicans on the issue, many of whom were also strongly conservative in their views. Sam's beliefs on such issues were normally more liberal, but the last thing he wanted was a divorce in which he might lose half of his hard-earned wealth and have his political career hurt to boot.

"I'm going to have to go now, Martha, I have other business to attend to." Puff, puff. And he really did, quite aside from Charise. A call had come in on his other line, so he punched that button.

Charise moaned.

"Hold it down, will you?" Puff, puff. "Hello, this is Clanton. What?" Puff puff. "You heard what?" Grunt, puff. "Teleportation? You must be joking. Hold on a minute."

Discharging in a rush, he basked in the glow for a moment while his heart and respiration slowed, then disengaged, stood and started pulling his pants on. Charise also got up and started looking for her panties, bra, and blouse. In a minute, Sam went to and sat down behind his desk. Charise finished dressing, wiped off the couch, straightened a few things, and sprayed some odor eliminator around the room from a small pressurized can she kept in her purse. Then she flashed him a smile he was too distracted to acknowledge, and left.

Sam picked up the phone. "Okay. Start from the beginning and tell me everything." He listened for nearly two minutes, asking occasional questions. Finally he was convinced.

"How the hell did this happen without me knowing about it?" he railed. "Never mind. I'm coming down to the floor. Round up the troops and tell them we're gonna cancel business for the day. I've got to call my broker."

*　　　　　*　　　　　*

It was about eleven o'clock when Gina Barlow found out that the world had changed. Senator Braxon had gone down to the Senate chamber earlier for debate on the Governor's bill to make the state income tax progressive, which was scheduled for a vote later in the week. The bill had been pushed through the finance committee rapidly by a Democratic Republican majority determined to ride roughshod over ALP resistance, but Bill Braxon was leading a strenuous floor fight, where the debate was more public and widely reported. Gina was at her desk in the office, inputting data into the statistical program on her tMac, which would allow her to estimate the demographic and economic effects of the proposed tax change. She expected to have those results for the Senator before noon, giving him plenty of time to assimilate, distribute, and employ them as ammunition before the floor vote. Kyle 'Spider' Webb was on the phone providing some kind of aid and comfort to one of the Senator's constituents and the other members of the staff were similarly engaged in one form or another of constituent or legislative task.

The normal chatter and background noise in the office had no effect on Gina's concentration, but suddenly she was distracted by some unusual noise and movement out in the hallway, almost as if a great many people had started rushing around out there. For a moment she wondered if there was a fire in the building somewhere, or perhaps a bomb threat, but realized she would surely have noticed an alarm. Spider, who had walked down to Gina's desk, also noticed the cacophony. He and Gina exchanged a curious glance before looking back at the office door. Suddenly it opened. Dexter Gibbs rushed in and down the aisle toward them.

"Spider! Gina! Did you hear what happened?"

"No. What?" They both spoke simultaneously.

"Somebody right here in California invented a teleportation machine!"

"What? Teleportation? You must be dreaming, Dex," Gina said, her work now forgotten.

Dex seemed almost offended that Gina would doubt him. "No, I'm not. It's all over the news. When they heard the news they took a vote downstairs, and canceled all Senate business for the day. I think the House leadership did the same thing. Bill's meeting with the RepubliCrat honchos for a few minutes to work out a rescheduling, and then he'll be up."

With that, Dex went to the wall and turned on the large inset 3-V. Nearly everyone in the office had already stopped work. When the three-dimensional picture came up on the seventy-six-inch wall screen, it showed a split-screen view of the primary CBC news anchor in New York, Chet Barker, talking to a local California reporter holding a mike. The local reporter was in an office building and seemed to have just concluded an interview.

"Are you getting the same story from all of these people, Wes?" the anchor asked the reporter.

"Well, yes, Chet, that's the amazing thing. It doesn't appear possible there's some kind of hoax going on here. This is the fifth person we've tracked down in San

Francisco, so far, who actually participated in the demonstration. They're all wealthy business financiers and they all tell exactly the same story: instant transportation up to Seattle, some kind of strange music in their heads, and so on. They *all* plan to invest heavily when the IPO comes on the market next Wednesday. The bankers handling the IPO though, Gates, Feldman, Vanderhoff, and Shapiro, have only been willing to assure us that the technology works and that it was developed in a research laboratory in Menlo Park called Universal Research and Fabrication."

The network anchor turned and looked directly into the camera. "Thank you, Wesley. That was Wesley Frickman in San Francisco. If you've been listening, you now know that we've gotten the same story from people in Seattle. We now go to Donald Burgley in Menlo Park, south of San Francisco, where Universal Research and Fabrication is located. Are you there, Donald?"

The reporter being addressed in this case was one of about two dozen such clustered around the front of what appeared to be a large hanger. "Yes, Chet. I'm out here at Universal Research and Fabrication, which I must tell you is not very impressive just to look at from the outside. As you can see, the lab seems to operate out of this large hanger located on an old airfield just outside of Menlo Park itself. We understand that the other building over there - that's it - is also part of the business and maybe those smaller ones here, too."

"Have you been able to talk to anyone there yet, Donald?"

"Well, yes and no, Chet, mostly no. People come and people go here, but none of them are talking to us much and they won't let us inside. It's a research lab, after all, and I guess they're worried about security. We did just learn that the head of the project is a guy named Tom Wright, but he seems to live on sight at the lab here and hasn't come out to talk to us at all, so far."

"Uh, tell me, Donald, does Universal Research and Fabrication have any connection to the Edison Institute there in Menlo Park?"

"Well, Chet, we don't know for sure, yet, but we just heard a rumor that Mr. Wright might have, or recently has had, some connection with the physics department up there. It's pretty hard to imagine a purely *private* operation inventing something like this without government contracts or subsidies of some sort. We're trying to check that out as we speak."

Gina listened in growing amazement at the possibility that someone might have actually invented practical matter transmission, which she immediately intuited would completely shake up and transform the whole world. As she did, however, a tingle went up Gina's spine when she connected several small bits of information. Menlo Park. The Institute. Someone named *Thomas* Wright. *That couldn't be.* . . she wondered. *No. It couldn't.* But later that evening, when some details on the academic record of one Mr. Thomas *Alvin* Wright became available and one of his old yearbook photos was shown on the news, she found that it could

Chapter 16: Media Madness

Tom and the Skeleton Crew were not without things that had to be accomplished in the two weeks between the demonstration run for the bankers and those for the investors. In fact, activity was intense. For one thing, organizational matters had to be settled. Board members had to be recruited. Articles of incorporation had to be written up and filed with the California State Commissioner of Corporations before the IPO could be offered. The Buzzard prepared the paperwork on the articles to be filed if and after the demonstration for the potential investors went well, while Tom and the Crew hashed out details on the initial corporate structure. Tom, of course, had already been chosen to be President and CEO of United Teleportation Transport, but that left much else to be decided.

A typical board of directors for a U.S. for-profit corporation averaged about seventeen members. In the nature of things, board members could not simultaneously be employees of the firm. Since the stockholders were the ultimate owners of the corporation, but the firm was run by professional managers, the function of the board was to see that the managers ran the firm profitably in the interest of the stockholders. Tom and the Crew decided to keep the board relatively small at first. Tom's first choice was Marlon Gates, who knew a great deal about how corporate Boards of Directors operated since he was already sitting on two others. Marlon, it turned out, was more than willing to sit on the board of UTT. Tom and the Crew all thought it would be nice, in a high technology firm, to have technical expertise on the board. Since Tom needed to go up and mend a fence or two at the Institute anyhow, with the Crew's assent he offered a board position to Jacob Hansen, who also accepted. Since it was highly important to have people with financial and business competence on the board, and he liked them personally, he also brought in Lewis Edleston from the economics department and Ludwig Rothman, an extremely competent business professor. None of the professors had been on a corporate Board of Directors before, but since boards met only intermittently, the professors could work around their University duties; and they found the salaries attractive, in addition to the idea of watching over a beyond-the-cutting-edge technology firm.

It was a given before anything else was done and before the board was even formed, that each member of the Skeleton Crew, in addition to being a major stockholder, was to be an employee of the firm if he or she wished. Nobody wanted to bail on that despite their likely impending millionaire status. Beowulf, Phil, Billi Jo, and Dave, still taking classes at the Institute, hence unable to administer any proposed corporate divisions, were simply put on salary as researchers in the R & D section. Managing Directors slots provisionally went to Hulio, Lynn, Parker Freeman, Angel, and Sean Nezbit.

Despite his lack of seniority in the Crew or business training, Derek was chosen by vote of a large majority of the Crew members to be one of two Vice Presidents of the firm with responsibility for the R & D, satellite operations, and transport divisions. The thought scared him and he wanted to say no, but reluctantly agreed, thinking that he did not want to disappoint people who seemed to have faith in him. Maybe the whole thing would flop before it even got going, anyway. The Crew decided that the other Vice President slot, with responsibility over the financial side of the company, should be filled by an outside hire by the Board of Directors. As physical science and math geeks, most Crew members felt they simply did not have expertise in everything needed to run what, with any luck, would very soon be a large corporate enterprise.

Those things decided, Tom asked Marlon to get as many of the board members as he could together and write up a set of bylaws so they would know their responsibilities and operating procedures. In the process they decided to limit the Board to ten members, with four-year alternating terms. They also decided initial executive compensation levels.

In the meantime, Tom, Lynn, and Angel went to New Mexico to get cost estimates and possible timetables from some private satellite delivery firms. With the abolition of NASA during the Second Great Depression, private industry had completely taken over satellite delivery. A cluster of such firms, constituting a sort of mini-Silicon Valley, had developed outside of

Santa Fe in recent years. Orbiting of relay satellites would be a priority if everything went as anticipated over the next few weeks. Another priority would be rapid production of teleportation chambers and field generators, which Tom and the Crew decided would best be farmed out. It was a judgment call, but it was either that or turn the fabrication shop into a mass production operation, which looked likely to involve much more time and trouble. When they got back from New Mexico, Tom and several other Crew members spent a lot of time contacting and comparing cost estimates from manufacturers capable of doing the work. They finally picked the two best firms and let out the contracts.

Derek stayed in the Asylum because he had to keep working on the specialized cube designs that had to be completed before anything more than the current manufacturing design specs could be sent to contractors. Beowulf, when he came back from Seattle, had rearranged his class schedule to leave Tuesdays and Thursdays free so he would be able to help Derek on the design problems on those days. He could sometimes also help for an hour or two on the other weekdays and even on a couple of Saturdays. A lot of the time, however, he had to focus on schoolwork as did other members of the Crew still taking classes.

The stress and strain might have become intolerable as the days passed, but it never quite did. Exercise, Derek realized, was not only good for the body, but a great stress reliever that took the mind off pressing business and worries. Three mornings each week he and Beowulf went for their run before Beowulf headed to the Institute and Derek to the Asylum. Alternate evenings they practiced Aikido, with Tom running the sessions when he was in town and Beowulf running them when he wasn't. Slowly Derek began to get the hang of the falls, positions, movements, and some of the basic techniques. Evenings when there was nothing worth watching on the 3-V - which was nearly always the case - and Beowulf was either too busy studying for conversation or was out with Billi Jo, Derek found he could avoid worrying about work by thinking through the Aikido moves he was learning. Sometimes he went through them alone in slow motion, either in his bedroom or in the living room. Beowulf always got a chuckle out of it when he passed and saw Derek doing that. He'd been through that stage himself.

Then word came from Gates, Feldman, Vanderhoff, and Shapiro that everything was ready with the financiers and it was time to make final preparations for the last teleportation demonstration. Several members of the Crew flew to Seattle to help those already there handle things at that end. Derek thought that was ironic since they could have teleported up from the Asylum, but with only a few going, airline tickets were cheaper. Derek, Tom and Dave went over to the control tower which Derek had never been in before and brought the old equipment on line. Some of the potential investors had actually decided to fly into Menlo Park and land at the Asylum runway in their private planes, having been given directions by the bankers. Tom had maintained licensing for the field and hired some retired air traffic controllers to run the tower for a day.

*   *   *

The morning after the investor's demonstration, the news media blitz began. Very little work got done as Tom and the Skeleton Crew watched in amazement. They did manage to get the table moved back from the chamber to the conference room where they crowded in and watched the large wall 3-V, switching channels occasionally to see what the different networks had to say. At first it was little more than interviews with amazed and enthusiastic investors, but the newsmen quickly quizzed them enough to get the official name and location of the Asylum.

"Well, the cat's out of the bag now," Tom said. He leaned back in his chair and propped his feet up on the edge of the table as he watched the news cast with the others. "Looks to me like we're off and running. I better get The Buzzard on the phone and make sure he filed the Articles of Incorporation. In five days, guys, we're gonna have a pot-load of money to invest. A very, very big pot load."

Beowulf was at the Asylum with the rest because he had no classes pending that day. He was sitting across the table from Tom. "Don't you have to have some kind of published notice before you do that?"

"Yeh, that's the law. Buzz did that." Tom chuckled. "You know, it's kinda funny. The notice that a firm to be named *Universal Teleportation Transport* was incorporating has been in the papers for over two weeks and nobody raised an eyebrow. Shows you how much people pay attention to those things."

"I think we're raising eyebrows all over the world this morning, boss," Phil commented, then high-fived with a grinning Hulio Sanchez who was sitting next to him.

"No doubt about that."

"What are we going to do when that mob gets here, Tom?" Angel BlackSnake waved at the network reporters on the 3-V screen.

That was a serious question that in the rush of business, Tom realized, he had not previously given adequate consideration.

"Tell 'em what you want when they ask. Just don't go into any detail about our technology. And we'd better keep 'em out of here for the same reason. There really are people out there who're desperately going to want to know how we do it, and we aren't set up to distinguish legitimate news people from ringers that are sure to show up. Beowulf, you're big enough. Are you willing to guard the door for a few hours, just let Crew members in and out? Any outsiders get obstreperous, you have my permission to throw a *Kote-Gaeshi* or a *Shiho-Nage* on 'em."

Beowulf grinned at the thought. "Sure, boss. It'd be my pleasure."

"Good. I'm going down to my office and arrange for some permanent professional security." Lifting his feet down from the table, Tom got up and walked out.

239

One eye on Tom as he left the conference room and the other on the 3-V screen, a thought struck Derek which he directed to the other members of the Crew. "You know, I've wondered for some time, but keep forgetting to ask, why that hasn't been done long before now. I mean, here we are revolutionizing human knowledge and technology and just anybody can walk into the place."

Angel BlackSnake shrugged. "Well, Tom lives here. When nobody else is around, he locks up and if he goes out of town, Parker does."

"And we're a small operation," Dave added. "We all know each other. Any stranger coming in would be immediately obvious."

"Plus, there's the shoestring factor," Phil said. "As in, we've always operated on a shoestring, and professional security hasn't been in the budget."

"Tom once told me the big thing, though," Parker commented, "is being innocuous if not invisible. Tight professional security itself sends a signal that there's something important to be secured. Tom didn't want that, but things have changed now."

*   *   *

Before eleven the first reporters had arrived out front and by noon the Asylum was besieged with them. Beowulf guarded the door with a little alternating help from Dave, Phil, and Derek, letting only Crew members come and go. Very few of the Crew members answered any questions they were asked by the news hawks on their way in and out. On Tom's instructions, any of the newsmen or women asking for an interview with Tom were politely told that he was too busy for now. Tom really had far more important things to do anyway.

Despite the growing intensity of the 3-V reporting on the teleportation story, most members of the Crew began to marginally lose interest in watching repeated analyses of the event by network talking heads who knew nothing of what they were saying interspersed with pictures of the scene in front of their own building. Several members of the Crew wandered off to their own offices and watched on their small 3-Vs, checked the internet news, worked, and occasionally dropped back to the conference room to see what the others had heard. So the crowd in the conference room thinned out.

At two p.m. Tom was on his videophone finalizing contract terms with Nucleonic Orbital in Santa Fe and preparing to fax them his signed copy. Nucleonic had a good business reputation and had put in the lowest bid to orbit the first three relay units. Just then Beowulf knocked and stuck his head in the door.

"Boss, there are a half-dozen guys in uniforms outside saying the Pinkerton Agency sent 'em. They the ones you ordered?"

Tom was surprised. "Wow. That's good service, already. I didn't expect them this fast. I'll be right with you." Grabbing a file folder from his desk he headed out the door after Beowulf. As he did, Parker stuck his head out of the conference room door and called down to him.

"Tom. Looks like the security guys are here. The talking heads aren't happy."

"I know," Tom said. "Beowulf just told me."

The two men walked rapidly to the front of the building. Outside, the scene was not as tense as Tom had imagined from Parker's comment, but the six uniformed men had positioned themselves in front of the Asylum door in a semicircle, pushed the reporters back, and clearly intended to prevent any closer approach. As Tom and Beowulf went out the front door, the guard on the end turned, saw Tom, smiled, and extended his hand. He was average height, about Tom's age, and built very solidly. He had lieutenant's bars on his uniform shoulder. Somehow his face seemed vaguely familiar to Tom, but he could not remember from where.

"Mr. Wright, I presume? I'm Harold Pinkerton. Did you get the files the agency sent down?"

Tom pulled the top file out of the folder, checked the picture against the man's face, then reached over and shook his hand.

"Yes. I'm glad you made it. Come on in."

They started toward the door, but Tom turned back. "Beowulf, until we lock up for the night, you'll still need to hang around to let these security gentlemen know who to let in and who not. I think we'll clear the building at five, so you can go home and they can take over. Tomorrow we should have a better arrangement worked out. That okay?

"Sure, Tom. Can I still throw a *Kote-Gaeshi* on those news types if they get out of line?"

"I don't think you'll have to now, Beowulf," Tom said over his shoulder as he and the Lieutenant went in. Inside, the Lieutenant scanned the building with the eyes of a security professional as Tom led him toward the offices. Tom noticed that the man gave more than casual attention to the mat and workout equipment, seemingly intrigued.

"Are you any relation to the original Alan Pinkerton?" Tom asked as they walked.

"Yes, sir, actually, I am. There've been descendants of his in the firm all the way down."

"I read a little about him once," Tom remarked. "He was an interesting character."

Harold turned his head and looked Tom in the eye as they walked. "You have no idea, sir. The firm has records that've never been made public. So does my family. Is there another entrance to this building, sir?"

"Yes, down at the other end there are hanger doors and a regular door. The hanger doors we keep permanently locked until we need to move something large in or out. The small door we also keep locked until we need it. Usually we use the front door we just came through."

"What about the other buildings?"

"This one's our research facility. The building across the field houses our fabrication business. It has a lot of valuable equipment and materials, so it'll need to be secured, too. None of the others have anything needing to be protected, but it wouldn't hurt to check them once in a while. Somebody we don't want watching might set up shop in one of them."

Lieutenant Pinkerton nodded understanding. As they came to the offices, he gazed down the hanger to Zelda and beyond. "Is that where you. . ."

"Yes," Tom answered. "We really did."

The Lieutenant shook his head. "Amazing."

Inside the main office door, Tom first led the Lieutenant down the hall to the conference room and introduced him to the members of the Crew who were still draped across seats or leaning on the table watching the 3-V, before leading him back to Tom's own office, meeting and introducing him to other members of the Crew along the way.

Inside Tom's office, the Lieutenant got right down to business. "Well, here's how I see it so far, sir. Once that madness outside settles down, you can make do with a minimum of two men on duty per shift. One to guard and patrol this building, one to watch your fabrication shop and occasionally check the other buildings. I'll check on the two on duty every shift, and they'll have radios and can call each other or those off shift, or even the police if they need help. Eight-hour shifts, six people plus me. Sound reasonable?"

Tom nodded. The Lieutenant continued. "Our closest office is San Francisco, as you know, so we'll rent a small house in the neighborhood. Every week six guys will be sent down and they'll rotate with assignments up there so they can be home with their families. I'll give you files with pictures of all our guys who are rotating in the assignments. If anyone shows up you think might be a ringer, you can contact me fast."

Again, Tom nodded assent. The lieutenant pulled out a pad and pen and began writing some numbers on it as he talked. "I'll need files on all of your people, of course, so that our guys can get to recognize them all and know who to filter out. Also, if you do decide to hire us, I'd recommend you let the company install retinal, DNA, and fingerprint scanners for the main doors, and work up identification badges and security passes for your guys. That's additional expense, though, and it's up to you. Here's the cost just for the manual security, and here it is with the hardware."

Tom looked at the numbers. "We better have the security hardware. I'd feel better, though, with three men on duty at a time. Can you give us a nine-man team, plus yourself, just to start? We're selling our stock shares in five days. With the technology we've developed, I don't think this is the time to scrimp on security. Plus, we're going to be hiring a lot of people shortly and we'll need your firm to do background checks on applicants and watch for corporate espionage. I'd pretty well like the full load."

"Yes, sir. We can do all that," the Lieutenant nodded happily and started working out the numbers. When finished, he filled them out on a basic contract form and showed it to Tom, who read it and signed.

The Lieutenant folded the contract and put it in his pocket. "We'll start now then, sir. I'll leave three of my guys and the rest of us will go make housing arrangements. I do have just one other request, though."

Tom was curious. "What's that?"

"Could I and any of my guys that are off-duty in the evenings work out with your Aikido club?"

"You're kidding." Tom was astonished. "You're an Aikidoka?"

"You don't remember me, do you?" The Lieutenant grinned like a Cheshire cat. "You came up and worked out with the Oakland club once last year. I think you brought the big Nordic guy outside with you. I was just an *ikyu* brown belt at the time, but I made *Shodan* last month. Wow. I've never seen *anyone* as good at *Randori* as you, sir."

You could not have pried the grin off Tom's face with a crowbar. He squinted at the man as he walked him back to the front door. "Now that I think about it, I do remember you, Mr. Pinkerton. I was wondering where I'd seen you before. I didn't know your name, back then, but I could see you were about ready for your black belt."

"I'd be honored if you'd call me Harry, sir. At least, when I'm off duty."

Tom decided that he liked Harry Pinkerton. "And you call me Tom, Harry. Did you say your guys wanted to practice, too?"

"Yes, sir. I've been integrating Aikido into the training at the San Francisco office. Even got our boss to hire Ishi Harada to run the training so I wouldn't have to do it myself after hours. You know Ishi, and he's good, but when the guys heard who was trying to hire us down here, I had to fight off volunteers."

Chapter 17: Incorporating Actions and Reactions

The world seemed to hold its collective breath the day before the UTT IPO went on the market. Since Tom and the Skeleton Crew weren't talking, the networks had run out of hard information to feed to the public within three days following the investor demonstration. They had been reduced to repeatedly interviewing their own talking heads about the implications of such a technological innovation, interspersed with interviews of various science experts on how such a technology and industry might work. None of them had more than the rawest speculation to offer. For the last two days prior to the IPO, all headline stories, whether 3-V, radio, or print, dealt with anticipations of that event. When it happened, it lived up to the hype. The ten million shares sold for more than a hundred NDs each and went rapidly up from there on the NYSE. Even after Gates, Feldman, Vanderhoff, and Shapiro's discount, UTT had an initial capitalization of over a billion NDs. On paper, at least, every member of the Skeleton Crew was an instant multimillionaire and any who wanted to sell part or all of their stock could certainly have cashed in. They watched it all happen on the big screen in the Asylum conference room, and then celebrated. The party lasted all day and most of the evening.

The next day, everyone who could be at the Asylum went back to work. Neither legally incorporating nor money in the bank from a successful IPO meant that UTT was in business, much less that it would be a *successful* business. Despite the fervent belief of Tom and the Crew, and the enthusiasm of investors, that still had to be determined. State licenses to enter the transportation business had to be acquired, investments had to be made, assets had to be put into place, schedules and prices had to be established, employees had to be hired and trained, and a thousand other details had to be attended to before either passenger or freight operations could begin and a dime could be earned. The bank account was going to deplete rapidly. It was going to *have* to deplete rapidly, for some time, or they would never *be* in business.

No small part of the initial load fell on The Buzzard. Since Tom's plan was to enter the passenger business between Seattle and San Francisco first, Byrd, Rand, Epstein, and Ely sent teams of lawyers to Sacramento and Olympia state Transportation Departments to file for licenses to operate. The extensive federal deregulation undertaken years back when the ALP controlled both Congress and the presidency, had only been partly matched at the state level. Some state governments that had remained in RepubliCrat control had actually taken up regulatory slack. They had suffered slower economic growth and loss of employment and population to other states since then as a consequence, but some states were only slowly learning those lessons.

Tom and The Buzzard, with a few of Buzz's law clerks and interns flew to Geneva, Switzerland to file and negotiate with the International Orbital Commission, a private organization which had taken over the coordinating and allocation of satellite orbits from the old International Telecommunication Union when governments wanted out of that business during the Second Great Depression. Dealing with a private organization was easier than with the state regulatory bureaucracies, and within three days they had their orbit authorization for the first three of UTT's relay satellites. It would take a minimum of three satellites in high, elongated geostationary orbits to provide world-wide teleportation relay coverage, and, for redundancy, Tom planned an eventual system of twelve. With the first one, though, UTT would be on its way. Tom immediately called Nucleonic Orbital to give them the go-ahead and headed back to Menlo Park. According to Nucleonic, there was an orbital window for the first satellite coming up in two weeks and the others would follow quickly.

Before Tom and The Buzzard left for Geneva, however, something else of significance occurred. As Derek was driving his *Banshee* to the Asylum and listening to the radio the morning after the party, the local news reported that Intermountain Airways, a regional airline operating along the coast and through the intermountain states, was declaring bankruptcy and was ceasing operations within a month. As Derek remembered, they did a lot of passenger transport in and out of Seattle, but had never been able to be really cost-competitive with the majors.

Parking and locking the *Banshee,* he walked around the corner to the front of the Asylum. Hulio and Lynn had arrived just before Derek did, and some other Crew members were pulling in after him. Lynn gave him a big hug and cheery greeting as usual and he followed them through the door that Hulio opened by sliding his security pass through the slot on the door lock. Inside, he waved at one of Harry Pinkerton's men who nodded in greeting and watched as they negotiated the fingerprint, DNA, and retinal scanning system the agency had installed.

"I already wish for the good old days," Derek remarked as the three headed for the offices.

"Progress has its costs," Hulio responded.

"Hey," Lynn asked, "did you hear about Intermountain Airways?"

Derek's eyebrows went up as he looked at her. "Oh, you heard that, too? I was just heading down to tell Tom. I think he'll wanna know."

"You gonna help me run those cube design simulations through Zelda today, Derek?" Hulio asked.

"Listen Hulio, You're Managing Director of Freight Operations now. You shouldn't be involved in this petty stuff. You're supposed to get other people to do it. Don't you know nothing?"

Hulio snorted. "Right now there ain't nobody in the freight operations division for me to manage and until we get those new cube designs you're supposed to be working on into production, there ain't gonna be no freight operations, anyway. So my question stands."

"I hear Sean's already working on the first part of that," Lynn commented. "He's interviewing a bunch of H-R people pretty soon. Get that set up, then they'll start hiring people like mad for every division. We'll be busting at the seams in a couple of weeks. If you think this place is already changed, wait 'till you see it then, guys."

Hulio and Derek just grunted and sighed.

"We'll do those simulations, Hulio," Derek answered, "but let's wait 'til Beowulf gets here. I got some other things to work on first. For now, let's *all* go see Tom."

Tom's office door was open and he was inside, apparently in the terminal stages of a conversation with Harry Pinkerton. As Harry nodded to the three, said "Good morning, gentlemen," and left, Lynn crowded in front of Derek and rapped lightly on the door.

"Morning, boss. Did you hear about Intermountain Airways?"

"Hey, good Morning." Tom waved them in. "No, I haven't heard anything. What happened?"

Lynn and Derek walked in while Hulio stood in the doorway and propped his arm on the frame.

"They're in bankruptcy and calling it quits," Derek interjected. "Not taking any more bookings and planning to sell off their fleet."

Tom's eyes widened. "That's an opportunity. Hold on." He picked up his phone and punched in a number, listened for a few rings, and hung it up. "Parker's not in yet."

"He was pulling in just behind us, boss," Hulio said. "Probably half way . . ." Poking his head back out and looking down the hall, he waved and called "Hey, Parker. C'monze here!" In a few moments, he moved out of the way as Parker replaced him in the doorway and scanned everyone's faces with a questioning look.

"What's up, guys?"

"Lynn and Derek just heard that Intermountain Airways is quitting business," Tom told him.

Parker scratched one side of his nose and nodded. "Yeh, I just heard a snatch of that as I was pulling in behind these three, Tom."

"I'm headed out to Geneva with The Buzzard in about an hour to clear things with the IOC, Parker. Could you and Sean run up to Seattle, see Intermountain's head honcho, and arrange to hire as many of their people as we're likely to need when we get set up? Ticket counter people, baggage-handlers, even any of their stewardesses living in the area. Heck, we might even want some of their managers; retrain 'em in teleportation operations. It won't really be all that different than what they're doing now. Use your judgment."

Parker's brow furled a little. "Well, sure Tom, but what are we gonna offer 'em? We haven't had time to think about wages and salaries, insurance, benefits, any of that, have we?"

"It's not that difficult, Parker. Simple economics. We're going to have to meet the market as soon as we start hiring anybody, or nobody will sign on. Offer 'em their current scale plus, oh, say, six percent to start with as an incentive to wait and not nail themselves down to other permanent jobs before we're all set up. Tell 'em we'll at least match their insurance, retirement, and vacation packages, too."

Parker nodded agreement. "Yeh, I can do it. I'll go see if Sean can break loose. He's trying to hire H-R people, but if he can reschedule those interviews for, say, three days from now, we should be back."

"Be sure you talk to the Airport authorities, too, Parker," Tom added. "Arrange to rent one of International's gates and its counter space and tell 'em what we'll need to do in terms of chamber construction to get into operation. When you get back we're gonna have to do the same thing at Intermountain's operation up at San Francisco International. I might be back about then to go with you if Sean can't."

"Right, catch you later then, boss," Parker responded, and headed down the hall to see if Sean Nesbit was in yet.

"Derek," Tom asked as soon as Parker departed, "how are you and Beowulf coming on some kind of passenger cube design? I know you two've been working hard on the freight transport designs we talked about, but it looks now like we'll be in the passenger business first."

"We're already on it, boss. It's a simpler problem and I think we about got it knocked. I'll bring you down our current design and a concept summary in a few minutes and you can look at the schematics on your way to Geneva."

Tom nodded, pleased. "It's good to work with efficient people."

"You know, boss," Hulio interjected, "this place is too small."

"Yeh," Lynn agreed. "We're already busting at the seams, and we're gonna hire all these people? Where are we gonna put 'em?"

"You're right," Tom agreed. "No getting around it. We always knew that if we got this far, we'd have to either find or build a larger facility. In fact, that's what I was talking to Harry about when you three came in, because we'll need security at our new offices, too. Derek, as Vice-President of Operations, you're in charge while I'm gone. If you can eke out the time to do it, contact management of the Galt Tower that just opened downtown and rent at least three floors for us, just to start. I hate to do it when we're in the middle of so many crucial things, but I think we'll start moving and setting up our corporate headquarters there next week. Actually, now that I think about it, the move won't be so bad. We'll keep running the R&D and the fabrication shop out of the Asylum for a while, at least, and we'll keep the gym here, too."

*　　　*　　　*

Mark Mason, a political aid on the staff of California State Senator Samuel Hamilton Clanton, was just finishing scheduling a lunch meeting for the Senator with a lobbyist from the California Dairyman's Association when Charise Meardon finished her late morning tryst with the Senator. She came out of the inner office and jiggled her way to the outer office door without bothering to stop at her own desk where she was supposed to do her official work. Senator Jake Gramm, the president of the Senate, and Gerald Foxly, the Majority Whip, just arriving for a strategy session with Senator Clanton, held the door for her as she left.

Perhaps what bothered Mark the most was that Charise did no real staff work around the office though she collected a full-time salary, just like everyone else. That wasn't fair to the rest of the staff. As for the sexual part, he was no prude and had no objection to a man having a mistress, or even using prostitutes as long as he was discreet and nobody else got hurt, but it didn't seem right to him that the satisfaction of the Senator's urges was being paid for by the public. Mark was suffering something of a crisis of faith and Charise Meardon was aggravating it. His idealism about the beneficial effects of government action - the potential to just *make* the world come out right by law - had been severely shaken over the years as he had gradually come to see the actual motives that usually dominated most reformist legislation and observe its effects.

*   *   *

"Damn, is she built," Senator Gerald Foxly said to no one in particular as he watched Charise Meardon walk down the hall. Senator Gramm was the only one close enough to hear.

"What, her? You ought to see the trick Bill Braxon put on his staff, Jerry," Senator Gramm said as the two men headed down the aisle toward Sam's inner office. "An intern from the Edison Institute in Menlo Park. Supposed to be an economist and political scientist, believe it or not. Named Barley, Brolan, or something."

Jerry's ears perked up. "Why?"

"That gal is hot, without trying. She'd make you forget Ms. Meardon in a hurry. I don't think she has the same . . . uh . . . 'staff function' though. Braxon's too straight-laced."

Jerry smirked. "Was that a Freudian slip?"

"No slip at all," Jake responded as he rapped lightly on Sam Clanton's inner-office door and went in.

Bill was still buttoning his shirt. "For hell's sake, Jake, shut the door!"

Jerry and Jake both laughed as they found chairs and made themselves comfortable. "If you think any of your people out there are unaware of Charise's 'staff function' by now," Jerry said, "think again, Sam."

"That doesn't mean I want an audience!" Sam finished buttoning up his shirt and pulled his tie knot up, then sat heavily in his office chair. "Well, let's get to it. How's it going down on the floor?"

Jerry and Jake glanced at each other and neither smiled. Jerry spoke first. "Hally Arkwright is down there giving us hell right now. Looks to me like the ALP has really pulled together on this one. I dunno exactly what's going on, but something has 'em energized. I talked to Governor Slanghorn a few minutes ago and told him he might not get his tax bill after all. He was pissed, but I didn't know what else to tell him."

"What's the count right now, Jerry?" Sam asked pointedly.

"Well, we're about two votes short if it was held now and that's the optimistic count."

"Shit," Sam Clanton swore. "It's already passed the House and we're gonna lose it here by two lousy votes? This is where it was supposed to be a lock! Who are we missing?"

Jerry and Jake glanced at each other again. This time Jake spoke up. "Well, yesterday it was Vin Turner and Julie Hicks. They've been getting a lot of constituent pressure. The ALP has been hitting every forum in their district, making their case. They've looked good on the news lately, too. We've taken a bruising when we've debated 'em publicly. We keep telling people we're just gonna shift the tax burden from the ordinary folks to the rich, like it otta be, but a lot of 'em aren't listening. The ALP crowd all point out that the rich are *already* paying proportionately more. They keep hitting the voters with the statistics on vertical economic mobility. They tell them how most people start out relatively poor and rise through the income quintiles over time, until they retire. Then they tell them that if marginal rates are raised on the rich, pretty soon they're likely gonna *be* the rich that are paying those rates if they aren't already. A lot of people are listening. Hell, even some of our own people are listening. There are at least three more of our troops that are marginal, at best."

Sam digested this, gritting his teeth. "Well, you get after all those people, Jerry, that's your job. You let Turner and Hicks and the others know they won't get a damn bit of party support next election if they turn on this one. In fact, you make 'em understand we'll see they have primary election *opposition* that *will* have party support if they don't get in line. We've still got time. You put enough pressure on them and we'll pull this out yet!"

Jerry and Jake were less sanguine than the Majority leader, but they nodded assent and Jerry said "I'll put the screws to 'em. But I'd like to know what's got the ALP crowd so energized."

Sam pursed his lips and thought for a moment. "I've heard rumors. Braxon put an economist on his staff. Some broad from the Edison Institute, supposed to be working part time and writing some kind of thesis or dissertation part-time. He's been taking her to their strategy sessions and she's been coaching them. Damn, I hate economists. They're always trouble. If I had my way, we'd shoot 'em all."

Jake nodded agreement. "Yah. Jerry and I were just talking about her. I know what you mean about economists. Always yakking about the 'laws of supply and demand,' the 'mutual benefits of voluntary trade,' and all that crap. As if most people know what the hell's really good for 'em in the first place."

All three of them laughed sourly, being, of course, absolutely sure that *they* knew *exactly* what was good for other people and should have absolute, unfettered power to *make* them do it.

Jerry decided to change the subject. "What's your take on this teleportation thing, Sam?"

"Yeh," Jake added, "It's all over the news and everybody everywhere seems to be going crazy over it."

All sense of humor left the Majority leader's face as he considered the question. "I dunno. The whole thing could be nothing - impractical, too expensive, or some kinda scam. Or - it could be the biggest thing in centuries. I don't know which, but so far it's blind-sided me. I don't know what to think, except that we ought to be thinking about the possible downsides and, of course, how we can benefit, one way or another."

"Weren't you about to buy in for a while there?" Jake asked.

"My broker talked me out of it," Sam confessed. "The share prices got so high so fast he thought it was overpriced, so I didn't. That's one of the things that bothers me. It came out of nowhere and I didn't get in early."

"So what do we do?" Jerry asked.

"For a while we just watch," Sam told him. "If it collapses from its own weight, we haven't lost anything. If, on the other hand, it goes like most people seem to think it will, well, then, I think I know how we can get our piece of the pie."

*   *   *

Kiyoshi Tomiki, a lab assistant at Sony Electro-dynamics, had been trying for five months to get a look inside Section Five, with maddening lack of success. Security was unbelievably tight to that part of the building and whatever the project was, it was in operation every minute of every day, with those involved working in shifts. He knew something big was going on, but nobody going in or coming out let anything slip to him or to anyone working in the less-secure section where he was employed. He finally decided that it probably would not do him much good if he did get a look. He knew more physics than his official record showed and might have been able to figure out some of what they were up to if he had gotten in, but he would get caught quickly. He suspected that his punishment might be something more than just getting himself fired.

Of course, information and reports had to be being transmitted somehow from the Section Five lab to the administrators higher up, but there seemed to be no connection between the computer networks in Section Five and the network in his work section. Kiyoshi's section chief also had to make reports to the executives, of course, and Kiyoshi finally decided to try breaking into his own supervisor's secure system and from there into the systems of Sony Electrodynamics' administrators. It took another two months to do so, working only in spare time between his official duties and when his boss had already gone home for the day, but he was finally successful.

When he circumvented the last firewall, he entered a file containing every communication over the last two years from Yukio Hasimata himself to the Chief Executive of the division and downloaded it to his own computer. After exiting carefully, he spent days going over the information in snatches of available time. What he found made the short hairs on his neck stand up and sent a chill down his spine. Even his real employers at Kubota Electronics, one of Sony's main rivals, had had only the barest clue. Kiyoshi himself had a hard time believing that Hasimata's crew was so close to duplicating the teleportation technology apparently created - if you could believe the news - by those crazy Americans, much less that Hasimata had gotten key pieces of the puzzle from a Professor at The Edison Institute in Menlo Park, who had apparently stolen it from the original inventor.

The problem for Kiyoshi was getting the information out of the building and to his real employers. He couldn't print it out and carry the paper documents, or carry a data chip with the information on it. He would get caught as he tried to leave. He also couldn't leave it on his computer, so he hid the chip in an old file cabinet kept by one of his associates and erased everything he had down loaded on his computer. After work that day, he went downtown to the public library, opened up an account that he had established in a fictitious name on a computer there, and e-mailed his supervisor at Kubota's unofficial industrial espionage division the basic outline, from memory, of what he had found. In less than fifteen minutes his handler e-mailed back and instructed him to bring them the chip by whatever means possible.

Two weeks later Kiyoshi faked his own injury by engineering a lab explosion that just *happened* to completely destroy his own workspace and computer. Kiyoshi made sure he was far enough away and behind a large enough piece of equipment not to be killed, but imaginably to be injured, by the explosion. A few minutes before the blast, he completely erased the hard drive on his computer - just in case somehow it survived - and then he swallowed a pill supplied by his boss at Kubota that would fairly quickly induce a temporary coma. It wouldn't be pleasant, but this was how a poor boy from Nagasaki had come to make the big Yen. The data chip was hidden in the lining of his lab smock and the emergency medical team that was called after the explosion carried him right through security without the slightest check. In the ambulance, one of the EMTs, who had been bribed by Kubota, secured the chip.

Chapter 18: Interconnections in Menlo Park

Early in March Gina got permission from Senator Braxon to take a day off and go down to Menlo Park on the Friday before spring break at the Edison Institute to report on the progress of her dissertation to the committee, or rather, to Professor Edleston, the Committee Chair. She actually drove down Thursday afternoon in her mother's Hyundai after calling Cindy. Cindy insisted that Gina stay a couple of nights with her, since Cindy's family lived in Oakland, a comparatively short distance away, and Cindy wasn't leaving for home until Saturday morning. When Gina got to the University she parked in a visitor slot by the student housing. Cindy was watching for her and rushed down the slight hill to greet her, followed closely by a pair of burley, good-looking male athletic types, who opened the back doors to the car and gathered up Gina's bags.

"Ooh, Gina," Cindy said as she practically dragged Gina out of the front seat and spun her around before giving her a hug, "it's sooo good to see you!" Then holding Gina at arm's length and taking a good look, she said, "Wow, have I missed you. You look great! Sacramento must agree with you, though I don't know how it could."

"You look really great, too, Cindy." Gina crinkled her eyes and grinned as she glanced at the two guys.

"I see you have your usual complement of male attendants. Who are Barney and Fred here?"

"Oh, 'scuse me, Gina. Fred here is Rod and Barney over there is Kirk. They're taking us to dinner at the SUB and then to the Spring Fling dance tonight." The two men nodded in turn as their names were called. They both seemed a bit bug-eyed at their good fortune.

Gina's eyebrow raised, and she decided to tease the guys. "Oh, they are? Well that sounds like fun, but are you sure football players can dance?"

"Yes, they can. I trained 'em both just for this occasion, but keep your hands off Fred, 'cause he's mine!"

The two guys followed behind with the bags as Cindy practically bounced up the hill, chattering excitedly, and Gina walked rapidly beside her.

*   *   *

Gina's appointment with Professor Edleston was at ten a.m. the next day. Misty Parker, Cindy's new roommate, had left early for spring break, and Gina was able to sleep in her old bed. She slept late and was still up by six-thirty. After she showered, dressed, dried and combed her hair, she looked in the refrigerator and found that Misty and Cindy kept little food there, so she drove to the Albertson's grocery at a nearby mall to buy a few things. Cindy was up when she got back. Gina fried them each an egg, with toast, orange juice, and peaches. Cindy had one last nine a.m. class to attend - nearly all professors canceled afternoon classes the Friday before spring break because they knew that students anxious to get out of town would not attend - and was gone by eight-thirty. Gina gathered up her materials, stopped at the campus library to check a few things, and was on the third floor of the Demsetz building in plenty of time. Professor Edleston was waiting in his office when she arrived.

"Gina," he called through the partly opened office door, seeing her before she even knocked, "Come on in!"

Lew stood and shook Gina's hand as she responded to his greeting, guided her to a chair, turned his office chair around, and sat facing her. Then he waved at his videophone.

"I just got a call from Bill, believe it or not. He wanted me to tell you Governor Slanghorn's tax bill went down in flames in the Senate this morning. Lost by three votes. He says Slanghorn and Clanton are both spitting mad. It's probably all over the news by now. Did you know, Bill went out of his way to give you some credit for that? What did you do?"

Gina shrugged. "I just ran numbers for 'em, Professor Edleston, and maybe helped tweak a few of their arguments. I doubt I really had much to do with it."

"Well, that isn't what Bill thinks. He's pleased as punch having you around. Says his wife likes you a lot, too."

Gina nodded. "She's a wonderful lady. You should taste her cooking. They have me out to dinner about every other Sunday." She put her fingers over her mouth and giggled softly. "It's funny. Barbara seems to think I'll be an old maid if she doesn't find me a man. She's got all her friends looking for one. But if I ate half of what she tries to feed me, I'd be fat as a pig!"

Lew barked a laugh. "That sounds like Barb, and I *have* tasted her cooking. I guess you can't blame her, though, taking a motherly attitude toward you, with only Amanda at home nowadays."

Gina just grinned briefly and nodded again.

"Well, what have you got for me? Are you finding the data you need?"

"Yes, sir, so far." Gina opened her backpack, slid out several files, and started laying them out on Lew's desk, pointing at various tables, graphs and text statements while he scanned them.

"I've got most of the data on reported lobbying expenditures for the last ten years, all broken down and tabulated. Though it's still a little incomplete, so far it's looking like it'll be about the same percentage of aggregate income that other researchers have found clear back to Laband and McClintock. Here's the draft of my first three chapters focusing on those expenditures."

"Umm," Lew mumbled as he scanned various pages of data and made shirtsleeve calculations on a notepad. "Are these copies for the committee?"

"Yes, sir. I have everything on my computer in Bill's office, and I printed these off for you. If you want, though, I can e-mail you copies of the files."

"That'd be nice, Gina. Then I can just copy the files for the rest of the committee, and I won't have to make paper copies for 'em. By the way, I don't see anything on rent-extraction. Have you found much of that?"

"Yes, sir." She flipped through some of the papers. "It's here in section three of the second chapter. There wasn't much clear legislative extortion when the ALP had majority control, but it was big before and it's been growing again for the last two years. Several forms of rent- extraction seem very important in this state. Fruit growers and vineyards get hit particularly hard by threats to regulate 'em. Dex says they call 'em 'milker bills'. They're withdrawn once enough money has flowed into the pockets of the committee chairs and leaders sponsoring the bills. Here's the table on that, though I'm still short some data. Or rather, I still haven't entirely sorted it out of the overall reported lobbying expenses for some industries."

"Ummm, I see," Lew nodded. "Still, it's looking good. You're further along than I thought you'd be by now. Looks to me like you're ready to start tackling the hard part."

"Yes, sir," Gina answered.

"Come on, Gina, I keep telling you to call me Lew. You know I'm not gonna bite," Lew told her before she could continue.

"Yes, sir . . . er. . . Lew. You're right. I've already started putting together data to correlate changes in legislator net-wealth over time with changes in power: committee leadership positions, party leadership positions, and so on. Calculating the effect of simply gaining election to the house or senate on their net wealth was easy. I already did that. Positive and statistically significant like you wouldn't believe, even after adjusting for enhanced retirement earnings already legislated and for other factors. But that's all preliminary, and it isn't in here yet. Plus, I haven't even started looking for information on legislator's stock trades, portfolio rates of return, and so on, to estimate their insider trading."

Lew nodded. "Well, you've got a lot left to do, but I think the committee will be more than pleased. Any other surprises?"

Gina thought a moment. "No, except I'm picking up a lot of anecdotal stuff. I've made some good friends on Bill's staff, Kyle Webb and Dexter Gibbs in particular. Amanda introduced me to 'em and they both know a lot of other staffers on both sides of the aisle. You wouldn't believe the rumor mill around that place. As soon as Spider - that's what they all call Kyle - and Dex got a fix on the ideas of rent-seeking and rent- extraction they started feeding every dirty little secret and rumor they heard right to me. Even some of the RepubliCrat staffers have been telling me things. Usually those people think it's funny, what the Senators and Representatives they work for are getting away with, almost like they're proud of it, and sometimes, of course, they're anxious to give me dirt on ALP members. It's all actually been very helpful in some cases, clearing up some mysteries in the data. Like, why Senator Gram's net wealth numbers didn't add up, and he had no housing expense or assets listed at all? Rumor was, and it turns out to be true, since his wife left him, he's been living rent free on a yacht out in the Sacramento boat docks owned by a union leader he does legislative favors for. I haven't nailed down just yet what all the favors are, but it looks like a payoff. It sure cleared up his balance sheet!"

Lew's laugh was chopped off as he thought about what Gina had said. "You know, I have two minds about that. On one hand, systematic data is always better than anecdotal data by itself, but the more anecdotal data you have to *illustrate* systematic data the better. Makes it real to readers. On the other hand, you ought to be careful. Some of those things sound like criminal violations, and you're dealing with powerful people. They might take offense if they heard you knew about some of that. Maybe you ought to be a little careful."

Gina didn't know what to say about that, so she just nodded.

Lew reached over, touched the space bar on his computer, and looked at the clock as his screen saver went off.

"Well, I'll take all this to the committee. We'll make notes and comments, suggest changes, and get back to you. Do you think you'll be able to make another trip down here before summer? Things get a little hectic then. I'll be around campus most of the time, but Marilyn Hauser will be off to Europe and who knows where Bickard will be."

Gina nodded again. "Yes, I should be able to come back sometime in May with a much more extensive draft. Bill keeps me busy in the mornings on staff work, mostly statistics, but he's been really good about letting me work in the afternoons."

She started to zip up her book bag and get ready to leave, but Lew seemed to remember something.

"Say, do you know what happened to me since you've been gone?" he asked.

The excitement in his voice piqued Gina's curiosity. "No, what?"

"I was offered a position on the Board of Directors of Universal Teleportation Transport. Took it, too. Jake Hansen, the Chair of the Math Department, and Ludwig Rothman, from the Business Department, were offered positions too. The Chairman of the Board will be Marlon Gates, the investment banker who floated UTT's IPO. It was on the news a while back. I thought you would have heard."

Gina was surprised and in mild shock as she tried to see the implications. "No, Lew, I didn't. I guess I missed the news that night."

Lew chuckled. "I take it as something of a compliment that UTT's share prices took another jump the day after the media found out and that I was on the board, though I suppose it could have been a lot of things besides that."

"H . . . How did it happen? The job offer I mean."

"Well, Tom Wright, the boy genius himself, came up on campus to see us all. Amazing, to think he was the Alvin Wright who was taking my classes and only getting B's. I should have put it together. I'd heard about a guy named Tom Wright causing a furor over in the Math and Physics departments a few years ago, but the B's in my courses and the use of his middle name threw me off, along with everyone else. He was actually a little abashed when he came to see me. Apologized for the whole thing. Of course, he explained why he was doing what he was doing: lying low and getting business and economic training while he and his people put the finishing touches on the whole teleportation thing. You never met him, did you? I remember asking before you left for Sacramento."

Gina was surprised at how jittery her stomach felt as she thought of her one experience with Mr. Thomas Alvin Wright. "No, not really, though he was in class the day I proctored that test for you last semester."

"Well, I've gotten to know him better since, and he really is an amazing guy. So are the rest of the guys and gals on his research and development team. Wet behind the ears, almost all of 'em, but geniuses or near geniuses, every one. I asked Tom why he only recruited young grad students. You know what he said?"

"No, what?"

Lew stared off in space, blankly, as he remembered. "Said he needed people who hadn't learned yet that it couldn't be done." Then he looked right at Gina, and smirked. "You know what those people call themselves?"

Gina shook her head. "No."

"They call themselves The Skeleton Crew."

That startled Gina. "Why?"

It was Lew's turn to shake his head. "I dunno. I asked 'em the other day, and they all just looked at each other, laughed like crazy, and gave me five different answers. You know, Gina, I think you'd like those people. They're a lot like you."

Gina thought it was time to divert the conversation. "Have you tried it or seen it, Doctor Edleston. . . Lew? Teleportation, I mean."

"Not yet. It's expensive, unless you move a lot of freight or people at once, then it's very cheap, or so they say. So I haven't had the chance. Marlon's done it twice. To Seattle and then back with the other bankers. Says it was the darnedest thing he'd ever experienced. He can't wait 'til they get it in operation. Says he's gonna take his family to Seattle just for the ride, if you can call it that. Can you imagine, go up there, tour the city and get back, all in one morning if you want?"

"Do you think it'll work," she pressed, "as a business, I mean?"

Lew nodded with determination. "Darned well will if I have anything to do with it. I mean, just think of what it'll do for tourism when UTT goes international. And they're certainly working hard at it. They've got two of the three relay satellites they need up now, and I guess you heard the other day they arranged to install teleport chambers at the Seattle and San Francisco Airports. What's more, yesterday, Westmark Inns decided to refurbish their hotel in Seattle and contracted with UTT to put chambers in several of their other hotels to see if that helps fill 'em up. That'll be in the news tonight. So far, UTT's got orders for more chambers than they can fill. Not long now and they'll be in business, then we'll see."

Gina just shook her head in wonder and swallowed a lump in her throat.

Chapter 19: Uncertainties and Opportunities

The east elevator of the Galt Tower was crowded with the eight a.m. rush. Marge Haskins, just out of school with her business degree and employed in the Human Resources division of Universal Teleportation Transport for all of a month now, nudged her new friend, Abbie, who had just been hired in the same division, and whispered quietly as she pointed to two of the men up front by the door.

"Do you know who those two guys are, Abbie?"

Abbie shook her head. "No."

"I think that's Beowulf Thorson and the other one's Derek Martin. They're members of the original Skeleton Crew! They say the whole thing wouldn't have worked without something those two invented. They're bigwigs now. And rich."

Abbie's eyes widened. "Gee, they're cute. Big, but cute.

'Specially the blond guy. With muscles like that, no wonder they call him Beowulf."

Marge smirked. "Don't get your hopes up too much. I hear one of the execs in the research and development division, who was also on the Crew, has her hooks into him pretty solidly. And vice-versa. On the other hand, Mr. Martin's still available, and I think he's dreamy."

Abbie nodded agreement, and then had a thought. "Don't forget Tom Wright himself. *He's* still single *too.*"

Marge rolled her eyes. "Parish the thought. That would be too much like dating God!"

The door opened. Derek and Beowulf, followed by the rest, headed for the fortieth floor UTT office entrance while fishing for their security badges and key cards.

"What I don't understand," Derek was saying, "is why, after we finally got home last night, you had to start playing the synthesizer. All I wanted to do was go to bed."

"Well, after all that, I couldn't have slept if I had gone to bed," Beowulf responded. "I had to do something to get my mind off of all that, or at least get the wheels turning in other directions. Music is relaxing. Besides, you and me, we've gotta make a decision about that thing. You've heard what I've been doing with it since we finally got it together last week. We can make sounds like nobody's ever heard before and mimic any instrument ever made *perfectly.* In fact, *better* than perfectly! Manufacturers will be falling all over themselves to make and sell 'em for us."

Derek shook his head. "Maybe, but I still think we ought to get some bands to try it out first. Get them enthused and the manufacturers will know there's a market."

Inside the office doors, Derek and Beowulf waved at the two Pinkerton guards as they went through the security screen. Beowulf called out "Hi Burt, Al."

Al Frantzen nodded. "Mornin' Mr. Thorson, Mr. Martin."

Derek shook his head as they passed the executive secretary's desk, waved at her, and headed down the hall to their offices. "That guy is not so polite when he's throwing a *Kote-Mawashi* on you. Which he did, to me, about a dozen times the other day. With vigor. My wrist still hurts."

Beowulf just raised one eyebrow and gave his head a small shake. "Knowing you, you probably gave just as good as you got when your turn came."

"I tried," Derek answered, "but I can't get the hang of it. You're gonna have to show me again. Al can do it, but he can't *explain* it worth a hoot."

Beowulf grimaced, as he reflected on something. "If you think Al Frantzen is good at that, you ought to have Billie Jo throw one on you. I gave her one little peck on the neck while we were standing in the theater line Friday night, and I thought she was gonna break my wrist! 'Course, she kissed it better and made up for it when we got back to the apartment."

Derek nodded. "I remember. I almost got up and left so you two could be alone."

"Well, I'm glad you didn't. I ever went too far with her, her dad would shoot me, and you know he would."

Derek laughed. "He likes you. Practically thinks of you as a son already. You and Billie Jo should just tie the knot and solve the whole problem. It isn't as if you can't afford a house between you. Heck, with what the company pays you, your share of the royalties we're already getting on the modulator, and what we're gonna get from the synthesizer, you two could buy a mansion right now."

"Yeh," Beowulf nodded, "but I wanna finish the PhD first and really see if this business is gonna take off. Then me and Billie Jo are gonna buy a humongous ranch outside of Bozeman, get Tom to build a chamber there, and just 'port into work every day."

"At the ranch or at Bozeman?" Derek asked.

The two men passed the CEO's suite, but did not stop to see if Tom was in or not. They had something important to tell him, but they had a scheduled meeting with him and several of the other executives at eleven a.m. anyway and both of them had other work to do until then.

*   *   *

Tom was actually a little late getting to work that day, but was in his office before nine, putting data together for the meeting between phone calls. At ten a.m. his Secretary, Maria Santos, who had been on the job for nearly two months now, buzzed him on his computer intercom.

"Yes, Maria?" Maria was in her early thirties and married to a Mexican-American engineer that UTT had hired right after the move to the Galt Tower. Her grandparents had emigrated from Mexico, but the family was close knit. She spoke in a pleasant, husky voice that still had a slight Latin accent. This time, however, there was just a hint of tension.

"Sir, the first mail distribution has come in. There is a rather suspicious package addressed to you."

Tom's ears picked up. "Have Harry's boys run it through the sensors yet?"

"Yes, sir. Everything gets checked, as you requested. They can't detect any explosives or anything. It's just that it's from Japan and doesn't seem to have any return address."

Tom thought a moment. "Isn't there an environmental biology firm down a couple of floors? Tell Burt or Al or whoever's on duty to run it down to their Lab, will you, Maria, and have those people probe it carefully for contaminants of any kind. Poisons, bacteria, whatever. Tell 'em if it's clean, bring it on up. I'm curious."

"Yes, sir," Maria responded, and clicked off.

Tom went back to work and forgot about the package for the next half hour. Then Maria buzzed him again.

"Yes?"

"Sir, Harry Pinkerton is here with the package. He says they checked it and there are no contaminants."

"Oh. Good. Have Harry bring it in, will you, Maria?"

In a few moments Harry knocked softly and entered the room with a large manila envelope.

"Good morning, Harry," Tom greeted him. "Doing your shift check?"

"Morning, Tom. No, Mark is the OD, but he called me when this first came in, and I came right up. I went down to the Pacific Biologic lab downstairs and watched the last few minutes of the tests. They poked

278

several sniffers in, but didn't find anything. Looks like its safe to open the rest of the way."

Tom took the package Harry handed him and waved him over to a chair. "Have a seat for a minute or two while I look this over, will you?" Using a pair of scissors, he neatly cut the top of the mailer off, extracted the documents inside, and started reading them. Harry Pinkerton watched; he saw Tom tense visibly after only a few moments, but Tom kept reading. After another five minutes, Tom put the remaining documents down. It seemed as if he was making an effort to stay calm. He picked up his phone. "Maria," he said, "can you get Buzz on the line for me?"

*   *   *

Lynn Yip Ki, Parker, Hulio, and Sean Nezbit were already in the plush conference room at five minutes to eleven when Beowulf and Derek got there, followed closely by Angel BlackSnake, who brought Phil and Dave with her. Sitting next to Lynn was Lee Bricker, an early-middle-aged man formerly employed by Intermountain Airways. Lee looked like the accountant he was, but had a powerful analytical mind with a cheerful disposition, and had consequently been recently hired to be the CFO - Chief Financial Officer - of UTT. Maria Santos booted up the main computer networked to the terminals in front of each chair and inserted the chip containing the day's reports. Officially, the meeting was supposed to just include department heads and chief officers, but Tom had made it clear that any members of the original Skeleton Crew were always welcome at staff meetings, and they often dropped in. Sean, Parker, and Hulio seemed to be hashing something out between them, but Lynn waved and gave Beowulf and Derek her usual cheery greeting.

"I still can't get used to all this," Beowulf said as he plopped down and leaned back in one of the plush high-backed office chairs at the table. Derek pulled the next chair out, put his notepad and files on the table, and eased his lanky frame down. "This much luxury seems almost sinful," Beowulf continued. "I sorta miss the beat up old chairs and clapboard walls of the conference room out at the Asylum."

Lynn smirked. "That's your Christian fundamentalist upbringing speaking. We should never have started calling you 'Beowulf'. If you were really Viking hero stock, you'd love all this. You'd be wearing filthy animal furs, drinking grog, and have your muddy boots up on the table - if you weren't chopping it up for firewood - but you'd love it."

Billie Jo, who had followed Dave into the room, sat down next to Beowulf, looked at him sideways, and smiled slyly as she arranged her stuff. "With his mug, we probably should have called him Grendel anyhow. But that's a cheap shot at us Baptists. We're not really ascetics at all. He's just incurably cheap. I think he has Scottish ancestry somewhere."

Lynn laughed at this. "So he's a Scottish barbarian rather than a Viking one. Or maybe both. Didn't the Vikings invade Scotland once or twice back when?"

"Wait a minute," Beowulf began defensively, "I resemble that remark!" Everyone's laughter was choked off as Tom came in, followed by The Buzzard. The looks on both of the men's faces were uncharacteristically somber. When those present saw this, it suppressed conversation.

As soon as they were settled, Tom started the meeting. "Welcome everybody and thanks for coming. Something serious just happened that, consequently, isn't on your agendas and I'm going to have to spend some time on it, but first I want to go through at least most of the scheduled agenda items. You're up first, Parker. Are we still on for Friday?"

Parker nodded. "We are. The San Francisco and Seattle airport chambers have been finished and we've made several test runs. All the data is here in the report. They're working perfectly and the public is chafing at the bit. We've sold every ticket in advance for every seat of every scheduled run for the next three months. We had to turn people away. Of course, we suspect some of that's novelty demand which may fade sooner or later. Then again, it might not since we keep running into the fact that the experience is almost, well, *addictive.* Everyone loves it. On your suggestion, Tom, we reduced the number of scheduled runs between Seattle and San Francisco for the second month by two-thirds, because the L. A., Vancouver, and San Diego gates will be done by then, but we've sold all the tickets for those initial runs, also. So far we haven't found the limit on how many seats we *can* sell, particularly at the prices we've initially set, which are about half of airline prices and still give us a large profit margin. We actually oversold seats we've scheduled between those locations by about five percent to account for estimated no-shows, in accordance with airline history.

"The travel agencies have been all over me to get our schedules and arrange to sell our tickets. It's a good thing we hired Lee and those other Intermountain Airways people so we didn't have to reinvent that wheel. The only question about airport gates now is: where do we go next? I know you want to open in Mexico City, Tom, but I've looked at the airline travel patterns and I frankly think we ought to go to Houston. It's the third largest city in the U.S. and there's a lot of traffic between here and there. After that I think we should go to Honolulu, and *then* Mexico City. Then we look at Chicago and New York before considering some of the other metro airports. Derek and I've talked it over and he agrees with me. What do you think?"

"Ummm," Tom responded noncommittally. "Until we can get enough passenger cubes built, those questions may be moot. Remember, we're con-tractually obligated for - what was it - five chambers for the Westmark Inns? That may have been a mistake, since we need them so badly for what might be higher volume markets."

"Probably not in the long run, boss," Parker responded. "It's true, Westmark is mostly a Western and Northwestern chain, but they do have one in Houston that's on their location list. The Seattle cube with the passenger redesign is still a few weeks from being finished. And it's six chambers, not five. The others are Portland, Seattle, Denver, Salt Lake City, and Boise. Admittedly, some of those are not the biggest cities, but they're all vibrant, growing metropolises, and we'll *help* them grow. Those markets will pay off big, over time. The contract says we have to install those cubes within the next year. And, hey, when we do, Tom, you'll be able to 'port home!"

Even Tom chuckled at that. "Well," he said, "we're contractually committed, so there's no point 'crying over spilt milk'. Okay Parker, anything else? No? Then you're up Hulio. Where are we on freight operations?"

Hulio straightened up, cleared his throat, and looked over at Derek. "Should I tell 'em, or do you want to, Derek?"

Derek shook his head. "He put *you* on the spot, not me, Hulio. Besides, it's all in the report, anyway." He waved at the computer screen on the table in front of him. "Go ahead."

"Well, good news and better news, boss, with only one major problem. As I'm sure Angel will tell you, all the basic first-generation freight chamber designs, like the one to work at the container docks, are finished. We've arranged for docks at the San Francisco, San Diego, and Seattle container ports. We're only about a month out on completion, or rather, on scheduled manufacture and transport of the cube components to the sites. After that, it's only a couple of weeks to put things together at the docks. The tricky part has been deciding on our rates. With those price- elasticity of demand estimates you gave us, our own cost estimates based on different chamber volumes, run frequencies, and some 'off the cuff' guesses, we ended up setting our rates at about a third of the level the ocean shipper's charge. Frankly I think we guessed too high, but we can adjust later, if we need to. In any case, manufacturers, retailers, and the trucking companies in those cities are already coming to us in droves to contract for shipping to and from the docks. Right now, it's like Parker was saying. We're already booked solid for as far ahead as we've been willing to contract."

"That's good," Tom nodded. "It's nice to see optimism and enthusiasm, but we all need to remember the old adage about counting chickens before the eggs hatch. How about package delivery?"

Hulio resumed. "Well, here's where the 'even better news' comes in. We've been trying to decide for a couple of months now how to go about package delivery, whether to rent facilities at the airports and contract with truckers ourselves or what, but that problem may be mostly solved now. Derek got a call from APS's regional manager yesterday about noon. He and Beowulf had been out looking over APS's operation up in San Francisco some time back. Apparently APS has been thinking about it, too. They don't like the idea of having to compete with somebody else who can teleport packages in, so they want to be the ones doing the teleporting, or at least, having it done for them. When they called here and asked for a meeting, Derek grabbed me, Beowulf, and Billie Jo, and we went up and talked to them.

"They had some knowledgeable people there. It took most of the afternoon and evening, and we got back late. We did manage to convince them we could design chambers that would work with their equipment and facilities, at least on their long-haul shipping, and save them a lot of money over airplane shipping. And I do mean a lot of money. We knocked their socks off, when they saw our numbers. Their regional manager has to get final permission from corporate headquarters, but it looks like they want us to set up and operate about ten chambers at their facilities to test things in this region. The only hang-up was the contract. They want a competitive alternative to keep us from becoming extortionate down the line, so they'll only contract with us for five years. On our part, we reserved the right to contract with other shippers. Derek has the details of their proposal, and he can distribute it right after this meeting. But if this works, and we'll darned well make sure it works, APS will go country-wide with it, and that means an awfully lot of revenue for us, boss. An *awfully* lot."

An audible, excited murmur went around the room. Hulio waited for it to subside before wrapping up. "I think, working with their people, we should be able to put together a cube design for them without too much trouble. We're getting better at that. We've got Zelda programmed to the point that she actually does most of the work for us. So the big hang-up is the same one

Parker's side of things is facing: we can't get the dang cubes built fast enough. Something's got to be done about that. That's all I have for now, Tom."

Tom waited for another murmur to subside. "Thanks, Hulio. Point well taken. We'll come back to that. Lynn, anything new on the satellite system?"

Lynn shook her head as everyone looked at her. "No, Tom, not since we got the sixth one up. We know the hardware is working perfectly, since we ran all the San Francisco and Seattle airport test runs through them. We didn't even have any trouble the day they had that nasty weather in Seattle. With six satellites we've already got way, way more signal relay capacity than we're going to be able to use for a long time, even if everything else goes the way we want. I think the only question now is whether to go ahead with putting the next three up, while the IOC is so willing to allocate the orbital slots to us, or wait and shift the money into chamber construction, and see if we can hurry that process up."

Tom rubbed his jaw and thought for a few moments before answering, while Lynn and everyone else waited in anticipation. "Actually, Lynn, for several reasons, I think we're going to make use of some of that excess capacity much sooner than you might think, though on balance you're probably right. It might be best to put the next three satellites on hold while we deal with the current bottleneck. What do the rest of you think?"

Some of those present murmured and nodded assent, but Derek stuck his hand up, and Tom quickly recognized him.

"I'm beginning to think we made a mistake, Tom, when we left the lab out at the Asylum instead of renting another floor or two here and moving it over. We didn't see how hard it was going to be to find firms that could gear up to manufacture the chambers for us. We would have had to farm a lot of it out anyway and take the security risks that entails; but if we had set up a manufacturing facility of our own out there it would probably be in operation by now, turning out about a chamber a week, and a lot of this bottleneck would be relieved. I don't think you need to worry about the satellites. Put 'em up if you see the need." Derek looked up the table at Lee Bricker. "The problem isn't money, as I'll bet Mr. Bricker will agree."

Lee looked at Tom to see if he should respond. Tom nodded. "Well, actually that's a good way of summarizing my report," Lee began. "I've only had a few weeks to get up to speed on things, but money really doesn't seem to be the problem. If you'll check page fifteen," he indicated his computer screen, "you'll see that for this stage of the business plan, we're keeping expenses very reasonable and are actually behind schedule on investments. We literally can't spend the money fast enough, right now, because of the slow chamber manufacturing; and money will be even less of a problem over the next few months as we start generating revenue, particularly in the amounts that seem likely. Of course, the two issues are connected. The hang-up in cube construction will restrict our capacity to increase operations and revenue. I don't know if I agree, though, with Derek's proposal to move the lab over here and gearing up at the old building to manufacture cubes. It seems to me the constriction on chamber production will probably work itself out before we could do that, anyway."

Derek reluctantly nodded agreement. "I wouldn't really argue that we ought to move the lab and set up a manufacturing operation now, just that we really don't need to worry about shifting money out of satellite delivery."

"In fact," Lee looked down the table as he continued, "didn't you tell me, Hulio, that A. G. A. Manufacturing and Hillsbrook Equipment both say they'll be on-line to double their chamber component production within six weeks?"

"Yeh," Hulio responded with some disgust, "but they've been telling me that for two months now."

"If I may, gentlemen." Buzz jumped in. "At Tom's instruction mah people have been in contact with both of those firms, remindin' them of their contractual commitments and, while Ah don't have the technical expertise to make a judgment, Ah think they mean it this time."

Tom apparently agreed and wanted to reinforce Lee and The Buzzard's assessment. "I also sent Dave down to look over Hillsbrook's operation and give them some technical advice," he said. "It's a whole new technology, and they *have* found it very difficult to reduce it to routine manufacturing operations. Dave tells me they have most of the problems licked now, however. They had to subcontract production of some of the piezoelectric subcomponents to do it and, actually, we're doing the most critical of those at the fabrication shop ourselves, so we *are, in fact*, at least marginally involved in the manufacturing process. The bottom line is that they're about ready to go for broke. We're getting the same story from A. G. A. So I think we're seeing the light at the end of *that* tunnel. Do you have anything more to add on the financial end of things, Lee?"

"No, sir," Lee shook his head. "All the numbers are in the report and pretty straight forward."

"Okay. I'll go over it and take it with me when I meet with the Board next week. Now, here's where I think we are, so far, today: Since we already have much more relay capacity than our own operations are going to need, let's put a hold on further satellite launches, just for a while. As for the lab, I think we'll leave it out at the Asylum for now. Buzz and Dave have me convinced we don't need to go that route. You might be right, Derek, that we should have done that in the first place and gone into our own chamber manufacturing. We'll just have to see. I just don't want to vertically integrate in that way. I don't think we'd be cost competitive at it. Innovation, not routine manufacture, is our comparative advantage.

"As for the metropolitan sequence in which we locate the chambers, Parker," Tom continued, "why don't you, Derek, and I meet separately to look over the passenger and freight-volume estimates again and sort that out? If the bottleneck in chamber construction really is ending, we'll actually be able to build in several of those cities simultaneously. So I recommend that we start arranging our contracts and government licenses right now for at least the top ten locations on our list."

Parker and Derek nodded agreement. Tom looked down at Angel BlackSnake and Sean Nezbit "If you don't mind, Angel and Sean, can we table your reports on R&D and Human Resources until the next meeting? I'm anxious to hear about progress on the Zelda upgrade and on second-generation D-R field physics, Angel. And Sean, I know you're worried about whether the baggage-handlers might try to unionize the Seattle operation, but I've got something of more immediate impact to discuss. Those reports can wait for a while, can't they?"

When Angel and Sean nodded assent, Tom looked around the table solemnly at each person present before he began speaking. "Those of us involved in this project have been acutely aware from the first that we were in a race. Other people have been working toward the same goal, and some of them are in large corporate enterprises with enormous financial reserves that we lack. Our success has depended on developing teleportation first, making it cost effective, and then growing rapidly, so that we can have a presence in the major markets before others get in. We accomplished the first two of those goals, but the third, which is what we're working on now, may be the hardest. Information spreads, even when you operate in secret, and it spreads more rapidly when things come out in the open. Just showing that - and how - something can be done, helps your competitors. A lot." He paused and grimaced before continuing.

"I've just gotten confirmation about how closely at least one firm is breathing down our necks. Some of you may have heard rumors this morning about a suspicious package I received and had checked out for explosives or biological hazards before I opened it. It turned out to be okay in that respect, but the contents certainly were a bombshell. It contained documents that seem to be printouts of internal e-mails, the last one time-coded about three months back, sent from Yukio Hasimata, a top physicist who heads research in a division called Section Five at Sony Electrodynamics, to the division head, Koichi Ono, reporting on problems and progress in Section Five's sole project. It's teleportation, ladies and gentlemen, and they're very close to making it work.

"The interesting thing is: how they got so close so fast. A lot of it, Hasimata and his team had worked out for themselves. Hasimata is a legitimate genius. I've suspected for some time that he was leading a teleportation project at Sony. But, according to the documents, crucial pieces of the puzzle were supplied to them beginning late last year by a certain prominent physicist here at the Edison Institute."

"Westholm!" Derek was so instantly startled and angered that he spoke out loud without thinking.

"That sssnake!" Beowulf's verbal ejaculation came only a moment after Derek's and, speaking through gritted teeth, the very word sounded like a snake hissing.

Tom only nodded in confirmation.

Lynn Yip Ki was mortified. "I knew that man was slimy, but who would have thought he'd sink that low!"

"Just what did they get, Tom, and how close are they?" Hulio asked.

"They got help on the field modulation equations Hasimata hadn't been able to crack, apparently from a part of my dissertation proposal that Westholm sent them. Somehow Westholm also got a copy of the schematics for Derek's field modulator. The e-mails make it clear that they intend to invent around Derek's solution just enough to claim they got it on their own before he did and challenge our patent."

Lynn was puzzled. "How did they get your dissertation proposal, Tom? I thought you got all the copies back."

"I tried. Westholm and his group didn't have cause when they cashiered me. I could have won a formal protest of the dismissal, or even sued them, and they knew it. By then I realized I didn't want it all public anyway and had started putting together the Skeleton Crew. I demanded all copies back for letting 'em off the hook, and I made sure that request for the copies and their formal agreement was documented. Apparently, Westholm kept at least one copy, though, because the e-mails mention it. It's also clear, and this is the one piece of good news in the documents themselves, that at the time all this was going on, they still hadn't solved for the necessary strong force harmonics, and were having to search experimentally. Chances are pretty good, though, that if they haven't found 'em by now, they're getting very close."

"So, what are we gonna do?" Beowulf asked.

Tom and Buzz exchanged glances. Tom nodded slightly and the Buzzard took his turn, speaking with his usual slight hint of Southern drawl, now tinged with overtones of resolution and even menace. "We're gonna sue the pants off of Sony Electrodynamics, with special emphasis on Hasimata, Ono, and Westholm, for conspiracy to commit fraud, patent infringement, theft, and about a dozen other violations of civilized law and conduct. As we speak, mah firm is arrangin' things with one of the top law firms in Japan to work up and file the necessary charges and subpoena the documents we need from Sony. Thanks to whoever sent us those e-mails, we know just what to ask for. Byrd, Rand, Epstein, and Ely will go after Westholm on this end. In a few weeks, those people are all gonna wish they'd never been born. We play this right, all this could actually turn out to be a *good* thing."

Chapter 20: Discovering Corruption

On Friday, Gina found it difficult getting much work done either for the Senator or on her dissertation. Everyone else seemed to be having trouble focusing on work also. The world's first commercial teleportation runs began at nine a.m. that morning between the Seattle and San Francisco airports. Everyone's eyes seemed to be glued either to their 3-V or computer screens, with few people even going through the motions of doing anything else. There almost seemed to be more news reporters than passengers at the airports in those two cities, or at least at UTT's gates. In fact, as it turned out, quite a few of the passengers on the first few runs *were* news reporters, many for the big national networks and newspapers. They had apparently either bought up tickets for the early runs at the counter, or contacted ticket holders and bought their tickets for large premiums.

In some sense it was all a little bit of a letdown, at least to Gina. There was really very little to see in terms of the teleportation itself. Passengers could be seen going through the gates into the teleport chambers and coming out after incoming runs. Many reporters stood around pointing 3-V cameras at the passengers and interviewing them and each other. Yet, the air of excitement about it all was palpable. The near ecstasy and excitement on the faces and in the voices of incoming passengers was infectious. They described it as an amazing experience involving astounding *musical* sensations they could hardly describe, and universally said they wanted to teleport again as soon as they could.

Gina, too, watched it for a while on the big screen in the office along with the other members of Bill's staff, until she began to feel guilty about not getting anything else done. Then, even though it was only ten a.m., she decided to go down to the office of the California Legislative Research Service and search through their files for some data she needed. Gathering up her stuff, she headed out.

For a while, after she got to the CLRS offices, Gina thought she was wasting her time yet again. She stopped to see Jim Jefferson, a friend she had made on the research staff, but he was not in. When she tried to get help from the clerks and secretaries, they also were glued to their 3-V or computer screens, many talking excitedly to each other as they watched. It took some time getting one to tear her attention away long enough to grant Gina access to the filing system that would allow her to find what she wanted. Finally, though, she was able to locate the general section she needed, put the briefcase with her stuff in it down at a desk, and begin looking for some of the raw data she needed in nearby stacks of files and books, periodically taking a book or file back to the desk. In a short time, however, she began to notice a man hanging around nearby. She glimpsed him several times, always behind her in the stacks, off to the side, or passing by the row she was in. She never got a good look at him, and thought little about it at first. Gradually, however, Gina began to get the eerie sense that he might not be researching, but watching her. Just as this suspicion became clearly conscious, though, and she began watching for *him,* he disappeared. After a few more minutes, she began mentally chastising herself for paranoia.

Having found much of what she had been after, or at least as much as she could tabulate in one day, she sat down at the desk, booted up the desk computer, opened up its statistical and graphics program, started leafing through the materials she had brought back from the stacks, and thought about what to enter first. CLRS did not let material leave the building, since the files and books contained data collected too recently to have been digitized. As a legislative staff member, however, Gina was authorized, once the data was tabulated, to send it from the CLRS computer to her own computer in Bill's office. As she began working, however, she noticed a note left in one of the primary data sources. A tingle went up her spine because it had not been left by some prior researcher. It was a word-processed note, with no date or signature, and it was addressed to her.

Miss Barlow: Look for Charise Meardon in the legislative staff employee records. Then check the employee files of Aphrodite Associates and go back through the lobbying expenses for the California Brotherhood of Teamsters.

Gina read the note several times while the shock wore off, and then looked nervously around her. No one was near. With trembling fingers' she carefully picked up the note by one corner and put it inside her own notebook where she would not contaminate it further. Taking the books and files she had collected one by one to a nearby Xerox machine, she copied all the relevant data tables. Then she carefully wrote down all the sources and put the Xerox copies into her case with her other stuff.

Once she left the CLRS offices, her nervousness began to abate; and Gina decided to go down to the cafeteria instead of to the office. It was lunch time, and some food might help settle her stomach. Besides, it would give her time to think. When she got there, the cafeteria was more than normally busy. A large 3-V had been set up on an unused counter so patrons could watch the teleportation madness still going on. Gina noticed Dex sitting alone at a table eating potato salad and some ham steaks, along with, of all things, a large piece of pizza and a side of ice cream while he watched and listened to the 3-V along with everyone else. He grinned and waved as she walked over and put her case down by one of the chairs.

"Dex, can you watch my stuff while I go through the line?"

"Sure, Gina. Spider will be here in a minute. He's over there getting some dessert."

In a few minutes, Gina was back with her usual lunchtime Chef's salad.

"Hey, Gina," Spider greeted her as he set his tray down. "You're missing all the good stuff. CBC actually got an interview with Tom Wright himself. Had to chase him down outside his place. He actually lives out at that old airport hanger outside Menlo Park where they built the first teleportation machine. But since UTT moved their offices into that new skyscraper in downtown Menlo Park, they caught him and one of his Pinkerton guards leaving to go to work this morning. The guard was about to put a hurt on the reporter, but Wright called him off."

Neither of them noticed the catch in Gina's throat. "I'm sorry I missed that. Did he say anything interesting?"

"Nothing much," Dex answered. "Just 'yes', 'no', and 'please excuse me so I can get to my car.' Spider's exaggerating by calling it an interview. I think maybe I like that guy. He's an odd duck. Polite, but reclusive, and he certainly doesn't pander to those news people."

"Hmmm," Gina said. "Maybe he doesn't need to. Not with all the word of mouth and news publicity his business is getting." The next part came out on impulse. "Say, guys, something very odd just happened to me. I wonder if you might know something or be able to help."

Her tone distracted both men's attention from the ongoing teleportation news reporting. They were always eager to help Gina - seeing themselves as aids, if not co-conspirators in her dissertation project.

They listened closely as she told them what had happened in the CLRS offices.

"So you didn't get a good look at the guy?" Spider asked.

Gina shook her head in the negative.

The three sat in silent contemplation for a moment, considering the possible meaning of the note and its mode of delivery.

"You know, Gina," Dex commented, "I've been to the CLRS offices a few times getting things for the Senator. I don't remember really noticing, but I'll bet there're security cameras watching those stacks. If we could get a look at those tapes, we could at least find out who the guy was."

"Trouble would be," Spider put in, "he didn't really do anything. Besides, it's even possible that somebody else put the note where you found it. Dex and I've talked to quite a few people about your dissertation project, and they talk to others. A lot of people know about it by now. In fact, there's something of a buzz about it around here. Plus, I doubt the CLRS would want anyone poking around in those tapes unless there was a legitimate stalking or harassment complaint or something."

"Oh, I don't know," Dex responded. "Bill might be able to get 'em to let *him* have a look at the tapes, just to identify the guy. It's an odd enough event. I think the real problem with that is, without clear charges and a formal investigation, the CLRS would feel obligated to inform the guy if we did ask them to identify him. That might put him in a bad spot, Gina, and I'm not sure you want to do that. Clearly, he wants you to know or find out something, and he's worried about someone else - maybe his boss - finding out about him putting you on to it."

Gina nodded. "Yes. I've been thinking about that. Do either of you know this Charise Meardon?"

Both men shook their heads. Dex snorted. "Do you know how many Senatorial and Representative staff people there are here, not to speak of Senators and representatives themselves and other legislative and maintenance employees? Figure about fifteen staff members per member of the legislature, then add separate committee staff members, legislative staff members, all the lobbyists walking in and out, bureaucrats here all the time, and so on. It comes to thousands. Spider and I know a lot of 'em, but not nearly all. We can ask around though. I'll bet that if we find out who this Meardon gal is, we won't be far from whoever it was that left the note."

Gina nodded agreement, leaned in, and spoke quietly. "Be discrete, guys. And for now, let's keep it between ourselves. Whoever it is, gave me several clues. I'm going to finish this salad, go back to the office, and see what I can find."

*   *   *

Bill was in his inner office involved in some kind of conference call. Most staff employees were still watching the Seattle - San Francisco teleportation madness on the news, either on the big 3-V wall screen or on their computer screens. Some others were tied up answering constituent calls, most of which also had to do with teleportation. It seemed everybody was either entranced or worried by what was happening. Nobody noticed Gina working intently on her computer, and it didn't take her long to begin striking pay dirt. Within a few minutes, searching the California legislature web site, she had found the legislative employee database. In only a few more moments spent scrolling down she found one Charise Meardon, listed in alphabetical order right where she ought to be. When she saw Ms. Meardon's job description, for the second time that day a shiver went up Gina's spine. Miss Meardon was Public Relations and Research Assistant to Senator Samuel Hamilton Clanton, the Senate Majority Leader. Her listed address was in the city.

That raised the stakes. By all accounts, Clanton was not someone you wanted to cross. Gina wondered if she ought to drop the whole thing. Curiosity impelled her on, however. An internet search engine made it easy to find Aphrodite Associates. As soon as she saw the web site, she knew a key part of what the anonymous note writer was trying to tell her. Aphrodite Associates was a high-class call girl operation, with branches in Las Vegas, San Diego, San Francisco, and Sacramento. A number of years back, after the Disorders when the ALP had gained control of a large majority of state legislatures, California and many other states had legalized prostitution. They had actually had the help of many liberal RepubliCrats in crafting the legislation. Defenders of legalization to this day cited a significant reduction in rates of rape that had followed. To get the California state law through, however, the state ALP had had to accede to at least minimal state regulation of the industry, requiring regular medical checkups for the employees and so on.

The industry was allowed to advertise in print and internet media, though not on home 3-V, except on selected premium channels. Gina had never before viewed such ads, but she did so now, going in sequence to the web sites of Aphrodite Associates' separate franchises. Each proudly displayed the names of the girls (and in some cases, men) available from that office, with brief biographies, recent medical certifications, full bodied pictures of them in alluring poses, and a list of the services offered by each along with an hourly price list.

Gina found it all repugnant in the extreme. She was a Libertarian but not a *libertine*. She believed that all peaceful human interactions should be legal, even if many others regarded them as immoral, unless they generated very heavy externalities. In her ideal world, though, people would have enough moral character to neither demand nor supply such services. Worse, there was no Charise Meardon listed as currently working at any of the Aphrodite Associates offices. Stymied only for a moment, Gina decided to run Ms. Meardon's name through the search engine. As she suspected, there were more than a few Charise Meardon's nationwide. Narrowing the search to

California, she still came up with five, but most were too young or too old. Lo and behold, though, one in the right age range (twenty-five as of now) was listed as having been a highly skilled employee of Aphrodite Associates a couple of years back. Unfortunately, the search engine results included no pictures of her.

Gina leaned back and thought. The man who left her the note either knew or strongly suspected Charise Meardon the call girl and Charise Meardon the Staff Aid to State Senator Samuel Hamilton Clanton was not only one and the same, but that somehow she was a payoff from the California Teamsters Union. If true, serious illegalities were involved. But how could Gina prove any of it? Even if she could somehow show that the prostitute and the Staff Aid was the same person, that fact might mean nothing more than that Ms. Meardon had changed occupations. The search engine biography actually showed that she had taken a political science course or two, along with a lot of English and Sociology, before dropping out in her second year of college. The note-leaver must suspect she was still actually employed at Aphrodite Associates, off the books, as part of the arrangement, but if so, how was Gina going to prove it?

Also: how would Gina prove involvement of the Teamsters? She had data on the officially listed lobbying expenses of the union, broken down by type, but an arrangement of this kind would probably be well hidden, past Gina's capacity to prove. It might be possible for a trained investigator with subpoena power to go at it from the other end, obtaining the records of

Aphrodite Associates to document Ms. Meardon's continued employment, along with payments to the company from the union, but Gina had no way to do that. And what did the anonymous note leaver expect her *to do?* Assuming all this came out, Gina's first inclination would simply be to list and describe it in her dissertation as an egregious example of pervasive rent-seeking payments and influence peddling in the California legislature. True, she was certainly morally offended by this sort of thing. Her second inclination would be to see legal action taken. But then, as a member of Bill Braxon's staff, her motives would be questioned and as she had already been warned by Bill, Lew Edleston, and others, serious retribution might result.

And why, why, if Ms. Meardon's sexual services were a payoff to Senator Clanton, did he put her on the government payroll as a staff aid? A possible answer to that question jumped out at her only a second after she formulated it, but the thought of someone doing such a thing for mere convenience and/or monetary kickback made her stomach queasy. Just then another niggling suspicion hit her, along with another angle of attack on the matter. Getting up, she walked to the desk of Bill's executive secretary at the front of his office. The secretary was a sweet and efficient second-generation Vietnamese-American woman in her early forties named Ly Cam Hoang. Ly handled his time-scheduling and incoming calls, other than those calls, of course, from personal friends and associates who had his NanoPod code. Gina asked

Ly if she could see Bill for a minute. Ly picked up the phone, buzzed the inner office, and ushered Gina in a minute later.

"Hey, Gina," Bill, who was leaning back in his chair with his feet propped up on a corner of his desk, waved his hand at his office wall 3-V. "Can you believe all this?"

Gina nodded. "Yes, sir. It's . . . astonishing."

Bill shook his head. "No way to get anything done around this place today. I've tried. Nobody on the floor downstairs. We can't debate. We can't vote. The RepubliCrat Committee chairs have suspended hearings. Just as well ride it out and watch this happen along with everyone else for the rest of the day. What kind of a guy do you suppose it takes to do something like this: start right from scratch; invent something that's utterly revolutionary like practical teleportation; then start mass-marketing it in nothing flat?"

"Someone a bit different than most of us," Gina responded. "Like Edison. He did that with the light bulb. He didn't stop when he invented it. He built Edison Electric and started wiring the East Coast cities in the 1890s. Sold the bulbs, I suppose, but more important, sold the electricity. I guess he saw that it would be used for a lot more than light. People like Edison and Mr. Wright seem to see a long way ahead."

Bill snorted, and turned to look her in the eye. "You know that's just what they're calling him now? 'The Second Wizard of Menlo Park'. Even his name's similar. I wonder if that was deliberate. His parents must be a little odd. You know, I'm a mover and a shaker. I know what that takes. But not on the scale this guy operates on. I'd kinda like to meet a guy who can change the world like that. Wouldn't you?"

The thought distracted Gina from her purpose at a disturbing level, and she didn't answer as she tried to isolate her feelings and refocus. Bill must have sensed something of that.

"Excuse me, Gina. If you're actually trying to accomplish something around here today, you're one of the few. What was it you wanted?"

With an act of will, she remembered. "Bill . . . Senator . . . when anybody enters or leaves the building and goes through security, the time must be recorded and a computerized record must be kept, right? Security would want that in case of any criminal or terrorist act, right?"

Bill nodded. "Sure. So?"

"I wonder if you could get me a look at that data base."

Bill thought that over for a moment. "Well, maybe, but why?"

"I. . . I think there may be some phantom employees on the staff payrolls. People who are hired full-time, but putting very little actual time in. One, at least. Maybe more. And there may be salary kickbacks involved. We don't formally punch time cards when we get to the office, but the security time codes on the DNA and retinal scans would at least tell us when any given person was in the building."

Bill's mouth tasted bitter. "Boy, I hope you're wrong. That looks like a can of worms. I don't know if I can get the security office to let us see the records on log ins and outs without starting a formal investigation with the ethics committee, but without the records, how could I make the charge credible? Where does this suspicion come from? Is there something you want to tell me, Gina?"

For a moment she debated with herself. "Not right now, Bill. I might be wrong. It's just a suspicion. Maybe soon I'll tell you the whole story. But I really would like a look at that data."

Bill nodded. "Well, okay. I'll talk to the Director of the security office. I get along well with him. Maybe if we tell him it's related to your dissertation research, we can justify it without generating too much suspicion and setting off too many alarm bells. It makes sense anyway as a form of rent-seeking or rent-extraction, so it fits. I'll let you know what he says."

Heading back to her desk, Gina decided it was time to go back to her regular work and let all of this gel in her subconscious for a while. She still wanted to enter at least some of the data she had collected from the CLRS into her computer this afternoon. Then she wanted to go home and get something to eat. She had an appointment to take Heather and Amanda to Heather's high school gym. Absorbed in her data, she hardly noticed when Dex walked by and asked if he could borrow the note. She mumbled assent, distractedly, reached into her case and handed it to him, not noticing that he took it gingerly, by one corner, just as she had intuitively done when she first found it.

*   *   *

"No, no, Amanda," Gina said. "You have to get more elevation on that jump and do the twist like this. Show her again, will you, Heather?"

They were working out in the gym at the private middle school Heather attended. Gina had started teaching Heather gymnastics several years back, and Heather, at age fourteen, was getting very good. In fact, she was one of the top gymnasts in central California for her age, having already won several inter-school competitions, and was giving at least some consideration to following in her big sister's footsteps and training seriously for national competition. Adam and Rachael had indicated willingness to foot the bill, if she wanted to do so badly enough.

A few months earlier, Gina, having already been invited several times to Bill and Barbara's home, had gotten Adam and Rachael to invite the Braxon's over to their place for Sunday dinner. Bill and Barbara had been glad to come. Bill, for one, had wanted to meet Adam for some time. Both sets of parents quickly became friends. Amanda and Heather formed a very strong bond. It didn't take long after that for Gina and Heather to talk Amanda into trying gymnastics. So they had been practicing several times a week, at the well-equipped gymnasium in the capitol building on

Saturday mornings, and a couple of evenings at Heather's school. Amanda loved it and was learning fast. She did find it frustrating at times, though, as did all beginners.

Heather lined up, sprinted down the floor, and sprung off the beat board into a perfect handstand on the vaulting table. Springing off the table, she twisted into a nearly perfect landing and immediately completed two more somersaults while Gina and Amanda watched.

"Ah, gee," Amanda complained. "You two make that seem so easy. But I'm getting tired. Aren't we about done? I've got some homework I need to do tonight."

Gina looked at the wall clock and saw that it was, indeed, time to quit. "Okay, Amanda, you're right. Let's do our stretches and go shower.

Gina and Heather usually drove over to the Braxon's and picked Amanda up to take to the workouts, but sometimes Barbara liked to come along and watch. As usual, she was watching from a chair a few feet away from the mat. Gina waved at her as the girls finished their wind-down exercises and the three of them headed for the shower room.

Finishing her shower and dressing a minute or two before the younger girls, Gina went out and pulled up another folding chair next to Barbara to wait. "She's getting much better, Barbara. She has a lot of native ability. Having been wrapped up in my graduate program for so long, and now with all of my dissertation and legislative work, I'd almost forgotten how fast kids that age can learn."

"You have the patience of Job," Barbara responded, "and the teaching ability of Socrates."

Gina laughed. "Well, I'll accept the Job compliment, but Socrates was no gymnast. And not even much of a political philosopher, if what Plato attributes to him is accurate. Did you ever actually read *The Republic,* Barbara? It's a text on the ideal elitist tyranny." She grimaced to emphasize her point.

"No, thank heavens, I never had to," Barbara responded. "I have Bill and Amanda for that sort of thing. But you really are doing wonders with Amanda. Now she has an interest in something besides boys and politics and it's a healthy one! The only problem is, I almost can't get her to wear dresses anymore. She wants to walk around the house on her hands about half the time and do front and back flips in the yard!"

They were still giggling when Heather and Amanda came out of the dressing room and looked at them suspiciously.

"Anybody want to stop at the DQ for shakes?" Gina asked the girls as she gathered up her workout bag and they all headed out of the gym. "I'm buying."

In the parking lot, Heather and Amanda jumped in the back of Rachael's Hyundai and began talking girl-talk while Gina and Barbara got up front, fastened their seat belts, and made sure the girls fastened theirs.

"Were you as excited by all this teleportation stuff today as everyone else seems to have been, Gina, dear?" Barbara asked as they drove to the Dairy Queen. "I watched for a while at home, this morning, while I got a white load together. Bill says that up at the capitol it was like the whole world just stopped and watched for most of the day."

"Yes," Gina reflected. "It certainly felt like something amazing and historic was happening. Of course, it wasn't as visually exciting as, say, something like the moon landing must have been. Like you, I just watched a while until duty called, but most other people seem to have been entranced."

"That guy who figured teleportation out, Mr. Wright, he must be an amazing young man," Barbara observed distractedly. Then a thought hit her, and she looked over at Gina. "They say he's only a year or two older than you, Gina. Didn't Bill tell me he was at the Institute there in Menlo Park taking economics courses just last semester, while you were there? Did you ever. . ?"

"No," Gina responded defensively, before catching and calming herself. "No, I never did, quite. But I *almost* met him once."

Almost instantly, Heather and Amanda leaned forward and only the constraints of their seat belts kept them from sticking their heads between the front seats. Their eyes were wide open as they spoke almost in unison. "You almost met Tom Wright?!!"

Gina smiled wistfully, as she glanced at the girls in the rear view mirror, before looking back at the road, though perhaps with more inward than outward focus.

"Yes. He was in a class one day when I proctored a test for Professor Edleston."

"Did you notice him?" Heather asked.

"Is he handsome?" Amanda asked.

"Well, yes, to tell you the truth," Gina responded, "I did notice him. And yes, he is handsome, if you like big, athletic, brainy hunks with eyes that look right through you and . . . and . . ." Her sentence trailed off.

Barbara looked at Gina sideways, with calculation, and debated with herself for several seconds before asking: "Did he notice *you,* Gina?"

Uncomfortable now, Gina swallowed before reluctantly answering, in a small voice. "Maybe."

Barbara turned her head to the front and shook it slightly in wonderment while Heather and Amanda just looked at each other with open mouths. "Gina," Barbara said, "somebody ought to tell you just once. You knock men over like bowling pins every day and you just don't notice. Sooner or later you're going to have to pay attention or the right one will get away. Or maybe I should say the *Wright* one." The girls laughed at that, and Gina blushed as she turned the Hyundai into the lot at the Dairy Queen.

Five or ten minutes later they were back in the car, sucking soft chocolate, strawberry, and caramel flavored ice cream through straws, and on their way again, headed for the Braxon homestead.

"Barbara," Gina asked, seeing a way to change the direction of the conversation as they cruised through the streets, "what do you know about Senator Clanton?"

"He's evil!" Amanda almost shouted from the back seat before Barbara could say anything.

"Shhhhhh," Barbara said, looking back at Amanda. "She asked me, not you! But Amanda's right, Gina. He really is not a very nice man. I try to be charitable with people and assume the best about them, but it's probably fair to say that he's not a good man."

"Is that Bill talking?" Gina asked.

Barbara was almost offended. "Heavens no. Bill tells me about a lot of bad things Sam does that go on behind the scenes in the legislature, but I'd know that about Sam even if Bill never said a thing!"

Gina was curious. "How?"

"Oh, I know his wife, Martha. We've both been in the state DAR for years, you know, and we've done some charity work together. We get along well. Martha was never a militant RepubliCrat like Sam anyway. She's kind of politically neutral, truth be told. And gals talk. She's told me some things, and the other gals have told me some. He treats her badly."

"How?" Gina asked. "I mean, in what ways?"

"Well, he's been domineering and abusive, both to her and to the kids. There even used to be some physical abuse, though I gather he quit that when he got into politics. But the worst thing is, he cheats on her repeatedly. Done so for years and years. It hurts her terribly, poor thing. They're separated, you know. He went up to a legislative session once and she changed all the locks on their home in San Francisco. Wouldn't let him back in. He had bought a condominium here in Sacramento before that and he lives there permanently now, though he's kept the whole thing quiet."

A small alarm went off in Gina's head and a thought started to crystallize. "Why doesn't she divorce him?"

"Oh, she wants to, but he won't let her have one. That's one of the nastier things he's done to her. You know the legislature got rid of the no fault divorce and community property laws last year. She says he admitted to her a while back he worked for that change so she couldn't divorce him, take some of the property, and hurt him politically. She'd have to have really good evidence of his infidelity. So far she doesn't have that kind of proof."

Several things came together in Gina's mind, giving her a possible solution to more than one problem. "It would be nice if someone could do something about that," she said.

"Yes, it would," Barbara said distractedly. "People like Sam ought to get their comeuppance once in a while."

Chapter 21: Covert Movements

The tension Gina sensed in the Senate Transportation Committee room seemed thick enough to cut with a knife as the committee chair was handed the final vote tally and looked it over. Gina, Spider, and Dex were sitting two rows back, just behind Roger Galbraith and two of Roger's key staff members. On assignment from Bill, the three had spent their mornings either in that room or one of the adjoining subcommittee rooms for the last two weeks, helping to shepherd the Braxon - Galbraith Automotive Deregulation Act through its hearings. Gina had testified twice, a nerve-wracking process subject to hostile interrogation from bitter opponents in the Democratic-Republican Party. Spider and Dex assured her she had done well.

Some murmuring among the various committee and staff members in the room had become audible as they waited for the decision. The chairman banged once with his gavel to cut the murmuring off before announcing the outcome. "The vote is six to five with one abstention to send SB-2044 to the floor with an unfavorable recommendation. Since it's so close to noon, the committee will adjourn 'til nine a.m. tomorrow morning."

The RepubliCrat opponents of the bill sighed with relief, while Gina and the ALP members in the room groaned with disappointment. The murmurs returned and about a quarter of the crowd immediately started to gather their stuff and leave the room while discussing the day's outcome. The last vote was a defeat for the ALP since they had wanted a favorable recommendation, but it had been expected. The surprising thing was how small the RepubliCrat margin of victory was, and even more, that the ALP had won a far greater victory earlier by getting the bill sent to the Senate floor where it still had a chance, even though it had gotten an unfavorable committee majority recommendation.

"Well, I'm glad that's over," Spider said, getting up. "All in all, Bill will be happy, though I still don't see how we can get it through the full Senate. I'm for some lunch before we head back to the office to see him. Serena, do you want to come?" Serena Michelo was a young member of Roger Galbraith's staff whom Gina, Spider, and Dex had become friends with over the last two weeks. Spider had actually started dating her. She was a cute brunette, a bit on the shy side, but she responded to Spider's attention and was fascinated by Gina's dissertation project.

As they were about to join the crowd beginning to head for the door, Dex nudged Gina and nodded across the room. "Gina, see that guy just to the left of Senator Jenks? That's Mason. Don't know why I didn't spot him earlier. I think he was hunkered down where I couldn't see him."

Gina saw Mason then, but didn't recognize him. As she had told Spider and Dex, she had never gotten a good look at the man in the CLRS office the day the note had appeared. Still, a small shudder went through her. Mason was almost certainly the man she had seen, and he certainly *was* the one who had left the note. Dex had scanned the note into his computer with one of the new bimolecular scanners and sent it to one of the commercial spy web sites. It had cost him nearly two days pay - for which he had refused to let Gina recompense him - but they had been able to bring up the fingerprints on the paper. Through comparison with police and private databases, they had identified all the prints other than Gina and Dex's as belonging to one Mark Mason, employee on the staff of Samuel Hamilton Clanton, California Senate Majority Leader. Dex had actually met him once or twice at social functions, and Spider had played against him in the annual Fourth of July RepubliCrat-ALP softball games. Both knew him on sight.

"Should we go corner him, Gina, tell him what we know, and see if he's willing to tell us anything else?" Dex asked.

"Ummm," Gina shook her head. "I don't think so. I don't think he wants any more contact. If he does, he'll make it. It's too public here anyway, and we're likely to get him in trouble if we're seen with him. Let's go grab a bite, like Spider says, then go back to the office."

*　　　　*　　　　*

Maynard Clairborne Hoffer, a former labor lawyer and now Director of the California Department of Transportation, adjusted his air purifier and took another drag on his cigarette. It was a filthy and unhealthy habit, he knew, but he only smoked occasionally anyway, and right now he needed something to steady his nerves. At any moment, three of the most powerful men in the state were going to walk into his office and he had a niggling suspicion they were going to want something from him. Most likely it had something to do with the Braxon-Galbraith Automotive Deregulation act which was supposed to have died in committee, but had somehow, just this morning, made it out to the full senate, albeit with an unfavorable recommendation. The news, which he had just heard, had been shocking. What more could he do? He had already done his best in testimony before the subcommittee, along with every expert he employed, to oppose the bill. He and his troops had deluged the committee with voluminous, mostly irrelevant, and obfuscating data. They had threatened that the bill would result in massive fraud by huge corporate insurance conglomerates and enormous increases in highway deaths. They had used every other tactic they could to oppose the bill. What more could they want him to do, other than keep speaking out and hammering it in the press, which he would do anyway? The whole notion of letting private insurers license drivers was repugnant; particularly since his own job, with all its perks and power to compel obedience from lesser employees and from members of the public, was on the line.

Maynard took another drag on the cigarette. It was illegal under California law for anyone to smoke in public buildings, of course, but such laws - indeed most laws - were really for other people and he didn't intend to let them stop him in the slightest. Just then the intercom buzzed and his secretary announced that the men he expected were there. He stubbed out the cigarette reluctantly and stood as she opened the door to his office. Senators Samuel Hamilton Clanton, the California Senate Majority Leader, Senate President Jake Gramm, and the Majority Whip Gerald Foxly filed in.

"Senators," Maynard said, walking around the desk and extending his hand, "a pleasure to see you."

"Maynard," Sam responded, and "Director Hoffer," Senators Gramm and Foxly chimed in as he shook their hands in sequence.

"Make yourselves comfortable," Maynard said, indicating several capacious chairs. "Can I offer you gentlemen drinks?"

"Yes, I think so," Sam responded as he made himself comfortable, "and maybe a cigar. One of those Cuban's you keep in your cabinet."

"Whisky for me," Gerald told him, "on the rocks."

"Me, too," Jake added. "And a cigar really would be nice."

Having distributed the drinks and cigars, Director Hoffer sat down and eyed his visitors, somehow even more nervous now than before they had arrived. "I suppose this visit has something to do with the disaster in the transportation committee meeting this morning, but I confess I'm at a loss to see what."

Clanton swallowed a sip of his bourbon, took a leisurely puff on the cigar, looked at it and seemed to consider things for a moment before turning his attention back to Director Hoffer. "Well, yes, it does, Maynard, and no, it doesn't."

"That disaster was something we allowed to happen," Jake Gramm noted. "We have more than enough votes to stop that bill on the floor," he added, then paused for a moment, "if we want."

Maynard's jaw dropped open with shock. "If you want? Wha . . . wha . . . why would you possibly want to let that bill *pass*? It'll gut this department! There'll be nothing left but . . . but . . ."

Senator Clanton cut him short. "Relax, Maynard. You've been a good party supporter. You'll remember I swung weight with the governor to get you this job. We don't want Braxon's bill to pass. Whether it passes or not, however, depends on you."

"Me?" Maynard squeaked.

"We have a proposition for you," Gerald Foxly said. "You're going to get a call from Governor Slanghorn in a little while, asking you kindly to go along with us on this," Jake Gramm added.

A sinking feeling told Maynard this is what he had sensed when they first called and told him they were coming over.

"What is it you want?" He squeaked again.

The three men looked at each other for several seconds, as if silently reaching a final conclusion.

"We want you," Senator Samuel Hamilton Clanton said after taking a large sip of his bourbon, "at a certain point in time that we'll specify later, to pull the licensing from Universal Teleportation Transport to operate within the State of California."

For several seconds, Maynard was aghast and speechless. He was completely blind-sided. He didn't see the connection at all between the Braxon-Galbraith bill and the licensing of UTT. Gradually it occurred to him that the whole fiasco this morning was a demonstration for *him.*

"Why?"

Again the three men looked at each other for several seconds before responding.

"Well," Gerald Foxly began, "we and the governor feel the licensing was granted too precipitously, without adequate consideration of many factors vital to the public well-being."

"Such as environmental hazards from Teleportation," Jake Gramm added.

"What environmental hazards?" Maynard asked.

"That's the point," Jake responded. "We don't know, and we *should have known* before they were licensed!"

"Then there's the safety issue," Senator Foxly added. "It's a whole new technology, never adequately tested. Who knows what disasters could happen to passengers if there's some kind of transmission failure or something, or how frequently such things might happen. There should have been a lot more testing before it was ever licensed. And hearings. Long, long hearings."

Unthinkingly, Maynard fell back on his law background and made a statement he regretted rather quickly. "But doesn't that all amount to presuming guilt without evidence of harm and punishing without due process of law?"

"Oh, for Chrissake, Maynard," Sam barked angrily. "You're a regulator. That's what all regulation does!"

Maynard choked on a response and, despite the voice of his conscience that had never quite gone away, simply nodded.

"And then there's unemployment issues," Jake Gramm said. "The Teamsters are afraid they're going to be losing long-haul jobs all along the coast now that APS and UTT are gonna team up to ship packages. The airlines are already losing business and laying people off like crazy, and the ocean shippers are scared to death of what will happen when UTT starts shipping in and out from Hawaii and then Asia. And don't even ask about the railroads. All that has to be considered."

"It all has to be considered," Senator Foxly added, "And it'll take some time to sort it all out. Their license needs to be pulled so that that can happen."

Maynard leaned back in his chair, eyed them cautiously, and tried to regain some of his internal equilibrium. "I can't just up and do it. I need at least a few days to get a case prepared, and I'll need public support. Remember, everyone that tries teleportation seems to go 'gah gah' over it. In fact I tried it myself a few weeks back. I 'ported up to Seattle for a meeting of the Western State Transportation Director's Association. Then I 'ported back and *I'm* 'gah gah' over it. This could bite us all."

Sam partly stood, leaned forward, crunched the remains of his cigar in Maynard's ashtray, and sat back down. "We've already talked to the environmental lobby, the Teamsters, the airlines, the ocean shipper's cartel, and the public safety crowd. Most of 'em are already on board and the rest will be soon. There're a few details that still need to be settled. Organizing and coordinating a 'spontaneous public outcry' isn't easy, but it'll all be ready to go soon. So you'll have your show of public support. One of the things they'll all be doing is lobbying hard on the hill for the continuance of the Department of Transportation as a bulwark against those kinds of dangers. So you've got a few days, maybe even a week or two, to put your rationale together before we give you the go."

Maynard noticed that he was chewing on one of his fingernails, but it was with calculation now, not nervousness. It was time to take the gloves off. "Yes. Okay. That'll help, but clearly you guys are up to something more or you wouldn't have gone to all this trouble, and you wouldn't be trying to get me to *time* the licensing withdrawal, because ultimately it won't work. For one thing, we won't find any significant safety problems. UTT has already done several thousand runs without a hitch. More important, they've already expanded beyond California. Remember, they *started out* running between San Francisco and Seattle. Now they're not only in operation out of San Diego and L.A., but Vancouver, too. They're just about ready to start up in Houston, Mexico City, and Honolulu. Hell, they're even building those chambers in the hotels in Idaho, Colorado, and Salt Lake, and I hear the one in the Seattle Westmark is doing almost as much business as the one at the airport there. No, even if I go along, you can't stop 'em. Assuming that most of their business still runs through California, as it probably does, that won't be true for very much longer. They can just run their business right around us if they have to. Pulling their California license might cripple them for a while, at most, but it wouldn't shut 'em down. *Somehow, I think that must be what you really want.*"

Clanton, Foxly, and Gramm looked at each other again and communicated silently for several moments before Jake broke the silence. "I told you he was no dummy, and we'd have to let him in."

Sam nodded and turned back to Maynard. "Those of us who work so hard for the well-being of the public deserve a certain. . . uh. . . compensation. Did you ever hear of a form of stock transaction called 'short sales'?"

*   *   *

True to his word, despite being extremely busy with legislative and party business, including managing the fight for his and Roger's Automotive Deregulation Act, Bill found time to talk to the Director of Capitol Security to see if he would allow Gina access to the building entry and exit logs. Beforehand, Gina had decided to tell Bill about Mark Mason, the note, and what she had learned and suspected about Charise Meardon. Bill had visibly shuddered and said, "Damn. Oops, pardon my language, Gina. I just keep hoping for better from that man and keep getting disappointed. Sad to say, I wouldn't put it past him. But we're going to have to play this very carefully."

Bill called Director Sherwood and asked if he could come to the security office for a face-to-face meeting. When the Director agreed, Bill took Gina with him. As his secretary let them into his office, Ben Sherwood greeted them warmly, but turned grim when they told him their suspicions and what Gina wanted to do. After considering the legal and political ramifications, including possible threats to his own job, Ben decided that the information they had was enough to justify looking up and printing out Ms. Meardon's time logs, but because of the legal ramifications he couldn't justify a more generalized search aimed at finding other possible phantom employees. Further, she would have to work from a computer in the security office itself, while monitored by one of the office's own computer specialists. That was fine with Bill and Gina.

It was several days later, actually, after the hearings ended and the Braxon-Galbraith bill went to the floor, before Gina had enough spare time to call ahead to the security office and make an appointment. She was greeted at the door by the computer specialist assigned to watch over her, a slightly balding forty-year-old officer named Jack something, who made her sign in at a desk manned by another officer. For a moment Gina was alarmed. Now there was a record of her having been here. She hadn't thought of that beforehand. When she had come with Bill, they hadn't made either of them sign in. *Oh well,* she thought, *too late to worry now.*

Jack took her to a computer workstation, pulled up an extra chair, sat down and showed Gina how to get into the building entry and exit logs. Then he sat back and watched silently while she did her work, occasionally answering her questions about how to manipulate the data base. The system was intuitively simple, however, and Gina soon tuned Jack out, as he just sat quietly and watched her. Finding the DNA and retinal scan time logs for Charise Meardon by name was easy. Gina saved the record for Charise's entire two years and more of employment at the capital on a data chip she had brought. Taking the chip, she thanked Jack for his help, went back to the registration desk, signed out, and took the elevator up to the senatorial office floor. Usually she used the stairs, for the exercise, but this time she was in a hurry.

*   *   *

As Gina left the security office, Jack watched, then wandered over and stood by the officer at the registration desk as he continued watching Gina recede. The other officer was also staring at her.

"Barlow," the man said. "Isn't she that economist everybody's talking about who works for Bill Braxon?"

"Yeh, I think that's her," Jack responded, still staring.

"Damn, I never pictured an economist looking like that. The one in my high school was an old wrinkled-up guy. In fact, I don't remember any of our *prom* queens looking like her."

Jack turned and looked at the guy. "If you had ever gone through high school, you wouldn't be doing desk security now."

"Well, I did," the man retorted, "and if Mr. Herker had looked like that, I would've paid attention."

"Yes, but to what?" Jack grinned. "You still wouldn't have learned any economics."

With one last look at Gina, standing sideways down the hall waiting for an elevator, Jack sighed wistfully, turned, and began walking away.

When Jack was out of earshot, the desk officer picked up his phone and dialed the code for Mark Mason's personal NanoPod. On the second ring, it was answered.

"This is Mason. Talk."

"Mark, this is me, Rick, at the Security office. The Barlow gal you paid me to watch for was just in here doing something on the computer."

"What was she looking for?"

"I don't know. Jack Walker, one of the computer guys, was with her. I could ask, but I don't think he'll tell me. He's one of Sherwood's golden boys and he's pretty tight-lipped."

It was five or ten seconds before Mason answered. "Don't bother. I already know."

Mason disconnected and immediately punched in the code for Senator Samuel Hamilton Clanton's personal NanoPod. Mark seldom used that number. It was normally reserved for fish that were a lot bigger and swam a lot deeper than him, but he had been given a dispensation for cases like this.

Clanton was in a strategy meeting with Gerald Foxly and several of his other party acolytes. Jake Gramm was out on the floor trading barbs with Hally Arkwright over the Braxon-Galbraith bill, and it was not going well. Sam was not in a good mood when his NanoPod rang and, in hopes that whoever the caller was would give up, he let it ring until it became an irritant.

"What?" he asked brusquely when he gave up first and answered the call.

"It's me, sir," Mark responded. "I just found out that Gina Barlow has been in the security office looking something up on the computers."

"Do you know what it was she was after?"

"No, sir, I don't," Mark lied.

Clanton thought for a moment. *What kind of information could she get there,* he wondered? *The only thing they would have would be. . .* A small alarm went off in his mind. *Could it be Charise?* He dismissed the thought, however. How could the Barlow woman know anything about Charise?

"Hmmm," he muttered. "That's Dick Sherwood's demesne and he's thick with Braxon. He won't tell me anything. The man has delusions of honesty. I should have gotten rid of him long since, and I would've if he wasn't a Civil Service employee. Well, keep an eye on Barlow, Mason. She's getting to be an irritant. Let me know if you hear anything else."

As Clanton rang off, Mark smiled to himself. He was covered now, on record as having tried to warn the Senator. Whatever happened, suspicion would not fall on him.

*   *   *

Back in the office, Gina waved as she hurried past Ly's desk, booted up her own computer and inserted the data chip, tuning out the normal office background chatter of ringing phones, conversations, and clicking keyboards. After maybe forty minutes, Dex, who had been busy with his own work, took a break, came over, pulled up a spare chair, and sat down. "Well, what did you find, Gina? Anything like we expected?"

Gina nodded. "Maybe worse. I'm still running the descriptive statistics, but I'm not going to get much out of it. At least, you can say this about Miss Meardon: she's reliable. Two hours and ten minutes a day, almost every day, with a very small standard deviation. Typically comes in at eleven a.m., leaves at one. The ten minutes is probably just the time it takes getting up from and down to the ground floor.

"What about her salary and job description?" Dex asked

"That's public enough. I got that from the employee database right from here, no trouble," Gina answered. "She's full-time staff, all right. Hired for public relations and research. In fact, she's one of the highest paid staff members Senator Clanton has, paid more actually than several with more seniority."

Dex smirked and quipped unthinkingly. "I don't think her relations are very public. Good pay for two hour's work mostly spent lying down." Then he remembered who he was talking to as he saw Gina redden. He reddened himself and began to stutter an apology. "S . . . sorry Gina, I didn't mean to be . . ."

Just then Spider came in the office door and rushed past Ly without even a wave as he spotted Gina and Dex. "Boy, you two should see what's happening down on the floor. Hally's up, and her and Gramm are going at each other like a couple of pit bulls. You'd think . . . What's wrong?"

"Nothing," Gina and Dex spoke simultaneously, and then glanced at each other before Dex continued. "Gina downloaded Charise Meardon's time logs. It looks like we expected. She only spends a couple hours a day here, probably on duties rather different from her official job description."

"Well, what now?" Spider asked. "Should we see if Bill wants to take it legal? Call for an ethics committee investigation?"

Gina folded her arms, sat back, and seemed to be thinking for a moment while the other two waited, then she shook her head slowly before she spoke. "I don't think so, guys. We haven't been able to make any connection with payments from the Teamsters. There aren't going to be direct witnesses willing to testify to exactly what services Ms. Meardon performs for the Senator. Clanton's too smart for that. With the fingerprints from the note, we could put a lot of pressure on Mr. Mason to talk, but I don't think I want to do that. I don't want to cause Bill a lot of trouble, nor you guys, nor myself. If we go public, it will just be seen as political. That's how Clanton will spin it and a lot of people will agree. There might come a time for an ethics investigation, but not right now. I have a different idea about how our information might be put to use." Her eyes glittered and a small smile came to her face. "I'm going to see if someone else entirely will do it."

*   *   *

For some time Gina struggled with the urge to simply take a day to go down to San Francisco, find Martha Clanton's place, introduce herself, give everything to her, and explain it all in person. She could certainly get the address from Barbara or out of the phone book. But even in her unfortunate circumstances, Mrs. Clanton, like anyone else, might reject it because of its source. So, Gina spent the rest of the afternoon putting it all together in a thick packet and getting it ready to mail. Taking a page from Mark Mason, it would go unsigned. Further, there would be a nonexistent return address on the mailer, since neither APS nor the USPS would take it without some kind of address. In an effort to improve on Mason's methods, she printed everything out fresh and touched none of it directly, including the brown mailing envelope itself, which she took from the office supply closet, holding it only with a cloth.

She typed out and included an unsigned letter explaining as much as she dared, along with her suspicions and recommendations, such as: subpoenaing personnel and payment records from Aphrodite Associates, particularly to look for payments from the Brotherhood of Teamsters or from Sam for that matter. Spider and Dex helped her carefully compose the letter to leave as few clues as possible as to the origin of the information. With any luck, Martha would conclude it came from some disgruntled member of Sam's staff, which was not entirely untrue. Bothered by the nonexistent address on the mailer, she apologized for that minor deception in the letter itself, leaving it clear by implication the necessity to maintain anonymity. Once the packet was finished and addressed, it went into her briefcase.

At about four-forty p.m., she pulled out of the capitol parking garage in her Hyundai - Rachael had wheedled Adam into buying her a new one last week and had given her old one to Gina, though Gina insisted on paying what she could for it, when she could - and drove to the mall to drop the package off at an APS pickup point, again being careful to touch it only with a cloth. Back on the street and headed for home, the drive was pleasant. The day was just warm enough, the sky was blue, the trees were magically green in the late afternoon California sun, and Gina felt as if a weight had been lifted from her spirit. It was up to Martha Clanton now. If Martha understood what she had been given and used it wisely, hiring an investigator (as Gina had suggested) to nail down some of the other details, Gina was clear of it. She could get back to serious work on her dissertation, which had been left hanging in the press of this and legislative work for Bill over the last two weeks. In particular, she needed to start putting together systematic data on stock trades of California legislators over the last few years, back to the time they had first been legally required to start reporting all transactions.

Absentmindedly, Gina noticed that it was nearly five o'clock. She told the car computer to turn on the radio. Usually she played music when she drove, often classical, sometimes light pop, mostly instrumental. For years, though, Gina had listened to broadcast news at least twice a day. She listened reluctantly, consciously forcing herself to do so, while applying a skeptical analytical focus. She liked to be informed as much as she could about what was going on, nationally, internationally, and locally, while recognizing that broadcast news was usually heavily biased, and that its worst distortions came not from what was said - though that was normally distorted enough, and always to the Liberal left - but from what was *not* said or allowed to be heard by the public. The kinds of things that were typically deleted a person had to find out about by searching other sources. Gina subscribed to and read a variety of publications and visited a variety of internet sites to help with that. In this case, though, the headline story immediately snatched her attention away from her dissertation project.

"Good afternoon, this is NBS News with Rexford Grumman. For months now we've heard nothing but good news about the teleportation industry. Two weeks ago was their first quarterly report showing UTT already enormously profitable. Last week it was the announcement of the contract between UTT and APS to supply teleportation package transport services in the Western U.S. But just this afternoon, in a startling turn of events, Buzz Byrd, senior partner at the San Francisco law firm of Byrd, Rand, Epstein, and Ely representing UTT, announced that UTT had filed suit this morning in Ninth District Federal Court against Sony Electrodynamics, a research division of the Sony Corporation, for fraud, conspiracy to commit fraud, and infringement of patents on UTT teleportation technologies. Byrd says a suit will also be filed in the Japanese courts in Tokyo later today. Specifically named in the suits are Yukio Hasimata, Head of Research, and Koichi Ono, Division Manager at Sony Electrodynamics.

"According to Attorney Byrd, subpoenas will be requested in Japan for numerous internal documents which Byrd alleges will substantiate the charges. Byrd says that under the Hanzo-Eckman Treaty all such documents acquired will be available for evidence in the Ninth District Court as well. And in a twist, a third, separate suit has been filed by UTT against Irwin Westholm, Chair of the Physics Department at the Edison Institute of Economics and Technology in Menlo Park for theft and conspiracy to help Sony Electrodynamics engage in fraud and patent infringement. Reached at his office on the EIET Campus by our reporter Lori Nichols from KJAB in San Francisco, Professor Westholm said he was shocked, since he had done nothing wrong, and had no connection with Sony Electrodynamics, but had no further comment. Let's go now to Bob Van Nef at our affiliate in Tokyo. Are you there, Bob?"

"Yes, Rex," another voice responded. "This is Bob Van Nef in Tokyo. Because of the time difference here and the late part of the day when the suits were filed in California, the people at Sony Electrodynamics have only just found out about it and have not had much time to respond. So, I'm afraid there isn't much to report here, yet. We did talk briefly with some of the people at the Japanese law firm working with Byrd, Rand, Epstein, and Ely, but they only confirmed that the suit would be filed here tomorrow. We might have a little more for you later, Rex, if the people at Sony have any response in time for the ten o'clock news. On the other hand, they may not want to say much before they see the legal particulars. So, back to you, Rex."

"Thank you, Bob. Let's talk now with Karl Rasmussen, economics consultant for NBS news here in New York. "What do you think of all this, Karl? What's this all about?"

Gina knew of Rasmusson, a minor economist of the left, who was a longtime RepubliCrat party operative and who had, therefore, become a favorite and highly paid analyst of the broadcast networks.

335

"Well, Rex, the most obvious thing here is that Sony must be just about ready to enter the teleportation business in competition with UTT, and this looks very much like an effort on UTT's part to maintain their current monopoly status . . ."

Gina was so immediately affronted by the absurd notion that UTT, which was *adding* to competition, and supply in the transportation industries and *reducing* prices, was some kind of monopolist that she almost ran a red light, stopping just in time to be embarrassed by a nasty look from an irate pedestrian. The lady quickly moved on through the crosswalk before the light turned green and Gina drove through the intersection, anxious to get home and turn on the 3-V, if it wasn't already on. Usually Gina stayed noticeably under the speed limit, but today she thought *maybe if I'm careful and watch the traffic I can get away with going just a little bit over.* As it turned out, either luck was with her, or the traffic police were also watching the news.

Chapter 22: A Chrysalis Opens,
but the Worm Turns

BAM! The sound of the .44 magnum revolver going off was loud even through the ear mufflers Tom had on. The big gun bucked and sent a commensurately satisfying shock down his right arm and through his shoulder. Twenty-five yards down range a chunk of the head of the loosely man-shaped black wood-backed target flew away.

Dan Hargrove, thirty-five year old founder and CEO of Nucleonic Orbital, standing to the left of Tom by the long range-bench, lowered the binoculars he was using to spot Tom's shots and shook his head slowly. Down the bench to Tom's right, four of Dan's kids kept blasting happily down range at their own targets while another, Dan's youngest girl, Kirstin, was reloading the clip of her .22 semiautomatic.

"I can't believe it," Dan almost yelled to be heard. "Another four in a row, right in the head. You don't group as tight as I do, but I spent three years on the 8th division pistol team. Where did you learn to shoot like that?"

Tom grinned. "Oh, my dad used to take us camping up in the Idaho wilderness country north and east of Boise, and he liked to shoot. Like your kids, I learned early. Then, there was the Fifth Rangers during the Disorders. For a while my life sort of depended on it, among other skills. Plus I've got a twenty-five yard range in one of the smaller buildings out at the Asylum. I used to take a sandwich out there at lunch time with one or two of the Crew members and bust a cap or two every few days. Good way to relieve tension. Don't get to do it much since we moved up town, though."

Putting the .44 down on the bench, pointed carefully down range, Tom turned to his right and looked back at Phillip Adobo, who was watching the whole circus from a few yards back, arms folded in front of his chest.

"Sure you don't want to try this, Phil? There're still two in the chambers. You could think of it as an exercise in geometry and ballistics."

"No, thanks, Tom," Phil smiled. "Not my thing. Guns make me nervous."

A female voice called from a distance and Dan, who somehow heard it through the thunder of pistol fire, looked back at the verandah of the large, spacious hacienda-style house highlighted by the late-afternoon New Mexican sun. "Sounds like everything's ready," he said to Tom. Then he put two fingers to his mouth and whistled loudly to cut through the gunfire. "Hey, Kids! Clear your weapons and pack it in. Time to eat!"

In another few minutes, with guns cleared and ammunition and other equipment gathered, the whole mob was headed up the slight desert incline between Dan's pistol range and the house.

"Quite a place you've got here, Dan," Tom commented as they neared the house. "Wide open space with lots of seclusion."

"Yeh, we like it. Nobody else for six miles in any direction. I can target practice whenever I want; trek out and hunt for agates and Jaspers, if I feel like it; shoot jack rabbits; or take my metal detector and look for treasure. And, the way my kids shoot, I don't have to worry about coyotes or snakes killing our family pets. And yet it's only twenty minutes to the big mall at the edge of town. You ought to get yourself a place like this."

Tom sighed, then nodded toward the verandah, where Dan's wife and a couple of their older kids were finishing up grilling the steaks and putting the food, drinks, plates, and silverware on the picnic style tables. "Someday I will, Dan, if I don't inherit my Dad's ranch first. I've been thinking about it, but first I'd like to find somebody to share it with. And when do I have time to look?"

Dan shrugged and grinned. "Well, I'll admit, really good women are a scarce commodity. But do you really mean to tell me that, as successful and famous as you're becoming, you can't find one?"

Feeling uncomfortable at the particular female image that Dan's question brought to his mind, Tom just shrugged.

Within a few minutes, all the guns had been safely stored, hands and faces had been washed in one or another of the house's four bathrooms, and everyone was seated at the tables. Dan asked his oldest daughter to bless the food - Dan and his family were very religious - and they all fell to talking between mouthfuls of barbecued steak, baked potatoes, corn, and salad, with Tex-Mex side dishes. After a while Dan's wife, June, gathered several of the kids and went into the kitchen and brought out apple pies and boxes of ice cream for each table.

"By the way, Tom," June said as she sat down again next to her husband, "we saw the article in *Our Times* magazine with you on the cover. *The New Einstein and The New Einstinians.* A wonderful title for a wonderful article. Congratulations."

Tom was slightly embarrassed. "Yes, well, they kept bugging us, so we finally decided to give them an interview. Better than letting them just say whatever they wanted. We recorded the whole thing ourselves and hinted that we'd sue if we were misquoted, so the part about us, which, of course, was most of the article, came out a bit more accurate and fair than a lot of what's been written before now."

"You should have seen Beowulf," Phil grinned. "He took his shirt off, posed like a weight lifter, and kept trying to talk them into putting him in a centerfold. Embarrassed poor Billi Jo, and the people from *Our Times* didn't know whether to take him seriously or not."

With the rest, Dan chuckled at that, and almost choked on a bite of apple pie and ice cream he hadn't yet swallowed. Finally he cleared his throat. "I noticed they included interviews with Hasimata and that German physicist along with those two guys from the Fermi labs. They even mentioned last month's issue of *Mathematica* devoted to whether a new Einstineian cosmology is emerging in physics."

"Yeh, well, demonstration is a powerful thing," Tom answered. "Pretty hard to fight what obviously works. And all four of those guys really had done a lot of work in the same direction as ours. If string theory really is on its way out, as I think we're seeing, even Hasimata legitimately deserves some of the credit."

"Speaking of Hasimata, how is your suit against Sony going?" Dan asked.

"Well," Tom thought about it for a second, "so far I'm impressed with Sony Corporation's CEO. He canned Hasimata and Ono right after he made them cough up the documents we asked for. Seems genuinely ashamed and angry by what those two did. I get the sense that he really didn't know. But he's ultimately responsible for keeping his people from doing things like that; and we're suing Sony for an awful lot of money, so I don't know whether he's going to fight it or not. We'll just have to see what he does next Friday when the trial starts in the Ninth District."

"Any more pie and ice-cream, Tom?" June asked.

"No thank you, June. I'm stuffed."

"You, Mr. Adobo?" She asked Phil.

Phil, leaning back in his chair, smiled and shook his head. "No thank you, ma'am."

"What say we three go back in my office for a little while and let June and the kids finish up here?" Dan asked Tom and Phil. "I got something to run past you guys." Then, "That okay with you, June?"

June leaned over and gave her husband a peck on the cheek. "Yes, I know, you guys want to go talk business. We can handle it here."

Extracting themselves from the table, the three men wandered into the house, Dan leading. "My office is back this way. I only actually go in to headquarters about every other day, unless we have a launch on. Rest of the time, I just work here and telecommute. I can manage things just about as well, and it saves on gas and time. Computers are wonderful things. Seems to me your business is gonna have some of the same effect, Tom."

"Oh, right." Tom responded. "Airplanes, trucks, and ocean freighters use a lot of oil. A couple of years of expansion at the rate we're going, and I think teleportation will noticeably reduce the demand for fossil fuels."

Dan's office was in a back corner of the main floor. It was spacious, with large - almost floor to ceiling - windows looking out on the twilight desert on two sides; indirect lighting; bookshelves; a large desk; and several comfortable chairs covered in leather. As Tom and Phil sat down and leaned back, Tom noticed that Dan had an old-fashioned blackboard on one wall. Dan stood in front of it and began pacing slowly with mild nervous energy.

"You may have thought, Tom, that the reason I asked you guys to come on out here was to try and talk you into going ahead with your next set of relay satellites. But I'm not worried about that. You'll do that when you're ready, and I've got enough other business for now. But I'm looking to the future. I'm trying to steal a page from you, rather literally, and see if I can leapfrog the competition in my business. You know

I've got some pretty good mathematicians and engineers on my team, too. In fact, I'm a more than fair engineer myself. I've stayed cost competitive by flying my payloads to near space and then just rocketing them the last increment. But all of that technology, no matter how sophisticated I and others have made it, has long since reached the dinosaur stage.

"Since you first contracted with us for satellite delivery and you and I clicked personally, so to speak, I've had a team of my top people studying everything we could about how you and your Crew did what you did, and all the math behind it that you've so kindly shown me. It's warped our minds, somewhat. It's such a radically different way of seeing things. We think we've just about got it down, though we've been looking at it with a rather different application in mind. So, the question I have for you is this: everything you've done you've done, ultimately, with strong force harmonics, but why haven't you thought about *weak* force harmonics? Look. What do you make of this, which my people came up with the other day."

Turning to the black board, he picked up a piece of chalk and wrote out a set of abstract equations, filling about a third of the board. Tom and Phil both stood quickly and moved closer to get a better look, as they saw where the logic was going. When Dan finished and looked at them questioningly, Tom picked up another piece of chalk and an eraser.

"No. No. No. This doesn't work." He erased the last third of Dan's equations and replaced them quickly with a modified set.

"Hold on," Phil interjected, pointing at part of what Tom had written. "Don't we need to integrate from here to here and. . .? Oh, oh, I see it. Okay. But you're forgetting Nylstrom's Symmetry, Tom."

"Oh, right!" Tom responded. Then he quickly circled another part of the equations "That would make this simplify to . . . this! He wrote out another set of expressions below, then stood back and all three men looked at it for a minute.

"I think we're missing a boundary postulate," Phil said, "and I think we've got the sine wave wrong."

Tom started to speak, stopped, looked puzzled for a moment, and then said, "No, it's not the sign wave, it's this. And we do need a boundary condition." He erased and changed another part of the equation, then wrote some more, further on down the board. When he was done he looked at Dan.

"Don't ask me," Dan said. "You lost me way back!"

Now, Tom and Phil looked at each other, with wonder on their faces. Phil slowly nodded. "They've almost got it."

"Right," Tom agreed. "It needs work, but I think it can be done." Turning to Dan, he said, "I think what you guys are on to is astonishing. The key insights are brilliant, and I'm embarrassed they didn't occur to me before now. Do I understand correctly, Dan, that you're proposing a joint venture here?"

Dan nodded quickly. "Yes, absolutely. Or at least some kind of cooperative effort. I don't think we can quite get there without your kind of help, both on the theoretical and engineering ends."

"Hmm . . ," Tom muttered. "Assuming we manage to make this theory really come together, the engineering is still going to be extraordinarily difficult. Tell you what. Phil and I will get a group of our math and physics people working on this," he indicated the blackboard, "and you show it to your group. We'll keep working on it from our respective ends and just e-mail things back and forth."

At that moment the videophone on Dan's desk buzzed, but only once as someone else in the house picked it up quickly; and after a quick glance, the three men ignored it.

"You don't think we should form a combined research group up front?" Dan asked.

Tom thought a second, and then shook his head. "Nah, let's do it this way. We'll actually have more people working on it. I know my guys; they'll keep running parts of it past the other R & D people on the Crew, and your guys will probably do the same. Once we really get the theory straight, we can form a joint group and start thinking about contracts; finance; budgets; work sharing; and the rest. At that point, I'll send some engineers over to work with your guys to develop a prototype. We can do some of the fabrication in our shop, too. In fact, I know just the guys I want to send over."

"Yeh," Phil chuckled. "Derek really hates administrative work, anyway. He'll be ecstatic to get back into R & D, even if it means a pay cut. Particularly when he sees this. And Beowulf should be free, at least for the summer, since he's planning on taking most of his classes over the internet anyway, if you want to send him along, too, boss."

"I suppose you're still thinking in terms of a satellite-delivery vehicle for the prototype, aren't you, Dan?" Tom asked.

Dan nodded. "Right. The prototype field generator and it's power plant will probably be too large for anything less anyhow. So I. . ."

Just then there was a rather urgent sounding knock on Dan's office door. As the three men looked over, Dan's oldest son, Mike, opened it and stuck his head in. "That call is for you, Mr. Wright, somebody named Derek on line two."

"Thank you, Mike," Tom said, then looked at Dan and indicated the desk videophone, where line two was blinking. "May I?"

"Oh, sure," Dan responded. "Or, if you want privacy, you can use the one in the master bedroom down the hall to the right."

"No, I think this will be fine, if you don't mind." Tom moved to the desk as Dan and Phil began going over the equations on the board again.

"Derek," Tom said after picking up the phone. "What's up?" From the screen he could see that Derek was calling from his apartment. Beowulf, Billi Jo, and Lynn Yip Ki were there, along with several others he couldn't make out. Something of a party seemed to be going on.

"Tom, while we were on campus this morning some executive from Sony called the office and asked to talk with you or me. I didn't find out about it until about one o'clock, when we got back to the tower after lunch, and by then it was after hours in Japan. The guy left his home phone number, but I decided not to call back until he's at work tomorrow. I wanted to talk to you first."

"What?" Tom asked, "Are they offering to settle? I didn't expect anything like that this soon."

On the screen, Derek shook his head. "No, Maria asked them, and it's apparently not about that. It's not about company business at all, really. Well, it is and it isn't. What they want, Tom, is to make you, me, and the Edison Institute a deal to lease rights to use our field modulator when they enter the teleportation business."

Tom's eyes widened. "They haven't found a solution of their own!"

"Apparently not," Derek responded, "and they don't think they're likely to find one soon. But the question is, should we do it? Beowulf thinks we should hold 'em up, you know, make it expensive enough to delay their entry or even keep them out of the business."

Tom shook his head. "I don't think we could keep them out for long. Not once they solve the other problems. We've shown them one way it can be done and sooner or later they'll find another way if they have to. My intuition is, if they make us a reasonable royalty offer, we should go ahead and make a deal. It's big money to you, me, and the Institute; and if Sony has to pay us to use our modulator, it might help us keep a cost advantage in teleportation, anyhow."

Derek nodded. "All right, then. I'll tell Beowulf what you think, then call Mike Zidelski and Buzz at home tonight and see what they say before I call Sony back tomorrow."

Derek looked like he was about to ring off, but Tom stopped him. "Hey, how did graduation go today? Congratulations *Doctor* Martin, I'm sorry I missed it. I wanted to be there."

Derek laughed. "Well, it was nice, but like when a toothache quits. I've never been much for ceremony myself and I'm glad it's over."

"How about Beowulf?" Tom asked. "How did he do on his qualification exam yesterday?"

"Well, they won't officially have them graded for a week, but you know how me and Billi Jo have been coaching him, and he says he aced it. In fact, Mike Zidelski told him afterwards that he thought Beowulf had learned more just from working with us and the rest of the Crew than he was likely to learn in the next two years at the Institute, anyhow. He actually offered Beowulf an opportunity to CLEPP out of several of the graduate classes in the fall, if he wanted. If that works, he could be done in a year or less, instead of two, at least with everything but his project. Beowulf's been on air ever since Mike told him that." Derek moved to the side and pointed at Beowulf, who stopped dancing with Billi Jo long enough to wave at Tom.

"Well, tell him congratulations, too," Tom said, "and tell him something important has happened here that I want to talk to both of you and the R and D people about as soon as Phil and I get back. Have Maria clear our schedules for tomorrow morning."

"Okay, boss," Derek said. "See you then."

Tom hung up and thought for a few moments, then looked over to Phil and Dan, who had apparently reached a stopping point in their own discussions and were looking at him.

"Good news or bad?" Dan asked.

"Nearly all good, I think," Tom responded. "And maybe for you, too, Dan. I've decided I'd like to go ahead with the next three relay satellites, as soon as you can schedule 'em."

*   *   *

In the morning, Dan drove Tom and Phil to the Santa Fe Airport. From Dan's place south of Santa Fe, it was almost as close to Albuquerque. There was a teleport chamber being built at the airport there, but it wasn't finished yet. So they took an early flight out of Santa Fe to Houston, then 'ported from the new chamber at the airport there to San Francisco International, where one of Harry Pinkerton's men was waiting out front of the terminal with a car. Picking up an hour by crossing a time zone, only the drive from the airport kept them from being at the office by nine a.m.

Phil dozed for most of the eighteen mile drive from the airport, but as they neared the Galt Tower on Santa Cruz he roused himself. "Tom, what would you think about gearing up to do a few scheduled passenger runs to and from the Asylum? Between Menlo Park; Stanford; North Fair Oaks; Atherton; and the other towns around here, there might be enough business to do four or five runs a day at least, and it would be handier for us than driving between here and San Francisco International all the time."

Tom thought it over for a moment, but no longer than that, and grinned at Phil's at least partly facetious question. "You know it just wouldn't pay, Phil. We'd have to move the lab, and I don't want to do that. We'd have to schedule runs from other 'ports, and we'd probably be displacing much higher volume runs since we're going twenty-four-seven on every big-city chamber we have open now and filling all of 'em. It'd be cheaper to just buy a 'copter, put a heliport on the top of the tower - in fact I think there's one up there already - and hire a pilot to ferry us out to the airport and back. But he'd have to be paid to be around full-time, too; and I just don't think it's worth it to save forty minutes per round trip in and . . . What the world is going on here?"

The Galt Tower was coming up on the right, and there seemed to be a rather large group of people milling around on the sidewalk in front. As the car approached the entrance to the parking garage, Tom, Phil, and the driver could see that most of crowd members were protesters or picketers of some kind.

Some of them, however, seemed to be news reporters taking pictures of and interviewing the others, who were blocking both the ground level entrance and the entrance to the parking garage. A small group of Harry Pinkerton's uniformed men were just coming up the ramp of the garage with evident intent to take control of the entrance. Recognizing their car, the officer in charge - who Tom could now see was Harry himself - waved them in. The five guards, with Harry and two others on one side and two more on the other started walking forward and to the side in an effort to move the protesters back and make room for the car to pass.

The crowd parted sullenly, and the driver turned the car and started driving down the ramp. Something motivated Phil to take his NanoPod out, set it to camcord mode, and start recording through the back window as the rear of the vehicle passed between the picketing protesters. Just as he did, one of them, a burly guy with a scraggly beard, turned his sign edgeways and slammed it angrily into the trunk of the car. Harry held his hands out, palms forward and seemed to be talking to the man in an effort to calm him down. Instead, the guy swung the sign violently, sideways and to the left at Harry. Harry stepped in, blocked the man's wrist with his left arm, and simultaneously whacked the guy in the face with his right open palm. The man's head jerked back in surprise and the sign flew behind Harry's back. Instantly, Harry gripped the man's wrist and twisted the arm counterclockwise; pulling it on through in the direction it had been swinging; and stepping *under* it to the man's left side, facing the same direction, doubling the man over from the waist. Continuing the move, Harry simply did a hundred and eighty-degree *Tenkan* to the left with his right hand on the man's arm above the elbow, swinging him forward and around in a big circle, face down and horizontal until he skidded face first into the sidewalk. The whole thing was like a smooth, intricate ballet movement that ended with Harry wrist locking the man's shoulder into the pavement with one hand from knee level. Unfortunately, the man knocked the legs out from under two or three other people who couldn't quite dodge back fast enough as he swung around. That set the whole crowd off. About thirty of them, with blood in their eyes, surged toward the five Pinkertons.

"Stop!" Tom yelled to the driver, jumped out the left side door, and started pelting up the ramp. The driver hit the brakes, jerking the car to a stop, threw it into park, jumped out, and began running after Tom before Phil could even think to move. But the driver was passed by a huge blond-haired guy running full tilt up the ramp on the *other* side of the car, ascending like Thor himself, toward the melee. In a moment, Phil could see through the viewfinder on the NanoPod that it was Beowulf Thorsen, who had apparently either followed the guards down from the UTT offices, or just arrived in the lot before him and Tom. Beowulf was only a step or two behind Tom and ahead of the driver when Tom reached the crowd. One of the five Pinkerton men was down, trying to block punches and kicks from several of the protesters. Harry was holding his own, slamming one attacker into two others. The other three Pinkerton men were about to be overwhelmed when Tom started going through the attackers like a whirling dervish, throwing three of them head over heels in about two seconds. Then Beowulf and the driver got there. Beowulf bowled three men over by simple mass and inertia before he actually thought to start using his Aikido, and about then the driver pitched in.

Phil dropped the NanoPod, threw his door open and headed up the ramp, but before he got there the protesters had second thoughts and started scattering back as Beowulf stood and glared at them.

Tom was helping the downed guard up when he saw Phil coming.

"Phil, take this man up to the offices and have the company nurse look at him. And have somebody call the medical center over on Willow Road. A few of these people" - he waved his hand at the eight or ten injured protesters, most of whom were sitting up or limping back toward where the others were now collecting themselves - "might have broken something when they landed."

Harry Pinkerton limped over, favoring his right leg, but determined to talk to Tom. "Tom, sir, you go, too. The reporter here seems to have had his camera smashed in the fight, but there are three more reporters coming down the block. You should get out of here now, or your face is going to be on the six o'clock news!"

Reluctantly, Tom took Harry's advice, following Phil and Beowulf supporting the battered and shaken guard down the ramp into the parking mall past the car, and toward the elevators.

Harry turned to the driver. "Dalton, get that car out of the road and parked. Other people need to get in and out of this building, and you're blocking things. Then get back up here."

Dalton turned to head down the ramp, but Harry stopped him. "And don't ever do that again. Next time anything like this happens, you just keep driving and get your passengers away fast. We're hired to protect *these* guys *not* the other way around!"

"Yessir," Dalton answered, and then muttered, "but I don't know how I can stop *him* from getting into it if he wants to!"

"Well," Harry partially conceded, "there is that! But if you drive fast enough, he won't get the chance!"

Turning away, Harry started reorganizing his troops to control the entrance and let some other arriving cars into the parking garage. Sirens were already blaring in the distance. The reporters had arrived, soothed their shaken comrades, and were recording everything. Harry pulled his CB off his Sam Brown belt, and called upstairs.

"Al, you there?"

"Right, sir," Al answered. "What's going on down there?"

"A mess, but we have it under control for now. Mr. Wright, Mr. Thorsen, and Mr. Adobo are coming up and bringing Joe with them. He got knocked around a little bit. I want you to call the off-duty guys on the GemCorp and Hallencamp jobs and get them over here fast. Tell 'em I'll authorize the overtime. When you've done that, call Ed at the San Francisco office and tell him we're going to need a dozen more full-time bodies down here for a while even if he has to hire some new guys."

"Will Ed go for that?" Al asked.

Harry grimaced. "He will when he sees the news."

Another thought occurred to Harry. "One more thing, Al. If Joe is okay, have him ask around the office for some old civie clothes. Jeans and a sweatshirt. If he can find some that fit, I want him to switch out of his uniform, go down and out the back, walk around front, mingle with the protesters, and see what he can pick up in the way of information. Something is going on behind all this, and I don't like it."

*   *   *

It was nearly forty minutes of uneasy standoff before Harry's reinforcements showed up and he could leave the line by the parking mall entrance and get back up to the fortieth floor offices. Until then he kept in radio contact with the thin Pinkerton contingent guarding the other two main ground level entrances to the tower, who had been augmented by a few Galt Tower security men. The city police had shown up fairly quickly and were still taking statements when Harry finally headed into the building and upstairs.

355

The cops didn't seem to know who to protect from whom, but their presence may have helped calm things down. Between them, the police, and the network reporters, the protesters were nearly outnumbered anyway and were virtually all getting interviewed.

Harry got interviewed twice. First the police took his statement, and then several national network reporters tried to interview him on his view of events. He told them just what he had seen and done. When the interview turned ugly as they started asking him to verify or refute charges of aggressive actions by the guards, he refused further comment, telling them that all UTT response would come through their Public Relations Officer. Actually, Harry didn't know if UTT even had a public relations officer yet, but it was as good a response as he could come up with on the spur of the moment.

Before he turned things over to Sergeant Slaughter (that was his real name, though he was a very mild-mannered fellow), who had come over from the GemCorp Job to help, Harry spotted Joe, bruised and battered in an old sweatshirt, jeans, and a pair of thongs, carrying a sign he had picked up somewhere. The sign simply said SAVE THE ATMOSPHERE: STOP TELEPORTATION NOW. It was so inane, Harry wondered if Joe had made it up until he read a few of the other signs. Joe was mingling and talking with the other protesters, none of whom seemed to recognize him as a guard they had been trying to stomp only a while back. Harry noticed Joe was subtly evading reporters and their cameras. Occasionally he glared at the Pinkerton men in feigned resentment right along with the others, though he winked once at Harry.

Exiting the elevator and entering the UTT offices, Harry checked in briefly with Al to make sure everything was in control. Al told him that the home office had authorized the increased contingent and that the men would be here tomorrow. That was the good news. The bad news was that there were pilot and baggage-handling union picketers at UTT's San Francisco, Los Angeles, and San Diego airport gates. *What in the world is going on here,* Harry asked himself before he headed for Tom's office, where he was stopped short by Maria Santos.

"Sorry, Mr. Pinkerton, but Mr. Wright is not in."

"Did he go home?" Harry asked. "I've been down by the parking entrance most of the time, and I didn't see the car leave."

"No, sir. He's had the physics, math, and engineering people down in the conference room for the last half-hour. Oh, maybe they're out now. Here comes Mr. Barret."

Harry turned and saw that, indeed, Dave Barret, whom he recognized but did not know well, was coming up the hall from the conference room.

Harry walked toward him and caught Dave's attention. "Excuse me, Mr. Barret, sir, is Mr. Wright going to be available anytime soon? I have some security matters I need to talk over with him."

"Hmmm?" Dave responded, as he slowed his pace to listen to Harry. "Oh, no. Too darned many things going on at once. Something big came up while Tom was in New Mexico, and we're trying to wrap our heads around that right now. We're going to be quite a while. Probably be about one or two before we're done. I just came out to make a pit stop, then I'm headed back. Tom told us what happened out front. Are you and your men okay?"

"A couple of us got banged up a little, but we're all right otherwise," Harry said. "The other guys got the worst of it."

"Good," Dave grinned and nodded. "That's what Beowulf said. Right now, though, we're focused on this other thing. Everything else is on hold 'til we get a grip on it. But I'm sure Tom will want to see you as soon as we're done."

"Okay," Harry nodded. "I think it can wait that long."

Chapter 23: The Jaws of the Trap

In the California Senate chamber the same morning, Bill Braxon was huddled at his desk with Hally Arkwright, the Minority Whip, while senate pages moved throughout the chamber distributing ballots for the final vote on HB 2044. In this day of computers, legislative votes could have easily been accomplished electronically, but in this, as in many other matters, tradition dictated other, time-honored procedural methods.

"Well, this is it, Hally," Bill said. "What's your final count?"

Hally shook her head. "As near as I can tell, we're still four votes short, Bill."

"How about Stiles, are you counting him? Since I talked reason to State Farm and Allstate, they've been leaning on him; and last I talked to him, he seemed to be coming around."

"Yes, that's counting him, even though he told me a few minutes ago he doesn't really know yet how he's going to vote and won't until he does it. He's afraid of bucking Clanton. Four short is the optimistic number, Bill. Actually, I'm surprised we got this close."

Bill sighed. "Me, too. Well, we gave it a good try. Too bad this isn't an election year. Public sentiment being what it is right now, I think we'd pick up enough seats to take control; and we could get this bill and a lot of others we want through. By the way, what did you think of our esteemed Governor Slanghorn's strange speech last night?"

A look of confusion lit Hally's face and she seemed to struggle for words for several seconds. "Well, we've always known he was a front man for the unions, the environmental wackos, and every other fear-mongering-big-government group in the state. But why he'd go on 3-V out of a clear blue sky and start yapping about economic dislocations and hypothetical environmental hazards from teleportation, I just don't get. It isn't as if something disastrous has happened, or is likely to happen anytime soon. Hell, Bill, all reports are that UTT is making the whole West coast boom, California in particular! State GDP is higher than expected, employment is up, prices of transportation and transported goods are falling, tax revenues are way above budget predictions. I just don't see . . ."

Roger Galbraith hurried up the aisle, sidled down the row, and joined their huddle, interrupting their discussion. "Bill, Hally, something's up. I've overheard several of Clanton's troops spreading the word that they were going to delay the vote."

"What?" Bill and Hally spoke simultaneously, and glanced at each other before Bill continued. "Why would they do that, Roger? They've got enough votes to kill it, unless there've been some defections we don't know of." He looked at Hally, but she just shrugged, and all three of them turned toward the podium where they could see Sam Clanton huddled with the Senate President. Sam turned, walked down the steps from the elevated platform, and went back up the aisle to his own desk where he stood and adjusted the microphone for a moment before speaking.

"Mr. President?"

"The floor recognizes the esteemed Senate Majority Leader, Senator Samuel Hamilton Clanton," Jake Gramm droned in response.

"Mr. President, as a result of certain urgent matters that were brought to light last night by our esteemed Governor Melvin W. Slanghorn that require the deliberation of this body and due to certain disturbing events that have since occurred, I would like to move that the final vote on SB 2044 be tabled until some more propitious time, to be determined by the joint leadership of this body, so that we can discuss these matters. As part of the motion, we should also reschedule debate on other matters pending this morning."

The Senate President looked around the chamber. "It has been moved that the final vote on SB 2044 be tabled at this time and that other matters scheduled this morning also be rescheduled. Is there a second?"

The call of "second!" came nearly simultaneously from several parts of the chamber. Bill was not entirely sure that some of them weren't ALP members. The presiding officer pointed to one of them arbitrarily. "I believe Senator Dickerson has seconded the motion. Is there discussion?"

Bill, already standing, felt a strong urge for reasons he did not entirely grasp - perhaps partly just because Clanton wanted it - to oppose the motion and actually opened his mouth and moved closer to his mike to speak, but nothing came out. For one thing, he did not know what to say since holding the vote now seemed to mean certain defeat. Also, Hally Arkwright whispered urgently in his ear.

"Don't do it, Bill. It will give us time to swing some more of the Senators from the central districts."

"Senator Braxon?" The presiding officer queried, seeing Bill leaning toward his microphone and thinking he was about to speak.

Still in shock and undecided, suspecting that somehow he was falling into a trap but not grasping its outlines, Bill finally shook his head.

Seeing this, other ALP members took their cue and also remained silent.

"There appears to be no discussion," the presiding officer droned. "Does somebody wish to call the question?"

"Question," somebody spoke loudly from several rows behind Bill.

"The question has been called by Senator DeLavega. All in favor say aye."

This time the response was thunderous from the members of both parties throughout the chamber.

"All opposed now by the same sign."

Only a very few scattered responses were heard this time and Bill had a sinking feeling he should have been one of them, though he didn't know why.

The Senate President banged with his gavel. "The motion passes. The floor will now entertain another motion."

By unspoken agreement, Hally Arkwright and Roger Galbraith headed back to their own places in the chamber. There was no point in further discussion between the three until they knew more about what was going on. Apparently a script had been written that they simply had to listen to for a while in order to learn the plot.

When the murmur in the chamber subsided, Gerald Foxly stood and attained floor recognition. "Mr. President, on behalf of the majority party leadership in the California Senate, I move that a special committee be established as soon as possible to hold hearings on the economic dislocations and environmental and safety hazards of teleportation, and to recommend legislation to ameliorate the threats hanging over us."

Gramm's proposal was quickly seconded and the presiding officer called for discussion. This time there *was* discussion, and it was very heated. Bill knew just where he stood on this proposal, but the RepubliCrats were unified and prepared on the issue while ALP members were split, some thinking that hearings could only ultimately serve to bring out the truth, whatever that was. What really swung things, though, was news reports - apparently only minutes old, yet quoted by several members of the Democratic - Republican Party - about peaceful demonstrators being violently attacked by vicious UTT guards at the Galt Tower. By noon the motion had passed by a significant majority. Bill had no choice but to round up the other ALP leaders, and then go talk to Clanton and his cronies to see when they wanted to meet to determine party representation on the special committee. He had a niggling suspicion that the other side already knew just who and what they wanted.

*   *   *

Gina, with Senator Braxon's permission, went to sit in the Senate gallery and watch the final vote on the automobile deregulation bill. Amanda, out of school for the summer, had come with her dad to hang around the office, and went with Gina. When they got to the gallery they saw Spider and Serena on the front row, peering between the railings down into the chamber. Dex had stayed up in the office to help manage things there. Serena looked back, saw Gina and Amanda, and waved them down.

As the four friends watched the last of the debate and the preparations for the vote, they bantered quietly in good spirits, despite their expectation that the ALP would lose. When the final vote was delayed by the RepubliCrat leadership, they were as surprised as were Senator Braxon and the other ALP leaders. The immediate call for the special committee to investigate the environmental and economic consequences and hazards of teleportation and following debate on the proposal made the short hairs on the back of Gina's neck stand up. She had seen a small part of Governor Slanghorn's speech the evening before and had turned it off in disgust. Nobody with any sense had taken radical environmentalism seriously since the Great Global Warming Hoax had been exposed, back when

Gina was a toddler. As for economic dislocations from the new technology, she had no doubt they would be significant, but new, advanced technologies and industries innovated by daring entrepreneurs like: John D. Rockefeller; Andrew Carnegie; Henry Ford; Malcolm McLean; Bill Gates; and yes, Thomas Alvin Wright; always displaced old ones in the process of improving the human condition. Now Gina realized how much she had underestimated the power of vested interests and old ideas, though she sensed something else going on behind and underneath the RepubliCrat rhetoric.

The real shock, though, was when the first Senator arguing that the committee investigation was necessary to establish the various threats posed by teleportation bolstered his arguments by reference to violent abuse of peaceful demonstrators by UTT guards that had supposedly just occurred outside the Galt Tower in Menlo Park. Gina felt an immediate, urge to get to a 3-V or a computer and find out what had really happened. She told her friends as much and headed up the gallery stairs and back up to the office, with Amanda in tow.

When they went in the office door, the phones were ringing off the hooks. Whatever had been happening was apparently motivating a lot of people to call their elected representatives. Almost every staff member was engaged in a conversation with a constituent, and as soon as they finished one, they had to answer another. Amanda went to find an extra desk and help. The office 3-V was on and tuned to CNABC cable news, but the sound had been turned down low and Gina could not really hear much through the cacophony. Worse, when she got to her desk her own videophone was ringing.

She snatched it up. "Hello." Gina immediately regretted the brusqueness in her tone as she saw that it was Jim Jefferson, her economic researcher friend over at the California Legislative Research Service. Jim had taken an interest in her project and was a bit smitten by Gina herself, who failed to reciprocate in that way, though she liked him.

"Gina, you okay? You sound a little stressed."

Gina consciously relaxed, feeling a bit guilty. "Sorry, Jim. Lot of things going on, but I'm fine. How are you?"

"I'm all right, despite my unrequited love. Hey, I wondered if you were still collecting and processing the data on legislator's stock trades."

"Yes, I am." Gina was interested now. "I'll probably be at it for another couple of weeks, at least. Why? Did you find something new for me?"

"I'll say. Some very recent trades. When you see what type of trades they are, and the magnitudes, and who it is, you'll be surprised. Or, knowing you, maybe you won't. The interesting thing is, the legislators didn't report them. I got wind through a back door from my friends at the exchange itself. I already e-mailed the data over to you, so check your mail. I'll be interested to see what you make of it."

"Oh, thanks, Jim. You really are a peach of a guy. Or maybe a coconut."

"So, either way I'm a fruit, huh? Well, do you want to go with a fruit to a movie Saturday night?"

Gina thought for a moment. "Would it be okay if we went earlier, and doubled? I sorta promised Spider and Serena I'd go with them to a matinee, and then back to Spider's place for a serious game of Scrabble."

"Well," Jim leered ostentatiously, "I'd rather get you alone and whisper sweet quotations from *Capitalism, Socialism, and Democracy* in your ear."

"Oooh," Gina squealed in mock feminine shock. "Schumpeter. You really are a bad boy, Jim!"

"Nah, I just know what turns you on. About noon then, at your folk's place?"

"Yes. That'll be fine."

"Okay, Gina. See you then."

When Jim rang off, Gina was torn as to whether to check the news first or the data Jim had sent her. Flipping a mental coin, she went to the CNABC web site on her computer for a live broadcast. She put the computer earphone in, so that she could hear clearly without having to turn the office 3-V up.

The network was running a video clip of the disturbance at the Galt Tower, which had apparently happened just after nine a.m. The clip was being repeated over and over while network anchors and talking heads discussed, dissected, and analyzed the chaotic events, occasionally breaking away for further commentary from outside 'experts'. The film itself, though visually interesting, was not particularly informative as to exactly what caused the furor. The first part was apparently shot by a cameraman who was filming a group of protesters in front of the parking garage entrance at the Galt Tower. A stir went through the group and the camera shifted and focused down the street as a limousine approached, then shifted back as what may have been a small line of guards - difficult to see from near the back of the throng where the cameraman was located - came up out of the garage and apparently started trying to part the crowd so that the car could go down the ramp.

When the car finally did pass through the crowd and start to disappear down the ramp, there was an audible thump of some kind and some form of disturbance up at the front of the protesters, which suddenly caused many of them, simultaneously, to surge forward with (as Gina interpreted it) apparent angry intent to swarm the uniformed guards. At that point the first clip ended as the cameraman was knocked down in the surge. The next segment of film was shot from up the street near the main pedestrian entrance. The cameraman swung suddenly away from the face of a leader of one of the protesting groups - saying something inane about 'long term human cell deterioration from teleportation' - as the disturbance started by the parking entrance. Many of the protesters at the ground entrance started moving down the street toward the disturbance, and the cameraman jogged across the street in hopes of getting a better angle while still filming. Consequently, the camera bounced so much it was hard to see anything clearly.

Once the cameraman stopped, what could barely be seen was that some kind of fight was apparently going on between the protesters and the guards at the parking garage, though mostly, all the film showed was the backs and sides of protesters trying to crowd forward to participate. Then something or someone, perhaps guard reinforcements, seemed to hit the crowd from the front. There were glimpses of a large blond man and another pair of darker haired men, surging into the crowd from the parking entrance. Several of the protesters seemed to suddenly get thrown head over heels, and the crowd had second thoughts, backing off. The cameraman moved down the street, still filming, but by then an uneasy standoff seemed to have been established. A third segment, taken some minutes later, showed ambulances arriving and EMT persons helping some of the injured while Menlo Park police milled around between the demonstrators and the corporate guards.

After repeating these films several times, the network showed interviews their reporters had taken with the participants, particularly with the protesters involved, several of whom were battered and bruised, and who excoriated Universal Teleportation Transport for sending "Ninja Pinkertons" (as one put it) or "a hoard of Karate trained guards" (as another said) to attack the demonstrators and deny their rights of peaceful assembly. Gina's ears pricked up as one of the protesters even alleged that Tom Wright himself had been involved in the fight, but she immediately discounted that. The newsmen didn't discount it, however. Though they admitted they had no direct photographic evidence, they promised to find out for sure who had been in the car.

Despite a brief clip of an interview with a young guard captain, who claimed that he and the other guards acted only in self-defense, the news analyst apparently took the protesters at their word and began calling the event the "Menlo Park Massacre," even though the network's own tally of injuries included only a dozen or so people with bruises and sprains, one with a cracked femur, another with a badly scraped face, and another with a suspected mild concussion. In all, the intensiveness and the tone of the reporting of the event seemed way overblown to Gina. Nobody at all had been killed or really seriously injured, and the whole thing seemed to have lasted less than a minute. The media seemed determined, though, to turn it into a major event reminiscent of the violent and bloody labor-capital disputes of the late 19th century or the violent civil rights conflicts of the 1960s.

Several questions tugged at Gina. For one thing, the media seemed to have arrived at the demonstration/protest just as fast as the participants themselves. Come to think of it, though, calling the media in advance was natural for protesters and demonstrators, who above all wanted publicity for their cause so maybe that was no mystery. There seemed to have been a great deal of advance planning, though. Several groups were involved that often had rather disparate agendas, and Gina suspected that there was some connection with Governor Slanghorn's speech the night before.

Such things were speculative, though, so Gina checked out the web sites of two more networks to see whether they had any more information than CNABC, which they didn't. All of them made pleas for contact from any citizens near the fracas who may have recorded it on their NanoPods. From the network films, though, it didn't seem to Gina that there had been many pedestrians along Santa Cruz at nine a.m. in the morning. Still, *maybe by tonight,* Gina thought, *they'll know more about what really happened.* So she took her earphone out, exited the internet, and opened up her mail to see what Jim Jefferson had sent her.

For some weeks now, Gina had been systematically tabulating data on stock trades of California Senators and Representatives over the last several years, for chapter seven of her dissertation. Several years back, the California ALP had gotten a law through that required all such trades to be registered with the state statistical office and made publicly available. Gina was processing the data to see if legislators made abnormally high rates of return on their portfolios while in office. Logically, legislators faced opportunities and temptations that allowed such abnormal returns. For one thing, stock tips by corporate insiders could be a form of rent-seeking payoff to legislators offering to grant special favors.

For another, legislators were the ultimate insiders even *without* help from corporate officers, because *as legislators,* they knew in advance of anyone else what firms and industries would be helped or hurt by their own proposed legislation. Indeed, they could even tailor their legislative proposals to *generate* such consequences. Often, powerful legislators at both the federal and state levels proposed excise taxes on specific products or regulatory laws on particular firms or industries specifically to motivate firms in those industries to lobby - and pay them - to withdraw the legislation. Back in the 1990s an economist named Fred. S. McChesney had termed this common practice *rent extraction* and identified it as a form of legislative extortion. But clearly, such politicians *could also profit from stock trades on either harmful or helpful legislation that they proposed.*

Researchers Alan Ziobrowski, Ping Cheng, and others, in the December 2004 issue of *the Journal of Financial and Quantitative analysis,* had shown, using data from 1993 to 1998, that members of the U.S. Senate had made abnormally high returns on their stock trades. Indeed, the rates of return obtained by U.S. Senators *far exceeded the above normal returns typically earned by corporate insiders.* Other economists had later extended this literature to other time periods, showing that the phenomenon persisted. It was a matter of unresolved controversy, though, whether the same thing could happen to any great degree at the state level. Most states had economies too small for mere state legislation to seriously affect either the stock values of large national corporations, or of the stock market overall. Of course, they could materially alter the value of firms and industries located mostly in state, but the sums involved were smaller than at the national level. But California by itself had no small part of the whole U.S. economy, and Gina suspected a lot of the same legislator behavior would be found here.

When she opened up the data file Jim Jefferson had sent her, Gina was surprised and did not at first know what to make of it. It showed a large number of recent transactions in the stock of Universal Teleportation Transport by a few key members of the California Senate, in particular, by Samuel H. Clanton, Senate Majority Leader, Jake Gramm, the President of the Senate, Gerald Foxly, the Majority Whip, and a few others. Oddly, the contracts were forward contracts, agreements to sell large amounts of UTT stock to specified parties a few weeks from now at what appeared to be bargain prices, given the ongoing run-up in UTT stock values since the firm began operations.

A suspicion slipped across the gap from Gina's subconscious to her conscious mind. Exiting the new data file, she went to the main file in which she had been keeping and statistically processing her accumulated legislator stock trade data and began looking for the trading records and current portfolios of those senators. It didn't take long to see that almost none of them actually owned any UTT stock shares. *Clearly, then, they were trying to sell UTT stock short.* They would have to buy between now and the delivery dates in order to sell at the contracted prices on those dates, and the only way they would make money would be if the UTT stock price *declined* so that they could buy low and sell high. They were betting on a steep decline in the price of UTT stock shares.

'Click' went a connection in Gina's mind: Governor Slanghorn's speech, implying environmental and safety problems with teleportation. She had no data showing stock transactions by the Governor, but the suspicion she suddenly felt approached *certainty* that he also had recently negotiated the same kind of contracts. Then 'click' went another connection: the hearings and threat of probably costly state government regulation of UTT's California teleportation operations in the Senate this morning. And 'click': the demonstrations at the Galt Tower. But doubts came. Something was missing. How could all of this, even together, be enough? She had heard nothing from any legitimate source about risks associated with teleportation, and it seemed to be about as clean a technology as ever existed. Unless there really was some scientifically known threat of which she was unaware, it seemed likely the hearings and threats to regulate would ultimately go nowhere. Plus, tele-portation was immensely popular. Gina had not had occasion yet to try it, but everyone she knew who had, seemed to love it. Dex had actually driven down to San Francisco and teleported from there to San Diego and back a couple of weeks ago on legislative business for Bill and had raved about the experience for days. She doubted the public would buy into a campaign of hypothesized dangers; and if they didn't, the price of UTT stock would not fall significantly, and the conspirators would lose their shirts.

Something else must be waiting in the wings, but Gina did not know what it could be. Unless . . . *Wasn't there a time back around eighteen sixty-three when Commodore Vanderbilt was trying to extend the New York & Harlem Railroad into the city from Broadway down to the Battery? What was it that those New York Aldermen did to him and how was it that he fought back?* Her attempt to remember the details of a story she had read several years ago was interrupted when Bill, Hally, and Roger entered the office, clearly agitated and speaking loudly enough that Gina could hear them even through the cacophony of ringing videophones and phone conversations going on in the office.

"Just how in *hell* are we supposed to prepare or decide who to put on the committee when we don't even know what this is all about?" Roger was asking.

"I don't know, Rog," Bill answered. "We don't know what's driving this, but we know what they're *saying* it's all about, so I guess we have to go with that somehow. We could put Fred on it. He's been on the Transportation Committee before. He knows about transportation issues, and he'd be happy to do it. And he's combative."

"But Fred doesn't know anything about science, technology, or safety regulation issues, does he?" Hally asked. "I think this whole thing is going to deal a lot with technical matters."

"Well, actually," Roger responded, "he might. He used to run an electronics firm. I think he has some background that might help. That would give us four, and only leave us a couple more to come up with. Besides, like Bill says, Fred won't take any guff from Clanton's cronies."

"Ly, cancel my appointments and divert all my calls to Dex until we're done in here," Bill said to Ly Cam, before his, Roger's, and Hally's voices faded as they disappeared into Bill's inner office.

For several minutes, Gina considered what she knew, what she suspected, and what her options might be. Then she instructed her computer to print out Jim's stock trade data, got up, and went over to the printer the computers in her end of the office were networked to and picked the sheets up. Walking back down the aisle, she passed her own desk and stopped by Dex's.

Dex was on the phone, apparently to a constituent, but he spotted Gina out of the corner of his eye and waved briefly at her as he continued talking. "Yes ma'am. I know, ma'am. Well I'm sure no teleport beams are going through your house, ma'am, but we'll look into it. Yes, goodbye." Putting the phone down, he ignored the other blinking lines as Gina stopped.

"Gina. The world is going crazy. I guess you saw what happened downstairs this morning, but did you hear about the riot at the Galt Tower down in Menlo Park? NBS News is calling it 'the battle at Galt's gulch'."

"Yes, Dex," she said, "I did. Could you do me a favor?"

Something in Gina's tone made Dex sit up straight. "Sure, what's up?"

"I need to get in to see Bill. He's in there with Roger and Hally, and he's not seeing anyone until they're done, but he needs to see me. I don't think Ly Cam will let me in, and I have information they need. It has to do with everything that's happening."

Dex's eyes narrowed for a moment. Then he took his NanoPod out and punched in Bill's private code. Nobody who had that code would use it frivolously at a time like this, so it only took a couple of seconds for Dex to get a connection. "Senator, Gina badly wants to see you, Roger, and Hally. Says it's urgent. Can she come in? . . . Okay."

Dex folded up his NanoPod and pointed toward the office with his thumb. "You're in, Gina. And you owe me one."

Gina nodded and flashed him a smile as she headed toward Ly Cam's desk. "Thanks, Dex, I do owe you one."

The door to the inner office was open and Bill was talking to Ly Cam a few seconds later when Gina got there. Bill saw Gina and waved her in after him. "Come on in, Gina. You need to be in on some of this anyway."

Gina smiled and nodded to Ly Cam, then followed Bill into the office. Roger and Hally were sitting close together, going over some lists. They looked up and briefly greeted Gina, who nodded back with a grim smile. Bill went back behind his desk, but stood and paced with his hands in his pockets, too nervous to sit, and though he waved her to a chair, Gina, too, remained standing for the moment.

"I'd like to get your take on all this, Gina," Bill said. "We're going crazy trying to figure out what the RepubliCrats are up to."

"Well, sir," Gina began, nervously fingering her print out, "I think I may have a piece of the puzzle. Would you take a look at this?"

Bill took the papers she handed to him and scanned down the first page for several seconds, then paused, trying to grasp what he was seeing. "What am I looking at here, Gina? Some kind of stock trades?"

"Yes, sir. Forward contracts, all in large amounts of UTT stock, for delivery in a couple of weeks. And what you want to notice, sir, is who is selling."

Bill scanned the sheets some more, his eyes widened, and his jaw dropped noticeably before he spoke. "Clanton! Gramm! Foxly! And, . . . It's the whole Clanton gang!"

"What?" Hally Arkwright asked, startled. "Let me see that."

Bill handed her the top sheet of the printout and the second to Roger, then went back to scanning the rest for several seconds as the others did the same. In only a few moments, though, Roger and Hally traded sheets, then after a few more the three senators looked up at each other in nearly simultaneous comprehension.

"They're selling UTT short," Hally Arkwright observed, almost distractedly.

Roger nodded grimly. "That explains a helluva lot!"

Bill sat down and slumped in his chair, scattering the remaining pages on his desk. "Just when you think you've seen the depths of that man's depravity, he surprises you." Then he sat forward. "Gina, where'd you get this?"

"I've been compiling stock-trade data for the Senate members for my dissertation," Gina answered. "You remember the law you got passed a few years back? All trades have to be reported. I thought I had all the data, including the most current, but a friend of mine, Jim Jefferson, a researcher over at CLRS, found these new ones, and sent them to me."

"What do you mean 'found them', Gina?" Hally asked. "Didn't Clanton and the others report these contracts?"

"No," Gina answered. "They haven't reported them. Jim knows some people who work for the exchange. He's taken an interest in my dissertation. In fact he told me once that, to his knowledge, nobody had ever looked at that data before. It's just been accumulating there and collecting dust. When I started compiling and analyzing it, he got his friends to look for stock trades by California Senators, so that my data would be as complete and accurate as possible."

"Wait a minute," Bill interjected. "I wrote that law. They have six months before stock trades have to be reported. All this will be long since over by then. So we can't accuse them of any infraction on failure to report, and stock trades by Senators *per se* are perfectly legal, even forward sales."

"Well, for hell sakes, Bill!" Hally raised her voice, she was so angry. "This all stinks to high heaven! Look at the timing!"

"Right," Roger agreed, also miffed. "The whole Democratic-Republican party leadership in the Senate short-sells UTT stock, and *then* calls for hearings on the hazards of teleportation?"

Bill threw up his hands. "I agree. Thanks to Gina and some random good luck, we now know what's driving all this. But they have a majority in the Senate! We'll never get an ethics committee hearing, and we might not win if we did! Timing alone is *not* proof of causal connection. Besides, there are too many things going on at once: the Governor's speech, the demonstrations at UTT headquarters, heck, I even heard there were union picketers out at the UTT airport gates and container docks up and down the state this morning. You really want to try proving that this is all a conspiracy by Clanton and his cronies? How many of those people are going to admit to that?"

Hally opened her mouth to make a possibly angry retort then controlled herself before speaking. "At the very least we should make a public stink about these trades! A lot of people will see what it means."

Roger nodded agreement. "Yes. They'll see the cynical corruption here for what it is."

"Maybe," Bill responded. "And maybe not. We'd get a lot of favorable play on the internet, and on radio, and maybe some on the local 3-V stations. But the national networks will spin it as a deliberate political distraction by us from the committee hearings and from the supposedly 'spontaneous public outcry' against the hazards and dislocations of teleportation. Maybe going public would allow us to cast doubt on the other side's motives, and it would certainly get us off playing defense. But I think we ought to hold back on doing that for at least a while. Like Gina said, this is a big piece of the puzzle, but I have a sense that we haven't seen the whole picture yet. What do you think, Gina?"

Gina's mouth was dry, and she licked her lips discretely before answering. "I don't know about going public, sir, or pushing for an ethics investigation, though it looks to me, if you do the one, you've got to try the other, or you won't be taken seriously. But I do think you're right that we haven't seen everything yet. Those people can only make money if they seriously hurt UTT, at least for a while, and what we've seen so far doesn't seem enough."

"So what else do we do?" Roger grumbled.

Gina and the three senators thought quietly for a while before Bill broke the silence.

"Well, all of this is a concerted attack on one business firm. By now the people at UTT probably know they're going to have to defend themselves at the hearings, and we need to start coordinating with them on that. But most important, they need to know about this short-selling. They may have answers we don't on how to deal with that. I'm calling Lew Edleston, right now. He's on UTT's Board of Directors and he'll know who to talk to over there." Picking up his vid phone, he began punching in code.

Suddenly Gina regretted that she had not thought of that first.

*   *   *

   With the spring semester over, Lew Edleston was enjoying the lull before the start of summer classes, taking the opportunity to make progress on his latest book. He had deliberately not scheduled summer classes for himself this year so he would have as few distractions as possible and could finish the project over the next two or three months. All he would have in the way of interruptions, beyond intermittent meetings with the three graduate research fellows who were helping him gather and process data, was an occasional UTT board meeting and the odd student coming into his office for help once the summer sessions did start. Lew was excited, of course, about what was going on at UTT, but today he wanted to work on his book. He had slept well last night, come to work early, and deliberately avoided listening to the news to keep his mind uncluttered with those kinds of distractions. So his mind was clear and focused and things had been coming together well all morning as he worked. The early afternoon sun, blue sky, and sculpted campus greenery observable through his south windows added to his feeling of wellbeing.

   When his vid phone buzzed, Lew naturally felt a pang of irritation, but he quickly scooted his office chair over to the other desk and picked it up. Immediately he saw it was Bill Braxon and his irritation evaporated

   "Bill, good to see you. Long time since we talked. What can I do for you?"

   "Lew," Bill asked, "have you been watching the news this morning?"

"Well, no. I've been too busy working, and I didn't really want to."

"How about the Governor's speech last night?"

Lew snorted. "Are you kidding, Bill, that fathead? You know, I'm getting older, and there's only so much nonsense I can put up with these days. My wife and I went to bed early just to miss it. Why, what's up?"

Bill could be seen shaking his head. "Too many things for me to explain 'em all, Lew, and I couldn't if I tried. You're gonna have to see for yourself. All of a sudden it seems like everyone in the world is coming down hard on UTT, including the California Senate. I'm surprised you haven't gotten a call from the company already. I've got Roger, Hally, and Gina in my office here, and we're trying to make sense of it all ourselves. We've come across one crucial piece of information that we thought you ought to know about, which helps explain a lot of things. You should get this information to Mr. Wright and maybe a few other key people, though my suspicion is, you might want to keep it a little tight beyond that. That'll be your judgment call, though."

Mystified, Lew really didn't know what to say beyond, "What is it?"

"Sam Clanton and several other members of the senate majority leadership are selling UTT stock short."

"What?" Lew's eyes widened. "You must be joking!"

Bill shook his head. "No, I'm not. We've got the documentation. Wait a second and I'll scan it in and send it over."

Lew laid the phone down, slid over to the other desk and picked up the sheets as they printed out, then quickly read through them. His hands were shaking and he felt chilled before he got back to the phone.

"Where did you get this, Bill?" He asked.

"Gina got it from a researcher in the CLRS, who got it straight from people in the exchange. Among the ten thousand things my people here are going to be doing in the next day or two, is to discretely check this for accuracy, but I think you can take it to the bank."

Lew Edleston struggled to pull himself together and a core of angry resolve began to grow and burn away the shock and chill that he felt, until in only a few seconds, only the resolve was left. "I know somebody who can get to the bottom of this fast, Bill," he said. "He knows the financial markets better than you or I ever could. If you don't mind, I'm going to ring off and give him a call. Thanks, Bill. Thanks a lot."

Hanging up, Lew immediately punched in another code. It buzzed for several seconds, and he thought that he was not going to get an answer, but then he did. "Marlin," Lew said, "if you've got a minute, we need to talk. There're things you need to tell me and something I very, very, badly need to tell you."

Chapter 24: Parrying the Thrusts

It was one-thirty when Tom's meeting with the R & D people, who were still mostly members of the original Skeleton Crew despite the recent hiring by UTT of about a dozen physicists, mathematicians, and engineers, finally broke up. Most of them left in small knots, chattering excitedly among themselves as they contemplated and discussed the possible applications and implications of the revolutionary insights Tom and Phil had brought back from New Mexico and the proposed joint venture with Nucleonic Orbital to develop the technology. Angel BlackSnake, as Director of R & D, would now have the difficult job of selecting the initial theoretical research team - which nearly everyone wanted to be on - without gutting the teams working on the Zelda upgrade, second generation D-R physics, or other ongoing projects.

Tom intended to work closely with the Weak Force Team himself as often as he could find the time and actually act as its *ex-oficio* leader. The ramifications were just too exciting to him *not* to be involved, even if he was CEO of UTT. For now, though, faced with the unpleasant necessity of dragging his attention back from the beautiful world of pure physics and math to the real world, he headed for his office to find out just what the current crisis was and deal with it. He had asked Derek, Hulio, and Beowulf to meet him there as soon as they could break free.

Maria stopped him as soon as he reached her desk, where a large man in a suit and tie was waiting. "Mr. Wright, there's a policeman here who wants to see you. Our legal counsel, Mr. Byrd has been trying to get hold of you. Harry Pinkerton is anxious to see you about some security matters. He's waiting out at the front security station. And Marlon Gates has called several times, sir. I told him you'd call back as soon as you could."

"Thank you, Maria," Tom answered. "Call Buzz and have him come over as soon as he can. By the way, was Harry's man - Joe is it? - hurt badly?"

"No, sir. A little shaken and bruised was all. The nurse fixed him up and he . . . uh . . ." she glanced quickly at the officer and back, "went right back to work, sir."

"Good. Derek, Phil, and Beowulf will be here in a short while, Maria. Let them right in, will you? Let Buzz in, too, when he gets here." Turning to the police detective, he extended his hand. "I'm sorry you had to wait. I'm Tom Wright, Mr . . . . ?"

"Devlin," the man said, "Detective Burt Devlin. I just need a statement from you, Mr. Wright. I understand you were in the car that went down the parking ramp just as the fracas broke out. I'd like to ask you a few questions about just who was in the car and what they each saw and did. I might want to get statements from the others, too."

Tom sighed. "Well, there were three of us in the car: myself, Phillip Adobo, who is one of our mathematicians, and the driver. I think his name is Dalton . . . something."

"Pinkerton," Maria said.

Tom was startled. "Pinkerton?"

"Yes, sir. He's Harry's nephew."

Tom blinked and turned back to the detective. "If you'll see the security officers out front, they'll tell you where he is and you can get his statement. I need an hour or two right now to deal with several things going on, but how about Mr. Adobo and I write out and sign our statements as soon as we get a little time and just have a courier take them to you? I think we should be able to do that by, say, four this afternoon. You'll probably have them before you're off duty. I'll also have Maria schedule you some time with Phil and me separately in the morning in case you have any other questions. Would that be okay?"

Detective Devlin pursed his lips for a moment as he thought that over, wondering if perhaps they wanted to coordinate their stories before talking to him. Some of the demonstrators involved in the fracas claimed that Mr. Wright and the others in the car had taken an active role. If so, they might have something to hide. But it wouldn't do them any good unless they had already coached the driver; and Wright looked like an honest sort, though you couldn't always tell. Finally, he nodded his assent. "I think that will work, sir."

Tom shook the man's hand again. The detective started to turn away, but then turned back. "One more thing, sir, if I might."

"Yes?"

"I drove to 'Frisco on my day off last week and 'ported up to Vancouver, just to see what it was like. Teleporting, I mean. Loved it. Saw my favorite brother-in-law while I was there." He shook his head and waved his hand to indicate confusion. "I don't understand what all this anxiety is about. I should tell you, though, that some of the injured protesters are talking about filing charges."

Tom nodded appreciation. "Thanks, Mr. Devlin."

As the detective walked away, Tom turned back to Maria. "What else do I need to know or do right fast, Maria?"

"Sir, I think you need to spend a few minutes looking at the news before you do anything else. Then you need to see Mr. Sanchez and Mr. Freeman. There are union picketers at the airport gates and the dock chambers. The managers there have been calling in all morning."

"Thanks, Maria," Tom said, and headed for his office, where he took Maria's advice. Making himself comfortable in his desk chair and turning on his big screen 3-V, he listened to the news with increasing astonishment and consternation as he learned for the first time about the Governor's speech the previous night, the actions the state senate had taken this morning while he was meeting with the Crew, and the angry network news reports of the "Menlo Park Massacre," precipitated by a "modern robber baron" who apparently thought he was above the law. Derek and Beowulf knocked and came in. He silently waved them to seats so they could sit and listen. In another minute or two, Hulio arrived, found a place to sit, and also listened. Finally Tom turned the 3-V off.

Derek waved his hand angrily at the set. "What's up with all this insanity, Tom? All of a sudden everyone in the world is going bonkers and it all seems to be aimed at us."

"Yeh, Tom," Beowulf seconded Derek's sentiment. "One day we're scientific titans and entrepreneurial heroes admired by everyone and the next we're being condemned in the legislature, picketed everywhere, and attacked by a mob in front of our building. I've never seen the worm turn like this!"

Tom shook his head. "It amazes me, too. But you'll remember, I've said repeatedly that we were going to upset a lot of people and make enemies. I've been expecting some kind of reaction, but maybe not this soon. All of this does seem awfully . . . organized... coordinated . . . and sudden. Before we try to sort it out, though, let me make a couple of phone calls. Buzz is already on his way, I think, and it might help to put a few more heads together here."

Picking up his vid phone, Tom called Parker Freeman. It only took a couple of minutes to get Parker's report. Tom hung up, and then turned to the others. "Some good news. Parker says the picketing at the airports is peaceful, so far. They're letting passengers go through their lines. The picketers are airline pilot and baggage-handler union members, but not any of *our* baggage-handlers. Basically, people who are worried about being displaced as we keep expanding. It's apparently having some effect. Parker says cancellations and no-shows are up, but not really much, so we're okay, so far. How about our freight operations, Hulio? Maria said your operations managers have been calling in all morning."

"That's one reason I skipped the meeting this morning, boss," Hulio responded. "They started calling not long after you, me, and Beowulf got up here. So far there's no violence at the dock teleport chambers either. The Longshore picketers don't really seem to have their hearts in it, and they're not interfering with operations. I think they're smart enough to see we've been hiring as many people as we've put out of work as we've expanded. The ones picketing just seem to be following orders, putting on a show. And like the airports, none of *our* employees are involved. We're paying 'em premium wages and treating them well. A lot of them dropped their union membership when they went to work for us. I think that's half or more of what has the union leaders upset. But it's a little different story out at the APS operations. Those pilots are threatened with big job losses and they're mad. Things are tense, and the APS honchos are worried."

Tom nodded grimly. "Okay. Keep a close eye on it. Let me know immediately if things turn any uglier. And as for things turning ugly, maybe we better sort out what happened here this morning, and how we're going to respond to it. First thing I want to know, Derek, is just when the picketers got here?"

"Not long before you did, Tom. Beowulf and I got here about ten to nine in my *Banshee,* and they were already forming up out front. They let us go down into the parking garage. When we got upstairs, we told Harry. We knew you were on the way from the airport, so Harry called the Galt Tower security office. They didn't have enough people to control the entrances downstairs, so he got their permission and headed down with everyone he could spare. Our big mistake, Tom, was not calling you and waving you off before you got there. For a while, though, they were just letting cars through. People kept coming up to work with no problem."

"Maybe next time you'll listen to me, Derek," Beowulf interjected. "I told you something might happen when Tom got here. It kept bugging me. That's why I decided to go down after Harry and his guys. Good thing I did"

Tom nodded. "A *very* good thing, Beowulf." Just then Maria buzzed the office to tell Tom that The Buzzard was there. Tom told her to send him in.

"I don't get it, Tom," Derek said. "What set that whole brawl off? You can't see anything from the network films. Beowulf says they were already starting to mob Harry's men when he got there and saw you jump out of the car and start charging up the ramp."

Tom shrugged. "I guess some of the picketers recognized me. One of them apparently hit the trunk of the car with his sign as we started down the ramp. I heard a thump. I looked back and Harry had one guy down. Then the whole bunch went after Harry and his men. I jumped out of the car and headed up to help and . . ."

Buzz opened the office door and walked in, found an empty chair and sat down just in time to hear Tom. He was aghast. "You did what? All morning Ah've been hearin' injured picketers say on national 3-V that you, Beowulf, and a hoard of 'Pinkerton Ninjas' attacked them. You mean to tell me it's *true?* Don't you two have a *lick* of sense? You know, don't you, that at least half a dozen of those people are gettin' ready to sue you, the guards, the company, the Pinkerton Agency, and everyone else they can put a name to? Public interest law firms are probably linin' up and biddin' down their *contingency* fees to get the cases! How am Ah supposed to deal with all that when most of mah attorneys are gonna be in court dealin' with Sony?"

For a moment Tom tried to speak and nothing came out. Then, "I don't know, but I'm telling you, Buzz, we didn't have much choice. If me, Beowulf, and the driver, Dalton, hadn't gotten back up there when we did, some of Harry's men might have been seriously injured and maybe even killed. As it was, we stopped the whole thing before anybody got badly hurt."

"Well," Beowulf smirked, "there is that guy with his face all scraped up. I don't know what Harry did to him, but it was effective. And that guy I threw who rolled twice and banged his head on the ramp abutment isn't feeling too good either."

"Anyway," Hulio said, "what's the big deal, Buzz? There certainly wasn't any *hoard* of guards. We were way outnumbered. And *everything* our side did, we did strictly in self-defense."

Buzz was dubious, to the point of snideness. "And you can prove this in court just *how?*"

"Well," Hulio thought for a moment, and then looked chagrined as he suddenly remembered, "I recorded the whole thing."

At least three voices spoke at once. "You what?"

"I recorded the whole thing. Out the back window of the car." Then he pulled his NanoPod out of his pocket. "Forgot all about it until just now."

The others looked at each other, and then Derek spoke. "Can we put this up on your 3-V, Tom?"

Tom nodded. Hulio quickly removed the visual recording data chip from his NanoPod. In a moment, they had it inserted into the 3-V, and for the next few minutes they played Hulio's twenty-second recording over several times in slow motion. Hulio had a high quality Texas Instruments NanoPod and the translation software in the 3-V had no trouble reformatting the data. After the third time through, Buzz was satisfied.

"Mr. Sanchez," he said, "you just put about ten years back on mah life that Ah thought Ah'd lost when Ah heard about the fracas this morning. First thing you do, Tom, is put this up on the UTT web site where everybody can see it. And Ah mean now! Then you send copies to the networks. Then Ah want a copy. This will take the wind right out of their sails. You just saved your company a lot of money, Mr. Sanchez. You otta get a bonus!" The others nodded enthusiastic agreement.

Hulio extracted the recording chip from the 3-V recording receptacle and headed out of the office. "I'll take this down to Sean. It's as good as done. I'll see that you get your copy, Buzz."

"Wait a minute, Hulio," Tom stopped him. "There was an MPPD detective waiting for me by Maria's desk when our meeting ended. He wanted our statements. I told him that we had some things to deal with first, but that you and I would write ours up this afternoon and have them delivered to him by courier. So, do yours as soon as you're done downstairs, and send it up to Derek's office. That means you better do one, too, Beowulf, since you were involved. And everybody be strictly accurate."

When the door closed after Hulio, Tom looked at Buzz. "We heard something on the 3-V just before you got here about the California Senate holding hearings on safety and environmental issues relating to teleportation. I didn't hear the whole report. Do you know what that's about, Buzz?"

Buzz shook his head in amazement. "Tom, Ah'd like to know what in the world was so important and kept you so busy this mornin' that you didn't hear any of this. You're just findin' out now? Particularly after what you went through just tryin' to get to work? Ah've been callin' all mornin' and haven't been able to get through to you."

"I learned something while I was in New Mexico yesterday," Tom told him. "A possible breakthrough application of my work that some of Dan Hargrove's people at Nucleonic came up with."

"He's not kidding," Derek added, as Beowulf nodded agreement. "It could be just as big as teleportation. It took Tom all morning to get the basic ideas across to us and map out an attack on the problem."

"Well," Buzz said, contemplating this. "Ah guess, then, you didn't hear about the Governor's speech on the threedevision last night either?"

"Just a brief mention on the news is all I've heard," Tom said. "What was it about?"

"Paranoid nonsense, mostly," Derek said before Buzz could answer. "Beowulf and I listened to part of it, Tom. He made a bunch of ridiculous allusions to unspecified public safety and health hazards from teleportation that somehow urgently had to be dealt with. He quoted a few loony claims that have been made by the usual crazies over the internet in the last few weeks. Then he mixed in some exaggerated Luddite fears about job loss and economic turmoil. We almost laughed ourselves sick, it was so stupid. But after a while it stopped being funny, and we just turned it off."

"So the legislature took him seriously?" Tom asked. "That's what this is about?"

"No, of course not, Tom," Buzz responded. "That's just what the public is supposed to *think* it's about. But it doesn't matter what the real motive is, for now. Let those people have their way, and UTT could lose a lot of money. If California decides to regulate teleportation heavily, other states could follow and compliance could be extremely costly. You're gonna have to defend yourselves at the hearin's."

Tom nodded. "I can do that. Right from the first, we've been keeping an eye out for safety problems and environmental effects. As near as we can tell, there *aren't* any of significant magnitude. It won't take me long to put the data we have together and make that case. I'll go up to Sacramento and testify. If you can spare one lawyer, it might help."

"Take a couple of Harry's Ninjas with you, too, will you, Tom?" Beowulf asked. Everyone guffawed briefly.

"Seriously," Tom said, "unless there really is genuine data we've missed somewhere on some important downside to teleportation, we shouldn't have much trouble making this look like the nonsense it almost certainly is. Since the picketing hasn't affected our ability to operate, my guess is, we won't even see our stock price fall much. But that's precisely what makes me think that there must be more behind this than we know, and maybe there's another shoe getting ready to drop."

Just then Maria buzzed Tom from the outer office. "Yes, Maria," Tom responded.

"Sir, Marlon Gates is calling again. He's on line one."

"Oh. I'd almost forgotten. Okay, I'll take it, Maria." He connected line one. "Marlon. I guess you've seen everything that's going on. Maria told me you called several times. I'm sorry I haven't gotten back sooner, but I've been busy. I'm here with Derek, Beowulf, and Buzz, trying to sort things out and come up with a strategy. What can I do for you?"

"Tom. I'm glad to see you're okay. Apparently you weren't hurt in that fracas you had over there. Say, I got a disturbing call from Lew Edleston about two hours ago. He told me something that might help explain a lot of this. Maybe you should put this conversation on speaker. Buzz and your guys need to hear this, too."

"Marlon has something he wants us all to hear," Tom said as he switched the phone to speaker. "All right, we're ready here, Marlon."

"Lew says he got a call from Bill Braxon this morning. I don't know how much you follow state politics, but he's the Senate ALP Minority Leader in Sacramento. Braxon told Lew that Sam Clanton and several other prominent Democratic-Republican Party leaders on the hill are selling UTT stock short."

To Tom, it seemed that the blood drained from his face, and he suspected that the others could see his pallor. Derek and Beowulf's jaws both dropped open, but nothing came out. Apparently they knew what short-sales contracts were, and what it meant. Likewise, The Buzzard sat forward and looked at Tom in shock.

"Are. . . uh. . ." Tom started. "Was Braxon sure about this, Marlon? This isn't just third-hand rumor?"

Marlon could be seen on the screen, shaking his head. "No rumor. Apparently it's true. Lew sent me a list of the contracts that Bill had sent him. It has delivery dates, who bought and who sold, everything. I'm scanning them in and sending them over to your computer now."

Tom found the documents as they came in and immediately began printing off copies and distributing them. For a few seconds the four men read in shocked silence.

"Marlon," The Buzzard asked, "are you *positive* this isn't some kind of hoax? What we've got here might explain a lot it it's true, but this sort of thing is easy to fake. It's hard to imagine even someone as corrupt as Sam Clanton tryin' somethin' like this. How did Bill Braxon get this stuff?"

"Braxon apparently got it from a CLRS researcher named Jefferson, Jim Jefferson, I think. Lew said Jefferson got it from some friends he had in the forward exchange," Marlon responded. "That's round about enough that I wondered myself if there was something funny going on, maybe even disinformation of some sort. But it's genuine. I've been calling around, tapping my own sources."

"What's the CLRS?" Beowulf asked.

"I think that refers to the California Legislative Research Service," Tom answered. "It's a staff agency that does economic research and compiles certain types of data for the legislature."

"Right," Marlon said. "But this isn't all of it. My contacts tell me Governor Slanghorn has also sold large amounts of UTT stock he doesn't own forward. Apparently they've been setting all of this up over the last several weeks."

Derek thought he saw it now. "By 'all of this,' Marlon, I guess you mean Slanghorn's speech, the demonstrations, the picketing, the hearings, all of it."

"And more," Marlon answered.

"More?"

"More. Exactly what, I don't know, but more. Think of what's happened so far as Fort Sumpter, or better, Pearl Harbor, with the invasion of the Philippines still to come. We're in a war, gentlemen, and we're going to have to take it to the enemy."

"Well, at least," Tom said with determination in his voice, "we know now who they are, and what they're after."

"Right," Derek added, "and we know who some of our allies are."

Tom nodded. "And that all helps."

*   *   *

Joe Bender came back upstairs at about three-thirty, still sporting his bruises and abrasions and carrying his sign. "Well, boss," He told Harry, "the only thing those guys know, or think they know, is that teleportation is another example of giant corporations ravaging the environment, destroying human health, and throwing people out of work. But something bigger is going on, because there are several different groups down there, all brothers under the skin, but the line troops were all surprised to see the others show up. They hadn't been told there was a coordinated effort going on. I talked to a couple of the leaders - just hinted I was with one of the other groups and they didn't know better - but they were pretty closed mouth. So, I guess I can't add much to what we already know. I had fun, though. They all thought I was one of them that got stomped by us, instead of one of us that got stomped by them. I'm a sort of a local hero with some of them now. You want I should keep playing that angle?"

Harry thought about it. "We'll see. For now, you're late getting off duty. Head home and rest up. You've done a good job, and I'm sorry you took a beating. I'll see there's a bonus in it for you."

It was nearly four p.m. before Harry got in to see Tom. Apparently, Tom had been in a meeting with Derek, Beowulf, and the lawyer the Skeleton Crew guys called The Buzzard. Those men were just coming out of the office as he arrived. He nodded as they passed him on the way to their own offices, they exchanged a few words, and Beowulf gave him a thumbs-up sign as he and Derek went down the hall.

Tom was waiting at the office door and hailed Harry in. Inside, He stood, hat in hand, even after Tom sat back in his office chair and motioned to him to take a seat.

"Harry," Tom asked, "weren't you limping a bit this morning?"

"Yes, sir, I was, just a little. One of the guys Dalton threw hit my knee with his leg when he landed. It's okay now, though, just a little bruised."

"Good. Maria said you had some security concerns to talk to me about?"

"Yes, sir, but. . . Derek and Beowulf just said that Mr. Adobo recorded our fiasco this morning."

"Yeh. Out the back window of the car. And I wouldn't call it a fiasco, at all, particularly after seeing Phil's recording. You and the rest of us acted completely appropriately, and we can prove it. Pretty soon it'll be up and running on our web site. We're sending copies to the media."

Harry sighed. "Well, that's a relief, sir, given what the networks have been showing and saying. But, in retrospect, I think I should have done things differently. I want to apologize for not thinking to call and warn you off. I was preoccupied with deciding how to secure the building and getting my guys downstairs. If I'd diverted you in time, the whole thing might not have happened. And having made that mistake, I probably shouldn't have taken that first guy down. Then you wouldn't have had to charge up there, save our butts, and get your face on national 3-V in the middle of a brawl."

Tom shook his head and chuckled. "Don't worry about it, Harry. That guy didn't give you much choice. Hindsight is always twenty-twenty. The best any of us can do is learn from our mistakes. Don't ever ask me to list all the goofs the Crew and I made trying to invent matter transmission before we got it right. Anyway, the only thing you and I have to worry about is what we do next."

Harry nodded, relieved. "On that matter, sir, I called the office and told them to send a dozen more men down for the duration. I can cancel that request if you want, but I think we need them. Things are still tense down on the street. With the networks whipping up resentment, we might even see more demonstrators show up tomorrow or the next day. Right now I'm borrowing off-duty men from other jobs around here and paying them overtime. We can't do that for long."

"What?" Tom joked lamely. "A dozen more 'Ninja Pinkertons'? What'll the networks say about that? Heck, if you think we need 'em, get twenty, Harry. Get as many as you need. By the way, apologize to your nephew for me. It was my decision to bail out of that car. I don't want him feeling guilty over it. He can drive me any time. And tell him I'm glad he jumped out and pitched in. It helped a lot. Anything else?"

Harry hesitated. "Just one, sir. I hate to do it with this all going on now, but I have to go upstate for a few days. The 'Frisco office called me last night. They're sending me to Sacramento to oversee a rather nasty investigation going on there. While I'm gone, they're sending an officer named Juaqine Menendez down to take over here. He goes by 'Jack'. Here's his file. He's a veteran with the agency. We hired him away from the military Special Forces. You'll like him, sir. He's one of Ishi's students, too. I should be back in about a week or ten days."

*   *   *

Gina and Heather got home just in time for supper with the family. Rachael had fixed creamed potatoes and peas, with pork roast, salad, and a banana cream pie for dessert. These were all among Gina's favorite foods. Rachael fretted when Gina, still a bit disturbed by the events of the day, only picked at her supper. Heather, with the voracious appetite and constitution of a teenager, ate both her own and half of Gina's portions. Adam had been doing surgery all day, and

Rachael hadn't heard the news either, so Gina and Heather told them everything that had been happening. Both Adam and Rachael expressed concern about Gina being so centrally involved

"Well, I really haven't tried to be, and nobody other than Bill, Lew Edleston, and a few others, knows that I have been," she told them.

Rachael pursed her lips and shook her head slowly. "These things have a tendency to come out, Gina, darling. You've got to be careful when you're dealing with people like them."

"Oh, come on, Rachael," Adam said, "You can't expect her to sit back and do nothing when she learns things like that! On the other hand, your mother's right, Gina, you have to be careful. Anyway, you've got me intrigued, so I'm going to go watch the news."

Against her protests, Gina and Amanda sent Rachael in with her husband and started clearing the dishes, swishing most of the detritus off, and packing them in the dishwasher. They were nearly done when Adam came back into the kitchen.

"Hey, kids. I don't get it. They're talking a lot about the proposed State Senate hearings and the picketing at UTT's teleport chambers, but they're not saying anything about any 'riot' at the Galt Tower."

Gina couldn't believe it. "What? Are you sure, Pop?"

Gina and Heather both followed Adam back into the living room to see what was happening. Sure enough, local news coverage focused almost entirely on the morning's State Senate action and the picketing at

UTT's airport gates, APS shipping points, and the dock chambers.   Only brief mention was given of a demonstration at the Galt Tower, with the barest hint that some kind of disturbance had occurred.   The national news spent a couple of minutes on coverage of the California Senate action and the picketing before turning to other national events.   Nothing was said either nationally or locally about a 'Menlo Park Massacre,' or any kind of 'riot' at the Galt Tower, as the networks had been calling it earlier.

Gina was mystified. Something had changed to mute the tone and coverage of the disturbance severely, and she didn't know what. She said as much to Adam and Rachael and excused herself to go boot up her computer and check the internet. Once she did, it didn't take long to find out what had happened. Virtually every web site dealing with political or economic issues was showing a recording of the Galt Tower incident that had been taken from *inside the car* that started down the ramp just before the brawl between the demonstrators and the guards broke out. The picture was perfectly clear except for a period of about two seconds when the driver apparently braked to a stop, and whoever was doing the recording was thrown into the back of the front seats, so that the camera bounced up and down and nothing but the car roof and back seat could be seen until he focused again. The recording completely exculpated the guards.

Gina was too fascinated to even notice that Adam and Heather had joined her and were looking over her shoulder as she watched the guard captain - actually a lieutenant whom some of the bloggers had identified as Harold Pinkerton - be viciously attacked. Almost casually he took his attacker down with some kind of intricate jujitsu move, which generated an angry surge of the demonstrators. She watched in horror as one guard was knocked down, kicked, and punched by multiple assailants. The other guards began backing up and frantically trying to block punches and kicks. Then, two men could be seen through the back window running up the garage ramp from the right side of the car, along with a huge blond man on the left side, to tear into the mob about to overwhelm the guards.

What Gina saw then astonished her even more. The man in the center of the three seemed to move through the assailants like a whirlwind, spinning off everyone he touched head over heels in different directions, all with the speed of lightning and the grace of a ballet dancer. Then, the others got there and began adding their own similar skills and energy to the fight. Suddenly the recording ended, possibly because the man making it had decided to go help his friends. But the bloggers, using enhancement software, had identified two of the three men who charged up the ramp to join the fray. Their pictures had been on 3-V more than once before, and even recently in a national news magazine. The big blond guy was Thad "Beowulf" Thorsen, one of the engineers on the original team that had developed teleportation, and the one in the middle was Thomas Alvin Wright himself.

*   *   *

Samuel Hamilton Clanton had a bitter taste in his mouth as he watched the news in the study of his condominium about the same time Gina was. Charise was puttering around out in the kitchen, looking for something to eat. Sam had not found time for her services earlier in the day, as sometimes happened in the press of Senate business, and had told her to come over for the evening. But right now he was not in the mood. All day things had been going well. The unions had sent their men to picket as planned. The environmental groups, public safety, and consumer organizations were doing their part. Sam and the others had been delighted by the brouhaha at the Galt Tower. It had happened just in time for Sam and the other majority party leaders in the California Senate to use in their call for a committee to investigate teleportation. They had not planned on generating overt violence at UTT headquarters. That had happened all by itself, much to their glee. It was icing on the cake, and their friends in the media had been playing it to the hilt, spinning it to generate as much public resentment of UTT as possible. And how sweetly ironic it was that UTT had actually hired the *Pinkerton* Agency to provide their security services. Pinkertons! Even in this day and age many people still remembered the historic role of the Pinkerton Agency in helping suppress the union movement in its infancy. Yes, everything was going their way, almost like clockwork.

Up until now. Now something had happened. The picketing of UTT passenger and freight chambers at the commercial and private airports and the docks was still being covered, but news of the brutal attack at the Galt Tower by the martial arts trained Pinkertons and the many innocent protesters injured, was being suppressed, and Sam did not know why. He reached over to pick up his vid phone and stopped suddenly, because it buzzed with an incoming call. Seeing who was calling, he picked it up.

"Jake. Just the man I want to talk to."

"I'll bet I know why, Sam. Have you seen the news in the last half-hour?"

"Yes. They've stopped showing any of the Galt Tower footage any more, or covering the story at all. Do you know why, Jake?"

"If you really want to know, Sam, go to the UTT web site, or almost any political site on the web, and you'll find out in a hurry."

"Don't jerk me around, Jake," Sam responded angrily, "I don't have time for it. Just tell me what the hell's going on!"

"Well, it turns out that really was Wright himself in that car that went down the ramp, and he really did take part in the guard assault, just as the news hawks have been saying."

"Then why have they taken the whole thing off?"

"Well, Sam, somebody in the car was recording everything from a NanoPod through the back window, and it shows our demonstrators starting the whole fight, just like that Pinkerton officer said."

Jake waited for several seconds for Sam to respond in some way, but Sam said nothing, apparently not knowing what to say, so Jake continued: "It's worse than that, Sam. Wright and the Pinkertons actually look like some kind of heroes on that film. You really need to go to the web and see it. The networks are actually doing the best they can by taking the whole story off the air. That recording is all over the web, and the networks can't show it without making themselves look like fools for everything they've been saying all day. They're hoping it'll all just go away. I don't think they'll manage, but we better hope they do."

Again Sam remained still and silent, long enough that Jake was beginning to wonder if he was having a stroke or something, but finally Sam spoke. "This doesn't change anything. We can't expect everything to fall our way. We'll just have to adjust, Jake. Are the demonstrators ready for the capital when the hearings start next Monday?"

"Yes. But you really have to see that recording, Sam. You don't know what that man Wright can do, and you are not going to believe me if I tell you unless you see it for yourself!"

"Are the unions gonna hold tough?"

"Yes. You were right, when you said this afternoon that their resolve might even stiffen when they heard Wright had actually hired Pinkertons."

"How about Hoffer?"

"He's still on our leash, Sam. Ready to move when we tell him."

Sam nodded grimly once, his eyes as hard as steel. "Then we're still on track."

Chapter 25: Ninja Pinkertons and Unexpected Allies

"It's my turn to drive this morning," Beowulf said as he and Derek went out the front door of their apartment and down the steps. It promised to be a beautiful day, with only a hint of the morning haze typical of Menlo Park, which nearly always burned off by noon anyway. The air was fresh with a light sea breeze, the sky was heart-achingly blue, and the California sun was shining through the foliage.

"All right," Derek responded. "But are you sure you want to drive your El Zorro *Blade* through that crowd at the building? Remember what happened to the company car yesterday."

"Yeh, well," Beowulf chortled, "Tom, Harry, Dalton and I taught 'em a lesson about that, didn't we? I bet they're meek as lambs today. Particularly the way Phil's video was all over the net last night. Besides, Harry's men will be out in force this morning."

"You might be overconfident, Beowulf," Derek said as he opened the passenger front door of the El Zorro and slid into the shotgun seat. "Some of those guys might be looking for payback."

Beowulf pulled out into the street, drove down the block, and turned right at the corner. In a couple of minutes he stopped in front of Billi Jo's place. Billi Jo was waiting. She greeted Derek as he stepped out of the El Zorro. He held the door and closed it behind her after she slid into the bucket seat next to Beowulf, then he got in back. After a quick and affectionate smooch between Beowulf and Billi Jo that made Derek a little jealous, they were on their way. They hit most of the traffic lights right and in only a few minutes were within sight of the Galt Tower.

The ranks of the anti-teleportation protesters had already formed up, in numbers easily as great as before, and they were milling around on the sidewalks in front of the building with their signs, along with several groups of 3-V network reporters. Beowulf was right in both of his predictions, though for the wrong reason. First, the crowd of protesters was notably subdued, and second, lines of Pinkerton men controlled the entrances, buttressed by several Galt Tower Security personnel. At least a squad of MPPD officers was also present. What was unanticipated, however, and actually appeared far more responsible for the apparently subdued attitudes of the protesters, was that there was another crowd about half as large on the other side of the street, which appeared to be picketing them! This group had signs with mostly hand-scrawled messages such as ECOFREAKS GO HOME, FREE TELEPORTATION NOW, and even NINJA PINKERTONS ROCK. Indeed, the MPPD squad seemed more concerned with keeping those two groups apart than with separating the protesters and the guards.

Amazed at this development, Beowulf powered his window down to get a clear view just before he turned toward the garage entrance, slowing almost to a stop to let the demonstrators move out of the way. Harry's men who were there moved forward and the protesters sullenly parted to let the car through. At the same time, many of the counter-demonstrators, more than a few of whom appeared to be good-looking young women, recognized Beowulf and began jumping up and down and cheering. One of them even jiggled coyly and blew him a kiss. Billi Jo leaned over and elbowed him in the side, none too gently. "Keep your eyes on your driving, buster," she said sweetly, but firmly.

*   *   *

Bill Braxon spent most of the morning on the phone in the inner office. Gina kept herself busy doing cleanup work on a legislative statistical analysis she had been running, while ducking for a minute or two every half hour or so to the CNABC or EAGLE/FOX web sites to see what was happening. About eleven, however, Ly buzzed her and told her the Senator wanted to see her. She grabbed a pen and pad to take along. Apparently Bill had also summoned Spider and Dex, since they were headed the same direction at the same time.

"Gina, have you seen the recording of the fight between the demonstrators and the UTT people in Menlo Park yesterday that's been all over the internet?" Dex asked. "I don't mean the network clips, but the one that one of UTT's people took from inside the company car?"

When Gina grinned and nodded that she had, he continued, waving his hands as he spoke. "I never saw anything so amazing. First time I saw it, I almost thought I was watching an old Kung-Fu movie or something. Now the networks literally don't have a thing to say!"

"It's worse than that," Spider contributed, with more than a little glee. "This morning counter-protesters started showing up at the airports and picketing the picketers! Incoming teleportation passengers have been borrowing signs and joining in. I hear they even had some counter- demonstrators over at headquarters. Clanton and his sycophants must be spitting nails!"

At the door, Dex knocked and led them in at the Senator's request.

Bill looked a bit haggard for this early in the day, but resolute, as he waved them to seats and told them to make themselves comfortable.

"Well, it looks like the hearings of the Senate Special and Select Committee on Teleportation Hazards are going to begin on Monday," he began.

"Isn't that a little soon?" Spider asked, surprised. "How are we going to line up people to testify, prepare to question their witnesses, and everything. Do it over the weekend?"

"We argued that point," Bill said. Then he picked a set of paper packets off his desk and handed one each to the three of them. "Clanton and his guys won't listen. They're claiming the threats of teleportation are too important to delay. I think pressuring us that way is part of their strategy. They already have all their

412

witnesses prepared, while we'll have to hustle to put anything together. It's obvious they've been working on this for some time. Here's their witness list, on page four."

"These people are almost all union leaders and technophobes, Bill," Dex said as he scanned the list. "Environmental radicals, public safety fanatics, and other professional pessimists!"

"That's right," Bill nodded. "Their witnesses on employment and industrial issues are going to go first, and take the first couple of days. Then we get a day of our witnesses, before the focus shifts to public safety issues, and it's the same rotation. Two days for their witnesses and one for ours. Then next Monday, we bring in Tom Wright and some of his technical people and whoever else we can think of in the meantime. I've been on the phone with Mr. Wright this morning, and he's anxious to help. Seems to be a nice guy.

"By the way, Gina," Bill continued, "he put me in touch with Marlon Gates over the weekend. Gates is senior partner in the investment-banking firm that floated their IPO, and now he's chairman of UTT's board of directors. His sources in the investment community confirm everything you got from Jim Jefferson, and more. As we suspected, Slanghorn is in on it. There might be others, too."

This enraged Spider. "Why not go public right now with what we know, Bill? Since we know this whole thing is a hoax, why not tell the public? That might generate enough voter pressure to kill this whole charade, and maybe even get an ethics committee investigation of Clanton and his cronies!"

"Well," Bill started, but then thought for a moment as he chose his words, "Hally's been arguing that way. I suspect we might have to, eventually. Roger and I are working up a bill of charges for the ethics committee and a statement for a news conference. But we want to walk softly and play the RepubliCrat's game for at least a while. For one thing, consider the fact that it might *not* be seen as a hoax by the unions or other groups involved. Oh, a few of their key players might be knowingly involved with the Clanton clan, but most are probably being lied to themselves. But they won't believe that if they're told. Besides, it is possible that there really *are* one or more large unknown hazards from teleportation. It's a new technology, and no technology is perfectly safe. Mr. Wright tells me their people haven't found any significant risk factors at all, and the few trivial ones they have found they've minimized further by every technical means they could.

"The point though, is that *Clanton and his gang might have entered into those short-sale contracts precisely because they found out about some genuine safety risk or environmental hazard that nobody else knows about.* That would still be unethical on their part, but an expose' won't have much bite in that case. As of right now, Rog and I have convinced Hally it's better to go at least a few days into the hearings, particularly the part dealing with public safety issues, and see what their hand really is, before we play that card. Mr. Wright agrees."

Gina found her heart thumping and her palms sweating as she thought about Tom Wright coming to the capitol for the hearings, and she was disturbed by how much she had to struggle, with only partial success, to focus her mind back on the issues and strategy under discussion. "Could I please attend, sir?" She blurted out. "The hearings, that is?"

Dex, Spider, and Bill all looked at her somewhat curiously. "Well," Bill said, "that's why I asked you in here, Gina. I need you there. I'm going to have to manage everything else going on, and Dex will be running this office. We've put six of our sharpest ALP people on the committee, including Hally, who insisted. I need you to advise them on all the economic issues. The hearings will run two hours in the morning and two in the afternoon every day, so you'll have to tear yourself away from dissertation work for a while, but I need you there. And you go, too, Kyle, to be a gopher for Gina and to keep me informed."

*   *   *

Harry Pinkerton, wearing a suit and tie designed to blend in with the legislators and staff people at the capitol, followed Charise Meardon at a discrete distance, out of the building and down the steps in front. He paused part way down, put on his sunglasses, and scanned traffic while she waited for a taxicab to pull up and got in. Then he walked the rest of the way down the steps and got into the front seat of the late model delivery van that pulled up in front to collect him.

"She came from the Senator's office all right, Rod," he said to the driver, a medium built man with unkempt dishwater-blond hair and thick glasses. "I see what you mean about how hard it would be to get in there. Could be done some night, but it wouldn't be easy with Capitol security the way it is. Let's see where she goes now."

The driver pulled the van out into traffic and followed the cab, about half a block behind. Harry pulled a file out of the big van console and scanned it as Rod drove.

"Did you and Pete have any trouble getting the equipment out of Clanton's condo this morning?" He asked Rod.

"No, sir," Rod responded. "In and out with all the goods in fifteen. He won't even know we were there 'till he sees it in court, or we show him."

"Did you get what you wanted?" Harry asked.

"Yes. All of the bank records off his computer, and a recording of him doing Charise in glorious color and three dimension. Boy, do I hate looking at that stuff. We really need to hire voyeurs for that part."

Harry grinned. "Hazards of the game, Rod. Sign on for private detective work and most of the time you end up looking at people's dirty laundry. Or worse. Still, you've got to admit this isn't your typical case. For one thing, we seldom get to investigate powerful state Senators. Usually that only happens in the dime novels. And for another, we don't usually have somebody we don't know doing most of our work for us."

Rod took his eye off the taxicab now about three cars in front of them long enough to glance over at Harry. "Are we going to try to find out who that was, Harry?"

Harry sighed. "I'm still thinking. It isn't as if we don't have clues, but it depends on how much trouble and expense that appears to be. Making that decision is one reason the office sent me up here. Mrs. Clanton's instructions are pretty clear. She doesn't want us looking into that, and won't pay us to do so. I have a suspicion, though, that it might be useful to know. There's kind of a disturbing peripheral connection to another job we have."

Rod knew better than to ask what job that was, but he thought he knew. He listened to the news, and was well aware that Samuel Hamilton Clanton was one of the principals behind the upcoming teleportation hearings, and that the Pinkerton Agency was doing UTT's security work.

"By the way, sir," he grinned, "you looked good on the 3-V. All that training with Ishi and Wright paid off big."

Harry looked and felt mortified. "Having my face on national 3-V just makes it harder for me to do my job."

"Say, Harry," Rod asked, "what is Tom Wright really like, anyway?"

Harry squinted at Rod for a moment. "You've heard of someone having a mind like a steel trap? Focused, powerful, penetrating?"

"Yeh. I've known some. You're a bit like that yourself, Harry."

"Well, men with minds like that only dream of having one like Tom Wright has. But the amazing thing is, behind that, he's just a regular guy, who likes people and takes what time he can to have fun. And he's an even better Aikidoka than Ishi."

Rod shook his head in amazement, and then pointed down the street ahead to the cab. "She's going home to her place," he said to Harry, "not back to the Senator's. Most of the time she does that."

Harry closed the file. "Okay. No mystery there. File says you've already been in there and copied her bank book. We know she's depositing her staff salary and withdrawing half in cash within the next day or two. The scatterbrain even labeled them 'Clanton'. And since his records show regular deposits of the same amount a day or two after her withdrawals, we're in like Flynn on that score. Break off and let's drive over to Aphrodite Associates. I want at least one look at the place."

Rod turned at the next light and headed across town. "Why are we doing all this, Harry? We've got signed statements from three of Sam's disgruntled ex-lovers, plus what we collected last night. Don't we already have everything Mrs. Clanton needs?"

"Sure, if all she wanted was a divorce. We've got more than enough for that, now. But apparently she wants everything hinted at in the information packet sent to her to be brought to light, if it's true. Call it revenge; call it social conscience, or whatever. I don't know since I haven't talked to her yet myself. But she's willing to pay, so we're going to do what we can."

They rode in silence for several minutes until Rod pulled into a parking space across from Aphrodite Associates. Harry was amazed. It was a large, beautiful two story building in modern Spanish architecture surrounded by lush, sculpted grounds. Several grounds keepers could be seen working on the greenery and the place looked busy, even though most of its business probably occurred at night.

"Now there's a business that has come up in the world," Harry noted. "So you got a good look around inside?"

"Yeh," Rod nodded. "We got the basic architectural plans from down town. Once we looked them over, Pete just put on a suit and tie and walked in. He told 'em he was a podiatrist, in town for a convention we knew was going on, and he wanted to shop before renting a few of the girls for the closing celebration. We made up a fairly convincing medical ID for him. They took him around to see all the girls that weren't busy, and he memorized the whole layout."

"So how are you going to get a look at their employee list and financial records?"

"Well, we've considered several options. We could try to get some of the girls to roll over. There's bound to be one or two a little miffed at the special treatment Ms. Meardon has been getting the last couple of years anyway. But that's risky and likely to take too long. So we thought we could go in like customers again, but with a pea shooter and an adhesive smoker button we could stick up on one of their fire alarms. Or maybe we could just call in an anonymous bomb threat. Either one should give us about ten minutes alone with their computers, which is all we'd need."

"Night or day?" Harry asked.

"I'm thinking night," Rod answered. "Lots of people there. Easy to get lost among the other customers running for the exits and make our way to their business office."

Harry nodded. "I notice they don't seem to have any real security on their parking garage. How 'bout we just drive in, call in the bomb threat, do our stuff, go back down to the garage afterwards, and drive away with everybody else?"

"We?" Rod asked, wide-eyed.

"Right," Harry affirmed. "I don't have enough excitement in my life. I'm going in with you guys."

*   *   *

Eleven lawyers from Byrd, Rand, Epstein, and Ely, led by Buzz Byrd himself, marched into the Ninth District Federal Courtroom Friday morning, carrying their briefcases and almost, if not quite, in lockstep. None of them were cracking even a hint of a smile. Sony's attorneys were already there, watching Buzz's troops walk down the aisle and take their places on their side in front of the panel of judges. Buzz thought that, behind their stoic demeanors, the other side looked scared. *Good,* he thought. He intended to keep them that way.

*   *   *

"Sure seems inconvenient, having to fly up here on a Sunday evening just to go to a set of ridiculous hearings we could watch on 3-V instead," said Ron Beck, as he, Derek, and Dave picked up their rental car at the Sacramento Airport.   Ron was a young attorney employed by Byrd, Rand, Epstein, and Ely.

"I guess this is what you get for being a junior member of the firm," Dave responded as they stuffed their bags in the trunk. "I know you'd rather be with your guys in Federal Court, but like The Buzzard said, we really do need somebody with legal expertise with us at the hearings, even if none of our people will be testifying for some time. Anyway, once we get to the hotel, you'll be able to go upstairs in the evenings, talk with your friends, and find out what's happening in court."

"I guess all I'm saying is you guys could have put a teleport chamber in this airport," Ron said, "and saved us all the flight."

"We *are* building one here," Derek said defensively, taking the keys from the lot attendant and walking around to get in on the driver's side of the car, "but it won't be done for a couple of weeks. We walked right past the UTT gate. Didn't you notice?"

"I was thinking of other things, I guess," Ron said as he got in on the other side of the car. Dave started the engine and headed away from the airport for the twelve-mile drive into the city.

"Do you know where the Sacramento Westmark is, Derek?" Dave asked. At Tom's request, the local Westmark Inn had been more than glad to give Dave, Ron, Derek, and the Byrd, Rand, Epstein, and Ely lawyers an extremely good deal on rooms. Installing teleport chambers in five of its hotels had already turned out to be very, very good business for the chain, and the Westmark Inns Corporation had been trying very hard to contract with UTT to install chambers in the rest of its units, including the one in Sacramento.

"No. Nearly six years in California and I've never been up here. Tom said it's over in the new section of town, rebuilt after the Disorders, and only a few blocks from the new Capitol building."

"I was raised in Rio Linda," Ron said. "We used to come over here a lot. I can find it."

It wasn't quite that easy, but with a little backtracking they did manage to find the hotel, get registered, and to their rooms with all their bags. Derek used his NanoPod to call Tom to tell him they had gotten there and to check for any new developments. Then he walked down the hall, knocked on Dave's and Ron's doors and the three headed down to the hotel dining room.

The food in the dining room was good so they also had breakfast there the next morning, with several of Buzz's troops who came down to eat with them. The hearings were set to start at ten a.m., and they needed to be seated beforehand, so Derek, Dave and Ron parted company with the lawyers, who needed to be at

Federal Court, and they grabbed a cab, leaving the rental in the hotel parking garage.

"Are you sure you want to go there?" The cabby asked when they told him to take them to the capitol. "I went past earlier. A pretty nasty anti-teleportation mob showed up this morning because of those stupid Senate hearings. You know, I bought a few shares of that UTT stock, and it was going up like crazy. With all this, though, it stopped, and now I'm thinking about selling."

Dave and Derek glanced at each other as if each had been half anticipating something of the sort. "Yeh, let's go take a look anyway," Dave told the cabby. "They can't keep people out, and they don't know any of us from Adam."

The cabby was right about the crowd being nasty. There were at least a couple thousand of them, clearly in an angry mood, shaking their signs and chanting anti-teleportation slogans. From the signs, many of them appeared to represent various unions. The environmental crowd was also well represented. Obviously the effort to whip up public opposition to teleportation had been ramped up for the hearings. Local and national news people in numerous knots were making the most of it, filming and interviewing. The Sacramento police were out in force, though, and seemed to have things under control. The street was being kept clear enough that traffic could go by, albeit slowly, and aisles were being maintained for foot-traffic up or down the steps of the building. The three men had the cabby stop half a block away, and had no real trouble walking through the crowd and up into the capitol building, despite the palpable feeling of tension and intimidation.

At the security station inside they gave their names, picked up their passes to the hearings, got directions to the committee hearing room, and headed upstairs. The room was already filling up when they got there, with some people seated, others milling around, and six or eight State Senators at the table shuffling papers and adjusting microphones. Derek was surprised to also see at least three major network news crews setting up elevated 3-V cameras at propitious locations. He hadn't realized the hearings were to be quite that open. The security man at the door made them turn off and surrender their NanoPods, then pointed to their assigned seats, which the ALP leadership had arranged to be only two rows behind Senator Fred Macklin. The three men headed over.

Macklin, who came from a district down near San Diego, was one of the main ALP members on the committee. Tom had suggested that Dave make the Senator's acquaintance before the hearings started, and provide the Senator with any advice he could on any technical issues that might arise during the sessions. Macklin was glad to see them and took a moment to introduce them to the senator seated to his right at the table, Hally Arkwright, who was actually the senior ALP member on the committee, and one of the ALP leaders. Senator Arkwright, tall and slender, in her fifties, with short tan hair, welcomed them cordially and briefly discussed strategy with them. She seemed tense with anticipation and determination, however, much like a fighter about to go into the ring.

Derek, Ron, and Dave were just turning away to go sit down, when Dave noticed one of the most strikingly beautiful young brown-haired woman he had ever seen, sitting right behind Senator Arkwright, with several other staff aids. Dave guessed her age at two or three years less than his own. The woman, who had almond-shaped eyes with long lashes, noticed Dave's attention and flashed him a somewhat shy smile. He only got to enjoy the view for a moment, however, before the committee chair started banging his gavel and asking everyone to please take their seats in preparation for the start of the hearings. It was only about another minute before things quieted down. At ten a.m. on the dot, the chairman banged his gavel again and declared the California Special and Select Committee on Teleportation Hazards in session.

*   *   *

"I'm telling you, Tom, things went a lot better for us today than the networks are spinning it. A lot better." Derek was pacing back and forth in his room at the Westmark as he talked on his NanoPod, oblivious to the late afternoon sun that could be seen through the window on the west side of his room, still visible as a spray of pink on the western horizon, but quickly dissolving into the encroaching dusk.

"Those union guys were pretty well coached by their economists," he continued, "and I'd say some of their

425

projections of future job losses by their members weren't too far off the mark. But the ALP people didn't back down a bit. Every time their turn to question came, they tore into those guys. Pinned 'em down with questions about likely expanding employment by major manufacturers and retailers as we add chambers and transport costs fall. And they backed it up with some very good estimates and data. Arkwright and Macklin were particularly effective. They put those estimates we sent 'em on our own past and projected future employment and wage payment growth to good use. They even had some impressive numbers on employment growth by our major instate suppliers, including Hillsbrook and A.G.A."

"They didn't get that from us, did they?" Tom asked, somewhat surprised. "I don't remember having data on Hillsbrook and A.G.A."

"No. The ALP here must have some pretty sharp people doing research for 'em." Derek paused, and chuckled briefly. "Dave thinks it's some brunette bombshell he saw there. Says she kept passing papers to Hally Arkwright, who passed them on down to Macklin and the others. By the end of the day, the union guys were reduced to whimpering about 'the horrors of uncontrolled technical and industrial change'. The exec from the ocean shipper's cartel was even worse. It was almost embarrassing. Anybody there sure got a different picture than you're seeing on the national networks tonight. As near as I can tell those network people have cut all the really effective ALP parts out and are just running clips of the testimony by the union leaders and some of the softball-questions asked by the RepubliCrat Senators."

"Is anything more accurate likely to get out on the net, Derek?" Tom asked. "That could make it difficult for the networks to keep distorting things. You noticed, didn't you, that they caved in and actually ran Phil's recording a couple of times yesterday? CNABC even grudgingly admitted some of their early reporting had been a 'little' inaccurate."

Derek chuckled. "Yeh, I saw that. But we're not going to have something visual like that going for us at the hearings, Tom, unless someone managed to sneak in a NanoPod. They made everybody check 'em at the door. So the network visuals are all that there are. I did ask Senator Arkwright to send us an official transcript. We can post that on our web site. But that'll be a couple of days coming, and how many members of the general public are going to plow through something like that anyway?"

"Well," Tom said, "I don't think we need to worry about it, Derek. In this case the entropy law is working for us. Information spreads, and it spreads fast. All afternoon everyone who was there has been talking to people who weren't there. Despite the way the networks have been reporting today's hearings, I concluded several hours ago that we must have come out at least even, when our stock price didn't fall."

"It didn't?" It was Derek's turn to be surprised. "I would have thought the national news coverage of the protests in front of the capitol building would have made it go down some, even if the hearings didn't."

"No. Well, a little in the morning, but then back up in the afternoon. Actually ended up a few cents higher than yesterday's close. On the other hand, Derek, remember, we never planned to pay out any dividends before we get through our primary expansion phase, at least a year or two from now. Our stockholders have been earning their returns in capital gains. So, if our stock price stays flat, like it's been since this mess started, our investors really *are* losing money."

At that cheerless insight, Derek had to look for some consolation. "Well, at least a flat share price means Clanton and his crowd aren't going to make money either!"

"True," Tom said grimly. "Let's keep it that way."

Chapter 26: The Jaws Close

Wednesday morning, when Gina got to work, she was surprised to see that there were counter-demonstrators forming at the capitol. There were only a couple hundred when she arrived; a rather thin crowd so far in comparison to the anti-teleportation demonstrators, but more seemed to be arriving, to the consternation of the anti-teleportation group. Police resources were strained, since they not only had to maintain lanes for pedestrian traffic in and out of the building and auto traffic in and out of the parking garage, but also had to keep the two crowds apart. Surprisingly, the counter-demonstrators seemed almost as angry and militant as the anti-teleportation crowd. Gina thought the Internet reporting of the hearings the night before, which had been far more complete and accurate than the network reports, had a lot to do with it. The tension between the two groups in front of the capitol was palpable.

It took longer than normal, of course, but Gina managed to get her Hyundai into the parking terrace and herself to Senator Braxon's office without incident. Hurrying to her desk, she first deposited the materials she had been going over at home the night before and then began booting up her own computer. Gina often treasured the few quiet minutes before the office officially opened. Over the next half hour other members of Senator Braxon's staff, including Spider and Dex, filtered in, phones began ringing, and people began working.

"Hey, Gina," Spider wandered over and asked, "what do you think of that new mob outside? Can you believe it?"

Gina shook her head. "It's amazing, Spider. I don't really know what to think. On the one hand, I'm delighted that people are seeing through all this propaganda, and some are even willing to publicly express their support for teleportation. But on the other hand. . ."

"Yeh," Spider completed the thought. "With the mood out there, things could easily get out of control. A lot of people could get hurt."

"You're not kidding," Dex added as he walked up and handed Gina a sheaf of papers. "I hope the police can keep that from happening. Here's some data UTT faxed in just after you left for home yesterday, Gina. That transportation department economist is testifying first today. More stuff on economic dislocations I guess. Apparently UTT thought this data might help."

"Thanks, Dex," Gina said. "Bill said that was coming, and I've been watching for it."

At nine a.m. the Senator arrived and called Gina, Spider, and Dex into the office for a brief strategy session before Gina and Spider headed down to the hearing room. It was already about two-thirds full when Gina and Spider got there. Taking their places after checking in briefly with Senator Macklin and Hally Arkwright, Gina looked over to see the three men UTT had sent to keep an eye on the early days of the hearings. She knew their names, now, though she had not spoken to any of them personally. One was a lawyer named Ron Beck. The tall one was Derek Martin, Vice President of UTT, and, by reputation, one of the key engineers on the 'Skeleton Crew' - a term which had become widely known by the general public due to various publications and interviews with the principals - responsible for actually transforming teleportation theory into reality. The other, rather intense man was Dave Barret, one of the major physicists on the Crew. Both were relatively good-looking young men. But Tom Wright himself, the genius behind the theory, the man who intermittently rerouted Gina's train of thought to romantic and erotic destinations, was not present, not having been scheduled to testify until the following Monday.

"Last day of this nonsense," Spider whispered. "Then at least we get a day of *our* witnesses before we move on to public safety issues and find out if there's anything substantive behind this whole thing. My guess is that'll just turn out to be nonsense of a different sort. Then we can expose this whole . . ."

"Shhhhh!" Gina said suddenly, looking at Spider, who then glanced quickly around to see if anyone else had been listening, and looked properly chastened.

BANG, BANG, BANG. The committee chairman pounded his gavel repeatedly to get everyone's attention, and the sound echoed through the room. "Could everyone please take your seats so we can begin? Thank you. The Senate Special and Select Committee on Teleportation Hazards is now in session.   First to testify this morning will be the Honorable Dr. Leon Edmunds of the California Department of Transportation . . ."

By three p.m., when the gavel sounded ending the second session of the day, Gina felt almost physically drained. Constant tension and *attention* could do that. The testimony and questioning had gotten more than a little rancorous. The ALP Senators had tried to counter what they saw as ephemeral projections of statewide economic disaster based on little more than anecdotal incidents of employment and output loss from the expansion of teleportation with more systematic data showing not just benign effects on the state economy, but large net benefits. The RepubliCrat senators then accused them of engaging in selection bias themselves. For a while, the whole thing had almost turned into a brawl, with Hally Arkwright literally threatening to "come over and smack" one of the RepubliCrat Senators if he didn't stop interrupting her as she questioned a witness. The RepubliCrats clearly did not want the recent data on price trends for heavy freight that Hally had been citing, in counter to the initial statement of the witness, to be entered into evidence.

Spider seemed almost as tired out by the day's testimony and debate as Gina was. Upstairs, Bill was waiting for their report. He ushered them right into his office, where they spent some time going over the main points of the testimony and debate. Despite, and maybe even because of the angry turn the hearings had taken, Bill seemed satisfied that they had at least stayed even on things.

"Oh, by the way, Gina," Bill asked, "did that stuff UTT sent down help?"

"Yes sir, it did," she responded. "It's one of the things that got Senator Mendenhall upset with Hally."

"Good," Bill chuckled. "Not everything is going their way. I checked the news at noon, then went and poked my head out front for a look. There are almost as many counter-demonstrators out there now as there are in the anti-teleportation crowd. That's becoming the news now."

"Have you heard a stock report, sir?" Gina asked.

"UTT shares were down a dollar as of a few minutes ago, about the time the hearings adjourned, but there hasn't been any trend all day. Just looks like random-walk fluctuations to me."

"So far this is turning into a stalemate, Bill," Spider observed. "Seems to me like they're going to have to play their hole card pretty soon, if they've got one."

Bill agreed. "Right. I think something more's coming. I just don't know what it is. But at least we have our own hole card."

On that note the meeting ended, and Gina went back to her desk. She spent an hour or so with Spider and Dex, going over copies of the prepared statements the ALP witnesses planned to submit in the sessions the next day, trying to figure out the likely points of attack the RepubliCrats would make on them.

When it came time to go home, she was more than ready to do so. Tension was added to her tiredness as she drove out of the parking terrace and through the lanes being maintained by the police between the angry anti-teleportation protesters and counter-demonstrators. She relaxed somewhat, though, when she saw that the mood of the latter group had turned almost festive as their ranks had grown. Some of the anger of the protesters might well have been a reaction to that. All in all, she found it cheering; at least once she was away from the Capitol. By the time she was halfway home, she felt better yet. She was supposed to take Heather and Amanda to the high school tonight for a gymnastics workout. She was beginning to think that with a little rest and some supper, she might just be up to going.

She received something of a jolt, however, after she told the Hyundai computer to tune the radio to a local news station. It turned out Bill was right about the UTT stock price. The station reported that it had bounced around a little, but not changed much over the day. Following reports on the hearings, demonstrations, counter demonstrations, and of a refusal by the Ninth District Federal Court to dismiss UTT's lawsuit against Sony Electrodynamics, however, there was brief mention of a bomb threat made the night before to a business downtown in the city. The building had been emptied for some time until the police bomb squad had arrived and conducted a thorough search. No bomb had been found. The business was Aprodite Associates.

Gina felt the short hairs on the back of her neck stand up. *I wonder what that was about,* she thought, *and whether I caused it.*

*   *   *

Charise Meardon was also disturbed by the report of the bomb threat at Aphrodite Associates, as she listened to a local news broadcast of the event on her 3-V while relaxing in the living room of her expensive condominium. She had not been to the Aphrodite office for over two years. The exclusive off-the-books contract with Senator Samuel Hamilton Clanton and the unusual (also off-the-books) nature of the remuneration to her employers, literally required her to stay away. Several of the other girls were still her friends, however; and since her services to Sam had been rendered earlier today, she planned on going out clubbing with some of them tonight. She wondered why anyone would want to make a bomb threat at a pleasant business like Aphrodite, which had so many satisfied customers, and she thought that question should make interesting conversation with her friends.

The sudden ring of the doorbell startled her. The girls were not coming for another hour and a half. She wondered who it could be. Salesmen never came to the condominium complex. The gate-guard saw to that. She occasionally had pizza delivered, but had not ordered any tonight. When she opened the door, she saw a rather pleasant looking young man, with an almost military bearing and intensity of gaze, waiting.

He had some kind of file, or folio in his left hand, and had apparently arrived in a late model Dodge sedan that was parked at the curb. The gate-guard must have let him in.

"Excuse me, Miss," he said, "is your name Charise Meardon?"

"Why . . . yes," Charise answered, somewhat reluctant to say more.

The man extended his hand, which she shook automatically. His hand was warm and grip firm, but brief. "My name is Harold Pinkerton," he said. "If I might have a few minutes of your time, I have a matter of some significance to discuss with you."

*   *   *

Tom was in his apartment at the Asylum, disposing of the paper and plastic remnants of a 3-V dinner, when his vid phone rang. It was Dan Hargrove, calling from his home outside Santa Fe.

"Dan. Good to see you," Tom said after picking his phone up.

"Tom. Likewise. Hey, we got the first report your team sent over. My guys are almost delirious with excitement. They say it gets us around several hurdles already. You're making me pay a lot of overtime. My people don't want to go home at the end of the day. I have to kick 'em out of the place."

"I know what you mean," Tom chuckled. "My guys are acting the same way."

"Glad to hear it. But I'm a little worried about what's going on over there. I mean, a lot of it I can't believe, even when I see it on the news. Ninja Pinkertons? Angry anti-teleportation protests? Pro-teleportation demonstrators? Riots in Menlo Park? An inquisition in the California legislature? Makes me glad I live in New Mexico, where at least a little sanity still reigns! What's all this about, Tom?"

Tom gritted his teeth and shook his head, before answering. "It's hard to explain, Dan, and parts of it I can't right now. But I hope I can when I see you again. Until then, don't believe much of what you hear."

"Well, how bad is it? I've got the orbit allocation and launch window for your seventh satellite. Are we going ahead? You know, if we start and then have to stop, that's very costly."

"I know," Tom nodded. "So we'll go ahead. Don't worry about what's happening here. We're still running passengers, packages, and freight just fine, and I don't see anything coming out of these hearings that will stop that. The company has more than enough cash reserves to cover the launch. When is the launch window?"

"Four days, Thursday through Sunday, three weeks down the road."

"Well, we're on then. If you don't mind, Dan, I'll come over and watch, if I can break free of things here. That'd give me a chance to bring my Weak Force Team over, anyway."

Dan's eyebrows went up, and he nodded once, quickly. "My guys would love that. Okay, then. We're on. Talk to you later."

"Right. Say 'hello' to June and the kids for me, will you Dan? Tell 'em again I had a great time over there, and I hope to see 'em soon."

Hanging up, Tom had to take a moment to mentally shift gears. Then he went to the bedroom to find his Gi. The workout was going to have to start just a few minutes late tonight, even though Ishi Harada was down for a visit with a few of his students, mostly Pinkerton men from the San Francisco office. Moreover, about twenty new people had joined Tom's club in the last few days. He was going to have to buy another couple of dozen sections of *Tatami* mat soon, and probably move the club to a place with more room. The Asylum just kept getting too small.

*   *   *

Sam Clanton was miffed. "What do you mean you don't know? Somebody's gotta know. She sure isn't answering my calls. You've kept the payments up, haven't you?"

The financial officer of the California Brotherhood of Teamsters, whose face could be seen on Sam's videophone, protested that there had been no interruption of scheduled payments to Aphrodite Associates.

"Well, something's up, and I don't just mean me! You don't suppose it could have anything to do with that bomb threat they had?"

This time the man was completely confused. He had not even heard of the bomb scare at Aphrodite Associates, but he promised to look into it. Besides, he pointed out, if Charise Meardon had taken off for some reason without telling her employers, another girl could be easily arranged for.

Just then, Jake and Jerry knocked briefly, opened Sam's office door, wandered in, and began making themselves comfortable. "Maybe that's what we'll have to do," Sam said. "I'm getting tired of her anyway. I gotta go. Jake and Jerry are here." With that he put the phone down, none too gently.

"What's the matter?" Jake asked Sam, speaking around the cigar he was lighting.

Sam waved his hands in both disgust and dismissal of the matter. "Charise hasn't shown up since Tuesday. For a while I thought maybe she was sick or something, but she doesn't even answer calls. I don't know what's happening with her, and I'm just trying to find out."

Jerry chuckled. "One of these days your personal arrangements are gonna get you in trouble, Sam."

"Oh, right!" Jake objected. "Like you don't have a tootsie on the sly, Jerry!"

"Well, I don't keep her at the office!" Jerry shot back.

"All right, all right, you two," Sam said, seeing the need to change the subject. "Let's get down to business. Where do we stand?" It was half past three in the afternoon and the last hearing of the committee had just concluded for the week.

Senator Gerald Foxly looked down and shook his head before looking Sam in the eye. "Well, according to Brad, we didn't get far in the morning. UTT has apparently looked pretty close at the risks of electromagnetic interference, sunspot activity, lightning storms, equipment failure, and such. They had a lot of frequency data put together on those things, plus their own operating experience. The people UTT sent down had the ALP crowd pretty well coached. I don't think they're lying at all when they say that passenger teleportation is about a hundred times less risky than airplane travel. We all know those risks have been accepted for a long, long time."

"Yeh," Jake added, "we couldn't even catch them on the terrorism threat. They thought of that one, too. Somehow they found a way to program their equipment to literally edit the signal and delete guns, most poisons, and radiological or toxic materials, so that they just don't get transmitted. Then they just store the energy. We got some traction out of the afternoon session though. Adding that Physicist from the Edison Institute - Westholm - at the last minute to testify that teleportation beams might ionize the atmosphere was a good idea. Sounds scary enough, doesn't matter if he's right or wrong. The ALP crowd didn't know what to say. The two guys from UTT kept trying to explain something about it to Hally, but she apparently couldn't follow the argument without a script. All she could do was impugn Westholm's motives for testifying against Teleportation when he's a defendant in a UTT lawsuit."

"Actually," Jerry added, looking at Jake, "I think we've been gaining traction over the last couple of days. I'll admit the public opinion polls don't look good. Only about a quarter of the public is siding with us, with about five percent on the fence. The rest think we're a bunch of idiots and tyrants out to get UTT. But the markets are getting the message that, win, lose, or draw, we're serious about regulating Teleportation. UTT stock shares were down four bucks at close yesterday, and I hear the price fell a couple more by noon today."

"At that rate, it'd take a month to get it down where we need it," Jake scoffed. "Remember, we have to buy over two hundred thousand shares! Unless it falls below a hundred-fifty a share, we'll never make it, even with the union pension fund money Rockfort and Ergley are kicking in."

Sam chuckled darkly. "Doesn't matter, guys. We've given Maynard enough public justification. Come Monday morning, UTT share prices will drop like a rock."

*　　　　*　　　　*

From the edge of the helipad on top of the parking terrace at the capitol Monday morning, Derek, Dave, and Bill Braxon had a good view of the demonstrators and counter-demonstrators marching, shaking their signs, and chanting taunts and slogans at one another and anybody else passing in front of the capitol. The mood of neither group was helped by the steady drizzle of rain that had been coming down for over an hour. There was an air of expectancy in both crowds, however, the news media having made it widely known over the weekend that the first witness at the Committee on Teleportation Hazards this morning would be Tom Wright himself.

Derek turned around as he thought he heard the faint eggbeater sound of the incoming helicopter ferrying Tom from Sacramento International. Some of the demonstrators, particularly the pro-teleportation crowd across the street who had the better angle, seem to have heard and seen something, too, and they started pointing at the sky.

"Here he comes," Derek said to the others, who were already turning around and looking into the sky in the same direction the demonstrators were pointing toward. Off in the distance, the 'copter looked like little more than a mosquito, perhaps lost and disgruntled in the drizzle; but it grew, as did the sound of its engine and rotating blades, until it loomed over them, settled gently onto the pad, and began powering down.

Before the blades stopped rotating, the three men began walking toward the 'copter and Tom got out.

"Tom," and "Boss," Derek and Dave called out simultaneously. "Good to see you," Dave finished.

"Guys," Tom responded. "Good to see you, too. And you must be Senator Braxon."

Bill shook Tom's outstretched hand. "Nice to finally meet you. I wish it was under better circumstances."

"Well," Tom grinned, but without much humor, "we have to deal with people and circumstances as they are, right? What say we get out of this rain and go see what we can do to improve things?" With that, the four of them headed toward the walkway connecting the top of the parking terrace to the capitol building.

"It's too bad we don't have the Sacramento airport chamber done yet," Tom said to Derek and Dave as they walked. "That flight time is a waste."

"Yeh," Dave snorted, looking over at Derek. "That's what we said last week."

There were numerous reporters outside the hearing room when they got there. The repeated camera flashes as the newsmen rushed to get pictures of Tom were nearly blinding. Inside, the hearing room was already packed, and the network 3-V cameras were all focused on Tom as Bill led him over toward the seats behind the chair at the table that the witnesses all used when their turn came.

"I guess you know you're first up," Bill told him through the din, "but wait until the Chairman calls you. I'm not on the committee itself, but I'm going over to sit behind Senator Arkwright - she's the slim lady at the table down there - and watch you while you testify. If you can spare a little time before you head back to Menlo Park afterward, let's talk. In fact, I'll buy you lunch, if you can stay that long. I'd like you to meet some of the ALP leaders here and a few members of my staff. Good luck!"

With that, Senator Braxon started making his way down the table, occasionally stopping to shake a hand and exchange a word or two with various people. Derek and Dave had already headed in that direction, and were just taking their seats next to Ron Beck, the junior attorney The Buzzard had sent down to help. Looking around the room, Tom could see that most people were watching him, some steadily and others intermittently, as if trying not to look, while they talked to each other. Nervously, Tom reached into his suit pocket and took out his prepared opening statement, thinking he might profit by reading through it once more. In a minute or two he found that he had been looking at the words without reading them, however, and felt foolish. He knew what he was going to say, cold, anyway.

Looking around the table, he examined the faces and demeanors of the Senators representing the two parties on the committee. When he came to Hally Arkwright, he looked in the seats behind her to spot Bill Braxon. Braxon was there, but it was not his face that suddenly attracted Tom's attention, like a quasar grabbing a passing asteroid. It was another face. The face of a young woman sitting next to Bill Braxon. A woman who was looking at Tom intently, with an expression almost as if she were afraid he would *not* see her. When their eyes met, an almost electric sensation went through Tom, as it had the first time he had seen her. His mouth dropped open in surprise at recognition, and her expression changed, too. Her face lit as if at some joyous secret pleasure.

Gina Barlow, he thought! *Here. With Senator Braxon!* And then, making a more intellectual and less visceral and physiological connection: *she's an economist!* And, *what was it that Derek or Dave said about a brunette bombshell coaching the ALP Senators?*

BANG, BANG, BANG! The sound of the Committee Chairman's gavel shattered the connection, jerking Tom's attention back reflexively. He felt a moment of consternation as he tried to refocus, but not forget. "Ladies and gentlemen, fellow Senators, please quiet down and take your seats . . . . thank you . . . thank you."

The din quickly subsided. The man continued. "The California Senate Special and Select Committee on Teleportation Hazards is now in session. Since we have no unfinished testimony or questioning left over from last Friday's session, we can begin with our first witness of the day, Mr. Thomas Alvin Wright, Chief Executive Officer of Universal Teleportation Transport. Mr. Wright, if you would . . ."

Just then the man was interrupted by another man who had entered the room a few seconds earlier, worked his way over behind the Chairman, put his hand on his shoulder and whispered in his ear. Tom was not sure, but he thought the man interrupting was Samuel Hamilton Clanton, the leader of the Democratic Republican Party in the Senate.

"Are you sure?" The Committee Chairman asked the man.

The man nodded and whispered some more in the Chairman's ear.

"Well, okay, if you say so, Sam," the chairman said, then turned back to the room as Senator Clanton walked back toward the exit.

The Chairman cleared his throat awkwardly as he thought of what to say. "Uh . . . ladies and gentlemen, fellow senators, in a news conference held just a few minutes ago, Maynard C. Hoffer, Director of the California Department of Transportation, announced a department decision revoking the license of Universal Teleportation Transport to operate within the state of California. Mr. Hoffer reluctantly made this decision in response to public demands and questions raised by numerous witnesses in these hearings about the safety, environmental effects, and adverse economic impacts of teleportation. As a consequence of this unexpected event, these hearings are suspended until further notice. Those of you scheduled to testify please remember that you may be asked or even required to do so at such time as this committee reconvenes."

Tom was stunned, as was everyone else. The room went crazy. Most people stood instantly, but none faster than Tom, who headed for the door, but was impeded by nearly everyone wanting to talk to him.

He worked his way to the exit as fast as possible under the circumstances. Derek and Dave, under less constraint, caught him before he got there, and he was glad they did.

"Derek," Tom spoke loudly to be heard over the uproar, "hang around here another day, will you? Take this, and if they decide to reconvene tomorrow, read it in and take questions for me. If they don't, come on back. I'm heading for the helipad. You might just as well come with me, Dave."

Tom handed Derek the written copy of his opening statement, and he and Dave began worming their way again toward the exit. Outside of the committee room, the crush was worse for Tom than inside. Every reporter wanted to question him and he had to turn away and squirm through them in an effort to make it to the hallway. It helped that Dave went first and began clearing a path; otherwise, Tom would have felt an almost irresistible temptation to begin clearing his own, by other methods. As he was nearly through, something, a strange and almost clairvoyant sensation, motivated him to stop struggling forward for a moment and look back. There, about eight or ten feet behind and reaching out with one arm between two reporters, was Gina Barlow. She was trying to hand Tom something. Tom was conflicted, his body locked between two urges, almost to the point of paralysis. He stretched out his left arm between several other reporters, barely reached, and took the small piece of paper from her hand. There was no time for words, which neither could have heard anyway amidst the shouted questions of the reporters. With an expression that was at once longing and promising, Gina turned away, deliberately severing the bond and letting Tom go. At first reluctantly and then decisively, he went.

Stopping for nothing and nobody but capitol security, Tom and Dave made their way back to the helipad. The pilot had been paid to wait, and he was still there, though surprised to see them back so soon. Intuiting that they were in a hurry to leave, he began firing up the engine as they piled in. In a few moments the blades started rotating, at first slowly, then more rapidly.

"Get us back to the airport as fast as you can," Tom said as he and Dave connected their restraining belts. In only a few moments, the copter was lifting off, the building was receding below them, and more of the city was appearing and beginning to rush by below.

"Our tickets are for this afternoon, Tom," Dave noted. "What if we can't catch an earlier flight?"

Tom nodded and leaned forward to talk to the pilot. "Could you take us where we can charter a plane to fly down to Menlo Park right quick? We don't necessarily need a jet, but something relatively fast."

The pilot nodded and changed course slightly as Tom leaned back in his seat and spoke to Dave. "If we have to, we'll land at the Asylum runway. No air-traffic-controller on duty, but we'll do it anyhow. If the FAA wants to get sticky about it, they can just fine me. We should call the company and have another helicopter waiting. Did you manage to get your NanoPod on the way out?"

"Rats!" Dave snapped his fingers in irritation. "No, I forgot. I'll have to call back and have Derek pick it up. Yours, too, right?"

"You can use mine, if you need to, sir," the pilot said, speaking to Tom.

"Thanks. I appreciate it."

They were on the outskirts of Sacramento before Tom remembered the note Gina Barlow had struggled so hard to give him. He pulled it out of his pocket. It was folded once, and he opened it. All it said was:

Cornelius Vanderbilt. The New York & Harlem R.R. into the city, 1863. Then again, merger with the Hudson River R.R. the next year.

I'll be darned! Tom thought. *That's the very first thing I thought about when Hoffer pulled the plug! But can I pull it off?* Then he smiled to himself as he thought of Gina Barlow. *Great minds. . .*

Chapter 27: The Best Defense

The flight from Sacramento to Menlo Park seemed to take forever to an anxious and determined Tom forced to wait and fume for the duration. Only a hundred miles south they were out of the rain and had no trouble landing the small but fast propeller plane on the Asylum runway. A helicopter was waiting and the flight from the Asylum to the helipad on top of the Galt building took only a few minutes. Tom and Dave were out of the 'copter almost the second it set down and heading for the elevator. Inside, the high-speed elevator seemed to Tom to descend toward the fiftieth floor main UTT offices at the pace of a piece of cottonwood fluff fluttering on a breeze.

"Dave," Tom said, almost desperate to divert his own attention from the wait, "I need you and Lynn to keep the Weak Force Team working. No matter what happens over the next few days, keep them focused and working. That goes for the rest of the R & D teams, too. You hear me? This is *not* going to stop us!"

Dave had never heard this kind of stress, barely suppressed anger, and determination in Tom's voice or speech before, but he understood. He was completely empathetic. He nodded in the affirmative. "I hear you, Tom."

When the elevator door opened and they could see the hall, it was immediately clear that the local and national news crews had beat them here. Once again they had to worm their way through the press of bodies who were shouting questions and endure the repeated flashes of camera bulbs like a massive first strike of mini A-bombs, on their way toward the main entrance of the UTT office complex. Harry's men, captained now by 'Jack' Menendez, had not let the reporters inside, but they did let Dave through, and Tom was about to follow him when he decided to stop and turn around. Gesturing for silence he waited for a moment while the reporters realized he wanted to speak and they needed to stop shouting questions in order to hear him.

"Thank you, ladies and gentlemen of the press," he began. "At this time, I'm not prepared to make any kind of formal statement. As you might understand, I have many things to do in assessing and responding to the situation resulting from this morning's unjustified action by the California Department of Transportation. At two p.m. this afternoon, however, I will have a formal statement and take a few questions. Since this hallway isn't the best place, and UTT has to maintain security in our offices, let's hold that press conference in the large conference room on the fifty-fifth floor. That floor is currently unoccupied, but I'll have arrangements made with the building management. For now, please clear this hallway so people can come and go as needed. Thank you." With that, he went inside, hurrying past security with only a nod to Jack and the others on duty.

Maria was on the phone when Tom came to her desk, but she put the party on hold as he approached.

"Maria, I need to see Parker and Hulio right fast."

"They're already on their way, sir," she answered. "I called them just now when I saw you out front. Marlon Gates and several of the other board members have called, sir."

"Has Buzz called?"

"No, sir. He's in court and probably hasn't heard anything yet."

"If Marlon calls again, tell him I'll get back to him just as fast as I can, but I have to do some emergency management first," Tom said as he went past the desk toward his office. Then he paused for a second and turned back. "In fact, call Marlon back and ask if he can get the board together for an emergency meeting here as soon as possible. This afternoon, or tomorrow morning at the latest. I also need to see Lee Bricker right now, too, if he's in."

Tom had not even gotten settled at his desk and booted up his computer when Hulio and Parker knocked briefly and came in at his call. Hulio, normally more placid and cheerful than most men, was unusually agitated as he flopped angrily down into a chair. "I can't believe this crap, Tom! Can you? Now I know what you meant the other day about 'another shoe getting ready to drop'. What kind of people think up something this slimy, and how many more are in on it?"

"More to the point," Parker said as he sat down on the edge of a chair, "what do we do now?"

452

Just then Lee Bricker, the CFO, stuck his head in the partly opened doorway, knocked briefly, and came in and sat down at Tom's wave and listened, intuiting that a conversation was already in progress.

Tom steepled his hands and rested his chin on the fingertips for a moment, thinking. "First things first," he said. "What's happening at our teleportation centers? You go first, Parker."

"Everything's stopped at the airports throughout the state, Tom," Parker lamented. "Transportation Department officers showed up with paperwork and orders to cease operating just *before* Hoffer's news conference. They must have been sent out already. My people have been on the phones since then, canceling all of the incoming and outgoing 'port transmissions, shutting down new ticket sales, and so on. Rebating ticket owners is going to cost us a bundle since we're still booked three months ahead. On top of that –"

"Have you got a copy of that paperwork with you?" Tom interrupted.

"Well, sure. They showed up here, too." Parker handed Tom the copy of the Transportation Department's cease and desist order he had brought with him. Tom read through it rapidly, and then nodded to himself.

"Okay, Parker, I'm going to have you reverse some of what you've done, and I'll tell you why in a minute. But first, it's your turn, Hulio. What's happening at the freight chambers?"

"It's the same thing, boss," Hulio answered. "Nothing is moving since they showed up with the orders and told us to stop. So, we've been on the phones canceling all transmissions in and out. Customers are already mad as hell, though it seems to me most of 'em are mad at the legislature and the Transportation Department, not us. It's not going to hurt us as much, rebating payments already made, as it does from Parker's side of the operation since freight isn't booked that much in advance the way a lot of passenger service is, but it'll still hurt. The revenue loss is gonna be enormous. What worries me most, Tom, is that APS is right in the middle of transition to our service. They've still got most of their pilots and planes. If this license revocation looks like it's going to hold, APS will just shuck our deal and switch back to their old operation as fast as they can."

Tom nodded grimly. "Okay. Here's what I want both of you to do. Get back to your people and tell them to *resume all passenger and freight teleportation transmissions that are interstate or international.* Stop *only* those that *both originate and terminate* within the state of California itself, say between San Francisco and San Diego airports, between docks along the coast within the state, between an instate airport and an instate Westmark, and so on."

Both Hulio and Parker were wide-eyed with surprise. "How can we get away with that, Tom?" Hulio asked.

"We can get away with it by interpreting their order literally," Tom responded. "Look. It says we have to cease operations *within* the state of California. It says *nothing* about transmissions between California and other states or other countries. Article one, section eight of the U.S. Constitution says the only the *U.S. Congress* regulates interstate commerce, not the states. That's been settled law in this country since the Supreme Court case of *Gibbons versus Ogden* in eighteen twenty-four."

"But that isn't what they meant," Parker put in, "and we know it, Tom! They mean for us to close down everything!"

"You're right, Parker," Tom responded. "But we have licenses to operate in all those other states. If Hoffer tries to interpret his order as requiring us to literally cease all operations in the state, *he'll be regulating interstate commerce.* I don't think he realized that, and it's going to make him sit up straight and think hard when he does. Besides, we have to minimize our losses. For the next few days we're going to need every dime we can earn so unless and until they literally turn out the police and credibly threaten to haul our people off, *keep operating those interstate and international teleport transmissions.* What I need from you, Lee, is an estimate of how much the loss of purely instate business will cost us. And I need it yesterday."

"You got it, Tom," Lee nodded, and then got up to leave. "I'll get my people right on it."

"Hold on a second, Lee, you need to hear this, too." Tom said. "Here is what has to be the central focus of our strategy: Stock markets work on expectations.

They capitalize people's present *estimates* of *future* net earnings of firms into current stock prices by discounting them at the market rate of interest. Slanghorn, Clanton's gang, and Hoffer want the public, our investors particularly, to think short-term, focused on the crisis and financial loss they're causing for us right now. We have to get people to think long-term.

Our message to all of our employees, our stockholders, and to our customers, to *everyone* we can possibly communicate with, has to be: This order, suspending part or all of our operations within the state, must and *will* be rescinded, and soon. We *will* be allowed to operate fully and openly.

The great genius of the Federal system established constitutionally at Philadelphia is that it allows the states to be mini-laboratories, experimenting with different bundles of legislation, taxation, and regulation. Combine that with free mobility of population, goods, and productive capital assets across state boundaries, and it means that states are *constantly in competition for population and business.* States that institute bad legal policies lose those things to states that institute good ones. That disciplines the former states and rewards the latter, minimizing bad policy behavior by the state governments. The key point is: other states *are* going to allow teleportation, *without* regulating it unnecessarily. The California government will *not* be willing to put the state to the disadvantage their current policy implies for long. I'm going to hold a news conference in a couple of hours, and that's *exactly* what I'm going to tell them! You do the same to *everyone* you talk to."

Hulio, Parker, and Lee all understood completely. Lee left immediately to begin putting together the estimates Tom had asked for. After a few more minutes spent discussing strategic and tactical management details for dealing with the crisis, Hulio and Parker also left. For a few moments, Tom simply sat back and breathed deeply, trying consciously to relax and think clearly about the order in which to do things. *First things first,* as he had told the three men. So first, on his computer, he checked his own financial records. As he had thought, he had a hair over a million NDs of his salary collected so far in personal savings. Next, after calling the offices of Gates, Feldman, Vanderhoff, and Shapiro, he asked to speak to Marlon and was connected almost immediately.

"Tom," Marlon's voice came on, "I've been following everything. I can't say 'good' afternoon, because it's not. We've all had a shock, and I guess you most of all. Are you holding up all right?"

"Yes. Thanks for asking, Marlon," Tom responded. "Are we on for this afternoon or tomorrow with the board?"

"Yes, we are. Nine a.m. sharp tomorrow. A couple of the members are out of town, but we'll have more than enough for a quorum. Do you have a strategy?"

Tom nodded. "Yes, I do, but how it goes and its likelihood of success, will depend a lot on whether the board will back me up. First, I need you to do something personal for me, if you can. I have a million

NDs and change in my savings account. I intend to spend the million buying UTT stock first thing tomorrow morning when the market opens. I could go to a regular broker, but I wonder if your people could take care of it instead. I'll pay the normal fees."

Marlon squinted slightly as he peered into Tom's eyes, then grinned wolfishly and nodded. "Yes, I'll take care of it. I already see what you're up to, and I'll back you to the hilt. In fact, if you're really serious about going that route, Tom, I'll put in a million of my own."

*   *   *

Sam Clanton was horrified when he heard on the 3-V network news how Tom Wright and UTT had responded to the Department of Transportation order. "Can he *do* that?" He almost shouted at Jake and Jerry, whom he had summoned to his office immediately. "You're a lawyer, Jake, how can he do that? I thought we were shutting him down completely!"

Jake shrugged and shook his head. He had been as shocked as Sam, but had had more time to regain some of his equilibrium, since, unlike Sam, he had seen Wright's news conference live. In fact, it was Jake who had called Sam and told him to check the news. "Apparently, he can, Sam. At least for now. You heard how he argued. The guy is smart and fast on his feet. But they're still hurt. Transit instate has to be a large part of their business. UTT's share price dropped over twenty NDs by noon, and it was still heading down last I heard."

"Not anymore," Jerry lamented. "It was back up three neobucks a few minutes ago. It'll probably close only about fifteen or sixteen down for the day."

"What?" Sam and Jake asked simultaneously. "It's gotta fall a helluva lot faster and further than that," Sam said. "We need to start buying as soon as possible. Remember, we've only got a few days to go before we have to deliver!"

"I know," Jerry responded. "Sorry, Sam. I just heard it from one of the ALP guys on my way up here. But it should drop a lot tomorrow. Like Jake says, they're hurt."

Sam fumed and paced in gloomy silence for nearly a minute, then decided. "It might not be enough. We've got to hurt them more. We've got to get hold of Maynard. I don't believe they can get away with that. Maynard has to stop it."

Picking up his videophone, he dialed Director Hoffer's number at the Transportation Department and waited while it rang several times. Finally Hoffer's secretary picked up. Sam's conversation with her was brief.

"His secretary says he left about a half-hour ago," he told Jake and Jerry as he put the phone down.

"I'll bet he heard what Wright did," Jake commented. "He should be home by now, though. He only lives out on Redlands Drive. Try him there, Sam. Use his NanoPod code. That should get him wherever he is."

Sam lifted the phone again and punched in Hoffer's NanoPod code. Again he listened to it buzz intermittently and repeatedly without response. "He's not answering. The S.O.B. might have it turned off."

Jake nodded thoughtfully. "Apparently, he wants to think things over for a while without any more pressure from us. But he'll be at work tomorrow. He isn't going to duck us for long, and he knows it. He's in this right along with us."

"What do you think Braxon's up to?" Jerry asked.

Both Sam and Jake looked puzzled. Then Sam asked, "What do you mean?"

It was Jerry's turn to look puzzled. "I thought you knew. That's the other thing I heard on my way up. The ALP leadership is holding a news conference at six-oh-five down in the press room on the main floor."

Jake continued to look puzzled as he pondered that information, but Sam simply shrugged. "They've been complaining about the hearings right along. You'd expect them to denounce Maynard's order. No surprise there."

"I don't know," Jake commented. "There's a cold feeling inching up my spine that they might have more up their sleeves than that. Maybe we ought to take a look."

*   *   *

"Are you ready for this, Gina?" Bill asked. He, Gina, Spider, and Dex were in his office, just about to head down to the news conference that Bill had arranged.

Most of the other staff members had gone home at the end of the normal workday and would catch it on the news.

Gina was just flicking a few errant dandruff flakes off the Senator's suit lapels before they started down. She smiled encouragingly. "I'm not the one who has to stand up in front of the cameras and speak to millions of people, Senator. You are, thank heavens."

"But you're the one who got us here, Gina. Without you, we wouldn't have known any of this."

"No, sir," Gina said, looking Bill in the eyes and speaking with a hint of sorrow in her voice. "Senator Clanton got us here."

"Well, Roger and Hally are waiting," Bill said grimly. "Now is the time to shoot our bolt. Let's go down and give Sam Clanton what he's been asking for." Stepping around Gina, he walked out of the office at a determined pace. Gina and the others hurried to keep up.

It was only a short walk from the main floor elevators to the news conference room. The room was nearly full when they got there. The reporters were seated and the elevated 3-V cameras were already set up. As Bill had hinted, Roger Galbraith, Hally Arkwright, and several other California ALP leaders were already seated behind the podium and waiting for Bill. Several flashbulbs from hand cameras went off as they entered the room. A row of seats at the right front of the room had been set up for favored staff members invited to attend and Gina, Spider, and Dex sat down there while Bill went up to the podium, arranged papers, and tested the mike. Red lights went on the overhead 3-V cameras as the live feed to national network news programs began, in some time zones interrupting other programming.

"Ladies and gentlemen of the press," he began, "I have a prepared statement which will take about five minutes, and then I'll be willing to take a few questions. Some time back, I and my colleagues in the leadership of the California Senate American Liberty Party came into possession of information indicating that certain leaders of the *Majority* party in the Senate, including Samuel Hamilton Clanton, the Majority Leader, and several others, had written contracts to deliver large amounts of Universal Teleportation Transport stock shares forward at a delivery date not long from now, at a price set when the contracts were written. In essence, these august gentlemen were betting on a large *decline* in the price of UTT shares, which had been rising rapidly and steadily over the several months since that firm had first entered business and begun rapidly expanding its teleportation operations. The men involved in these short- sales do not currently own any appreciable amount of UTT stock. A large price decline between the time of negotiation of those contracts and the time the shares have to be delivered will be necessary for those involved to be able to profit from buying the contracted shares and delivering them at the specified prices. We have documentation of these transactions, including the persons, the stock volumes, and the share prices involved, which will now be passed out to you by some of our staff members."

A nervous stir began among the reporters as many sensed where Senator Braxon's revelation was going. He paused for a moment to let it abate, while the sheaves of data were being handed out, and then started again.

"The first thing I wish to stress is that we have delayed making this information public because we wanted to completely confirm its accuracy, which took some time. We were reluctant even to believe in what appeared to be corruption on the part of our esteemed colleagues. In addition, events now seem to have confirmed our suspicions and forced our hand. In that regard, it is important to stress that these contracts were written *before* the Senate hearings on alleged teleportation hazards were initiated by *the very men who wrote the contracts,* and before the actions taken by the Transportation Department today, which have combined to start forcing down the value of UTT stock shares. In short, we believe that these men, probably including Transportation Director Hoffer, have engaged in a corrupt conspiracy to profit by entering into those forward contracts then using their political, legislative, and regulatory power to injure UTT and force down the price of its shares. As such, we, the leaders of the ALP in the Senate, will introduce a resolution on the floor tomorrow morning calling for a Senate Ethics Committee probe into the behavior of the men engaging in these transactions. Thank you. I will now take questions."

Pandemonium ensued, as every reporter in the room tried simultaneously to gain recognition.

*　　　*　　　*

Sam Clanton was white and shaking as he danced around the office uncontrollably. "How did they find out?" He screeched. "How?"

Jake felt nearly as bloodless and shaken as Sam, but in contrast, he was almost paralyzed. "I don't know, I don't know," he whispered, before speaking louder. "But we have to get hold of ourselves. If we panic now, we're dead!"

Jerry was sitting down on Sam's couch, head in hands, and seemed to be having trouble breathing, but then he raised his head. "It could have been one of the buyers," he croaked. "They probably figured out this morning, if not before, that they were being had."

"No," Jake shook his head. "No. You heard him. Braxon and his guys found out before the buyers could have figured it out. Besides, the buyers don't really lose anything from the whole deal. They were happy to buy UTT stock forward at the price we offered. I think it was the Barlow woman. Somehow she found out. That's what she does. It's time to stop playing nice with her."

Somehow, by an iron act of determination, Sam regained control of himself and stopped dancing around and shaking. Some of the color came back into his face, though he looked like he had just swallowed something very bitter. "We can salvage this. Jerry, you get down there. Stop *any* of those news people from leaving. Tell them I'll be down in twenty minutes with a statement."

*   *   *

Nearly everyone but a few staff and support personnel worked late at UTT headquarters, trying to deal with the crisis. It was not clear that many of them would get home before midnight. Keeping one eye on the 3-V, however, Tom took long enough off the phone to catch the ALP news conference and the impromptu response by Sam Clanton. Afterwards, most of the national network news analysts quickly leaped to the defense of the Democratic Republicans in the California Senate. Disgusted, Tom turned the 3-V down, picked up his videophone and called Derek at the Westmark in Sacramento.

After only two rings Derek's face was on the screen as he picked up, saw it was Tom, and answered. "Hey, Tom, I'm glad you called. Looks like you're still at the office. I'll bet it's hectic there. What can I do for you?"

Tom ran his fingers through his hair and sighed. "Mainly I just wanted to see whether you know any more than I do about what's going on up there. Have they said anything about restarting the hearings?"

"No. Certainly not tomorrow and no word if, or when, at all. Really, I don't think there's much point to that whole charade now, anyhow, Tom. It served its purpose."

"Right," Tom nodded. "I should have just had you come back with Dave and me. You might as well catch a flight back tomorrow if you want. I can use the help here."

"Okay. I was going to anyway. By the way, Tom, that was a brilliant move this afternoon, keeping our interstate and international transmissions going. I'd never have thought of it. That'll reduce our losses a lot."

"Thanks," Tom responded, "but I don't think they'll let us get away with it for long. Clanton and Slanghorn have to get our share price down a lot and soon. They'll send in the police to shut us down if they have to."

"What are you going to do then?" Derek asked.

"Whatever we can. I'll fill you in when you get here tomorrow. By the way, did you catch Bill Braxon's news conference?"

"Yes. I did. He told me right after the hearings were canceled that they were going public with it. It's all out in the open now. I thought he did a good job. It's good that it was carried live. A lot of people will see through the network spin."

"How about Clanton's response a few minutes ago. Did you see that?"

Derek gritted his teeth and grimaced as if he wanted to talk, but was temporarily unable. "You know, Tom, I try to be a decent guy. In my whole life, I've never *really* wanted to kill someone. But if I had my hands around that guy's throat right now, I swear . . ."

Tom nodded tightlipped bitter understanding, if not agreement.

"I mean," Derek continued, "certainly you'd expect the guy to say that the contracts are perfectly legal, even for state senators, under California law, which

466

they probably are. And you'd expect him to deny any conspiracy with Hoffer or any foreknowledge of how Hoffer would respond to the hearings. But the gall of the man, the sheer evil *brilliance* of claiming that they entered into those contracts to *protect our stockholders,* to minimize the shock on UTT share prices from revelations of teleportation risks at the hearings by buying large numbers of shares at the right time! So instead of being sinners, he and his cohorts are *saints,* having nothing but altruistic intentions! And the most disgusting thing is that the network talking heads have already begun parroting all that!"

"No," Tom shook his head in the negative. "The saddest and most disgusting thing is that some people will want to believe them. But you know, Derek, he's right on one point. *Nothing they did was illegal.* It really wasn't illegal for them to write those forward contracts. It wasn't illegal for them to hold hearings and threaten to impose costly, unjustified regulations on us, or even to do so, on whatever pretense they might imagine. It wasn't and isn't illegal for Hoffer to withdraw our license. And even if it could be *proved* that they had conspired to do all this purely for their own profit, as they certainly did, it *wouldn't be illegal,* because *conspiracy to commit legal acts can't be illegal!*

"You know, Derek, if you think about it, the central problem, the initial corruption, is *precisely the existence and accrual of those kinds of governmental powers.* Our existence and operation as free persons running a business, selling a valuable service to other free and willing persons, should *not* depend on arbitrary legislative or regulatory *permission,* which can be withdrawn at their will. Nor should how we run our business be subject to their arbitrary regulatory dictate. That's the corrupting factor that enables the Clantons and Slanghorns to do this kind of thing. And none of it is necessary. Any real business malfeasance can be dealt with by other mechanisms. Market mechanisms, particularly the threat of losing business if you harm customers, act to inhibit and minimize such behavior. That's why you and I tried so hard to anticipate risks and side effects of teleportation. Plus there are civil and criminal mechanisms like tort law or prosecutions for false advertising, which, unlike regulation, at least allow the accused a defense in court with a presumption of innocence. If we hurt any of our customers, not only would we lose business, but they or their relatives could sue us. That threat adds even more incentive to minimize bad business behavior."

"Well, you're right, of course, Tom. But are you saying Clanton, Slanghorn and the rest are just going to get away with it?" Derek asked. "There's no way for us to get justice?"

Tom's eyes crinkled in the hint of a grin. He shook his head slowly. "I didn't say that, Derek. Come back tomorrow and I'll show you how maybe, just maybe, we might be able to get justice, or at least get even."

Chapter 28: Desperate Measures

"Is that her?" Rod asked. The morning sun was behind them and from their van parked half a block away they could see Gina Barlow as she came out of the front door of her parent's home and walked toward the Hyundai parked at the curb.

Harry leaned forward to get a good look. "Yeh, that's her."

"Wow," Rod said, "you didn't tell me she looked like that, Harry."

Harry shrugged as he raised his NanoPod, adjusted the focus, and recorded. "I didn't know, but everyone I've talked to said she was a heart-stopping knockout who didn't seem particularly aware of it herself."

Gina opened the front door of the Hyundai, got in, started it up, and pulled out into the street, almost certainly headed for the Capitol.

From the back seat, Pete gave a low wolf-whistle. "You know, I like old movies. There used to be this Italian actress, way back in the twentieth. Sophia Loren. I always thought she was the most gorgeous gal I ever saw. Now, I'm not so sure."

Rod glanced over his shoulder at Pete. "I don't see the similarity with Sophia. This gal looks more like Yasmin Bleeth to me, only . . . athletic."

"Yeh. Well," Harry said, "apparently there's a lot more to Miss Gina Barlow than her looks. Not only is she almost certainly the one who compiled and sent that information to Martha Clanton, but she seems to be involved in this whole teleportation mess, too."

"Well, what do we do now?" Rod asked.

Harry shrugged. "Nothing. I know what I wanted to know, and we don't have a client. I need to have one more talk with Charise Meardon, and then I'm heading back down to Menlo Park. Ed is after me to do that anyway. You two guys have taken enough of your vacation time helping me off the books, and you need to get back to some real work. I just wanted a look at Miss Barlow for future reference. She's like a human catalyst. Things happen around her."

Rod pointed down the street. "Who are those guys? I didn't see anybody get in that car."

A dark gray sedan with dark-tinted windows parked at the curb a couple of houses the other side of the Barlow homestead pulled out into the street behind the Hyundai. The sedan had been parked there since before Harry, Rod, and Pete arrived; and none of them had seen anyone get in or out. A small alarm started tingling in Harry's head.

"Follow them, Rod," he said. "Not too close, but don't lose sight."

Rod started the van and pulled into the street behind the sedan. Through a couple of miles of suburban neighborhood, they just kept the van in sight, often letting one or more other cars get in between, but not enough that they lost track or got left behind at traffic lights. It became abundantly clear that the sedan was following Gina Barlow's Hyundai.

When they got on the new parkway, they hung back for a while. All three cars were traveling in the far right lane. As Gina Barlow's car started onto an overpass, Harry saw that the sedan, which had been following at a discrete distance, was now pulling dangerously close to the rear of the Hyundai.

"Close up some, Rod," Harry said, and Rod accelerated, starting to close the distance. Just then, in a burst of power and exhaust, the sedan swung into the middle lane, pulled up next to the Hyundai, and swerved to the right, forcing Miss Barlow to swerve in reflex onto a narrow safety lane and nearly into the overpass side rail.

"Go, go, go!" Harry shouted and Rod punched the accelerator pedal to the floor. The van responded and shot forward, closing rapidly on the sedan. The driver of the sedan apparently saw them and punched the gas peddle of his own vehicle, swinging back into the middle lane and accelerating rapidly. Following the sedan, the van zipped past Gina Barlow's Hyundai. In the right side rearview Harry could see the Hyundai stabilizing and getting fully back into its lane as Gina Barlow regained control. The Hyundai dwindled in the rearview, though, as Rod tried to chase down the sedan. After a few miles, however, it was clear that that effort was futile. The sedan was just too fast, and Harry told Rod to slow down to highway speed.

"What just happened?" Pete asked from the back seat.

"I don't know," Harry answered, "but I know what I'm going to do about it."

"What's that?" Rod asked.

"I'm going to deliver a message."

*   *   *

"Do I understand correctly, Tom," Ludwig Rothman asked in his rather thick Austrian accent, "that you intend to buy large amounts of this company's stock to prevent its price from falling and keep those people from profiting by what they've done?" His incredulity was matched by that of several other members of the board.

"That's right," Tom responded. "It's the only way. I've already almost emptied my personal savings account and started buying. If I have to, I'll borrow as much more as I can, personally. I created this company, and I'm going to defend it."

"I'm supporting him on this, Ludwig," Marlon Gates put in. "Tom and I discussed this yesterday. I've already invested a couple million of my own money. And didn't you tell me, Tom that Derek and Beowulf are kicking in another million out of their own pockets?"

"Yes. Each."

"But you know that's not going to be enough, don't you?" Lew Edleston asked.

Both Tom and Marlon reluctantly nodded agreement.

"So," Ludwig made a statement, not a question, "you want us to let you use company funds, cash reserves, and current cash flow."

Again, Tom nodded. "Yes. Even if that means we end up going private."

"But will even that be enough?" This time Ludwig did make it a question. "With our cash flow severely reduced by our inability to make instate transmissions? Even given your brilliant action, Tom, in minimizing those losses so far, and much of our cash reserves committed to satellite launch, new chambers in construction, and so on, are the earnings we're generating on international, interstate and out of state business enough to support the share price?"

"I don't know," Tom reluctantly admitted. "Right now, I think maybe. It depends on the public reaction. If the selling panic gets any worse, I don't know. Maybe not. Long-term, of course we couldn't. It'd cripple us if we survived at all. But remember, those people have to deliver on those contracts in just another few days. All we have to do is keep the price up 'til then. If things don't get any worse, it might be enough."

For a moment nobody spoke as everyone pondered the risks.

"Have you considered the alternative, Tom?" Jake Hansen asked. "I don't like it any more than you do, but you know, you could just let the price fall. Let Clanton, Slanghorn, Hoffer, and the others get what they want. I don't think they intended to stop us from operating permanently in the first place. Once they have their money, all this will go away. It might be cheaper in the long-run. When we get back on track and start earning money again, the stock price will go right back up, so our investors won't be permanently hurt."

"But they will be, Jake," Tom answered. "This is happening to us because we've done something tremendously productive, and for that people are compensating us, willingly and highly. We're *earning* our money. That eats the Clantons, Hoffers, and Slanghorns of this world up inside; because they don't do anything productive. All they know how to do is coerce, compel, and steal. That's the nature of government when it loses its constitutional constraints. If we let them get away with this, believe me, it won't be the last political raid on our earnings, but just the first of many: threats of regulations, excise taxes or antitrust prosecutions by people with discretionary political power who will subtly invite us to buy them off, and a million other things. There are lots of people like Clanton and Slanghorn around. I want to stop it right here and teach those people a lesson that will make other political predators, state and federal, think twice before going after us. In my opinion, that'll be cheaper in the long run. I know that I'm asking to use investor money, but it really is in their interest. The only question before this board is: will you help me?"

When the vote came, a few minutes later, it was nearly unanimous.

*   *   *

Gina was still shaken when she made it to work, though not as badly as she had been immediately after the incident. It didn't help that the pro- and anti-teleportation crowds, though just forming up, seemed to have been agitated by everything that had happened yesterday. Gina wondered if they could be kept under control much longer. The pro-teleportation crowd seemed to be particularly surly, probably angered by the actions of the Transportation Department, and seemed to be growing in numbers rapidly.

Dex and one or two others were in the office already when Gina entered and made her way shakily toward her desk. Dex swiveled his chair, took one look at Gina, and got up, concerned, knowing something was awry. "What's wrong, Gina? You don't look well."

"I'm. . ." Gina started, "I'll be all right. Somebody almost ran me off the road on the Parkway overpass. I could have been killed."

"Wow. Bill is always saying that California drivers are the worst. Here, gimme that stuff." Dex took Gina's purse and briefcase in his left hand and helped her to her desk with his right hand. "Why didn't you stop at the medical office downstairs? Do you want me to go get a nurse up here, or at least get something to calm your nerves?"

Gina sat down and leaned back. "No, really, Dex. Thanks, I'll be fine. I just need to sit here for a while and relax. I'm already much better."

"Well, okay, Gina; but I'm right over here if you need anything." Reluctantly, Dex turned away and went back to his desk. In a few minutes, the Capitol operators would start routing calls into the office and the phones would be ringing, on top of which, he had a ton of other pending work.

On the hour, Bill came in with Amanda in tow. He went into his office, but was only there for a few minutes before heading down to the floor. Amanda, having heard something about Gina's incident, came over to commiserate for a few minutes before going back to her desk and answering phones, which were ringing off the hooks. It continued that way all morning, more intensely than Gina had ever heard it. Apparently, a huge number of people wanted to talk with the Senator, or at least register some kind of comment or complaint about yesterday's events.

About eleven-thirty, Bill came up from the floor and stormed into his office, obviously out of sorts. He had Ly call Spider and Dex in for a brief session. After a few minutes that broke up, however; and Bill walked to Gina's desk, pulled up an extra chair and sat down on it backwards, his arms propped on the backrest and a look of concern in his face. "Dex told me what happened, Gina. You feeling any better now?"

Gina smiled weakly. "I'm fine now, sir. Almost normal."

"Tell me exactly what happened, will you?"

Gina described the events as best she could. Bill listened carefully. "Are you sure that was an accident, Gina?"

"I. . . I'm not sure, sir. People do crazy things."

"Yes," Bill responded, "particularly in this state. But that sedan pulling up suddenly and swerving over doesn't really sound accidental. I'm fairly sure there are people on the other side who know about your role in things, Gina, and don't like it. The really puzzling thing, though, seems to me to be that van. I wonder if whoever was driving it was just a good citizen, or if you've got some kind of guardian angel. In any case, I think you ought to make out a police report. The van driver, whoever it was, might have gotten a plate number off the sedan. Take the rest of the day off. In fact, you could stay home until this whole crisis sorts itself out one way or another. Just work on your dissertation full-time for a while. Give you a chance to pull it all together."

Gina shook her head in the negative. "I can't live in fear and stay locked up at home, Senator. And I like being part of what's happening here, as long as you'll let me. I will make out a police report, though."

"Well, at least let me see if Spider or Dex will drive you to work in the mornings, and take you back home afterwards for a few days. I'd feel better if there was somebody with you."

Gina liked that idea. "That will be fine, sir. I can talk to Dex and Spider. I'll be glad to share the cost of gas. By the way, what happened downstairs this morning?"

Bill sighed and waved a hand in frustration. "Well, our call for an ethics committee investigation lost by one vote. We pounded 'em hard, and I really thought for a while that we would get enough to win."

"Well, that's good enough, isn't it Bill? They have an eight seat majority."

Bill grinned, slightly. "Well, if you look at it that way, you're right, Gina. We did get several RepubliCrat votes, and Clanton almost didn't hold enough of his people together. We're going to see how things go and try again tomorrow or the next day. There is some good news, though."

"What?"

"These phones," Bill waved a hand and glanced around to indicate the constant ringing in the office. "Those are constituents calling in, and they're running ten-to-one against the Hoffer's withdrawal of UTT's operating permit. They want the legislature to do something about it. I don't think the ratio's much different in Sam Clanton's or any of the other RepubliCrat senator's offices. If this keeps up for long, they'll have to cave in."

*   *   *

Though it was cool and comfortable in Sam Clanton's inner office, and he could barely hear the constantly ringing phones in the outer office, he was sweating. It had been a very near thing on the floor. Only some severe pressures on several Democratic Republican members of the Senate had kept the ALP from getting their ethics investigation into the financial activities of Sam and the other leaders. Other things were not going particularly well either. He had still not been able to contact Charise, and he desperately needed some release of tension right about now. Worse, Maynard Hoffer was still not taking his calls. On top of that, he had just heard on his office 3-V that UTT share prices had actually risen a few NDs for an hour or two after the opening this morning, though they were drifting back down now, and it looked like that might continue for the rest of the day. But it was not the panic selling that he and the others needed.

One more time, he thought. *He's got to answer.* Reaching to pick up the videophone to call Director Hoffer again, Sam was surprised when it rang. Startled, he hesitated, wondering who it might be, and then picked up when the caller ID gave him the name and the face of the person trying to make contact.

"Sam?" the man asked once he could also see Sam's face.

"Hello, Gene," Sam acknowledged the Chairman of the California Democratic-Republican Party, Eugene Neely. Sam decided he had better establish a confident tone up front. "How are you this morning?"

Gene wasn't having it. His face was dead serious. "Not so good to tell you the truth, Sam. I've been talking to our House leadership, other party leaders, and several of our biggest party backers. They're all concerned, Sam. We supported you on the hearings. We all understand that dangerous new technologies have to be regulated for the public good and shouldn't be allowed to throw the economy into total chaos. I do have to tell you, we were all disturbed by Braxon's revelations about your . . . uh . . . financial activities, though at least some of us are willing to give you the benefit of a doubt about your claimed motives, even if we don't really understand why you'd be concerned with 'limiting harm to UTT stockholders'. But this whole thing is rubbing the public raw. Particularly

Director Hoffer pulling UTT's license. I just got a call from a reporter for the L.A. Times. They conducted a big phone-poll last night, and people are turning against us. It isn't just the pro-teleportation demonstrators, it's a big public-attitude shift, and next year is an election year."

"So what are you saying, Gene?" Sam asked grimly. "What do you want me to do?"

"Well . . . Sam, a lot of us think you should get Hoffer to rescind that order. We know he's always been a flunky of yours, and he'll do what you tell him. Let UTT operate so that this public furor can go away, and people can start to think a little more rationally. Restart the hearings, and once everything is sorted out, institute a regulatory regime for the industry. Think about it, Sam. Tom Wright wasn't wrong yesterday when he said that California would be at a severe disadvantage relative to other states if this goes on. None of us wants that, do we?"

Sam shook his head. "Of course not, Gene. But we can't just cave in. That'll make Jerry, Jake, and I look guilty. It'll make the party look weak and vacillating. It'll confirm once more that big corporate slugs like Wright can push the government around whenever they want. I won't stand for it, the unions won't stand for it, the railroad execs and the ocean shipper's cartel won't stand for it, and the *Governor* won't stand for it! If we cave, that will hurt us more with our constituents in the long run than if we hang tough."

"Is that your final decision then?" Gene asked.

Sam hesitated. Neely was powerful and was probably telling the truth about the pressures he was getting. This might be the time to show just a little willingness to compromise. "I'll tell you what, Gene. I'll restart the hearings. I'll even put a word in Hoffer's ear that not too long down the road, maybe a few weeks, after we've thought out a regulatory regime and it doesn't look like we're caving in, he could think about restoring UTT's license. Not now, though. Okay?"

This time it was Sam's turn to wait, as Gene thought things over and decided how to respond. Finally he did. "I'm not sure that's good enough, Sam. Things are moving too fast and public opinion is swinging too much. I'm going to call Mel. If he really is backing you, though, I guess the rest of us will just have to wait and see what happens, for now."

"Okay, Gene."

As soon as the screen was blank, Sam punched in the Governor's personal NanoPod code. Maynard Clairborne Hoffer might not be willing to take calls from Sam right now, but he would certainly take one from the Governor, who could fire him at will. If Gene Neely knew what Hoffer was going to be told to do, however, he would not be happy at all.

*   *   *

Gina found it hard to concentrate on her dissertation work the rest of the afternoon. She found herself sneaking repeatedly to the web sites of various news bureaus, CBC, NBS, CNABC, and EAGLE/FOX, for updates on the California UTT story, and to the NYSE and other stock exchange sites to see what was happening at the moment to UTT's share price. She had been astonished when she had watched Tom Wright's news conference the day before and had seen how he had responded to the Transportation Department's order. Clearly, his announcement and actions had had a profound effect on Director Hoffer, who had remained unavailable for comment all day, despite repeated efforts by the network reporters to contact him. Gina understood exactly why Hoffer was conflicted and she smiled every time she thought about it. On the other hand, she found herself almost desperate to know if Tom Wright had understood her note, and was nearly crushed with disappointment at the missed opportunity for Bill to introduce her to him.

Finally, she gave up all pretense of work, and simply switched back and forth between web sites to follow what was happening. The markets were in turmoil. UTT share prices in particular were on a roller coaster, up, then down, then up, then back down, with only a slight declining trend. This apparently undecided and even conflicted state of investor attitudes actually heartened Gina. Clearly, the panic of some investors over UTT losses was being largely offset by large demand by other buyers. She suspected, though nobody had yet reported it, that one of the main buyers might be UTT itself, which might mean that Tom Wright had grasped her message after all. She wondered how long it would take UTT's enemies to tumble to that, if it was indeed true.

About two o'clock, Spider, who had been downstairs running errands for Bill, came back upstairs and excitedly announced that the RepubliCrats had formally decided to restart the hearings next week; and the committee was directed to make recommendations for regulatory legislation. Despite knowing quite well - at least in theory - how stock markets work, Gina was astonished at how fast that information was capitalized into UTT's stock price. Only ten minutes after Spider told everyone in the office the news, CNABC had a news flash on the restart of the hearings, and only five minutes later UTT share prices dropped five NDs. After that, it started falling more rapidly than before. Then the up and down pattern reasserted itself. The decline stopped, and the price bounced up and down around a slight rising trend over the next hour, before resuming a moderate rate of decline.

It was nerve wracking. Gina would certainly have gone home for the day feeling depressed, were it not for one other event. Someone, some kind of delivery person, had entered the office and was talking to Ly. There was a stir among the staff members up front who could see what he had brought, or Gina would not have noticed amid the clangor of ringing phones and the cacophony of conversation permeating the office. Ly pointed down the office aisle in Gina's direction. The man started down the aisle and walked straight toward Gina, distracting her attention from the web site she was watching. As he approached, she realized he was carrying one of the most beautiful bouquets of orchids Gina had ever seen. He stopped at her desk.

"Are you Gina Barlow?" He asked.

"Well . . . er . . . uh . . . yes," she stammered in amazement.

"These are for you." He put the bouquet down on her desk, carefully shuffling a few things to the side to make room next to her computer.

Gina found her purse and with some trouble, nervously managed to find a tip for the delivery man, who quickly departed. Everyone at the surrounding desks on both sides of the aisle, including Spider and Dex, who had followed the delivery man part way down the aisle, seemed to be watching as she opened the card that came with the flowers. It simply said:

> Dear Miss Barlow:
>   I understood your note.
> I sincerely hope to be able
> to meet and thank you
> personally someday soon.
>
>   Tom Wright

"Are you going to tell us who they're from, Gina?" Spider asked.

When she did, Gina blushed as nearly everyone in the office cheered, whooped, and clapped.

*   *   *

Samuel Hamilton Clanton was relieved. He sighed and leaned back in his office chair before speaking into his videophone again. "So he finally listened to reason?"

Governor Melvin Slanghorn's head, visible on the screen, nodded. "I had to threaten the stick, too, but yes. He came around on condition that I would make it a formal executive order. My people and his are having all the paperwork done, and we're already calling the networks to set up a news conference. We won't be able to make the six o'clock news - it's almost that now - but we'll certainly be on by ten. By noon tomorrow, UTT won't be moving anything or anybody in this state."

"That's good, Mel," Sam responded. "I don't understand why their stock price has been holding up the way it has, but I guarantee this will do the trick."

Governor Slanghorn looked dubious. "It had better, Sam. We don't have much time, plus I'm under a lot of pressure from within the party and it's only going to get worse when we do this."

Sam nodded. "I know. But that will go away once we've won and we can let UTT go back into operation." Then he smiled and barked a laugh. "Shucks, Mel, it might even be smart for a guy to put some money into UTT stock himself, just before we have Maynard issue that order. We'll certainly have plenty to invest. We could end up owning the company!"

Slanghorn refused to have any of the humor. "Maybe. But my mother used to caution me about counting my chickens before the eggs have hatched. I don't like the way this whole thing has gone so far, and

I think this may be our last chance. Keep in touch, Sam." He rang off, and the screen went blank.

Immediately Sam speed dialed Jerry and Jake, who were waiting for his call, and let them know it was on. They agreed to meet at Jake's place, on the yacht, to catch a bite and listen to Governor Slanghorn's announcement. Then he sat back and relaxed for a few minutes. Despite Mel's pessimism, Sam was heartened. Things were going the right way again. He had dealt successfully last night with Braxon's revelation of their short-sales. He had beaten back the motion for an ethics committee investigation this morning, even if narrowly. He had the Governor's news announcement to look forward to this evening, which would certainly send the UTT stock price into a tailspin tomorrow; and before the trading day was over tomorrow, the group should be able to make their purchases. Plus, the Teamsters Union had arranged for another girl to come over to his condo tonight. In fact, they were sending a series of girls over for the next week. He had told them he wanted to sample several before choosing a replacement for Charise, who had still not shown up, thus making it necessary for him to remove her from the staff payroll.

Sam logged out of his computer, shuffled some papers into his briefcase, and headed out the door. It was after time for the office to close, and most of the staff employees were already gone. With a wave to his secretary, who was also getting ready to depart, Sam walked out of the office and to the elevators, which took him down to the bottom floor of the Capitol, then he went down the hall through the security station to the lower floor of the parking terrace.

Sam liked to go home either early or late to avoid the rush from the parking garage. Early was better, of course, but as Majority Leader, he couldn't always do that, so more often it ended up being at least a little on the late side. As usual at this time, the garage was relatively empty, with only a few seemingly lost souls looking for their cars. Sam, of course, went right to his reserved spot, got in his car, started the engine, and backed out. The guard at the ramp to the street level saw his legislator's sticker and raised the barrier without asking him to pay the visitor's parking fee. The pro- and anti-teleportation demonstrators seemed to be thinning out as most headed home for supper, almost as though they were intelligent people. He sneered a little bit at that thought. Both groups really were, of course, little more than 'cannon fodder'. Or at least that was true of those on his side. The appearance of the counter-demonstrators had disturbed Sam. Nobody seemed to have organized them, at least at first. Neither he nor his cohorts had anticipated such a thing, and it bothered Sam a great deal that the sentiment motivating those people seemed to be growing.

In any case, Sam had no trouble getting out to the street and on his way to the boat docks. Jerry and Jake were waiting when he got parked, walked out on the dock, and made it to the tethered yacht. Jerry had already ordered in Greek food. They ate and listened to the Governor's news conference with growing satisfaction. Things were set now. Mr. Tom Wright, CEO of UTT would not be able to wiggle out of this. Jerry and Jake wanted to continue the conversation afterwards, but Sam decided to head home early since the call girl was coming to his condo at nine, and it was already near twilight. It was a pleasant fifteen-minute drive across town in the cooling part of the evening.

Sam enjoyed his condo, and he felt a minor surge of pleasure when he turned off the street into the complex. He had originally bought it to live in just when the legislature was in session. It was also an investment he could cash in on if he ever left politics. Martha had usually just stayed in their house in San Francisco and left the kids in school there, rather than move everyone up to Sacramento during the sessions, but Sam had had no trouble arranging for female companionship at those times. Of course, it had not been pleasant that time Martha had flown up without warning and walked in on him. When she subsequently locked him out of their house in San Francisco, he had simply moved into the condo permanently, though he kept it quiet and still retained residency in his San Francisco district. Nowadays, to say the least, he didn't miss Martha, or the house, or the kids, who all took after her in their attitudes anyway. He had power, the greatest thing a man could have, and he had independence, and he had all the sex he wanted. Before long he would have all the money he wanted. Life was good.

Parking the car in the condo carport, he took the stairs up to the deck, unlocked the side door and went in. Sam was surprised to notice that it was darker than usual inside. He often left one light on when he went to work. He must have forgotten this morning. As he fumbled for the switch, a shadow loomed out of the darkness. Suddenly his wrist was twisted in an unnatural and painful way, outward and up toward his ear, so that his arm doubled. Then leverage was applied and somehow he was flung forward, head over heels, to smash into the floor with a crushing impact in his back and kidneys. The odd thought flashed across his mind, despite the pain, that he was lucky he had not hit the coffee table. Then the shadow spun around in front of his head and, somehow, another leverage was applied to his wrist and arm that lifted him off the carpet and spun him over in midair to land face down with his arm straight up in the air above and behind him, an excruciating downward pressure being applied to his wrist, pinning his shoulder to the floor.

Sam wanted to scream, but the impact on his kidneys left him with no breath to do so; and he struggled to control his terror and racing heart and regain capacity to breath. After a few moments that seemed endless, the pressure on his wrist eased a little, the pain in his kidneys lessened enough so that he could breathe shallowly, and a voice came.

"Do you know what's wrong with guys like you, Mr. Clanton?"

"Wha', wha', what?" Sam wheezed, not understanding the question.

"What's wrong with you. I mean aside from your brutality, moral corruption, and egotistical belief that you're smarter and better than everyone else and should be able to push them around. What's wrong with you?"

"What?" Sam managed to gasp, this time understanding the question. He tried to turn his head far enough to be able to see the man with his right eye, but the effort resulted in a hint of more pressure being applied to his wrist, and with a gasp, he stopped. Anyway, it was too dark to discern features.

"What's wrong with guys like you," the man continued, in an almost pleasant conversational tone, with only a hint of menace behind it, "is that you think you're the only ones who know how to be ruthless and nasty. Once in a while you have to be taught differently."

"Wha' . . . wha' . . . what do you want?" Sam croaked out between gulping breaths.

The man leaned down a little closer to speak, but Sam could still not make out any facial features in the darkness.

"Oh, that's simple. I want you to leave Gina Barlow alone."

"But that wasn't . . ." Sam tried to object, "I didn't . . . It was Jake that . . ."

"Doesn't matter," the man said. "Those men are your flunkies. They do what you tell them. You *will* tell them to *leave her alone.* I'm going to be keeping an eye on her. If anything unfortunate happens to Miss Barlow, *anything unfortunate at all,* the consequences to you, *personally,* will be, well, let's just say, *more* than proportionate. Do you understand?"

"Yes."

"Okay. There's just one more thing."

"What?" Sam asked.

"You have to know that I mean it."

It was at that moment, just before extreme pressure was applied to Sam's wrist, and things began to tear, and he began to scream, that he realized that he was not going to have a good evening after all.

Chapter 29: The Night is Darkest

Tom had decided to set the board room up as a war room and coordinate all of their operations from there. Videophones had been brought in for everyone, and each executive's table computer had been networked with their office data nets. It had been an exhausting day, but they had managed to keep many freight and passenger operations going despite enormous and ongoing confusions. With fast talking and hard bargaining, including an offer of a twenty-percent price reduction for teleport shipping, Derek and Hulio had convinced APS to delay, at least for another day or so, any irreversible decision to back out on their contract and resume wholesale airfreight transport of their packages. Most important in Tom's view, was that at his direction, Lee Bricker had been able to reroute enough incoming revenue and existing cash reserves into stock purchases arranged by Gates, Feldman, Vanderhoff, and Shapiro, to keep the share price from collapsing wholesale.

All satisfaction at such accomplishments faded as they watched Governor Slanghorn's hastily announced news conference on the big 3-V screen on the wall of the boardroom. Their mood was glum afterwards, and when the network talking-heads began dissecting the Governor's action and its implications, Tom turned the set down.

"Well, I guess that's it," he said. "Parker, Hulio, you'd just as well start calling your managers. Tell 'em to close down and send their employees home as soon as the authorities show up in the morning. I don't want anyone going to jail over this, even for a little while. Tell them to let their employees know that it's just temporary. We expect to be back in full operation in a matter of weeks, if not days. Then we'll call 'em back. When you're done you two should go home and get a good night's sleep. In the morning, have your people start rebating the additional passenger tickets and payments for freight we can't deliver now. Tell you what, though, Hulio, you might try offering anybody from other states who bought tickets for California destinations tickets to other destinations instead. That could save us a little money."

"Will do, boss," Hulio nodded, and he and Parker went to work.

"You know, Tom," Derek commented, somewhat disgustedly, "You have to hand it to Slanghorn and Clanton. They timed this just right. Even six months from now, maybe only three, we'd have expanded enough internationally and out of state that they couldn't have gotten away with this. California would be generating too small a fraction of our earnings. They couldn't depress our share price enough just by shutting us down here, and we'd have plenty of money being earned elsewhere to buy stock back with and hold the price up anyway. "As it is, though, . . ."

"Hmmph," Beowulf snorted. "Don't count us out yet. Tom'll think of something." He had come over from the

R & D offices, where he had been working on components for the Zelda upgrade and hardware designs for the Weak Force Team, to hear what Governor Slanghorn had to say, and to see if Derek was ready to go home yet. The air of crisis had taken hold even in the R & D section, and most people had already left.

"I think Derek's right, though, Beowulf," Lee Bricker lamented. "Slanghorn has probably sealed the deal now. When the markets estimate what we've got left in the way of reserves and cash flow, I don't see how we'll be able to stop a landslide tomorrow."

Tom nodded dejectedly. "We'll try, but we've already tapped every source I can think of. I don't see how we can do it. For the same reasons you're talking about, Lee, there's no way we could even borrow what we need at any interest rate that wouldn't kill us to pay back. I suppose I better call Dan and cancel the satellite launch. That would give us some money to work with. I hate to do it. I gave him my word. But that might get us through one more day."

This depressed even Beowulf. "It's too bad nobody owes *us* a lot of money we could collect," he mused.

Derek sat up straight as a thought hit him, and then noticed that Tom had done the same thing.

"Are you thinking what I am?" He asked Tom.

Everyone else just stared, wondering what was going on.

"Yes, I'll bet I am." Tom answered.

"Could we do it in time?"

"There's only one way to find out." Tom picked up the videophone in front of him and began searching through its computerized directory, looking for the code for the Sacramento Westmark Inns Hotel.

*　　　　*　　　　*

"I just don't understand it, honey," June Hargrove said, as she sat at the dresser in her nightgown, brushing her hair before going to bed.

Dan was already in the bed, leaning back on a pillow against the headboard, reading while he waited for her. As was often the case with women in Dan's experience, his wife was continuing a discussion they must have been having some time before, as if no time had intervened, and somehow was expecting him to know the reference.

He had no option but to ask her, not being able to intuit well at this time of night. "What's that, June? What don't you understand?"

"Men like this - what's his name? - Clanton, and Governor Slanghorn. Why do they do the hateful, evil things they do?"

Dan smiled to himself. This one he should have intuited since it wasn't an hour or two ago when they had heard of Slanghorn's announced executive order on the news, with all the discussion and analysis of UTT stock price movements, etc. One of the reasons he had turned off the 3-V set and begun reading his book was to distance himself from the whole thing and suppress the anger it generated in him. Then he stopped smiling as he seriously thought about the question.

"I don't know what to tell you, dear. You and I both know there's evil in the world. I guess it all comes down to twisted values. Some people want to earn their way productively in life. They get satisfaction dealing fair and square with those who'll deal fair and square with them. They like being able to handle life's problems and make a living honestly. But there are more than a few people like Clanton and Slanghorn, who just seem to enjoy getting what they want by hurting others. The very worst are those who pretend to be benefactors of mankind and a lot of them gravitate toward government. That's where the power of the gun is, the power to *legally* take from others. Some people say that power corrupts, but I think it's more a matter of the corrupt people seeking power."

June kept brushing and brushing. "I just hate to see someone like Tom be hurt by this kind of hateful thing, Dan."

"I like him too, dear."

"Do you think he'll be able to go ahead with the satellite launch, honey?"

Dan thought for a moment. "I don't know, June. He has to be under a tremendous financial strain right now, but he hasn't called and canceled. Maybe he just hasn't had time to think about it or he would have. I don't know. You know, if he asked me, I'd put that satellite up for him and let him pay when he could. I wouldn't do something that costly for many people."

June stopped brushing for several moments and looked at Dan in the mirror. "You'd do that, honey? How do you know he'd *ever* be able to pay?"

Dan put his book down. "Two ways, dear. For one, I know Tom, and the kind of man he is. For another, nothing Clanton and Slanghorn can do is going to stop that firm from growing and prospering. Slow it down for a while, set it back maybe, but not stop it. Their technology and their service is just too beneficial to mankind and to people *personally*. Most people see that. Even if the California government was stupid enough to make that ban permanent, UTT will just operate everywhere else. Move clear out of the state if they have to."

June began brushing again. "Isn't there any other way we can help him, honey?"

Dan thought about it. Somehow, it had not occurred to him to consider the possibility, since Tom was so extraordinarily independent and competent. "You know, maybe I ought to just listen to myself. I *know* that firm is going to prosper, and its stock is a bargain right now. It'll probably be a bigger bargain tomorrow. How much savings do we have, dear?"

"Oh, I don't know, Dan. If you count our stock and bond investments, and *don't* count what we've put away in our college funds for the kids, isn't it about nine or ten million?"

"What would you think, then," Dan asked, "if we took two or three out in the morning, maybe by liquidating a few of the dogs in our portfolio, and invested it in UTT stock?"

*   *   *

Adam had already gone to work, having a full day of surgery lined up, when Spider and Serena pulled up in front of the Barlow homestead. Gina hugged and kissed her mother, gave Heather a hug, and went out the door. Spider got out, walked around, and held the back door open for her as she walked to his car, then slid in, and buckled up. After what had happened to her yesterday, it relieved her anxiety considerably to be riding with her friends. Frequent glances by Spider and Serena at the rearview mirrors and the rearview 3-V screen on the dashboard, and out the back window by Gina, failed to reveal anyone following them suspiciously. More than a little anxiety remained, however. The three had all heard Governor Slanghorn's announced *diktat* the night before and had already listened to the early news this morning. UTT was closing down all operations in the state and the markets were responding. The NYSE had opened for the day with UTT stock down ten NDs a share from yesterday's close, and it immediately started falling from there. The feeling that this was the day things would be decided, and that they might be decided badly, was ominous.

Only one thing relieved their feeling of gloom for a few minutes, like a ray of bright sunshine piercing through fog. When they got to the capitol, the crowd of pro-teleportation demonstrators was nearly twice as large as it had been yesterday morning and seemed to be growing rapidly. Indeed, the crowd of anti-teleportation demonstrators, though still forming up, seemed thin and haggard by comparison. But the gloom returned by the time Spider and Gina got into the office, and seemed to be shared by everyone else, including Senator Braxon, as they began to work. Gina struggled to focus on her statistical and analytical legislative work to keep from thinking about it, but could not keep from hearing of the continuing UTT stock price slide, even though the main office 3-V stayed off. Other staff people around her kept checking the news. With only intermittent fluctuations, reversals, and pauses, UTT share prices fell all morning in a near panic. The network news analysts at NBS and CBC could hardly contain their glee, while those at EAGLE/FOX seemed almost as distressed by it as Gina felt.

*　　　*　　　*

"Sam. Are we ready to . . ." Jerry and Jake entered Sam's office without even knocking this time, but stopped short as soon as they saw him. He was wearing a wrist brace and wrappings on his right hand. In addition he had several bruises on the left side of his face, his eyes were bloodshot, and he looked generally disheveled. He was sitting at his desk watching the stock report, however, while puffing on a cigar.

"What in hell happened to you, Sam?" Jake asked. "You look like you were hit by a truck!"

Sam waved them to seats, diverting his attention only briefly from the office 3-V. "I slipped and fell on my steps after I left you guys last night. Tried to catch myself and sprained my wrist. Had to spend an hour in the emergency room over at the UC Med Center, and I'm doped to the gills with pain killers. Sit down, will you?"

"Are we there yet?" Jerry asked as the two made themselves comfortable and focused on the 3-V. "It's been free falling all morning!"

Sam took another puff on the cigar he was holding in his left hand, removed it a few inches from his mouth, and slowly blew out a large cloud of blue smoke.

"Not quite, but soon. Drops another twenty neobucks and we can cover all our contracts. We'll be filthy rich. I figure another half hour at this rate, maybe less. See?" He pointed his cigar at the screen. "See that? It just fell another buck!"

Jake and Jerry reached over and high-fived each other like a couple of teenage kids, chortling.

"Hey, Jerry," Sam said. "You remember the van that ran off the guys you had the union send to teach that Barlow witch a lesson?"

"What about it, Sam?"

"I'm thinking they might not have just been good citizens. There might be somebody keeping an eye on her. Maybe even Feds or somebody. I think we should leave Barlow alone."

Jake was incredulous. "That's ridiculous, Sam! Why let her off scot free after all the trouble she's caused us?"

"Because I say so, Jake, That's why!" Sam snapped.

Jake shrugged. "All right, if you say so, Sam. You don't have to get huffy. Give me a second, and I'll call Rockfort." Fishing his NanoPod out of his pocket Jake unfolded it and punched in the union leader's personal code. After only a few rings the man apparently answered.

"Earl, this is Jake. . . Yes, it won't be long now. Me and Jerry are here with Sam doing a little early celebrating while we watch it fall. It's almost there. Say Earl, Sam thinks there might be somebody, maybe even Federal heat, watching that Barlow broad, and he wants us to lay off her. . . Yes."

At that moment Jerry and Sam, listening to just one side of the conversation, saw Jake's face go pale. "What? . . . You're kidding! . . . Well then maybe Sam is right. . . Okay. Yes, we'll get back to you as soon as it's a done deal. The share price only has to fall a little further."

"What did he say about Barlow?" Sam asked, feeling a sudden chill in his spine as he watched a disturbed Jake try to fold up his NanoPod.

"He agrees. Seems that somebody, and they don't know who, put one of the guys he sent after her in the hospital yesterday. Caught him coming out of a bar, broke his Jaw, broke his arm, and threw him back into the bar upside-down through the front window."

Jerry and Sam looked at each other for a moment, trying to assimilate this information. "Weird," Jerry mumbled, half to himself, deliberately looking down and away from Sam's wrist and face.

Sam shuddered visibly. "Yes. That doesn't sound like the Feds."

The phone rang. Sam punched the caller ID. The Governor's face appeared on the screen, with parts of the great seal of the state of California visible on the wall behind his face and upper chest.

"I gotta take this, it's the Governor," he told them as he picked up, awkwardly, with his left hand. "Mel, what can I. . ? Well, I had a little accident. Don't worry about it. Yes, almost. . . Well, we still need it to fall a little more, or we can't cover all the contracts. . . There are? He did? Well, we're almost there, Mel! Just hang tough! We should be able to buy in just a little while. . . Yes. . . Okay, Mel. . . Yes, I'll call you immediately."

"What's up with him?" Jake asked as Sam put the phone down none too gently. "Getting anxious?"

Sam was grim. "A pro-teleportation crowd has showed up and started picketing the Governor's mansion. The crowd is growing, and they're mad. He thinks they want to lynch him. He called out the state police. Plus, the *Times* just put a new poll out. The public isn't reacting well to what he did last night. There are recall petitions starting to circulate all over the state, and Neely called him, in a panic. It's all adding up, and Mel is really feeling the pressure."

Jerry swallowed and looked pale. "I know what he feels like. Have you looked outside in the last little while? Believe me, you don't wanna go out there. People are taking their *lunch breaks* from offices for three blocks around, and going and joining in with that pro-teleportation mob!"

Sam shook his head and half mumbled. "Just a little longer. Just a little more. We're almost there."

*   *   *

Tom put the phone down. With the disconnection, The Buzzard's face disappeared. The relief he felt was palpable, and a good deal of tension drained from his body. But he still had to act, and quickly. He picked the phone up again and punched in Marlon's code. Marlon was waiting, and picked up immediately.

"Marlon, Buzz did it," Tom told him. "Signed, sealed, and delivered. We're taking a beating, doing it this way. Probably less than two-thirds of what we'd have gotten if the trial went its whole course. The only problem is, it'll be days before the funds are transferred."

"It doesn't matter, Tom," Marlon answered. "The paperwork is good enough for me. Just scan it in and we'll front you the money. I've already cleared that with my partners. I can take it from here. There might still be time."

*   *   *

Bill came up from the floor, spent a few minutes watching the news on the 3-V in his office and talking on the phone to Roger Galbraith, then he wandered down toward Gina's desk, stopping on the way to nod

503

to or speak briefly with the staffers who were not on the phone or otherwise extremely busy. Gina turned her attention from her work as she saw him coming, wondering if he wanted her to do something in particular. She sensed, from his ambling pace, that he did not, and might simply want to talk. Nearly always, when Bill walked, he was energetic and focused, with purpose, heading somewhere to do something. Now, he seemed desultory, almost aimless, and perhaps even defeated.

"Nice flowers," he said, waving towards the bouquet.

"Thank you, sir. It was nice of Mr. Wright to send them to me."

"Hmm. Someday you'll have to tell me how he knew your involvement in all this. I didn't tell Lew, didn't tell Marlon, didn't tell anyone. Do you mind?" He indicated that he would like to pull up a chair.

"Of course not, sir. Is there anything I can do for you. . . Bill?"

Bill pulled a spare chair around, sat down and leaned back, hands behind his head, and shook it slowly in the negative. "No, I've about decided there isn't much any of us can do. Hally is downstairs trying to get another vote on an ethics hearing, but that's going nowhere. Boy, I hate to see those SOBs win. Pardon my language, Gina."

Gina simply pursed her lips and nodded slightly in agreement. "It's okay, sir."

"Do you have any idea when they'll jump in?" He asked.

"No, sir," she said as she closed out her statistical program and opened up the NYSE site so they could see the ticker. "They have to buy about two hundred-thousand shares, but I don't know how much money they've put together so I don't know what their target share price is. One equation, two unknowns. Maybe even three, since I don't know their target rate of return, either. My guess is, though, they're getting close. Of course, they might actually want to wait for the price to fall *below* their target, because their large purchases should make it go up a little."

Bill smiled weakly. "You mean that rat Clanton wasn't *entirely* lying when he said they were actually going to *support* UTT's share price?"

Gina nodded. "Not entirely, sir. Just ninety percent. My dad always says the most effective and dangerous lies are those that are partly true. We should see at least a little upward bump when they start buying in, and maybe even a rise for a short while when they do." She pointed to the ticker, then looked closer, blinked, and did a double take. "There. Did you see that, Senator? It just jumped up five NDs. Must have been a large set of purchases. I wonder if that's them."

*　　　*　　　*

"Okay, Sam, it's time to break out the Champaign. Only five more NDs to go, and it's falling like a rock." Jerry was standing, too nervous to sit as he pointed at the ticker showing UTT stock prices on Sam's 3-V screen.

"Call the brokerage first," Jake added, "and tell him to buy as soon as it gets there."

"I don't have to," Sam responded, smiling hugely despite the pain in his wrist. Some of the pain pills were wearing off, but a little alcohol would substitute, and he had been awaiting the opportunity. Lifting his feet down from his office desk and putting his cigar in the ash tray, he swiveled his chair around and rolled over a little to reach his small office wet-bar. "They're all ready to go. I told them when to buy last week."

Sam found three glasses and put them on the desk, using his left hand, then did the same with the Champaign, which had been chilling all morning. "Here, Jerry," he said. "You'll have to open this."

Jerry popped the cork and poured the wine, then the others stood, everyone took theirs, the three men clinked glasses in an unspoken toast, and simultaneously each took a big sip. Savoring the taste of the Champaign and the glow of the alcohol, their attention wandered back to the 3-V just in time to see the share price of UTT stock jump up by five NDs.

"What the hell?" Senator Foxly expostulated.

Sam was startled into near paralysis for a moment, and then shook it off. "Relax. Probably just a few people with more money than brains jumping in at the wrong time. Random fluctuation. Happens once in a while. It'll go back down."

As they watched, though, the price rose three more NDs a share.

*   *   *

"Is that what you expected, Gina?" The Senator asked, watching her computer screen intently.

Somewhat puzzled, Gina's eyebrows went up and she shook her head slightly. UTT shares had risen by more than ten NDs. "I'm not sure, Senator. It's a bigger initial jump and a faster rise than I expected. Maybe there were more people in on the conspiracy, and they committed for more shares than we know about."

"Could something else be going on? Some change in market psychology, or expectations, that would turn things around?" Bill sounded hopeful, or at least, as if he was looking for hope.

"It'd have to be based on something, recent news of some kind," Gina answered. Closing out, she skipped to CNABC's website, scanned the news there, then went to EAGLE/FOX, scanned that, then to NBS cable. "I don't see anything, sir. UTT is still closed down, or closing down. Neither the Governor nor Director Hoffer has changed their minds. Of course, they're coming under increased public pressure; but, by itself, I don't think that would change investor expectations."

"So you think they've won?"

"I don't know, Senator. There isn't any site I know of that will tell you who's buying." As Gina spoke, she dropped off the NBS news site and shifted back to the NYSE. UTT shares were up another five NDs. "But look, Bill, it's still going up and rapidly. This really doesn't look like just the conspirators buying. Maybe something else is happening."

Just then Spider and Dex came over, obviously excited. "Excuse me, Bill, Gina," Dex said, "but have you two noticed that UTT stock prices turned around a few minutes ago?"

"We noticed," Bill answered. "We're trying to figure out whether it's just Clanton and his gang buying in, or if something else is happening."

"You know," Gina said, "assuming for the sake of argument that general investor sentiment hasn't shifted and the Clanton people aren't in the market yet, there could be one other possibility."

"What's that?" Bill asked.

Gina was reluctant to tell them, because she was not entirely sure of her own motives for what she had done. "Well, when Mr. Wright came to the hearings the other day, I . . . sort of . . . advised him to have his company buy back their own stock. If they could buy enough, they could prop the price up, or at least keep it from going as low as the Clanton conspiracy needs. They wouldn't be able to buy low and deliver high on their contracts. That would take lots of money, though, and the problem is that what Hoffer did caused UTT to lose a lot of their revenue."

All three men looked slightly shocked and perplexed, as if they wanted to speak and couldn't decide what question to ask or response to give. Bill made his decision first.

"How did you do that, Gina? I didn't even get to introduce you to him, and he left immediately when Hoffer pulled their license!"

Gina shrugged slightly. "I. . . gave him a note as he was leaving."

Dex smirked. "That's why he sent you the flowers!"

"Yes, well, maybe." Gina answered, and then shifted back to the main discussion to get away from that thought. "They would have had to use uncommitted reserves and cash flow from out of state and interstate operations. I think they were actually doing that all yesterday, and that's what kept it from turning into a rout."

"Well, then I still don't get it, Gina," Bill said. "If all they could do yesterday was prevent a more rapid decline, and they have even less to work with today, how could they be turning things around all of a sudden? Where would they get the money?"

Gina was just as puzzled, particularly as she watched UTT stock prices jump up another five neobucks per share. "I don't know, sir, but look. It's still going up."

*   *   *

"It's still going up!" Gerald Foxly shrieked. "How can it keep going up?"

"I don't know. I don't know!" Sam's white and pasty expression made him look even worse than he had when he first came in to work that morning. He was wracking his brains, looking for an answer, and gradually, a glimmering came. "They. . . they must be buying their own stock!"

509

"How can they do that?" Jerry waved his hands in frustration as he yelled the question. "Didn't we take away their business? How can they do that?"

"I don't know! Of course we did. I don't know!" Sam yelled back, and then realized he sounded like he was contradicting himself. "They must be spending every spare dime they have. It's their last shot! They can't keep it up! It'll go back down!"

Jake Gramm had gone from shocked paralysis to an almost icy calm, oddly resulting from a feeling of near certainty that they were doomed. "Buy now, Sam! I know we gave you control of the money, but call that damn broker and tell him to buy now! We can at least cover part of the contracts, and we'll make enough on those to cover some of our losses on the rest. *Buy now,* while it's still below the delivery price!"

"No!" Sam yelled. "They'll run out. They can't possibly keep it up. If we hold on, it'll go back down!"

"Arrgh!" Jake's response was an incoherent verbal and physical expression of rage and frustration. Turning, he stormed out of the office, slamming the door behind him.

The videophone rang and Sam snatched it up angrily, without even checking first to see who it was. "What?" Listening, for a moment, his pallor worsened. "You can't do that! . . . We had an agreement . . . Listen, if we just hold on . . . But you can't do that! It'll ruin us!"

As Sam tried to hang up the phone, left-handed, while staring blankly off into space, it slipped and clattered on the desk. Finally noticing, he picked it up and seated it. Gerald Foxly watched glumly, wondering what Sam had heard, but afraid to ask.

"That was Ergly," Sam said, barely more than whispering. "The unions are taking their money and backing out."

*   *   *

In the war room at UTT headquarters, the mood was cautiously optimistic. Despite the horrible losses the firm was suffering as every operation in the state of California was being shut down, at least the slide in their stock price had been reversed. By three o'clock, the ticker on the big wall 3-V screen showed that all the morning losses had been made up and the price had reached yesterday's closing value, still going up. Tom was still nervous, however, over a key question. He had tried repeatedly to call Marlon Gates to get an answer to it, but was unable to get through. Finally, however, Marlon called back, and Tom put the phone on speaker.

"Tom, sorry for taking so long getting back," Marlon said, "but I've been busy spending your money to buy your stock. You might be unhappy if you knew just how much I've spent, but so far I've bought about a million shares. You can do the math. And, of course, it gets more expensive the higher the share price gets. You sure you want me to keep going?"

Tom nodded. "Yes. Unless we were too late, we're going to have to hold the price up until the delivery date on the Clanton gang's forward contracts. Do you have any idea whether Clanton and Slanghorn bought their shares?   If they have, we're just spinning our wheels for nothing, right?"

"I can't be positive, Tom, but I think we caught 'em napping.   I didn't see any indication in the price movements of them buying in before we started making our heavy purchases this morning.   Plus, nobody we've bought from tells us they've sold any shares yet to those guys.   In fact, I'm surprised if Clanton and Slanghorn haven't bought.   You'd think they would have by now, just to reduce their losses. They must be counting on us running out of money and waiting for the price to go back down."

"In that case, Marlon, just keep buying.   In fact, I was wondering if we shouldn't buy those forward contracts, too.   I seem to remember Vanderbilt did that to the New York Aldermen."

Marlon laughed.   "Yeh, well, Tom, Vanderbilt had a mean streak.   Plus, in relative terms, he was better financially situated than you've been in this instance.   If the Clanton and Slanghorn gang really haven't bought their shares and they default come delivery date, you'd just have injured yourself more if you had me buy those contracts."

*   *   *

By late afternoon, nearly all pretense of work in Bill's senatorial office had ceased, other than a few routine intermittent answers to constituent calls. Even those had fallen off considerably, as the public too, became entranced with what was happening in the market and on the streets. The amazing turnaround and rapid rise in UTT share prices had become the story on the network news. Nearly all the staffers were standing in knots in front of the main office 3-V listening. Bill, too, came out of his inner office to watch what was happening on the big screen.

At the moment, it showed Rexford Grumman, the main NBS News anchor at the network's headquarters. ". . . going on for over three hours, now, and - uh - just how to account for it is the question on everyone's mind. . . uh. . . I'm hearing now that we have a report from Sloan Brinkerhoff on the floor at the New York stock exchange, . . , are you there Sloan? What do you have for us?"

Sloan Brinkerhoff was a relatively young blond woman who would have been attractive except that, like many feminist professionals aspiring to act like men, she chronically wore a severe pantsuit with a hair style and facial expression to match. "Yes, Rex, this is Sloan Brinkerhoff at the New York Stock Exchange. We've been getting reports here, unconfirmed as yet, but we think that they're reliable, that Universal Teleportation Transport has - uh - been buying, through intermediaries, large amounts of its own stock. There certainly are some other transactions going on, Rex, but - uh - this appears to be the main factor behind the astonishing upward swing in UTT stock prices over the last several hours, despite everything to the contrary, or, rather, that you'd think would be operating to lower its value over the last several days, and seemed to be doing so."

"So, Sloan," the picture swung back to Rexford Grumman, "what you're saying is, if I may paraphrase, that this run up we're seeing is not due to any fundamental change in investor estimates of the likely profitability of UTT, but simply, uh, a big corporation using its investor's resources to manipulate its stock value? I mean, can that be legal? Doesn't this kind of corporate falsification of stock values sound a lot like the old 'Enron scandal'?"

"Well, Rex, strictly speaking, it is legal for a corporation to buy its stock back, with the authorization of its board of directors. I mean, if they can sell stock to raise capital, they can use capital to buy it back. That's not illegal. But you certainly are justified in questioning the propriety and ethics of possibly corrupt corporate officers misusing their own investors resources to - uh - I guess there's no other way to put it than you did, manipulate their own stock values for possible personal gain."

"But don't you think, Sloan," Grumman asked, "that the political dimension of this is also important? That this may somehow be aimed at fending off the legitimate efforts of the California governor and the legislature at establishing some kind of reasonable regulatory regime over UTT's obviously dangerous and environmentally hazardous technology?"

"Well, Rex it's, . . . yes, it does seem to be part of some kind of coordinated effort with the - uh - the growing protests that have been organized here supporting the resumption of teleportation transport operations by UTT, along with, the uh, . . . the petitions to recall Governor Slanghorn we've been hearing about all day, that are circulating rapidly through those crowds and around the state, and - uh -"

"Excuse me, Sloan, but I've just received word of breaking news at the Ninth District Federal Court in Sacramento. We have to break away to Bob Van Neff, our legal correspondent who has been watching the litigation between UTT and Sony Corporation over patent infringement, technology theft, and related issues. Are you there, Bob?"

Bob stood woodenly for a moment, waiting to be sure that he was live before answering. "Yes, I am, Rex. This is Bob Van Neff at the Ninth District Federal Court, where, within the last half hour, the Court has been shocked by a request from UTT to drop all charges and further litigation against Sony Corporation. We understand that a similar request is being issued by UTT in the Japanese courts. This all appears to be the result of some kind of out-of-court settlement reached this morning between UTT and Sony, possibly involving a great deal of money, though neither side is talking . . ."

"That's how they did it!" Gina whispered to herself, but apparently loud enough that Bill, standing next to her as they watched the news, heard, since he nodded understanding.

Dex apparently also heard her and understood, as he also nodded before commenting. "Now if they just beat Sam Clanton and the gang into the market, those guys are done."

*   *   *

"We're done," Gerald Foxly whispered, staring blankly at the floor of Samuel Clanton's senatorial office.

"No!" Sam said. "We've. . . we've still got the hearings! They start again next week. We can threaten severe regulation. We can. . ."

"We tried that, Sam!" Jerry somehow summoned the energy to reply vehemently. "It wasn't enough even before this settlement. They can buy as much as they need as long as they need, keep the price up until we have to deliver. Jake was right. You should have let us buy when we could have this morning and still limited our losses. Now we've had it. The share price is already above our delivery price. You've ruined us all!"

Jerry stood, turned, and shuffled dejectedly out of the office, closing the door quietly behind him. Sam simply sat numbly behind his desk, tried to ignore the pain in his wrist, and wondered where and why everything had gone so wrong.

*   *   *

Early in the evening, Governor Melvin Slanghorn called a hasty news conference, this time held in the pressroom at the Governor's mansion. Some wags among the national network technical teams, while struggling to get their 3-V cameras and other equipment set up in time, remarked that they thought it was because he was afraid to leave the building. The crowds outside were not in a pleasant mood, where the Governor was concerned.

At the appointed time, the red camera lights went on and hand camera flashes began going off as the Governor entered the room, walked to the podium, and began composing himself while making sure the teleprompter was working. Then he began speaking.

"Ladies and gentlemen of the press, thank you for coming and allowing me to speak to the citizens of the great state of California. To you citizens, let me begin by saying how much it has been my pleasure to serve as your Governor for the last two-and-a-half years. In this time it has been my constant effort not only to serve the public interest, but to instill the will of the public into law and policy. Events today have convinced me that I severely misjudged the public will in my hasty decision last night to support and reinforce the misguided directive from Director of the California Department of Transportation Maynard Clairborn Hoffer, to stop all operations of Universal Teleportation Transportation in the boundaries of the state of California. Consequently, I have decided to repeal that directive as of tomorrow and have asked for, and received, the resignation of Director Hoffer.

"I still firmly believe that a potentially dangerous and environmentally harmful technology that is deeply disruptive of traditional transportation industries must be regulated in the public interest. However, the form and magnitude of such regulations can be determined only after fair and orderly hearings that will determine the exact nature and severity of the threats, followed either by considered legislative actions or due deliberation by the Department of Transportation. While this is happening, UTT will be allowed to resume full operation. Thank you."

The Governor turned and walked out of the room without stopping to answer any of the simultaneously shouted questions about the effect of the circulating recall petitions on his decision: Why Director Hoffer and not he, the Governor, bore responsibility for the temporary shutdown of UTT; the implications of the run up in UTT share prices; the Governor's own short-sales of UTT stock; or, for that matter, any of the dozens of other questions on people's minds.

*   *   *

Practically everyone had crowded into the UTT 'war room' when word had spread of the Governor's hastily called news conference. The cheer that went up at Slanghorn's repeal announcement was deafening and lasted for over a minute, only gradually settling down into excited and cheery conversation.

"Well, Tom, it's back to business now!" Derek said as he and Tom shook hands while Dave slapped Tom on the back.

Beowulf stopped hugging, dancing around, and cheering with Billi Jo long enough to put his two cents worth in. "Yeh, we really kicked their butts."

"Well, it's a huge victory, but it's only part of what we wanted, right?" Phil asked. "We still don't know for sure those guys weren't able to buy their shares, do we, Tom?"

Tom shook Phil's offered hand. "No, not for sure, though Marlon doesn't think they were able to. We should find out pretty soon, though, certainly no later than a few days from now when those contracts mature. But like Derek says, at least we're back in business."

Chapter 30: Even Some Mighty Have Fallen

The next morning, Wednesday, Tom slept in, making up for sleep lost over the last several days. For Tom, however, sleeping in meant coming wide awake at six-thirty and feeling rejuvenated. Having missed workouts also, he decided to jog a few miles around the runway. Going out the front door of the Asylum in his running gear and waving to the Pinkerton guards at the front station on the way, he was surprised and cheered to see Derek and Beowulf outside, also dressed for running.

"Hey, guys. What are you doing here? Don't you usually terrorize your own neighborhood streets in the morning?"

"We figured you could use some company," Derek grinned.

"And, somehow, we just knew you'd be out here this morning," Beowulf added. "Besides, I'm gonna be here at the Asylum all day, anyway. I can just shower here when we're done running. We're finishing fabricating the prototype graviton wave generator this morning. Then we're gonna run a little current through it and see whether we can actually make some."

"Darn!" Tom said as the three men started jogging over to the runway. "If I wasn't going to be busier than a one-armed paperhanger making sure our operation gets everything and everybody up and running again today, I'd like to be here for that."

"Well, now you know how I feel, Tom," Derek said. "I'll tell you what. You let me, Phil, and Parker take care of all that at the Tower today, and you just go ahead and have fun with Beowulf and the other guys out here. You deserve it. But then you gotta find a replacement for me and put me back into the R & D, so I can have fun, too. Administration is driving me crazy."

Tom barked a laugh. "It's a deal, Derek, if you're serious. Not that you're not a good administrator, because you do fine, but, the truth is, I need you back in R & D. When we take the Weak Force Team over to New Mexico next week, I need a couple of our best engineers there. Besides, Sean has been talking with a guy at the Intermountain High Energy Lab who has a lot of administrative experience in high tech operations. He badly wants that kind of job with us. You do know, though, Derek, that if we do that, you'll have to take a pay cut?"

Derek grunted a half-laugh as he jogged. "Believe me, Tom, money doesn't worry me. I just want in the worst way to be where the action is."

"Yeh, Tom," Beowulf added, "You know we've had manufacturers busting down our doors to make our synthesizer, don't you? We made a deal with one the other day, and they sent us a check with so many zeros on it that it was a foot long!"

Tom barked another laugh. "Now if you guys would spend a little of that money, instead of just hoarding it all and living forever in that two-bit apartment."

"You should talk, Tom," Derek responded.

"Hey, Tom, you going to be at the Aikido workout tonight?" Beowulf asked. "It's not the same when Billi Jo and me or Jack Menendez has to run it. Besides, if you keep missing practice, you'll get sloppy."

"I've been a little busy," Tom said, sounding mortified.

A car passed them on the road just as they were starting their last leg down the runway. When they finished, and were walking the last little way back from the runway to the Asylum door, they were surprised to see Harry Pinkerton, in uniform, waiting for them.

"Hey, Harry," Tom called when he recognized him, "you're back!"

"Yes, I am, sir," Harry answered, nodding also to Derek and Beowulf.

"He must be on duty, Tom," Beowulf smirked. "He only calls you 'sir' when he's on duty." All three men chuckled and shook Harry's hand before Beowulf and Derek headed inside.

"I got bacon, eggs, and stuff in the fridge, guys," Tom called to them. "You get showered; then let's have some breakfast before we go to work."

The two waved and nodded agreement as they entered the building. Tom turned back to Harry. "You missed a lot of excitement around here. I'm glad to have you back, even though Jack did a good job while you were gone."

Harry's military bearing did not change, but there was a hint of satisfaction with life in his eyes. "I'm glad to be back, sir, though, believe it or not, I did manage to find a little excitement of my own where I was."

*   *   *

Bill Braxon smelled blood in the water by mid-morning when it became clear that none of the members of the Clanton cabal were even present on Capitol Hill. They were not on the floor, nor were they in their offices. The Democratic-Republican Party was almost bereft of its entire leadership, and several other key members of the party were also missing. Floor business was being conducted by a junior RepubliCrat senator. There were more than enough senators in the building for a quorum, however. Striking before the opportunity passed, Bill, Hally, and Roger got every ALP senator they could downstairs and called for a vote on his automotive deregulation bill. The RepubliCrats were too weak to stop them. Before noon the bill had passed by two votes.

Senator Braxon practically floated upstairs to his office, where he spent some time on the phone with several members of the American Liberty Party leadership in the House. They assured him that the House version of his bill was on track to pass within a few days. Jubilant despite the near certainty that Governor Slanghorn would veto the bill when it got to his desk, and leaving Hally and Roger to take care of business on the floor for a while, Bill grabbed Gina,

523

Spider, and Dex, and took them downtown to a classy restaurant for an extended lunch.

"Well, even if he vetoes it, it wasn't all for nothing," Dex was saying as they drove back toward the capitol afterward, speaking over the sound of the radio on which the news was droning in the background. "I heard this morning that the groups circulating those recall petitions already have more than two-thirds of the signatures they need. I don't think what the Governor did last night is gonna stop them from getting the rest. If he's recalled, we'll have an ALP governor before next year."

"Yeh," Spider interjected. "I hear that Rafe Brown, Eleanor Vixer, and Mickey Chin are already jockeying to be the ALP candidate."

Bill nodded, keeping his eyes on the road. "True. They're all good people, too. I particularly like Mickey. But we'll still have to herd the whole bill through both chambers again, and even with the strong shift in public sentiment we're seeing now, we won't likely have an ALP majority in the senate until after the next general election, nearly a year and a half out."

Spider was about to say something when Gina leaned forward. "Excuse me, Bill, but could you turn the radio up, please? I think they just said something about Sam Clanton."

Rather than verbally telling the car computer to raise the radio volume, which might itself cause him to miss something, Bill simply reached over and spun the dial to the right. There were still some advantages to old ways of doing things.

". . . reported that several members of the California Senate, including Majority Leader Samuel Clanton; Majority Whip Gerald Foxly; and Senate President Jacob Gramm; along with four others, have filed this morning for bankruptcy protection. There is also a report, as yet unconfirmed, that Governor Melvin Slanghorn is seeking help from the Democratic-Republican Party for payment of his debts and may have to file for bankruptcy soon if he is not able to . . ."

The silence from those in the car was almost eerie as they listened, and it continued for some time after the news turned to the rapid reopening of UTT passenger and freight centers all around the state, and then to more mundane matters. Bill finally turned the radio off.

"You know," Gina finally broke the silence and apparently expressed a common sentiment, "I thought I'd be happy if I found that out, but I'm not."

Bill nodded a qualified agreement. "I'm not either, Gina. It's not a sweet victory. But that doesn't mean I won't take advantage of it if I get a chance. Nobody who knew what they were talking about ever said that politics wasn't a blood sport."

When they got back to the office, everyone had already heard the news about the bankruptcy of the Clanton/Slanghorn cabal and a somewhat less charitable and more jubilant mood prevailed. Bill stayed only a few minutes there basking in the glow before going back down to the floor to deal with pending legislative business. Spider and Dex went back to work. Gina decided to work hard on her dissertation. She was on the edge of finishing the statistical work and would soon be able to start pulling the whole thing together into its final form. So she spent the remainder of the afternoon crunching numbers, constructing tables and graphs, and writing.

Gina was so intent on her work, she was surprised when Serena and Spider came to see if she was ready to go home. Reluctantly, she logged off her computer, packed up her stuff, and headed out with them.

"Did you hear the news, Gina?" Serena asked as the three walked down the hall towards the elevators, her hand in Spider's.

"Yes, I did." Gina responded. "This morning, when we were in Bill's car on the way back from . . ."

"Oh, that's not what she means, Gina." Spider interrupted in typical male-fashion before Gina could finish. It did not bother her though. She had realized long ago that it was a minor expression of natural male aggressiveness and usually wasn't meant to be insulting or demeaning. "They had it on the news a little while ago that Martha Clanton filed for divorce this afternoon."

Gina was so shocked that she almost stumbled, barely catching herself.

"Oh, and that's not the worst for Sam Clanton!" Serena pitched back in, having apparently learned that you had to be willing to do that to get a word in edgewise with opinionated men, including Spider. "The state Attorney General's office is filing charges of corruption in office against him, including: misuse of public funds, accepting bribes, false employment, salary kickbacks, and about a dozen other charges. It seems some as-yet-unnamed call girl is offering state's evidence in exchange for immunity from prosecution. They're also charging several officials in the California Brotherhood of Teamsters with bribery."

"Wha. . . why didn't you tell me all this when you heard earlier, Spider?" Gina asked.

"Well, I thought maybe you already knew." Spider had a smug expression on his face as he looked at Gina. "This is all your doing one way or another anyway, isn't it? That information you put together apparently got put to very good use by somebody. Besides, you were so busy working when Serena came up and told Dex and me, neither of us wanted to bother you. Anyway, this is going to change everything. Bill will have a field day tomorrow."

Somehow Gina was not really cheered by this news any more than she had been by that of the Clanton cabal's bankruptcy earlier in the day. The thought of Martha Clanton receiving the divorce she deserved was indeed cheering. It was also comforting to learn that, in at least part due to Gina's own efforts, Sam might be brought to justice for his other crimes, and his power to hurt others would be ended. But the thought that a man of talent would do such things as Sam Clanton did, and have to be faced with such consequences, struck Gina as sad.

*   *   *

Having heard of Sam Clanton's indictment on the evening news, Bill had his agenda for the day all planned long before he got to the office Thursday morning. Huddling briefly with Roger and Hally before the morning's session began, the three descended to the floor and began organizing the ALP troops in preparation for their assault. Surprisingly, Clanton, Gramm, Jerry Foxly and the other members of the cabal were also there, apparently anticipating what was to come and intending to mount a defense. This time it was not enough, however. Despite impassioned and angry debate, in which Sam and his cohorts tried every form of twist in interpretation to justify their actions, and Sam denied any wrongdoing in the employment of Charise Meardon, blaming everything on an ALP conspiracy to defame him and the Democratic-Republican Party, the ALP call for an ethics committee investigation passed by four votes.

The real surprise for Bill came afterwards. He was in his office, about to go out to lunch, when Ly buzzed him and said that three Democratic-Republican Party senators were asking to see him. Everyone else in the office saw them go in, and saw Roger and Hally come up and be ushered into Bill's inner office a few minutes later. Dex recognized the three Democratic-Republicans as among those who bolted that party to vote with the ALP for the ethics investigation. For the next half hour the office buzzed with speculation and rumor over what was going on. Then the three RepubliCrat senators came out, smiling and shaking hands with Bill, Roger, and Hally before leaving. A few minutes later Roger and Hally came out, and Bill spoke to Ly as they left. Then Ly buzzed Gina, Dex, and Spider to tell them the Senator wanted to see them. The three went to Bill's office with some anticipation.

Inside, Bill, standing behind his desk with the chair pushed back, as if too excited to sit, waved them to seats. "Normally I don't condone drinking at the office during work hours," he said, "but would any of you like a little sherry?"

Spider and Dex eagerly assented. Gina asked if she could have seven-up instead, if he had any, which he did. Bill got them their drinks, and then raised his glass, leading them in an unspoken toast. They all took a sip, and then he spoke. "You three may be looking at the new Majority Leader of the California Senate."

Gina drew her breath in sharply and Spider and Dex, as wide-eyed as Gina, both said "WHAT?"

Bill grinned at their surprise. "Hadly, Redford, and Tilden are switching parties. They're going to announce it tonight. It'll be a done deal in the morning."

"But. . . But that still won't give us a majority," Dex objected.

Bill's grin only got wider. "They say there're two more for sure, maybe three. A couple of them may just be in because they see which way the wind is blowing politically and want to survive. Hadly and some of the others are sick and tired of the corruption. Tildon and Redford have been closet Libertarians in RepubliCrat districts for years, and I've been after them to switch for a long time. They finally figured the time had come. If even two more do come over, we'll have a slim majority."

Gina raised her glass again. "Congratulations, Mr. Majority Leader!"

They all took another swig. Bill swirled his remaining sherry for a moment. "You know, I think it's time for a little celebration. I'm thinking maybe a barbecue out at my place tomorrow evening after work. We may even knock off a little early. You three up for it?"

They chorused their assent, then Spider asked, "Can I bring Serena, Bill?"

"Sure. In fact, we might as well make it a fairly big bash. Roger and Hally, of course; your folks, Gina; and I'd like to invite Tom Wright and a few of his people from UTT, if I can get 'em to come. I hear they'll be testing the teleport chamber out at the airport tomorrow. Mr. Wright is scheduled to testify at the committee hearings on Monday anyway. I've decided that even if we do take over, we'll just let those things play out. Tom might be willing to just come early and stay over the weekend."

Gina's heart leaped, and she struggled to compose her expression. Maybe the third time would be the charm.

"In fact, I think I'll invite the whole staff. Of course," Bill continued, thinking out loud, "with that many I might need an extra grill. I'm not sure mine would be enough, even as big as it is."

"I can throw my charcoal grill in the back of my pickup and bring it over, Bill," Dex suggested.

"I got one, too," Spider added enthusiastically. "They'll both fit in Dex's truck."

"We're on, then," Bill announced. "For now, let's get back to work."

*   *   *

Frederick M. Carmody III, U.S. Senator from Massachusetts, was the last to arrive at the meeting of the Commission, held in the subbasement three hundred feet below the lowest publicly known floor in Rockefeller Center. The Chairman of the Federal Reserve Board, the presidents of all of the American 3-V networks but one, the Vice-President of the United States, and the Triumvirate itself, those three who were themselves mere members of the World Commission, were already present.

Though Senator Carmody was still a minute ahead of the appointed time, the others stared at him in stony silence as the secretary ushered him in and he walked over and seated himself at the table. The Triumvirate liked people to be early and the rest all knew it. They also knew that each and every one of them held their own positions and power at the will of the Triumvirate, and that it's will was not to be flouted or even tested in the slightest. The experience of Fred's older brother Jack, a prior member of the commission who was assassinated in bed along with his mistress, the voluptuous actress Mary Beth Grabel, after Jack had

531

introduced a bill in the Senate to reduce personal and corporate tax rates, attested to that.

Of course, the power of the Triumvirate and of the Commission itself was not what it had once been. That power had declined significantly in the Second Great Depression and the Disorders and was only with great difficulty being rebuilt. It had first been weakened by the failure of major statist policies of regulation, income redistribution, and monetary management they had implemented in the 1970s, which led to the election in 1980 of a U.S. President they did not control. It was weakened further by the failure of their effort to assassinate that President, so that one of their own assets could assume power. As a result, that President did all too much damage to their cause before he left office. Indeed, he had been partly responsible for the collapse of the communist empire that the World Commission had cultivated for so long.

In addition, the unanticipated discovery and development of the personal computer and the Internet, giving people access to too many information sources the Commission did not control, had marginally weakened their power to manipulate public opinion. That and many similar, earlier experiences, had made the Commission leery of new technologies and industries that disrupted traditional economic and industrial patterns, all too often weakening their established power base. Precisely for the propensity of free markets to repeatedly generate such disruptive new technologies and industries, America had always been difficult to control. When such inventions and innovations could not be co-opted by the Commission and bent to its use (as they had done with broadcast radio and television), it tried to suppress them.

But new technologies and industries were not the only threat the Commission had faced. After some advance in its power by successful manufacture and propagation of an Islamic terrorist threat, and later of a financial crisis during a crucial election, a powerful blow to the Commission had come by defection and betrayal from within its own ranks. As a result, the Second Great Depression they had engineered had not led to a strengthening of central government control over the American people and of the Commission's power over that government, as had the First Great Depression they had engineered, but instead had led to a severe weakening of both. Indeed, the Commission had subsequently lost even its capacity to control the content of basic education, which for over a century and a half had insured that succeeding generations of the young were inculcated in the appropriate statist doctrines. Now, he, Carmody, was in the unpleasant position of having to confirm that they might face yet another setback.

"This meeting of the Commission is now in session," came the unmistakable voice of the Chairman, "and your report is first on our agenda, Mr. Carmody. Do not make us wait."

Fred cleared his throat and tried to compose himself before beginning. "Over the last several meetings we have all heard numerous reports concerning the corrosive and disruptive economic and political effects of this unanticipated new teleportation technology. First, we underestimated the threat. For one thing, since our own experts could not follow the math, we did not think it would work. For another, Mr. Wright and his colleagues have proved singularly ingenious at overcoming obstacles naturally existing or placed in their way. We also had no idea the extreme attraction the experience itself would have. That, combined with our failure thus far to control the public perception of Tom Wright and his people, and the failures of our unwitting tools in the California government, has resulted in a strong shift in public opinion. It appears unambiguous now, from all data, that unless we develop an effective strategy soon, we will not only lose California, but several other states in the next general election. The ALP will retake control of Congress and maybe even the Presidency."

Chapter 31: Barbecue, Badminton, and Romance

Gina and Heather got in Gina's Hyundai and left early for the barbecue, because Gina wanted to help Bill, Barbara and the others with the preparations, and Heather wanted to go with her rather than wait for Adam and Rachael, who would come later. Before leaving, Gina had agonized more than usual over what to wear. Bill's social gatherings were nearly always somewhat casual and this one even more so than most since it was being held in Bill's huge back yard and on the deck at the back of the house. Most people would wear jeans for comfort and many would wear hats to shade them from the late afternoon sun. Gina didn't want to be overdressed, but on the other hand she wanted to look presentable in case Tom Wright and his colleagues actually did come. She finally found a pair of pants and a white top with blue flowers that she thought both appropriate to an outdoor gathering and at least mildly flattering, and off she and Heather went.

Gina parked behind Dex's pickup at the curb in front of Bill's place. Barbara and Amanda opened the door at their ring of the bell, and the two girls ran ahead as Gina and Barbara made their way through the house and out back where Bill, Spider, and Dex were setting up their grills and getting ready to start cooking, with Serena looking on. After happy greetings, Barbara,

Gina, and Serena spent a while preparing salads and vegetables, then ferrying them, along with various meats, from the kitchen to the back yard. Roger and his wife, Lillian, showed up, followed shortly by Hally Arkwright, in time to help set up plates and utensils on the wooden picnic tables that were on the second story deck and the lawn next to the grills. Heather and Amanda, at Bill's instruction, brought out horseshoes for Bill's horseshoe pits, then started setting up a badminton net and laying out a court on the lawn behind the tables.

Soon other guests began to arrive. When Adam and Rachael showed up, coming out of the back door of the house with someone unexpected - a tall blond girl with penetrating gray eyes - Gina was shocked with delight. "Cindy!" She squealed, and ran to meet Cindy, who had squealed "Gina," simultaneously, and was doing the same. They hugged and danced around excitedly for a moment before holding each other at arm's length.

"What are you doing here?" Gina asked, amazed.

"Summer vacation!" Cindy told her. "My folks parked our motor home at a campground outside of town. We're going camping up at Crater Lake, then over the Lolo pass through the Idaho wilderness and then down through Yellowstone Park and Utah before heading home in about three weeks. I talked them into letting me borrow the car and come in to see you. Adam and Rachael were just leaving and insisted that I come along so I could at least get to see you for a minute."

"Oh, no, Cindy. You have to stay," Gina urged her. "Let me introduce you to Senator Braxon. Here he comes now. Bill?. . Bill, this is Cindy Markham, my roommate and my best friend at the Institute. Cindy, this is Bill Braxon, Majority Leader of the State Senate."

Bill shook Cindy's hand warmly, and Cindy, a bit abashed at meeting an important person, curtsied slightly. "Nice to meet you, sir. Gina has told me about you. I just showed up unexpectedly at her house and Adam and Rachael sort of - uh - drug me along. I don't mean to impose. . ."

"Nonsense," Bill grinned. "Believe me, any friend of Gina's is a friend of mine and welcome at my home. Particularly one as beautiful as you. Stay and have a good time. I always plan for an extra ten or fifteen people showing up, anyway. 'Scuse me a minute, though, I think some other people have just arrived."

* * *

"I think this is the right place," Beowulf said from the back seat, removing his arm from around Billi Jo's shoulder and leaning down a little to look out of the window.

"Yeh," Derek said from the front passenger seat of the rental. "Finally found the right address, and there're lots of cars. Looks like our bash to me. I think there's room to park in front of that Hummer, Tom."

"I hope these people have plenty to eat," Beowulf said after Tom parked and they got out of the car. "I'm getting hungry."

"Are you ever *not* hungry, hon?" Billi Jo kidded him playfully.

"What can I say," Beowulf grinned, "I'm a growing boy."

Before they got to the door, it was opened by Senator Braxon, who must somehow have seen them coming and been waiting. "Hello, Tom," he said. "Welcome. Glad you could make it."

"Good to see you again, Senator," Tom responded as he shook Bill's hand. "I'm sorry we didn't get to talk more the first time. I really appreciate you inviting us. This is Derek Martin, whom you met briefly before, and this is Billi Jo Jensen, one of our best engineers. That big ogre is Thad Thorsen. We call him Beowulf. You probably saw him on the 3-V, howling at the demonstrators outside the Galt Tower. Somehow he recently managed to persuade Miss Jensen here to tie the knot with him a few weeks from now."

"It was her doing," Beowulf said as he shook the Senator's hand. "She took a club, hit me over the head, and made it official."

"I didn't," Billi Jo said as she took her turn, "but I *will* if he keeps embarrassing me in public like this."

Bill laughed. "Congratulations. I know you all by reputation. I sincerely hope you two will invite me to the wedding so I can at least send a gift. Now if you'll follow me, I have a lot of friends who are anxious to meet you folks."

They followed Bill through the house and to the back where there was a crowd of about twenty or thirty people, some sitting at picnic tables, some standing, and several others pitching horseshoes near the back of the yard. A pair of teenage girls was batting a shuttlecock back and forth across a badminton net. Bill started taking Tom and the others around to make introductions. Many of the people there wanted to talk, however, about their own experience with teleporting, about how Tom and the others had managed to invent and innovate it, about the fall of the Clanton conspiracy, the effort to recall Governor Slanghorn, national politics and economics, and so on. Efforts at organized introductions broke down as Bill had to go check on other matters, and Tom and the others were left to make acquaintances on their own.

Gina saw Tom when he and his friends came with Bill into the back yard, but others had crowded forward. She felt an odd reluctance to initiate an introduction, so she sort of stood awkwardly with Cindy, sipping lemonade she had gotten somewhere, and looked in his direction, hoping he would see her and come over. It struck her as silly, since she hadn't felt that socially awkward since about the eighth grade, but the inhibition persisted.

Beside her, Cindy leaned over and spoke in Gina's ear. "Isn't that Tom Wright himself with Senator Braxon, Gina?"

Gina nodded. "Yes, that's him."

"Wow." Cindy's eyes were big. "You've really made important friends. But look at that long, tall guy next to Mr. Wright. Isn't he a gorgeous hunk?"

"Yes, I suppose so," Gina said. "I think his name is Martin. Derek Martin. They say he's some sort of engineering genius."

"Wow," Cindy said again. "Somebody sure did a good job of engineering him! Can you imagine if he's proportionate?"

Gina's ears burned and she flushed. "Cindy!" She said, shocked.

Cindy giggled at Gina's embarrassment, but then looked thoughtful. "You know, I think I may just go ask him," she said and headed off on a direct course toward Mr. Martin.

Gina was mortified, half jealous of Cindy's straightforward approach, but still inhibited. She simply watched as Cindy walked up to Derek Martin. She couldn't hear how Cindy introduced herself, but Mr. Martin was apparently more than pleased by the company. In a minute or so the two of them sort of drifted away from the others, deep in conversation that was intermittently interrupted by Cindy's feminine giggles and Mr. Martin's hearty laughs. Just then Bill came by and Gina caught his attention again. "Bill, could you introduce me to Mr. Wright?"

"You mean you haven't met him yet, Gina?" Bill was startled. "I apologize. I thought you had. Come on."

Bill sensed a certain tense anticipation in Gina as they walked over. He also noticed that as Tom saw them coming, his eyes locked onto Gina's with a rather singular focus, and an odd sort of half smile of anticipation lit his face and eyes. For a moment, sensing something going on, Bill was tempted to just walk on by, feeling that if he did, neither of them would notice. But Gina had asked him for an introduction.

"Tom," he said. Tom broke the lock long enough to look at him for a moment in response, before looking back at Gina. "This is Miss Gina Barlow. I guess this is the first chance you two have really had to meet."

"Actually," Tom said, reaching out and taking her hand, but just holding it, not shaking, "I'm sad to say we missed at least three earlier opportunities. Two were due to my own stupidity and bad judgment and one to unavoidable circumstances. I'm charmed, Miss Barlow, more than you know."

"Thank you for the flowers, Mr. Wright," she managed to breathe, wondering if he could feel her tremble. "They're beautiful."

Tom did sense her tremble as he gazed into her eyes, and was incredibly touched. "Thank you again for the advice. It worked."

Again, Bill felt motivated to leave, but decided to add one more observation. "You know, Tom, Gina was the one who found out about the Clanton gang's short-sales."

Tom was startled. He released Gina's hand and looked once again at Bill. "I thought that was some researcher at the CLRS."

"He was helping me," Gina said, almost embarrassed.

"I can see why he'd want to," Tom observed, making Gina flush a little. On her, he decided, it looked good.

"I . . . was putting together time-series data on stock trades of the senators," she stammered, a little disconcerted as she finally pulled her hand back.

"Aha. Looking for excess returns like Cheng, Boyd, and the Ziabrowskis."

"Yes, and I found them," she said, feeling herself relax just a little as this intellectual connection absorbed just a little of her visceral turmoil.

"Were the adjusted r-squares high?" He asked.

"Yes, very. But I'm also using a special neo-Bertolian Clex-Hagnon filter I designed, to test for . . . "

Just then Billi Jo, who seemed to have noticed and recognized Gina from across the lawn, came over and put a hand on her arm.

"Gina. Remember me? We met that time in the gym at the institute.

"Oh, yes," Gina said, distracted. "It's Billi Jo, isn't it? I remember."

"Tom," Billi Jo said, "if you think you're good on the uneven bars, you ought to see her. She's fantastic!"

Gina was embarrassed and Tom was startled again. Gina seemed to surprise him repeatedly. He thought back for a moment, searching his memory. His chin dropped a little as he looked at Gina in amazement. "You mean, on top of everything else, that you're *that* Gina Barlow? Second in the junior nationals back in . . . I almost went that year! I wouldn't have done as well as you did, of course."

Just then Beowulf came up with a Badminton racket in his hand, listened for a break in the conversation, then decided to make his own and nudged Tom's arm. "Hey, Tom. The Badminton court's free. You wanta play a game before we eat? I don't think the steaks are ready yet. I'll bet I can whip you."

A flash of irritation dissolved as Tom saw an opportunity in Beowulf's challenge. "How *is* the food coming, Senator?" He asked. "Do we have time?"

"Oh, probably," Bill shrugged. "I think they're just starting on the steaks, burgers, and brats. "You could play a game or two."

"I have a better idea, Beowulf," Tom said. "How 'bout a little mixed doubles. You and Billi Jo against me and Miss Barlow here. Would you be willing to be my partner, Miss Barlow?"

Gina didn't have to think twice, grasping immediately the advantage of being able to be close to Tom, yet harmlessly burn off some of the erotic energy and tension he was generating in her. "I haven't played Badminton in years," she said breathlessly, "but that sounds like fun!"

"Wait a minute," Beowulf started to have second thoughts. "Two Olympic quality athletes against me and . . . Ow! I'm gonna have to start practicing some defenses against that elbow of yours, hon!"

"Excuse us, Senator," Tom said, as the four started walking toward the Badminton court marked off with chalk dust on the lawn. They found their rackets and flipped a silver quarter ND to see who would serve first. Beowulf and Billi Jo won. Tom and Gina spoke briefly and reached agreement on how to divide up their side of the court; she would defend short, he long; and she would serve from the left side, he from the right. Beowulf whacked a monster serve that sent the birdie over the net and near the back line with the velocity of a missile, Tom slammed it back like a bullet about an inch over the net, and the game was on. In less than a minute, about half of the other guests had gathered to watch them play.

Gina was feminine beauty in motion. Rapid motion, with amazing grace and balance. Her backhand was perfection and her forehand even better. She caught virtually everything that came close, or that she came close to, darting from one side of the court to the other and repeatedly reaching out to make seemingly impossible returns, whether high or low. Tom was so entranced watching her from behind that he almost missed several serves and returns that came long. On the other side, Beowulf had all the power in the world, but less control. Billi Jo had a ton of control, but needed a little more power. Tom and Gina beat them rather handily by several points, and the game ended with all four laughing and panting as they shook each other's hands.

"We get to play the winners!" Tom looked to see who had called out. He should have known. It was Derek, standing next to a startlingly attractive gray-eyed blond girl who stood nearly to his shoulders. They had picked up two extra rackets.

"Are you up to the challenge?" Tom asked Gina.

"Sure, if I can breathe for a moment," Gina nodded.

"Do you know that girl?" Tom asked.

"Yes. That's Cindy Markham. She's my friend and roommate at the Institute, or was, 'til I went to work for Bill."

"Okay, you're on, Derek," Tom called, and with the usual preliminaries, they started, Tom serving first this time. Derek had both power and precision. It strained Tom to the limit to return Derek's serves and slamming returns, which always seemed aimed just within the boundaries. The blond, Cindy, turned out to be amazingly agile and coordinated, gliding from one side of the court to the other with grace and balance that rivaled Gina's, to bat almost everything back. She had a killer short lob, from one side of the court to the other, just barely over the net, that kept Gina hustling to reach and return, and left Tom with the problem of returning the powerful long shots that Derek would so often slam back.

In a momentary lull, Tom, already breathing hard, asked Gina, "Where does that gal get her energy and coordination?"

"She's a dance major," Gina answered, eyes twinkling and grinning. "She loves sports, and athletes." The game resumed with Derek and Cindy a point ahead. Tom and Gina lost another point when one of Cindy's lobs came down in between them and they both went for it. Backpedaling, reaching back, and turning sidewise, Gina reached it first and knocked it back over the net, but stumbled. Tom caught her in his left arm. She seemed to rest there against his chest for an extended moment, and Tom could feel her heart beat. He did not even notice Derek's return shot that hit just inside the back boundary before careening on across the lawn. Then Gina looked up at him, grinned, giggled, and bounced back to her position. After a heroic battle that threatened to leave Tom seriously winded, and aching in muscles he had forgotten he even had, he and Gina eked out a slim victory. The four laughed, joked, congratulated each other, and were about to head for the tables when another young man and woman Tom didn't know stepped forward holding rackets they had apparently gotten from Beowulf and Billi Jo.

"Hey, you can't stop yet," the young man said. "We challenge the champs!"

"Give us a break, Spider," Gina said. "We're tired, after that last one!"

"Well, okay. We'll give you a couple of minutes to rest. But this is me and Serena's game, and you two are going down!"

Tom and Gina looked at each other. Tom shrugged. "I guess we can't turn down a challenge like that." Without further ado, they began. This game turned out to be as fun as the others, though more relaxed. Neither Spider nor Serena were outstanding athletes, so the game simply became one of relaxed play, batting the birdie back and forth with nobody trying too hard and everybody laughing at everybody's mistakes. Viewers, however, began drifting over to the tables where food was being set out.

About halfway through the game, with Spider and Serena up a point, Bill's voice boomed out from over near the grills. "Okay, you four, that's enough of that. The food is ready and you're holding everything up." With good cheer Tom and Gina conceded the game, shook hands with Spider and Serena, and headed over with the others to find a place at the picnic tables. Bill guided them up the stairs to a pair of tables on the deck he had reserved for the guests of honor and set Tom and Gina next to each other. Then Bill called the whole crowd to silence, blessed the food, and everyone dug in.

After a minute of passing things around and loading plates, the pleasant looking woman sitting next to Bill reached over and offered to shake Tom's hand. "I suppose you know Roger, Lillian, and Hally, Mr. Wright," she said, "but since my husband is too oafish to introduce me I'll have to do it myself. I'm Barbara Braxon, Bill's wife. And if you call me anything but Barbara, or Barb, I'll put poison in your steak sauce. It's really wonderful to have you here."

Tom grinned and shook her proffered hand. "It's an honor to be here, Barbara. Over the last few weeks I've become a great admirer of your husband. The two of you remind me very much of my parents, in Idaho. I guess you know Gina Barlow well, and she tells me that the stunning blond next to her is her college roommate, Miss Cindy Markham. Don't ever play Badminton against her. Then there's Derek Martin down there, Beowulf Thorsen next to him, and next to Beowulf, his beautiful bride soon-to-be, Billi Jo Jensen. Those three are all engineers. I don't know why I brought so many of those up here with me this time."

"I came because you said there'd be food, Tom," Beowulf loudly interjected. Everyone laughed and congratulated Billi Jo and Beowulf on their impending nuptials. When Barbara and some of the others began quizzing them about details, Roger Galbraith, sitting on Bill's other side, leaned over toward Tom. "How much has this fight, resulting in you having to buy back so much of your own stock, really hurt UTT, Tom?" He asked.

Tom swallowed the piece of steak he was chewing before answering. "Maybe not as much as people expected, including me, Senator. Of course, it absorbed a lot of our cash reserves and a big chunk of our settlement with Sony. We needed all that for expansion. But I talked with Marlon Gates just before we left this morning. He says he hasn't had to buy a share of our stock since Wednesday afternoon. As soon as Slanghorn restored our license, the public came back in the market with a vengeance. Marlon's been *selling* shares back off since yesterday morning and at higher prices than he had to pay to buy. He says that in a few weeks we could have virtually everything we spent back and then some!"

"But what about the hearings, and the state regulation that might come out of that?" Hally Arkwright asked as she buttered a roll. "Couldn't you take a hit from that?"

"Well, maybe," Tom responded. "But with you ALP folks in charge now, I think the hearings will be fair. As long as UTT keeps its safety record as good as we have so far, which I'm going to demonstrate to the committee on Monday, I just can't see anything onerous coming out of either the legislature or the Department of Transportation. And I expect most other states to be reasonable, too."

"But don't you think, Tom," Gina interjected, "that the cost effects of a certain anticipated mild level of regulation might already be capitalized into the value of the stock, so you wouldn't see much effect if or when it happens?"

Tom looked thoughtfully at her, thinking more about her use of his personal name for the first time than about her logical argument, which made intuitive sense. "Good point, Gina. Could well be."

"But what about federal regulation?" Hally persisted. "Couldn't you run into that, and isn't that another whole ball game? Interstate business and population movements can't operate to keep that reasonable. Remember the ICC and the railroads."

"Yes," Bill grumbled in support of Hally's point. "And remember the trucking industry after its leading firms *asked* to be brought under ICC regulation clear back in the *First* Great Depression, when they saw the advantages of government enforced cartel restrictions."

"Well, I'll never support any government monopoly or cartel," Tom responded defensively, "but it does seem possible Congress could force some sort of teleportation regulation agency on us, particularly since the RepubliCrats are in the majority. It's hard to predict what the Federal government may do as we expand nationwide."

"But what about the thirty-second amendment?" Gina asked them both. "Federal regulation declined a lot once that was ratified at the end of the Disorders. And hasn't it stayed moderate even under the Democratic Republicans? It seems to me they're very careful about regulating much of anything these days."

"Hear, hear, Gina," Roger Galbraith said, waving his fork to emphasize his agreement. "That's one of the very best things we got done back then. I was a younger man in the California state ratification convention that put it over the required three-quarters of the states."

"What's the thirty-second amendment?" His wife Lillian asked. "I hadn't met you yet, dear. I remember you talking about being involved but I forget what it was about."

"Isn't that the 'takings' amendment?" Derek asked, joining the conversation.

"Yeh," Beowulf jumped in. "That's the one that forced the courts to recognize federal regulations as partial takings of property, compensable under the Fifth Amendment takings clause. In other words, when they partially take people's property by dictating its use or nonuse, they have to pay 'em for any resulting loss in value. That hits congress and the regulators right where it hurts. Makes 'em think more than twice."

"How did you know that, hon?" Billi Jo asked her intended. "You're an engineer, not a political scientist."

"Because I read all the time," Beowulf answered in mock offense. "And you know what that great

American philosopher Groucho Marx said about books!"

After a pregnant pause in which everyone waited for Beowulf to continue, Hally Arkwright asked, "What *did* he say, Mr. Thorsen?"

Beowulf looked smug. "He said, and I quote, that 'outside of a dog, a book is a man's best friend, and inside of a dog it's too dark to read'."

Everyone at the table cracked up. None who had heard Beowulf could eat, and a few threatened to fall off their bench seats. It was nearly thirty seconds before anyone regained control. Finally, Derek commented, "You and I are way too young to remember Groucho Marx, Beowulf! You must have read that somewhere, too."

"Oh, I don't know," Gina said as the laughter started to fade, and people were nearly finished wiping their eyes. "Even I've heard of the Marx brothers; Groucho, Zippo, Harpo, and Karl."

That set everyone off again, making people at the other tables wonder what was being served for drinks up on the deck. It didn't help when, just as they were starting to regain control, Tom chimed in. "Yeh, I remember them, too. Wasn't Karl the funny one? Didn't he write some jokes that ran over a thousand pages - in German?"

This time, everyone's stomach's hurt long before they stopped laughing and started breathing again. Conversation and laughter continued, along with the eating. Gina and Tom engaged in a good deal of small talk, as he asked her about her family, work, doctoral dissertation, and life. He was astonished to find out just how key she had been to recent events, and was highly disturbed, on a very visceral level, when she told him what had happened to her on the Parkway overpass.

Eventually, Barbara and some of the other wives went into the house and brought out ice cream sundaes for everyone, with a variety of nuts and toppings for garnishment. Even Gina figured she had burned off enough energy in the Badminton sets for her calorie budget to afford one. But in the middle of eating her sundae, she noticed something odd. She was eating left-handed. She never ate left-handed. She was right-handed. And she was sitting much closer to Tom than might be thought appropriate with a man she had just met, almost nestled against him. And she was having a little trouble breathing. And Tom seemed to be having a little trouble speaking in his turns at conversation. He slurred a couple of words and seemed to search for others. Then she noticed that somehow, she didn't know how or when, her right-hand had become intertwined with his left one, and she was holding them both in her lap. And she didn't want to let go. But for the sake of propriety, and with an act of will, she forced herself to do so, and inched discretely away. Her breathing and his speech improved almost immediately.

The rest of the evening was spent likewise in pleasant conversation, some on serious topics, some in light-hearted banter, extending long after most people stopped eating and the food was removed.

Eventually it got late enough that some of the guests started to thank the hosts and leave. Tom leaned over to Gina and whispered, "Aren't those your folks, Gina, down at the end of the other table, just getting up?"

"Well, yes," Gina answered. "That's Adam and Rachael."

"Do you mind if I go down and introduce myself before they leave?" He asked. "I've heard of your dad, Adam, many times."

"Sure," she said. "Should I. . ."

"No. That's all right. I'll do it myself. I'll be right back." Getting up and out - no easy task from the bench seat of a picnic table with a full stomach - Tom walked down to where Adam and Rachael were similarly extracting themselves and saying their goodbyes to others. Gina watched him introduce himself, shake their hands, and engage them in a brief conversation that seemed to be pleasant for all concerned. Then Tom waved goodbye to them and walked back, stopping on the way to engage in whispered discussions with Beowulf and Derek. When he reached Gina, he did not sit down. He leaned his head down near Gina's instead.

"Gina, do you mind if we talk over here for a minute?" He asked.

She let him help her up and out from the picnic table, and guide her by a hand on her lower back over to the edge of the deck, where he leaned on the rail, and looked over the back yard and the neighborhood, now visible only by the light from windows, streetlights, and stars. The air had a bit of chill; and Gina bravely stood close enough to Tom to feel just a little of his radiating body heat, and catch a hint of his male musk scent.

"Have you had a chance to try teleporting, Gina?" He asked.

"No," she answered, somewhat surprised at the question.

"I have to be in town Monday, of course, but, Derek, Beowulf, and I have tomorrow and Sunday relatively free. They've been testing the teleport chamber out at the airport here all day and it's working fine. Derek likes to go rock climbing in the summer. He's something of an expert. Beowulf, Billi Jo, and I thought that sounded like fun so we arranged a special teleport run early in the morning over to the Boise Westmark. We'll eat breakfast there, rent a car, and drive out to my folk's ranch. There's a good climbing rock, actually a cliff face, on a corner of our place. On top it levels out and there's a nice, shady, wooded spot, with a spring, for a picnic. We figure we could 'port back tomorrow evening, or sleep over at my parent's ranch and come back Sunday. Derek even managed to talk your friend Cindy into going. She's going to arrange it with her folks tonight. I can get my parents to drive her over to Crater Lake to meet her folks on Monday. Or maybe meet them in Caldwell a few days later on their way up to Lolo Pass. Would you like to go with us . . . with me?"

*   *   *

"Well, Adam, what do you think about Mr. Thomas Wright?" Bill asked as he and Barbara walked Adam and Rachael to the front door on their way out.

Adam shook his head. "He's an amazing young man in every respect. Know what he did, when he came over and introduced himself?"

"What?" Barbara asked.

"He asked us," Adam said, "if it was okay if he took our daughter out, assuming she was willing."

"We've never had one of her boyfriends do that," Rachael added, with a hint of wonder in her voice.

*　　　*　　　*

"So did she say 'yes'?" Beowulf asked from the back seat as Tom pulled away from the curb and started to think about finding his way out of the Braxon's neighborhood and back to the Sacramento Westmark.

"Yes, she did." Tom answered. "She's going to clear it with her folks - she's living at home after all, and she's that kind of girl - but she seemed eager. I didn't have to ask her twice."

"That's great. Now all three of us are fixed up. This otta be fun. Hey, Derek. You ever gonna get that grin off your face? 'Cause if you don't, it's gonna drive me crazy!"

"I've never met anyone quite like that Cindy," Derek answered. "So no, I may never get this grin off my face, Beowulf!"

Billi Jo laughed. "I'll say. The way she jumped up and down and jiggled all over and hugged you shamelessly every time either one of you made a point. There was a time or two I thought you were going to stop and make love right there on the Badminton court!"

"It wasn't every time," Derek said, looking into the back seat at Billi Jo. "But believe me, I sure wanted to make a lot of points."

"That explains a lot," Tom responded. "My arm is still sore."

"But underneath that - ah - well - shall we say, demonstrative veneer," Derek continued, "Cindy is really a very sweet, religious girl. Not a tart at all."

"How do you know that?" Billi Jo asked.

"We talked. You were there. Plus, Gina told me."

"Now there's another case," Beowulf commented. "Strange those two would be such good friends. That Gina is wound tight. I don't think I ever saw a girl with quite that combination of intelligence, natural sensuality - no offense hon - and inhibition. But did you guys see how she smoldered like a volcano about to go off every time she looked at Tom?"

The other three laughed and pointed at Tom's silent embarrassment.

"On the other hand, there's nothing inhibited about the way she plays Badminton," Derek complained, having second thoughts. Then he looked at Tom sidewise. "In fact, it looks to me like you get her doing *anything* physical - or mental - she loses a lot of those inhibitions."

"Seriously, Tom," Billi Jo said, giggling, "you're going to have to be *very* careful, the first time that girl gets *you* alone!"

Tom glanced at her in the rearview. "*She's* going to have to be very careful the first time I get *her* alone. And that's why I think I'll be sure we're around other people for a while. Besides, that reserve of hers is part of what I find so immensely attractive. Don't you think, Beowulf, that inhibition is a *good* thing, at least up to a point? Isn't the whole sum and essence of civilization a matter of people internalizing constructive inhibitions? Didn't whoever invented the very term know that, since it refers to people *becoming civil?*

Derek nodded. "You've got to admit he has a point, Beowulf. But what about things like writing and technological artifacts, Tom?"

"Well, It seems to me there's a direct connection," Tom responded. "All these technical toys that we and others keep coming up with, wonderful as they are, they aren't the essence of civilization at all. But aren't they a natural expression and *consequence* of those constructive inhibitions in people? The focus of a significant portion of their vital energy in productive ways, rather than squandering it all in reflexive responses to random stimuli? The willingness to forgo immediate satisfaction to invest for long-term productive gains?"

"Yeh," Beowulf quipped, pulling Billi Jo close, "but we do it for the women."

"Then why do *we* do it, hon?" Billi Jo asked him, laughing.

James Rolph Edwards

Beowulf shrugged and pecked her on the cheek.
"For the men!"

"But aren't you the one always saying, Tom," Derek
asked once they stopped laughing, "that getting the
institutions right is what's crucial?   Constitutional
government, private property, free markets and so on?
You're always citing that old economist Douglas North
- you better turn to the right here, Tom, or you're going
to miss the cutoff - on how those things are necessary
in order to provide the right incentives."

Turning right up the ramp, Tom shrugged. "Well,
institutions *are* crucial, Derek.   I just think the right
culture, the proper social, moral, and political ideology,
civilization in the correct sense, comes first.   Aren't
constitutional limits on government, so that its coercive
powers are focused on *protecting* people's rights and
maintaining the conditions of mutually voluntary social
interaction that are the essence of a free society
themselves just expressions of a culture of
constructive restraint and inhibition?"

"Yeh, okay, I guess you're right, Tom," Beowulf
conceded. "My mom says people in this country lost a
lot of that, in the last half of the twentieth century and
the first part of this one.   Morals, civility, and
government degenerated and ultimately that's why we
went through the Second Great Depression and the
Disorders. I think some conservatives may have had a
little better fix on that than us Libertarians."

Billi Jo, snuggled in Beowulf's side, nodded
thoughtful agreement. "You are right, Tom. It's good
that manners and morals have been making a

comeback. But I never saw that connection with constitutional constraints before. It makes sense."

"It seems to me, though," Derek observed, "that demographic changes in the Disorders played a role in all that. Particularly the population decline from the riots, starvation, and burning of so many of the big inner cities."

"Sad to say, that's probably true, Derek," Billi Jo agreed, and the others nodded, too. There was silence for a minute as everyone pondered that unfortunate history solemnly.

"Hey, Tom," Derek broke the silence. "Beowulf and I think we almost figured out why our Graviton wave generator melted down the other day!"

"Yeh," Beowulf added, "we all did some heavy thinking, and then sent our data and conclusions over to Dan's team. That Kumar Banerjee kid in their bunch came up with several insights. E-mailed 'em back to us this morning. First chance I get, I want to meet him. He's sharp."

"Well," Tom said, "you can do that on Thursday when we go over. The launch is Saturday, and we'll be 'porting home that night."

"Do I get to go?" Derek asked.

"That's why I have to be back in Menlo Park Tuesday," Tom answered. "Sean has that Mathews guy coming in for an interview. If he's our man, he can take over for a few days and you can come with us. Otherwise you'll need to stay home and run the shop while we're gone."

"Wasn't it nice having Harry back at the workout the other day, Tom?" Beowulf asked, switching topics again after another brief silence broken only by road and traffic noise. "He showed me that variation of *Ikkyu* he did on that first demonstrator at the Tower that day. Very nice. Billi Jo got it the first time she tried it. Put me flat on my face."

Tom grinned into the rearview. "Yes, it is nice to have Harry back. He's a good Aikidoka and one heck of a guy. The way he's learning I might let him test for *Nidan* next year. I'm beginning to wonder what he was doing while he was gone, though. He said the darndest thing to me after the workout."

"What was that?" Derek asked.

"We were getting dressed. You guys were still in the showers. I happened to mention that there was an attractive woman named Gina Barlow working for Senator Braxon that I badly wanted to meet when I came up here, and he gave me this strange look. When I asked him what that was all about, he just said that several things in the universe suddenly made sense to him."

*　　　　*　　　　*

All the guests had left, and Gina, whom Bill and Barbara regarded more like family than a guest, was just leaving, walking with Heather down the sidewalk toward Gina's Hyundai. Typically, those two had stayed later than the others to help the Braxons with cleanup, but Bill and Barbara had finally shooed the two of them out. They stood, now, watching Gina and Heather through the front window.

"You know," Bill said, putting his arm around his wife and pulling her close, "I think we can stop worrying about that girl now."

Chapter 32: Weak Force Teamwork and Inspiration

Early Thursday morning Tom, Derek, Beowulf, Phil, Dave Barret, Angel BlackSnake and the other members of UTT's Weak Force Team 'ported from the newest UTT gate at San Francisco International - there were three there now - to the newly finished Albuquerque, New Mexico airport chamber. Renting three cars, they convoyed up I-25 to Santa Fe where they checked into a hotel before heading out into the desert to the Nucleonic Orbital facilities. The guards at the gate of the two-hundred acre complex were waiting for them. The guards gave them passes, checked them through quickly, and directed them to the main office building, a modern three story structure. Dan Hargrove, having been notified of their arrival by the gate guards, met them outside and led them in.

The rest of the morning was spent in a joint meeting between the two groups, first getting everyone acquainted, then lining out the work and organizing the two teams into a set of subgroups with no fewer than two members from each team, to meet separately in the afternoons to work on the unsolved problems that had been identified. After the initial Thursday afternoon meetings of the subgroups, the plan was to have reports from those subgroups in a two to three hour joint meeting each morning Friday and Saturday, then get input from everybody on each report and run the separate meetings again the rest of the day. For at least the first two days, Tom intended to rotate through the afternoon sessions, sitting in part of the time with the specialized teams he deemed to be dealing with the most difficult theoretical problems. He had other plans for Saturday, however.

At noon Thursday, UTT's team members were given sack lunches and taken on a rather quick guided tour - essentially a driving tour - of the rest of the Nucleonic facility before initial subgroup meetings were scheduled to begin. Dan drove the car that Tom, Derek, and Beowulf rode in. The tour was timed so that they pulled up with the other cars following behind and parked not far off the runway just before a satellite launch plane took off. The plane was huge, aerodynamically sculpted with swept back, curved delta-wings designed to carry both the plane and its payload to the edge of space itself. Even from five-hundred yards away, the roar of the plane's engines as it powered up was almost deafening.

"Where's the final stage booster, Dan?" Beowulf asked. "I thought it would be mounted above or below the fuselage, but I don't see it."

"That's done both ways using somewhat smaller planes by some of our competitors," Dan answered, "but we designed our launch plane to carry it inside. We drop it out near apogee, depending on the orbital requirements, and light the rocket up for the last leg. We think it pays off in reduced drag, more wing surface to get higher, and in lower fuel costs even if our plane has to be larger. Our plane almost glides back, after all. The old space shuttles used to drop like a rock. Not ours. Carrying and dropping the orbital booster from inside solves some other problems too."

"What's the payload in this one, or can we ask?" Derek did.

Dan chuckled. "Asking's free, but I can't give you an answer. This one's a military contract, and we don't even know for sure what the payload is. We almost never do on those. Oh, I could make some educated guesses, but I prefer not to speculate. They like it that way. In fact, from the time they bring their insertion rocket with its payload to us, their own people watch everything like a hawk to make sure we don't even . . . Oops! There it goes!"

With an unbelievable roar, the huge plane began taxiing down the runway, clawed its way into the air and accelerated at an increasing angle toward space. In a minute, it was no longer even a speck in the sky.

"Wow," Beowulf commented. "That's something. I'll almost miss that when we make it obsolete. If we do make it obsolete, that is."

"Usually I watch all this from launch control in that building over there," Dan pointed. "Tom has been in there several times with me to watch. How 'bout next we go over to where your relay unit is being loaded into our insertion rocket. Tomorrow we'll be mating that up into the bay of that one's sister plane. If everything works the way it should, it'll be ready to go on Saturday. We can take a quick look before heading back to the offices." Dan backed the car out of the parking space diagonal to the runway and headed for another part of the facility. The other cars followed.

*　　*　　*

The afternoon sessions were intense. With very few exceptions, Tom's team members and Dan's got along and worked well together. Their shared passions, interests, and goals combined with their distinct personalities and perspectives to generate useful and productive scientific and intellectual synergies. Though no crucial breakthroughs occurred, significant progress was made on several fronts; and before the end of the day, Tom felt that such breakthroughs were inching closer. At five o'clock the sessions reluctantly broke up and the UTT people piled in their cars and convoyed back to their hotel in downtown Santa Fe.

Tom intended to simply change clothes, go downstairs with some of the team members for a quick supper in the hotel dining room, and then come back up to his room. Some of the others wanted to sample a little of the Santa Fe nightlife. A few wanted to stick close and keep mulling over the problems they had been working on in their afternoon sessions. Tom badly wanted to call Gina, who - given the time difference - should be home from work soon, and talk to her about her day and his. Day by day, he had found her intruding more and more on his thoughts whenever he relaxed attention in the slightest from other things. Everything about her struck him as perfect, attractive, and disturbing to his mind and body at sometimes inconvenient moments, enticing him to think about things very distracting to his scientific and business focus.

Their trip to Idaho with Beowulf, Billi Jo, Derek, and Cindy, had been wonderful. Tom's folks, Vernon and Alexia, were delighted to have Tom bring his friends and colleagues home, and particularly delighted with Gina and with the thought that she might be a very special friend indeed. The rock climbing expedition was a ton of fun. They drove his dad's Jeep to the cliff and practiced climbing techniques. Tom and Beowulf had done some climbing before. Derek was an excellent teacher and practitioner of the sport. When they felt ready, Tom, Derek, and Gina went up the rock face to the top, while Beowulf, Billi Jo and Cindy drove the Jeep around the back way and up the slope over the rough Jeep trail to meet them. After that they laughed, talked, ate their picnic lunch in the grass by the spring, explored the surrounding terrain, and simply had fun.

Tom showed Gina how to shoot a .22 pistol, which gave him an opportunity to stand close behind her, put his arms around her, and show her how to hold it, aim it and squeeze the trigger properly. Derek did the same with Cindy. In no time Gina and Cindy were delightedly punching holes in tin cans at twenty yards right along with the rest. Later, after driving back and having a wonderful supper at the homestead with Tom's folks (which Gina and Cindy insisted on helping prepare) they put out mosquito traps, sat on benches on the back porch, and simply talked until it got late. The smell of Gina's hair, the warmth of her body, the feel of his right arm around her waist as she nestled against him and he held her left hand in his, simply refused to go away. Even more memorable was the passionate and prolonged kiss they had shared on the porch before reluctantly going in for the night. That first kiss neither of them would ever forget.

On Sunday, they all went to church with Tom's folks in the morning. Afterwards, back at the ranch, Alexia and the girls cooked a large chicken dinner with all the trimmings. Then after a rest to let the food settle, they said their goodbyes, and the five leaving - Cindy had called her folks on her NanoPod and arranged for Vern and Alexia to take her to meet them in Caldwell, so she was staying for a few days - took their bags and drove back to the Boise Westmark. Tom had not known exactly when they would be going home, but the Westmark managers were glad to accommodate them in working in an extra transmission to Sacramento when they were ready.

To Tom, one of the most delightful things about the whole trip was Gina's reaction to teleportation. Her soul seemed to sing in harmony with the subatomic resonance, even more than was true of most people. Her own delight stimulated his. The thought that he had invented this wonderful technology seemed to attract her to him even more. She sat with Bill while Tom testified at the hearings on Monday, and afterwards begged him to stay long enough to have supper with her and her parents. When he asked, on her parent's doorstep just before he left for the airport, if she would like to teleport over to Albuquerque Friday night, stay overnight with Dan's family, and see the launch with him on Saturday, she had eagerly assented. He had called her every night since, and they had talked about shared interests: economics; politics; teleportation; and most of all, each other.

So Tom took a quick shower, dried, combed his hair, pulled on his clothes and was headed for the door when someone knocked. It was Derek, Beowulf, Billi Jo, and Dave.

Tom was surprised. "Hey, I thought you four were going downtown."

"We were," Derek answered.

"But you better turn your 3-V on right fast, Tom," Dave added. "Any news channel will do." All of them crowded into the room behind him and spread out to watch as Tom quickly walked over, turned on the set, and selected a news channel. As usual, the sound came up before the picture.

". . . repeat, Reuters has just reported that the German electronics-industrial combine, Daimler-Krupp, has announced that it is entering the teleportation business, having already acquired licenses and contracts to install beam-transmission chambers at airports in Germany's four largest cities. The firm also says it is currently engaged in negotiations for chamber installation at several other European airports and plans to have a system of at least three teleport relay satellites in orbit within . . ."

"Darn!" Tom said. "Hard for this to happen at a worse time. I really need to be back at the Tower to deal with this. I guess I should have left you home after all, Derek. Dick Mathews really isn't up to speed enough yet for something like this. Now I'm going to have to spend time on the phone with him tomorrow that I need to spend in those R & D sessions. Maybe I better call him and do some of that tonight."

The others pointed at the 3-V and Tom stopped talking to listen again. "This report by Reuters," the network newsman continued, "comes on top of the announcement by the Japanese corporate giant Sony earlier this afternoon that, now that it has settled in UTT's lawsuit and contracted the use of several UTT technologies, it is starting within the week to build teleport chambers in Tokyo and other major Japanese cities. The firm expects to expand into Asia and Hawaii within a few months. Further, Sony's CEO, in an exclusive interview with our own Donald Burgley . . ."

Tom was almost too astounded to speak. *Two at once! And those two American firms will almost certainly be in business soon.*

"Looks like you were right about why the Tokyo authorities were stalling on that contract you offered 'em, Tom," Beowulf commented.

Tom nodded grimly. "Yeh. They wanted to give Sony first grab. I expected that. Even though they were hit as hard by the Second Depression as anyone, the Japanese are still a bit mercantilist. It's a good thing, though, that we got the authorities in Taiwan and mainland China to sign the other day. They still don't like the Japanese very much. We can go great-guns in that market, and it's huge."

"I don't know, Tom," Derek objected. "We're already stretched pretty thin, trying to finish the chambers in Denver, Chicago, New York, Quebec, Miami, DC, and Santiago. Even with Marlon selling our stock back off at a steady clip, where's the money going to come from?"

Tom pointed at the 3-V. "A lot of it is going to come from them."

*   *   *

The first breakthrough came Thursday morning in the joint meeting, when Tom pointed out that several of the unsolved obstacles in the reports of the specialized teams had a common element in failure to correctly understand the graviton wave pitch in the fundamental space-time harmonic. Running back through the equations, Kumar Banerjee - the kid from Dan's team who had been working with Beowulf and Phil on reconceptualizing the gravity wave modulator that had failed at the Asylum - suggested a modification. Tom immediately saw several implications. Kumar, Tom, Dave, and Phil took turns for several minutes extending the logic, briefly arguing modeling points but quickly reaching agreement as they saw where things were going.

"That gives us the E-H action," Angel BlackSnake observed as they paused, "and now it balances."

"And now - poof - we don't need the dark energy postulate, or brain cosmology," Dave added. "I always thought that was essentially mystical."

From there it was like one falling domino knocking over another, and several perceived obstacles found at least hints of theoretical solution. Indeed, enough of the previously intractable problems now so obviously had solutions that Tom reorganized and retasked the subgroups. The general meeting broke up early and everyone headed for the cafeteria excited and anxious to get started on their afternoon sessions.

"We told you that Banerjee kid was smart didn't we?" Beowulf said to Tom as he, Derek, Tom, and Dave set their trays down at one of the tables.

"And you were right," Tom agreed as he speared some of his chef's salad with his fork. "I wish I could have found and recruited him for the Skeleton Crew before Dan got him. I'd offer him a job now, but Dan would just pay him more to keep him. I'll bet Dan will want him in on the R & D in the joint venture anyway."

"What do you think we should call it?" Beowulf asked.

Dave snorted. "Seems to me that's getting way ahead of things. We're still a long way from even thinking about practical hardware. Look what happened to your try at a gravity wave generator. Are there even materials we can use as electrogravitic wave conduits?"

"Well, I don't think we should use material for that at all. We can use energy field conduits by . . ." Derek started, and he, Beowulf, and Dave fell to arguing and drawing engineering designs and equations on napkins between bites of food. Tom only watched with one eye as his mind partly wandered to thoughts of Gina and what she might be doing at work this morning. In a few minutes, though, he focused, finished his food, and excused himself. Wandering back to the conference room that they had been using for the joint sessions, which was now empty, he took a seat, leaned back, put his feet up on the table, pulled out his NanoPod and punched in Richard Mathews' code.

It buzzed several times and Tom nearly disconnected, but Dick finally answered.

"Good morning, Dick. This is Tom. Did you manage to get hold of any of those people at Daimler-Krupp or Sony yet?"

Dick Mathews was a big redheaded man with a jovial disposition and a distinctive voice, combined with the mind of an engineer and a crackerjack business manager. "Well, yes and no, Tom," he answered. "Sony let me through to their CEO, but he didn't know enough about the technical matters to know whether it was feasible, despite my assurances, or want to make a decision even if he did believed me. But I haven't been able to get through to the guy he passed me off to at their electrodynamics division. It's so late there now; I'll have to wait until tomorrow. Come to think about it, late tonight would be even better. Catch 'em early in their morning."

"How 'bout Krupp?"

"I just got off the phone with them, and I did get to talk with a manager in their technical division who was able to see the advantages and pass our proposition higher up for consideration. Personally, he was very interested, especially when I told him we'd be willing to leave the relay unit we're putting up tomorrow untasked long enough for them to experiment with it, even though it had to be a limited time offer, in the nature of things. He did seem worried about what tests like that might reveal to us about their technologies, though."

"Humph," Tom snorted. "I can see that. Not that it'll turn out to be that different than ours, but precisely because it won't, in the nature of things. They're afraid they'll end up in litigation with us when we find that out. But they should recognize *that* as a different issue, since we'll find that out sooner or later anyway. They have to see the financial advantages to them of *this* offer. Renting excess relay capacity from us rather than putting up their own satellites could save them a lot of money, and it'll sure be good for us!"

"I agree, Tom," Dick responded, "but they won't see that until they run it through both their technical and financial people. Even if they understand that they have to hurry or the offer is off the table, my guess is it'll take a few days."

"Okay, Dick. I don't mean to press you so quick on this. I'm really not normally that kind of micromanager, I'm just anxious. If we can get either one of them to bite, the other one will, too."

Dick laughed. "That's okay, Tom. I'm new on the job and right now I don't mind a little bit of micro-management."

"Well, I'll try not to be overbearing anyway, but keep me appraised until I can get back there, will you Dick? By the way, what happened to our stock price this morning? I haven't heard."

"Down ten percent at the opening on the news, but inching back up now. The market seems to realize we still have a big head start."

"Okay. Keep in touch." Tom disconnected, thought for a moment about where he wanted to be next, and went back to work. The afternoon sessions went well and more progress was made as everyone assimilated and applied what had been worked out that morning. Quite aside from the practical issues, several people on both teams made plans for research publications. At the end of the work day, Tom and his team gathered and convoyed back to the hotel again. This time Tom went downtown to a restaurant with several of the guys before going back to the hotel and calling Gina at her folk's home.

*　　　*　　　*

Tom found out about the second breakthrough at four a.m. Friday morning, when his room videophone rang. He was not too far from being awake anyway, and was able to claw his way to full consciousness fairly rapidly, roll to a sitting position on the bed, and reach for the phone.

The face in the screen was Derek's. He, too, was in his bed clothes, but he looked excited. "Tom. You know that problem Beowulf, Dave, and I were working on yesterday? I figured it out! We can do it!"

"What have you been doing, Derek, working all night?" Tom asked.

"No. No. But it drove the three of us crazy last night. Beowulf and Dave finally went back to their rooms. Something one of them said made me think about Tesla, though, and I spent an hour or so rereading parts of that biography of his that you gave me. Finally, I went to bed. In the middle of the night, I started dreaming about Cindy. She had this sheer negligee on, and she was. . . anyway, just when things were getting really interesting, she stopped and told me the whole solution. We can do it. I know how we can control and conduct the Graviton wave flow and focus the field. You and Tesla have it right, Tom. I woke up and spent the last hour writing it all out!"

Neither of the men got any more sleep, though both tried for a while. When they did get up, the preliminaries of showering, dressing, and getting through breakfast so the team could get on the road seemed to take forever. Before going down to eat, Tom called Dan at home, told him something important had developed, and asked if he could come to the morning session to hear Derek's presentation. As it turned out, no launches were on tap for the day and Dan could leave all other matters to lesser managers. At breakfast, Derek couldn't help telling the others his story about what had happened and dropping hints about his solution. Beowulf, Dave, and the others teased Derek unmercifully about how he had gotten the answer, to the point that he was sorry he had told anyone. That was particularly true when Phil pointed out that it would now almost certainly become part of the legend. In any case, everyone on Tom's team was psyched as they loaded up and convoyed out to Nucleonic.

At the morning session, astonishment at the brilliance of Derek's solution was followed by fevered discussion as everyone assimilated the insights and struggled to grasp the implications for their own parts of the problem. Before lunch it was clear that all other problems were now tractable. Only one major obstacle remained: While they now knew they could do it *technologically,* they still could not do it *economically.* The power and materials costs would be inordinate. Further refinements and solutions were necessary. But they were close.

Chapter 33: Nexus Attained

The San Francisco teleport chamber disappeared and the Albuquerque chamber appeared around the passengers instantly in its place. Every atom of Gina's mind and body vibrated in the wondrous harmony of the teleportation. It took several seconds to fade, leaving her and everyone else in an elevated mood, though some with a sense of loss as the feeling passed. Gina stood, gathered her purse and her carryon bag, and walked toward the exit with the others. Outside, in the gate area, Tom was waiting. She saw the grin of pleasure light his face as he saw her. She wanted to run to him, but controlled herself and walked demurely to him, not conscious at all that the same type of delighted smile was on her own face. Since airport gates were one of the few public places where it was considered socially acceptable to hug, even with a crowd around, she dropped her bag and purse, and they did.

"Have you missed me?" She whispered in his ear as he held her tightly.

"Yes," he answered. "Almost intolerably."

A mildly humorous thought wormed its way into her mind. "Did you manage to get a lot done anyway?"

Tom couldn't help chuckling. "Well - uh - yes. I did. But it wasn't easy." With that he released her before they began offending other people and embarrassing themselves. That, too, was not easy. Picking up her bag with his left hand, as she picked up her purse with her right and slipped her left hand into his right, they headed out of the gate area and down the concourse. When they got to the baggage carousel they had to wait a few minutes before the bags from her transmission arrived.

"All these just for one night?" Tom asked, kidding her.

"Well, in case you didn't notice, I am a woman," she said demurely as she helped him take the bags out of the carrousel.

"Oh, I noticed," he said as he tried to figure out how to carry the three in addition to the one she had carried on with her. "I could tell by the luggage."

Gina smirked. "Is that the only way you know? I'll have to show you some others. Here. Let me take that one." In a moment, having redistributed the smaller bag to her, they were heading toward the ticket area and the main exit. Outside, he led her across the street to the short-term parking and across several aisles to where he had parked the rental car he had driven over from the hotel. Putting the bags down, Tom unlocked the doors and they stowed the bags in the back seat. Then he walked around and helped her into the car, before going back around, fishing for the keys in his pocket again, and getting in behind the wheel. Before he could do anything else, Gina turned, stretched out over the console between the bucket seats, reached behind his neck with both hands, pulled herself up, pressed herself tightly against him, and kissed him long and passionately, as he reciprocated.

"Any doubts now?" She asked after some time, whispering in his ear, her eyes closed.

"I never had doubts," Tom breathed back. Then after several moments, "But you can't be comfortable this way."

"I am," she affirmed, "more comfortable than I have ever been, in my whole life."

"Me, too," he answered, breathing heavily. "But woman, if you don't get back over there on your side, I won't be able to drive or get in or out of this car and we'll be late getting to the Hargrove's. You'll like them, and supper is waiting. Everyone is waiting. So. *Please.* Go. Back."

For a few moments Gina held him even more tightly. Then she, sighed deeply, relaxed, and playfully rubbed her chest against his before shifting back to her seat. She wanted him never to forget for a moment that she was, indeed, a woman. In less than a minute, however, mostly by struggling to review what he knew about Boolean functions, Tom was able to regain enough objectivity and control to fumble the key into the ignition, start the car, and head for the parking ticket booth. Getting out of the Albuquerque metro area and on the way to Dan's desert estate during late afternoon traffic took some doing, particularly with Gina's left hand seemingly unconsciously resting on his leg, when it was not nestled in his right hand, but he managed. Tom turned the air conditioning on low, and the drive across the desert in the gathering twilight was pleasant.

"I guess you heard about Daimler-Krupp and Sony," Tom said.

"Yes," Gina answered. "You're going to have competition, but you must have expected that, Tom. Are you worried?"

"Yes and no. It'll have its challenges, but challenges are a big part of life." He glanced at her and grinned. "You're a gymnast, and a social scientist, so you know that. Without them the whole thing wouldn't be much fun at all. Tell me again how your week has been."

"It's had its challenges, and been exciting," Gina answered brightly. "All week, Bill's been reorganizing the Senate leadership, reallocating the committee memberships and legislative agenda, and so on. I've been busy helping him with some of that, and working on my dissertation, too. But did you hear about the Governor?"

"No, what?"

"He resigned this morning, effective the first of next month, to avoid being recalled."

"Tsk, tsk, tsk," Tom responded, shaking his head sadly. "So he avoids recall and an untainted lieutenant governor of the same party takes over. That's probably the best solution for him. My guess is, though, it just delays things. Next election, they'll lose."

Gina nodded solemn agreement, and they rode in silence for a few minutes. Then she spoke again, and he listened close. There was a note of doubt, sadness, and hurt in her voice he had not heard before.

"Tom," she asked him for the first time, "when you were in that class that day and you saw me and I saw you, did you feel what I felt?"

Tom was almost shaken, remembering. He had to compose himself a little before answering. "I may not have shown it, Gina, but you can't imagine how I was affected the second I saw you. It was like I had been waiting my whole life for you, just you, and I hadn't known it at all. Suddenly there you were, and I did."

"Then why," she asked, "why didn't you find me afterwards, for so long?"

Tom felt shame and turmoil, but answered as best he could. "I. . . I didn't know for sure how you felt. I suspected, but I didn't *know.* And you moved to Sacramento. And I didn't know that. And I was very. . . It was a crucial time for. . ."

Gina squeezed his leg briefly. "It's all right. I understand."

"Besides," Tom continued after a moment, wanting to explain even though her assurance had relieved him, "I knew I'd find you again. I don't believe in fate, Gina, or in destiny, but I believe in *plans* and in *will,* often operating at levels far beyond my own. And I knew what *my* will on the matter was, too. And then, of course, I was in the news, so you had to know a lot about me and where I was. If you felt at all like I did, I knew that between us, we'd seek each other out and come together."

Gina unfastened her seat belt, slid across the separation and on to the console between the seats, nestled her head against his shoulder, and her shoulder against his side and sighed with pleasure. "That was cute, what you did."

"What?"

"With the test computer in the desk that day."

Tom shrugged slightly. "I had to communicate something, somehow, and I very much wanted you to understand certain things."

"You sent so many messages, on so many levels," she said, smiling to herself while absent-mindedly tracing a pattern on his leg with her finger. "Some of them I didn't understand at the time. But it was cute."

After a while, Tom put his arm over her shoulder then moved it down to where he could hold her right hand in his, keeping only his left hand on the wheel, and snuggled her in closer. "That was wonderful what *you* did, Gina."

"What?" She asked, puzzled.

"That day at the hearings. With the note as I was leaving. It sent several messages."

He felt her shrug, slightly. "I had to communicate, and I very much wanted you to understand certain things. But of course, you already did."

"Not all," he said, "and it *was* wonderful."

*　　　*　　　*

In a few minutes, Tom turned off the highway onto the graveled road on Dan's property. From there it was only a three minute drive to the house, and Dan's electronic security system had long since told him they were coming before they arrived. Consequently, Dan, June, and about half the kids were out front waiting. Tom pulled into the big graveled circular driveway - Dan liked things rustic and refused June's intermittent entreaties to pave the road in and out to keep the dust down - and parked. Going around and helping Gina out, Tom and the Hargrove's exchanged greetings and Tom made introductions while some of the kids hauled Gina's bags into the house and back to a bedroom made available because two of Dan's middle boys were off on a weekend camp-out with a Boy Scout troop. Actually a selection of bedrooms was available since some of the other kids liked to sleep out in the Hargrove's big motor home on summer evenings. Consequently, Dan and June didn't have to talk long or hard to convince Tom to stay overnight, too, rather than drive back to the hotel in Santa Fe at the end of the evening. Half expecting that they might do that, he had brought an overnight bag along.

Initial acquaintances made and arrangements settled, they went inside, and the rest of the evening was wondrous. They ate, joked, laughed, and talked, getting further acquainted. Mostly they talked, about themselves and their families; about the Weak Force Project and the prospective joint venture between Nucleonic and UTT that might come of it; about the Clanton Conspiracy and UTT stock purchases; about the new competition now entering the teleportation business; and a dozen other subjects. Long after several of the kids, at June's direction, had cleared away and stowed the dishes and utensils in the dish washer, then drifted off to play video games, watch television, or read, Dan, June, Tom, and Gina talked. They shifted early from the kitchen to the huge family room, where Dan and June took their favorite easy chairs, leaving Tom and Gina sitting closely together on a couch. Nor did the Hargroves, amidst the conversation, fail to note the affectionate touches and hand holding that Tom and Gina could not help engaging in as the evening went on.

Dan and June seemed genuinely enchanted with Gina as did, Tom had long since noticed, almost everyone who met her. They were particularly amazed when Tom told them everything she had done in uncovering Senator Clanton's personal corruption and conspiratorial political efforts to manipulate UTT stock prices. Gina, of course, tried to modestly minimize her role, an effort Tom gently countered. Tom had his turn at being surprised and delighted when Dan and June told him how much they had enriched themselves by adding UTT stock to their own portfolio at the bottom, just before Marlon Gates started buying, using prospective settlement money from Sony. Dan complimented Tom on the brilliance of that tactical response to the Clanton cabal's depredations.

Eventually the conversation began to wind down. Most of the kids had already gone to bed, and Tom and Gina noticed that June had started trying to hide yawns. So with a glance of understanding between them, they told the Hargroves they would like to get just a little air before calling it a night. Getting up, June led them through the house and showed them a few last minute things about bedrooms, bathrooms, towels, etcetera, before saying goodnight and discretely getting herself out of the way, leaving Tom and Gina to wander hand in hand to the front door. Outside, the heat of the day had burned off. The air was crisp and cool, and the surrounding desert lit by a brilliant half moon. Tom and Gina strolled, his right arm and her left around each other's waist, his over hers, close together for warmth, and, of course, for the closeness itself, until they were past the circular driveway and nearly to the edge of the desert, where scrub brush, sage, and cacti started in earnest. A bit to the right and down the slight incline was the family firing range, though Tom could not see it now. For some minutes they simply enjoyed the scenery around them, the desert smells, and the closeness, wishing for more of the latter. Finally, Tom, unable to resist, turned and pulled her close, his arms under hers. They hugged and kissed long and passionately, the feel of their hips, chests, and lips in contact yielding indescribable pleasure, comfort, and longing.

Finally, they had to breathe, though they continued to hold each other. Gina gently turned them slightly, so she, too, turning her head to the right, could look back at the house. Tom slid his right hand up, and ran his fingers through her hair, holding her head gently against him. Her hair was silky and smooth with an intoxicating scent, and he marveled at the highlights imparted to it by the moon. Only a few lights were now on in the house. The rental car they had come in was simply a shadow off to their right side, though its outlines could be seen. Reflected moonlight made several other vehicles parked in the concrete driveway in front of Dan's huge four car garage on the right side of his house barely discernible. Off to the left of the house was Dan's motor home. For a moment Tom thought he heard the sound of kids giggling from that direction.

"I think we have an audience," Gina commented, grinning slightly, apparently unconcerned, since she did not release her grip on him in the slightest.

"Maybe that's best," Tom sighed, "given what you do to me every time I even see, much less touch you."

Gina's grin just broadened for a moment before a more serious train of thought crossed her mind. "Tom," she asked softly, "life is about choices and values, isn't it?"

"Yes, of course," Tom responded, wondering where she was going. "You're an economist and your folks raised you religious, so you know that. Values, choices, and actions: they define who we are and determine a huge part of what happens to us."

Gina looked into his eyes and he wondered again at how wonderful and melodious the sound of the female voice was, most particularly hers. "Do you know what I want, more than anything else in the world?" She asked. "Far more than any wealth, fame, or accomplishment I might have? And even if all that disappeared?"

"Almost certainly," he answered, "the same things I do."

"I want what my parents, Adam and Rachael, have. I want what your parents, Vern and Alexia, have. I want what Bill and Barbara have, and what Dan and June have. I want it with you, and I want some of those." She nodded toward - but did not mean - the motor home.

Tom ran his right hand down her hip, felt her arch her back, then pulled her even tighter, however much it made him ache. "I know," he whispered in her ear. "I've known from the first."

*   *   *

June brushed her hair at the dressing table while Dan read in bed, as so often happened at this time of night before the lights went out, she snuggled into bed with him, and they held, whispered their feelings to and loved each other until they went to sleep.

"Do you know, dear," June began, between strokes, "I think we can stop worrying about Tom now. He's going to be all right."

Dan turned a page without looking up. "June, I stopped worrying about him the second that girl stepped out of the car."

*   *   *

It being Saturday, Gina slept in a little, but it also being a big day, not too late, waking at six to find the desert sun, though low on the horizon, already streaming into the bedroom window. Putting on her robe and slippers, she gathered her other necessities and walked down the hall toward her designated bathroom. Her hopes *not* to see Tom - or for Tom to see her in her frumpy, unmade-up condition - were disappointed when he walked by the other end of the hall, already showered and dressed, caught a glimpse of her, grinned and waved. But the obvious delight in his expression at even a glimpse of her, and his cheery "Good morning, Gina" as he went on his way with only a slight pause to get a look, dispelled any worries she may have had as to how he might react to this sight of her and left her feeling warm inside.

When nobody answered at her knock, she went into the spacious bathroom and spent the next forty minutes doing what women do to ready themselves for the anticipated events of the day. Then going back to the bedroom, Gina repacked her hair dryer and other necessities and started to get dressed. It struck her then, as she thought about what to wear, that Tom had seldom her in a dress, unless she had been wearing a skirt rather than a business pantsuit at the hearings that day, and she couldn't remember for sure. Likewise, she couldn't remember what she had been wearing in the classroom the first time they saw each other. It was probably a nice pantsuit, or a chaste skirt and blouse, since she liked to dress a bit on the classy side. But every time since and including Bill's barbecue she had been wearing pants and a blouse.

Only when he came to her parent's house had she worn a dress, and that very modest.

Of course, Tom had already made it abundantly clear that he found her so attractive he had trouble controlling himself when the two of them were alone, and the thought that she could have that kind of effect on him (and that he could have the same effect on her) gave her goose bumps. Perhaps precisely because of that, someday soon she wanted to wear a very sexy, slinky dress for him. Perhaps, best when they were with someone else, at a dance or restaurant, to provide needed social restraint; but definitely slinky, definitely sexy, and definitely for him. Nevertheless, what she anticipated for today seemed to call for another pantsuit, and even then she might be overdressed, so she started making her selection.

In a few minutes she found her way to the kitchen, where June and several of the older kids were busy putting the finishing touches on breakfast. The very smell of bacon, eggs, pancakes, and jam was delicious in the morning desert air.

"Good morning, Gina," June said warmly as she busily distributed plates around the huge dinner table, followed by two of her children carrying knives, forks, spoons, and glasses. Michael, her oldest, piled hot pancakes and fried eggs from the stove onto a large plate, helped by one of the older girls. "Did you sleep well?"

"Yes, I did. Thank you, June. Good morning. May I help?"

"No, Gina, dear, you're a guest. We're almost ready anyway. Sit yourself down. The men are out in the yard doing something or other. They'll come in in a minute. In fact, go get them when you're finished there, will you, Michael?"

Michael, who had long since reached the age of appreciation of young females of the species even if they were a few years older than him, came around, said 'good morning' to Gina, and held a chair for her, before going outside. The other kids also greeted Gina. Several of the younger ones, who apparently had indeed been watching from inside the motor home, began kidding her unmercifully about Tom and her kissing out in the yard last night until June, somewhat embarrassed, shushed them into silence - at least on that subject. Gina got the impression that it had been a hot topic before she had arrived at the kitchen and dining room.

In a few minutes Dan, Tom, and Michael did come in, and everyone began settling at the table and passing around plates of food. Dan took his place at the head of the table next to his wife. Tom sat down next to Gina, looked in her eyes and grinned while he squeezed her hand briefly under the table, then started loading up his plate. She watched as he lavishly buttered two large pancakes, put three eggs on top and then added several pieces of bacon. Gina took an egg, a small bowl of breakfast cereal with milk and artificial sweetener, and a small glass of orange juice. In a few moments, Dan called everyone to order and asked Michael to bless the food, after which everyone fell to eating and talking.

After a few minutes, watching four adults and eight children and young adults chow down happily, Gina could not help catching June's attention and remarking, almost jealously, "June, with your family, your food bill must be huge!"

June swallowed a bite of pancake and suppressed a laugh. "It looks like the national debt, or it would if food wasn't cheap these days, and the national debt hadn't been paid off over five years ago! Fortunately, Mr. Midas, my husband here, can afford it. Anyhow, it'll go down a lot in the fall when Michael and Kira start at New Mexico State."

"Mom, I've already been going a year!" Mike complained.

"Yes, but you're home now and you eat like a horse," June giggled.

Michael and Kira, Mike's just-younger sister who would be starting her first year of college at summer's end, were embarrassed to be subjects of discussion at breakfast, but they dutifully reported that he wanted to be an astronomer and she a music major following in the footsteps of her mother, who was an excellent pianist. Then the proud parents reported on the abilities and talents of all the other children, embarrassing them each in turn, before the conversation turned to other things.

"Are you ready for everything today, Gina?" Dan asked.

Gina nodded affirmation as she quickly swallowed a mouthful of cereal and milk. "Yes, I'm excited."

Dan had an odd, sly grin on his face. "Good. We need to be there about nine. The physical exam by the company medical staff shouldn't take too long, but we need to get it done. The plane goes up a little after one, and the booster launch is about twenty minutes after that."

Something made Gina hesitate as she tried to interpret Dan's statement, a spoonful of cereal halfway to her mouth. "Physical? Oh. I see. For the pilots."

"Oh no," Dan said, seemingly surprised at her response. "*Your* physical."

Tom put his spoon down, apparently mortified. "Oh come on, Dan. A joke is a joke, but now you're scaring her. You know I was just going to give her the option!"

Dan's face broke into an uncontrollable grin and he laughed as Tom turned to Gina to explain, and she turned to him for an explanation.

"Well, Gina," he started in an apologetic tone, "when I asked if you wanted to come over here and watch my satellite launch, I didn't really say we'd necessarily be watching it from *outside* of the plane!"

Gina was shocked. Her mouth was open but incapable of speech for several seconds. ". . . You mean. . ." She finally stammered.

"Well, yes," Tom said, still in apologetic mode. "We can watch it from the control room, if you prefer, or even from next to the runway. But if you want, we can go up with it. Dan does that all the time. He takes up millionaires for big fees. That's one of the ways he offsets launch costs. I know you don't get motion sickness, and heaven knows, you're in good condition, Gina, you're a skilled gymnast. We'd get to see near-space, watch the orbital launch, and there's a period of zero gravity on the plane's parabola. It'd be fun!"

All doubt and indecision left Gina's face. "Oh, yes. Yes!" She said as she did her own launch: arms up and around Tom's neck, to hug herself to him tightly, almost knocking herself, him, and his chair over, to the unrestrained laughter and hoots of the Hargrove clan.

*   *   *

Gina did have to submit to an extended physical, but so did Tom and the others going along. By about noon they were suited up in flight pressure suits similar to what the pilots wore, just in case. Then Dan led Tom and Gina and three other passengers - two bankers (one of them Japanese) and the CEO of FredMart, the giant retailing corporation - out to the hanger where the plane was being readied. They went up the movable stairs into the hatch forward of the launch vehicle bay and behind the cockpit. Inside, the chamber was highly padded: floor, ceiling and walls. There were only two rows of four seats, facing forward, one along each wall. They also were highly padded. Each seat had its own window. The glass in the windows was deeply inset below the padding. Dan told them it was a special form of glass, very hard and two inches thick. There was a similar row of windows, though larger, in the ceiling.

"You see those indicator lights just below the ceiling above the front hatch to the pilot's compartment?" Dan asked as they each took a seat. "When the blue one goes on, the plane is getting ready to take off. Fasten your seat belts and harnesses. When the plane approaches the upper edge of the stratosphere that one goes off and the red one goes on. That means the booster with the satellite is about to drop out and light off. That happens fairly quickly, so watch close. A couple of minutes after that, the red indicator light will go off and a white one will go on. That signals that the zero-gravity portion of the plane's arc is starting. Then, and only then, you can undo your harnesses and float around the compartment.

"You'll have maybe forty seconds to do that," he continued, "then the blue one will come on again, giving you maybe another ten seconds to get back to your seat and strap in before zero-G ends. Otherwise, you'll fall down. It's only a seven-foot drop at most, but despite the padding, a few of our passengers have managed to bang themselves up. Once you're back in your seats, keep the belt and shoulder constraints on from then until the plane gets back to the ground, lands, and stops. You've all signed liability wavers, so if you get injured from failure to follow instructions, too bad! You'll notice everything I just told you is replicated on the back of the seat in front of you, and on the wall facing the front seats. I hope you all have a good time, and I'll see you when you get back."

With that Dan left, closing and locking the padded hatch behind him, and the passengers began talking among themselves. Gina was nervous with excited anticipation. It helped her some that Tom, though also excited, seemed relatively calm. It struck her, then, that one of the most important things she felt whenever she was with Tom was *safe.* She wished the seats were arranged in rows, instead of columns, so she could sit next to him and they could hold hands. Such an arrangement, however, would cut down the room, the spatial *volume* clearly needed for people to float and maneuver around in when the inertia imparted to the passengers by the plane's upper arc was just sufficient to counteract gravity.

Before Gina was quite ready for it, the blue indicator light went on and everyone strapped in. The engines started and with a faint rumbling roar suffused throughout the plane and felt in vibration, the plane taxied out of the hanger and onto the runway, where it stopped again for a few minutes.

"Look, over there," Tom said, turning his head and pointing over to the edge of the runway to a set of cars parked on the other side of a chain link fence. "There's the guys in the cars over there. They knew you were coming and they begged me yesterday to let 'em delay the afternoon sessions so they could watch us go up."

Gina did not know what to say. She did not know many of Tom's friends and associates yet, having really only had time to become acquainted with Derek, Beowulf, and Billi Jo, but she liked them a lot.

"Poor Derek is really miffed," Tom continued. "When I told him I was going to try to talk you into going up with me on this launch, and he realized he couldn't do the same with Cindy because she's still in Idaho, he took it hard. I told him I'd give him time off to do it on our next launch if he wanted."

"What about Beowulf and Billi Jo?" Gina asked.

"Well, she's back at the Galt Tower, and the whole prospect didn't particularly interest Beowulf anyhow. Zero-G through parabolic inertia somehow strikes him as a little too mundane, given what we've been working on. Oh, oh, here we go!"

The engine roar increased by several orders of magnitude, the brakes were released, and the plane taxied down the runway, accelerating rapidly, and shoving Gina back into the seat as the scenery outside rushed past faster and faster. Then with an enormous surge of power, they were airborne and rising fast, the ground receding far more rapidly than she had ever experienced in a commercial airliner, buildings, streets, and other objects becoming smaller and smaller. For a short time, patterns of land use became visible that could not be seen from ground level, but within a few minutes those patterns themselves became too small to distinguish as the engine power increased even more and the plane climbed towards the sky.

The ground got further and further away. For the first time in her life, Gina, by looking backward and *downward* through her window, could begin to see first-hand the continental outlines. The back of the seat was now her support as they continued to accelerate upward. In just a few more minutes, by looking forward and *upward* through the window, she could see the blue of the sky thinning out, becoming black, and stars appearing. The red indicator light went on. In a few moments, she felt a thump somewhere in the compartment behind theirs. Looking down and out through her window, Gina caught a glimpse of the insertion booster dropping below and falling behind, becoming smaller, before a brilliant flame lit up the sky and the booster caught up and accelerated below and past them, imparting enough turbulence to the thin atmosphere to make the plane shake briefly. Then they could see the flame of the booster through the *ceiling* windows, as it rose above them and accelerated rapidly toward orbit. In another minute or so the plane began to noticeably level out on its arc, the pull of gravity disappeared, and the white indicator light went on.

Gina was caught by surprise and she fumbled with the catch on her belt and shoulder restraints. Tom had already released his. With a slight push, his body inverted as his legs went upward. He kept a grip with one hand on his seat so that he appeared to be doing a handstand. With the other hand he reached down and released Gina's restraint, then pushed himself gently away, folded into a fetal position and did several rolls in the air as he drifted slowly toward the ceiling. Being brave, Gina also pushed off and began doing slow rolls and flips in the air, laughing giddily with the others and occasionally bouncing gently off the ceiling or wall. The Japanese banker seemed to have lacked the bravery to release his seat restraints and was taking pictures of the rest. Then Tom, floating near Gina, caught her by her left hand, pulled her around in mid air, and seemed to slip something on her finger before pulling her close to him where they spun slowly together. She looked down at her left hand curiously and in growing wonder as he spoke.

"Gina, I love you more than life itself. Will you marry me?"

The Japanese businessman got it all on camera and that also became part of the legend.

7585143R0

Made in the USA
Lexington, KY
04 December 2010